ONE SUMMER AT HELGEVELD FARM

A novel of 1917 Illinois

JOHN BLOIS

JOHN BLOIS
For information or permissions, contact the author through:
johnkblois@gmail.com

Printed Worldwide
First Printing 2025
First Edition 2025

10 9 8 7 6 5 4 3 2 1

ISBN: 979-8-9992653-0-2

Interior Book Design by Walt's Book Design
www.waltsbookdesign.com

Cover concept by John Blois. Final design by CC.

ACKNOWLEDGEMENTS

The author gratefully acknowledges the assistance of the following individuals whose comments helped nudge and ease this debut novel into its final form. Thanks to Kern Philgence, Hillary Blois, Julia Blois, Ethel Bowden, Jessica Smith, Katrina Ray-Saulis, Richard DePetris, Tish Gadsby, and to Charlie Britton, who, somewhere along the line, said I ought to write a book.

CHAPTER 1

Thursday, October 20, 1949 5:40 p.m. Chicago, Illinois

William Parlor hustled through the unfamiliar city. He turned left instead of right on Ashland Avenue, recovered, and dashed across Vernon Park. He ended up on the wrong side of South Loomis **Street**, three blocks down from Milo's Deli which closed at 6 p.m. Traffic was thick. Will checked his watch and hurried along the sidewalk, scanning for a place to zigzag through the rush hour to the other side of the street.

But he stopped and stood straight. Across South Loomis, between the parked cars, he saw a familiar stride, a silhouette that disappeared, then appeared, disappeared, then appeared, sparking a thirty-two-year-old memory, still fresh.

Holding up his left hand to stop traffic, Will stepped into the street and darted across South Loomis to another lifetime, to the summer of 1917.

Friday, April 6, 1917 11:10 a.m. Peoria, Illinois

A work wagon pulled by a single horse eased to the curb outside Block & Khul's department store in downtown Peoria Illinois, *Helgeveld Farm* painted on the side. That name drew six boys to the curb.

The wagon driver looked down at the assembled group. "You the boys headin' to Helgeveld Farm?" asked Alwin Helgeveld, a mild Dutch accent surrounding his words. The six of them nodded.

Jumping off the wagon, Alwin faced the boys on the sidewalk. At twenty-three, Alwin was the oldest of the eight Helgeveld children and made the frequent trips to Peoria to collect the latest group of summer farm workers.

The boys formed a crooked row. They were strangers to each other, but all had managed to be on time outside of Block & Khul's, heading for a summer of long days and hard work. Alwin gave the group a quick scan and then pulled a folded piece of paper from his back pocket to check the names. He read the list not waiting for answers. "Owen Whitcomb, William Parlor, Isaiah Butler, Moses Butler, Roy March, and Elmer Duggan. You all here?" Each nodded or replied, "Yes, sir," except one, who leaned against the wagon and stared at Alwin.

Alwin took stock of the outlier and walked over to him. "You must be Roy March. I got a letter about you, Roy. You Roy?"

The boy pulled up his shirt and blew his nose into it. Then he stared at Alwin. "Yeah, I'm Roy." Roy was a skinny kid, about average height, with pants that were dirt stained and too big. His brown hair stuck out beneath an oily hat and Alwin saw that his shoes didn't match.

Alwin stood in front of Roy. "Well, Roy, someone from a state school out there in Pennsylvania, a Mrs. Atwell, asked that we give you a chance over the summer to pull yourself together and figure things out. You ready for some work?"

Roy stayed silent, but bit off a fingernail, looked at it, and flicked it across the sidewalk.

"Okay, Roy," Alwin said. "You remember this. It's gonna be an easy summer or a tough summer for you. Your choice."

Helgeveld Farm had taken in boys from state programs before and most worked out. But in 1915, Gerard Malloy from Cincinnati got sent back for constantly spitting in the food trays. And last year, Gregory Dunkin was sent back to Des Moines for jumping on other workers when they were asleep. Alwin wondered if Roy was this summer's Malloy or Dunkin.

Alwin stepped back and addressed the group. "Looks like you're all here. I'm Alwin Helgeveld. It's my father who owns Helgeveld Farm and you boys signed up for a summer of farm work. But it's good work." Alwin nodded toward the wagon. "Climb on up there and wait for a bit. I'm heading into the store to get some things for the farm. Might be half an hour or so."

"I gotta sit with them?" said Roy, nodding toward two colored workers.

"No, Roy," said Alwin. "You don't have to sit with them. You can take yourself over to the train station and go back to Philadelphia. How does that sound?"

Roy glared at Alwin, but followed the other boys who scrambled into the wagon. After getting settled, they sat in silence hoping that someone would be the first to speak. It didn't take long.

"Where y'all from?" asked Owen Whitcomb, the largest of the group. Owen was just plain big, a half-head taller than everyone else in the wagon. He had short blond hair, and although his blue-checkered shirt covered his arms, the sleeves bulged enough to suggest he could likely lift the wagon they were all sitting in. Owen bent forward, elbows on his knees, hands clasped. He'd never described himself to others and wasn't sure what to say. "Me, I'm Owen. Owen Whitcomb. From Chesterfield Township, out near Cleveland, Ohio. Worked on the family farm my whole life. Probably always will. It's called the M&W farm. That's from my father and uncle, Martin and William. But folks in town said the letters stood for *Moonshine and Whiskey* farm." Owen smiled at his joke, then said, "My father wanted me to see another farm over the summer, see how it worked. Guess the only difference working here is that I'll make my own money. And I gotta admit, I ain't never really been away from home before."

The confession surprised everyone, but it encouraged the others who, with a nod or a grunt, admitted that it was their first time away from home, too. Other than Roy, each boy nodded their welcome to Owen and he leaned back, glad his introduction was over.

After a time, a tall, lanky colored teen sitting next to Owen spoke next. He slightly rocked in his seat, realizing this was the first time he'd introduced himself to a group of boys, white boys. "I'm Isaiah Butler. Me and my brother Moses right there, we live with my Granddaddy and my Gramma down in Alabama. They took us in when momma died." Isaiah nodded toward his brother Moses, who sat next to him. "They sent us up here, up north. Said we might get a better deal." Isaiah had an easy manner but looked down as he spoke. His pants appeared almost new and his shirt was worn but clean. He wore shoes that had some shine and looked a little big for him.

Elmer and Will nodded at Isaiah's story and this encouraged him. "Me and Moses, we got a little schooling. First in our family that can read and write. Learned some math cipherin', too." Motioning to his brother, Isaiah continued, "Moses' story 'bout the same as mine. You wanna say anything else, Moses? Whaddya think? Good summer up here?" Isaiah turned to the others. "Moses, he usually got something to say about things."

Moses sat up and smiled, all teeth showing. "You told the story, Isaiah. Mighty good to see a new place like this. And yeah, gonna be a good summer here. A good summer. I can feel it." Moses was a year younger and half-a-head shorter than his brother, and although Isaiah was older and spoke first, Moses spoke sure and confident. Truth was, Isaiah was proud of his younger brother, fondly jealous that Moses could somehow walk and talk past so many barriers put in their way. His hair curled tight against his scalp and a faded scar above his right eyebrow gave a hint of past mischief. Moses had the same clean clothes as his brother, except for an added pair of suspenders that crossed in back of a dark green shirt and attached to his pants in front.

Will and Elmer nodded a greeting, but Owen leaned over, looking at the floor of the wagon. Back home, Owen's father and uncle would never hire a Negro to work on the farm. Owen's father told him, "They're different from us and you can't trust 'em. Best we keep our distance." Yet over time, Owen noticed that each story his father told about Negroes, he nudged the facts this way or that. But he was still his father, and Owen wasn't sure about working with Isaiah and Moses.

It was Will's turn. Will had sandy brown hair that curled slightly over his ears and gray-blue eyes that squinted when he smiled. He was taller than everyone except Owen, and he might have looked a little older than his seventeen years, but two deep dimples seemed to keep him there. In school, he was teased about them, but Will's size kept the teasing at a distance. His attitude toward his dimples changed in eighth grade when Molly Cunningham turned around in English class and told him she thought they were cute.

"My name's Will Parlor. Came here from Pittsburgh, Pennsylvania. First real time away from home for me, too. My father said it was time for me to do some hard work on a farm. That's what he did when he was my age. Got a brother and a younger sister. I work in my father's feed and supply store after school." Will thought he'd have more to say but couldn't think of anything else right then. After a pause, the other boys nodded at Will's story. Everyone but Roy said it was good to meet him.

The only boy left to tell his story, besides Roy, was Elmer Duggan. Elmer was thin with a nervous grin that came and went. He wore a new outfit: collared shirt, cuffed work pants, and high-rise work shoes for his summer of hard labor. His sandy hair was slicked back, almost reaching his shirt collar. Elmer knew he'd have to tell his story but he dreaded it, dreaded saying anything about himself. He leaned forward in his seat, his left hand cupped over his right, but the boys had long seen that Elmer Duggan had just a thumb and first finger on his right hand.

"My name's Elmer Duggan," Elmer said, rocking slightly. "He went silent and the others wondered if that was Elmer's whole story. However, he continued. "Lived in Milwaukee, Wisconsin my whole life and never worked on a farm before. Just went to school and worked in my uncle's hardware shop. Last year, he told me there's more to life than city living, so here I am. I got...."

"Hey, Elmer!" Roy interrupted. "Show us that blasted hand! I almost retched when I saw it back in Peoria. Rats chew them fingers off? Or maybe you lost 'em down the privy?"

Everyone sat straighter, but Elmer kept his head mostly down. He uncupped his hand for everyone to see, but kept his finger slightly bent to lessen the shock. "Nope," said Elmer, "I was born this way. And I suppose you'll see at some point. Only got three toes on my right foot."

"Three toes?!?" Roy laughed hysterically. "I swear, you're a whole circus side-show, you are!"

Owen inched up on his seat, leaned over and stared past Elmer to Roy. "You keep that up this summer and there's gonna be a problem."

Roy sat back and stared out the back of the wagon, trading his out-loud laughing for a silent, body-shaking snicker. No one expected Roy to share his story.

The tension in the wagon brought silence, but introductions had been made, and as people do, they considered each other, wondering how they'd fit together over the summer.

After another ten minutes or so, Alwin returned to the wagon, a large parcel nestled under his arm. He swung it into the front of the wagon, hopped onto the driver's seat, and gave a quick look at each boy, a little extra time looking at Roy. Alwin took the reins, looking back at the approaching wagons and motorcars, searching for a space to pull from the curb into Main Street.

The sound of a shovel turned Alwin toward the sidewalk and he saw the divide between past and future, wagon and auto. At the request of motorcar owners, Peoria had hired a team of street cleaners whose sole job was to clean up after horses, keeping the streets, and the new automobiles, clean. Alwin saw the approaching man and he glanced down at the street between his horse, Lily, and the wagon. There he saw the pile of work that called the street cleaner over. Alwin tipped his hat to the city worker who readied his shovel and brush. He'd be sure to tell his brothers about this new trend in town.

After the clean-up, Alwin breathed deep and again faced the traffic chaos. He struggled to pull the wagon into Main Street until a draft horse and carriage let him go in front. Alwin nodded his thanks and shook the reins. "Heya! Come on, Lily," and the wagon slid into traffic as smooth as a Model T. They traveled through several intersections, some with a police officer directing motorcars and occasionally pushing horses forward to keep traffic moving. The horse vs. motorcar turmoil was apparent, and the divide between them was a chance for auto drivers to blast their air horns over and over at a past that was quickly vanishing.

The wagon moved through and past the downtown commotion. Lily trotted between rows of stores that gave way to large homes, then smaller homes, then farms and fields, ready for the spring seeding. Alwin breathed deep, took off his hat and wiped his brow. Saying mostly to himself, "Gettin' in and out of Peoria is harder than tamin' a horse that can't be tamed." He turned to the group of boys in the back. "'Bout a 25-mile trip to the farm. It'll take a few hours. I'll make sure there's some lunch for you when we get there."

Alwin could relax in a wagon surrounded by farmland. There was a 1916 Dodge 30 Roadster back at the farm, but Alwin wanted no part of it. His father, Joren, had ordered it in mid-1915. At $795, it was quite a bit more expensive than the popular Model T Ford Town Car, but the Dodge promised better reliability. That never happened. Any trip to Peoria in that shiny black Dodge was a gamble. Generally, it would start and immediately stop. Then it wouldn't start at all. Several weeks ago it stopped for good, and two draft horses dragged it behind the back barn for now, crumpling the front fender on the way. For Alwin, and most of the farmers in the area, the wagon was still faster and more efficient.

The group of workers bounced and swerved over the poorly maintained road, cutting past fields that were brown and bare. There were small farms, an occasional draft horse and plow, dirt roads that wandered to the horizon, and flocks of crows feasting on any leftovers from last year's harvest. Will had never seen land so vast and thought that it would take everyone in America to plant and pick the nation's food with open spaces like this.

After about half an hour, the left rear wagon wheel squealed and shook, causing Alwin to slow down, jump from the seat, and look under the back of the wagon. Isaiah glanced at his brother Moses who leaned over the side for a better look. "That don't sound too good," Moses said.

Alwin shook his head but hopped back into the seat, moving Lily forward at half speed. Less than a minute later, the back spring, along with the axle, began to break and push up through the wagon floor. At the same time, the left rear wheel bounced up, then down, shattering the spokes, and destroying the wheel. The wagon listed left and Isaiah looked back over the side. "We better jump on outta this wagon or that other wheel's fixin' to bust off, too."

The boys and Alwin hopped out of the wagon and examined the predicament. There was no repairing this, at least not here. "That axle's been complainin' for some time," said Alwin. "Thought we could make one last trip before workin' on it. Guess not." Alwin took off his hat and ran his hand across his head. "Not even halfway to the farm. I'll lead Lily and pull the wagon on the three wheels. Looks like you all have to walk from here. Won't likely be anyone along this road to pick us up."

While Alwin was figuring, Isaiah crouched under the wagon and eyed the rear axle and leaf spring. He crawled out and walked over to Alwin. He scratched his head and looked toward the ground. "Mr. Alwin, sah. No disrespect, but it looks like they's put the wrong size spring underneath the wagon, not by much, but by enough. It's just too small. The weights is wrong and that put too much pressure on the bottom of the wagon and on the axle. Some rot under there, too. Might have worked for a quick fix, but I ain't surprised it didn't last." Isaiah looked up at Alwin then quickly back down toward the ground.

Alwin put on his hat and looked at Isaiah. "How'd you know that, son?"

"That's what me and my Granddaddy do. Moses too. Fix things in town. Almost anything, but mostly busted wagons, plows, farm stuff that folks bring in. Moses and Granddaddy even work on engines and motorcars." Isaiah looked toward the wagon, nervous to speak up to his new boss, a white man he'd known for barely an hour. "Seen this happen all sorts of times. People, they put the wrong sizes of everything on to keep their wagons goin'."

Alwin took a deep breath and looked off toward the horizon. "Not that surprised, I guess. Took it into Peoria a time back and went with the low price on a used spring. Looks like I got taken." He turned back toward Isaiah. "What's your name again?"

"Isaiah, sah." Isaiah looked toward the ground but was proud of having spoken up.

Alwin nodded and turned toward the rest of the boys. "Alright, I'll lead Lily best I can. If the other wheel breaks off, maybe we'll drag it." Alwin breathed deep, looked up at the road and shook his head. There would be no helping his father prepare the seed today.

Isaiah spoke up again, surprised at his boldness. "Mr. Alwin. We run into this same thing a few times back home. I believe we can balance this out if we wedge some of the broken wheel parts between the axle and the solid bottom part of the wagon. That should level it so the right rear wheel rolls clean and we can run on three wheels. Maybe a couple of us might could ride up front in the wagon to get the weights right, keep it balanced. Horse'd probably like it too, wagon not pullin' on that leaning rear wheel." Isaiah turned toward his brother, Moses. "You remember old lady Morgan's wagon?"

Moses laughed. "Sure do. We got that wagon rollin' on three wheels and she rode it like that for most of the summer." Moses, glad to be involved in the process, pointed to the broken wheel pieces strewn in the road. "Between that metal and the busted spokes, I believe I could jam it up under there and strap it together just like with old lady Morgan."

Alwin looked under the wagon, considering Isaiah and Moses' plan. "Worth a try. We'll see how your plan works, Isaiah, Moses."

"Okay," said Isaiah. "Just needs all of us to lift the wagon on this side to level the axle out." The boys put their backs against the side of the wagon and their shoulders pushed it level.

Alwin and Moses picked up some broken wheel pieces and Moses crawled under the rear of the wagon. He wedged several wooden spokes between the axle and wagon floor, bracing them with fragments of the broken iron rim from the wagon wheel. He secured it all with rope that Alwin provided. Alwin gave the axle-fix a shake and Moses pulled himself from underneath. They all stood back and the wagon rolled a few feet and stayed stable. Alwin shot Moses, then Isaiah, a smile and a nod.

Pointing to Will who was standing next to Isaiah, Alwin said, "Isaiah, you and this fellow, Will is it? Grab your travel bags and scramble up front in the wagon. We'll see what happens."

Alwin strolled to the side of the road, happy that they might make dinner after all. He picked up a brittle piece of hay, snapped it to size and nestled it into the right side of his mouth. He hopped into the wagon and turned to the two boys behind him and the four still on foot. "Okay, boys. Hang on." Alwin looked back at the other four boys. "We'll switch you around in a while so you all get to ride some."

The wagon made steady progress with Alwin weaving Lily to the smoothest parts of the road and the other boys hurrying alongside.

Nothing was said at first, but everyone was content with this outcome. Will turned toward Isaiah sitting next to him in the wagon. "That was all right."

Isaiah nodded, feeling an honor he seldom felt back home.

Will continued, "When'd you get to Peoria? I got there three days early. My father gave me $5 so I stayed in the Lud Hotel. Fifty cents a night. I think I saw you and Moses while I was walking around the town."

"Yeah," Isaiah replied, "Granddaddy, he sent us early. Got to Peoria six days back and walked around the town some. Nights, we stayed down near a river or a lake, next to piles of junk. Moses and me slept in one of the busted-up cars there. That way didn't have to spend no money for a hotel." Isaiah shrugged his shoulders. "Didn't imagine there was no hotel that would let us stay anyways." Isaiah reached into his left pocket and pulled out a $1 bill. He opened the folded bill and showed it to Will. "But I got this dollar left just in case. Granddaddy gave me two $1 bills for me and Moses. Said to make 'em last. We used the other dollar to buy some food." Isaiah carefully folded the remaining bill and slid it back into his pocket.

Then Isaiah reached into his right pants pocket and pulled out three pennies. "Here, looka these." Isaiah held them out for Will to consider. "These is the new one-cent pieces with President Abraham Lincoln on them. Granddaddy went down to the bank and got us three with some shine on them." Isaiah picked up each penny for a closer look. "Got one here from 1916." He held up another. "This here one is from 1912." Then he held up the last one for Will to see. "Lookee here. This one's from 1909. Tha's the first year they's made. Granddaddy said don't spend these for nothin' since Abraham Lincoln's on 'em. He's the president that changed things and got freedom for my Granddaddy."

Isaiah put the 1909 penny in Will's hand and he examined the date and President Lincoln. "Yeah, looks just like him." Then Will pointed above Lincoln's head. "And there, right there, says *In God We Trust.*" Guess the government agrees he's pretty important, Isaiah."

Will handed the penny back to Isaiah who sat a little taller and nodded. "Yes, indeed. Granddaddy said keep 'em close. Said if the Lord above can't bring you good fortune, who can?"

Isaiah turned and looked out the back of the wagon at his brother, Moses, who was hustling to keep pace. "Granddaddy and Gramma says I'm supposed to look after Moses the whole time I'm here, but he's gettin' old enough to look after hisself."

Since settling behind the wagon, Moses had been skipping, hopping, and singing a little loud. "Moses!" Isaiah lifted himself up and yelled to his brother. "Whatchu doin'? Whatchu singin' now?" Moses looked up, smiled back at his brother, cupped his hands around his mouth and kept singing.

The fare is cheap and all can go
The rich and poor are there
No second class aboard this train
No difference in the fare

Isaiah nodded at his brother and then turned toward Will. "Moses, he's a little noisy, always singing songs my Granddaddy sings from before the Civil War. Moses, he remembers all the words."

Isaiah's mood changed and he continued. "I know it's tough for Granddaddy, us being away and all. And Gramma's not doing too good. Something wrong with her breathin'. Granddaddy's got to keep fixin' things and takin' care of her by hisself."

"But he still wanted to send you up here?" Will asked.

"Sure did," Isaiah said, "All his life been given to others. First, raisin' a family on the plantation, then takin' in Moses and me. Now, he's takin' care of Gramma and doin' everything to give us all a good life." Isaiah paused and nodded to himself. "Before we left he told me and Moses, 'We got our freedom now, but it ain't everywhere. Bunch of colored families from Selma headed north last year lookin' for some of it. Make me mighty proud if you two boys go off and try to find some, too.'"

The farmland kept passing by and there was an anxious optimism that the three-wheeled wagon might make it back to the farm. After a time, Will and Isaiah hopped out of the wagon and Owen and Elmer jumped into the empty seats, keeping the un-wheeled back corner almost level. They were off again.

Will wandered to the side of the road and picked up a couple of hay stems leftover from last year.

He offered one to Isaiah. They snapped the stems to size and eased them between their teeth and cheek. The boys and the stems bounced up and down along the road to Helgeveld Farm.

CHAPTER 2

C oming to Helgeveld Farm had been six months in the making for Will. An ad in the Pittsburgh Post-Gazette in late 1916 was looking for summer workers on a 1,500-acre farm outside of Peoria, Illinois. Robert and Sarah Parlor decided that their eldest son, Will, would benefit from a summer of hard work.

His mother told him, "it would be good for you to meet other people, Will. See someplace other than Pittsburgh."

"Best thing I ever did as a young man," Will's father said. "Those summers in 1895 and '96 when I worked on that farm down near Cincinnati. That's what got us to where we are now."

Will's father had done well. After those summers at the farm, Robert Parlor turned a part-time job into Pittsburgh's largest feed and supply store, using the direct farm-to-store strategies he learned those summers outside Cincinnati. Now, Robert owned two stores in Pittsburgh and, in another few years, was planning another store in Chicago to be run by Clive, Robert's younger brother. Robert assumed that his children, Will, James, and perhaps even Annie, would continue on with the business.

*   *   *

The wagon rolled on and Will hustled up alongside Alwin as he continued to maneuver the wagon around the ruts and holes that threatened their uneasy journey.

"When do we reach the farm?" Will asked.

Alwin pointed to both sides of the road. "This is it." He paused so Will could take it all in. "We'll reach the house in a little short of an hour at this pace."

"Farm's pretty big," Will said. "Heard it's the biggest in Illinois."

"Not the biggest, I don't think. There are a couple between here and Chicago gettin' close onto 2,000 acres. One near Springfield well over 2,000, I heard. We're right around 1,500 acres. We lease out about 400 acres and farm 900. There's another 200 or so acres behind the farmhouse that haven't been farmed for years. The whole farm, takes the good part of a morning to circle it all on horseback."

Alwin paused and gave a quick glance over his shoulder to see how the wagon was holding up. Turning back, he continued. "The original family farm, about fifty acres, was a little south of here, but that got broken up and sold ten or fifteen years ago. My grandfather bought this land here in 1869."

The wagon rolled on and Will kept up the pace. "All of this is part of our leased land," Alwin said pointing to the tilled ground on the right. "Another half mile or so, we get to the land you'll all be working."

The plowed earth on Will's right went to the horizon. He looked to the left where there were waves of green. "What's that?" he asked Alwin.

"Mint. Peppermint," said Alwin, keeping his eyes forward, finding the safest path.

"Peppermint?" asked Will. "My mother does some veterinarian and nursing," he said. "She talks about peppermint sometimes and gives it to the sheep, horses, cows, even people. She says it's good for your stomach."

"Yup. That's it," said Alwin. "A few farmers are trying it out. It's pretty popular out East. California too. Smells good. Might be medicine, like you say. Good for desserts, cookies, cakes and such. My father and I looked into it, but it seems a risky crop. No plantin' mint for you. We plant corn, and over the last few years, added in some soybeans. That's where we think the money might be."

Will was settling in, happy to hear Alwin talk about the farm.

"Next year," Alwin continued, "the Department of Agriculture is sendin' a few farmers around here something they call 'hybrid corn.' Want us to try it out. They say it's a new combination of two types of corn in one seed. Supposed to help against drought and corn borers." Alwin kept looking forward, but shook his head. "Different corn in one seed. What'll they come up with next?"

Alwin was tall and blond and he wore working clothes, clean and ironed. The reins wrapped around his index finger and he moved the wagon left or right with a slight tug. While Alwin spoke strong, it wasn't hostile. Will liked him.

The one good rear wheel dragged into a rut. "Whoa, Lily." Alwin jumped off the wagon and examined the wheel and the pothole. He hopped back into the seat and eased the wagon to the right, back to flat road

Will looked to both sides of the road. "Where are the poles? You have electric lights at the farm?"

Alwin laughed. "Too far out of town to run electricity wires. Can't see how we'll ever get them way out here. There was some talk about running poles for telephone lines. Most farmers say they'd rather have a telephone than electric lights."

Another wagon approached pulled by a single horse. Alwin waved, the other driver returning the greeting and slowing his wagon. There were several milk churns behind him in the wagon, full and sloshing.

"Whatcha got here, Alwin?" the driver said, pointing to the three-wheeled mystery wagon.

"As you see it, Matt. She ain't that fast, but I think we'll make it home."

"Seems like there's one thing after another breakin' down on this road to Peoria," said Matt. "Auto, wagon, doesn't matter. Sometimes feels like it'd be quicker to walk." He turned and looked at his cargo and wagon. "I've been lucky with this setup. Other than that broken wheel last month, she gets to town and back every day."

"Right about that, Matt. See you later on," Alwin said.

Alwin waited and let Matt's wagon pass. "That's Matt Gorman. He runs the dairy business at the farm...come on, Lily. Over there!" Alwin continued. "We got fifty head of dairy cows and we get 'em milked twice daily. Matt brings near onto 150 gallons to Peoria every day. They pasteurize it and it's into stores the next day. Heard they're even makin' ice cream with some of it. Everything's goin' modern."

Will nodded, stopped, and let Alwin pass by. He walked across the road, picked a few leaves of mint and rolled them into a bright, wet, green swirl. He sniffed it, then pushed it inside his cheek alongside the hay stem. It was fresh and sweet and he kept it there.

Will eased back next to Isaiah who was keeping up just behind the wagon. They kept their heads down and scuffed at the dirt and stones in the road. "Where's home for you, Isaiah?" Will asked.

"Me and Moses, we's from Florence, Alabama." Isaiah answered slowly, but more confident after the wagon fix that he and Moses had provided. "That's up north in the state, right along the Tennessee River. Mamma died when I was little, but I remember her. She had a problem with her heart and one night they took her to the colored hospital, but there wasn't no doctor there. Then, they took her over to the white hospital, but no doctor would see her. She died in my Granddaddy's wagon. My two sisters and a brother went to live with my Aunt Myrtle down near Tuscaloosa. Moses and me, Gramma and Granddaddy took us in." Isaiah paused and breathed deep. "I don't remember my daddy. But I think somethin' bad happened to him and two of his friends. Granddaddy won't tell us."

"You been away from home before?" asked Will.

"Not like this," Isaiah said shaking his head. "Not where I don't know nobody. And I got to tell you, I'm a little...scared. Don't know what's gonna happen. Don't know what people will think about workin' with me and Moses." Isaiah chuckled and nodded. "But things already feel a little different up here." Isaiah pointed his thumb back over his shoulder. "Back there on the road when we was talkin' about the wagon, I looked Mr. Alwin straight in the eye by accident and he didn't say nothin'. Didn't seem to care. Never had that happen before."

They walked with an easy silence, staring across a landscape that had no end. This was their home until the crops were harvested and the farm was buttoned down for the season.

Roy March walked behind everyone. Will's impression of Roy wasn't a good one, but they'd be working together all summer, so Will slowed and let Roy catch up.

"What you want?" Roy asked as Will got a little closer.

"Nothin', really. Just to know where you're from, Roy."

"None of your business. Why don't you go back up there and talk with the other ladies." Then Roy laughed out loud and said, "And when you get to the farm, be sure to wash some of that colored off ya."

Will stopped and looked at Roy. "Really, Roy? Not that surprised, I guess."

Will had grown up hearing that talk float through the neighborhoods of Pittsburgh. But Will knew several colored farm workers who'd come into his father's store and order supplies. Each month, he'd look for one of them, Ezekiel Williams, who'd come in and ask Will, "Why did the chicken cross the road?" Will would guess and each month Ezekiel would say, "Nope, that's not it," and he'd have a different answer to the joke. Will still laughed when he remembered Ezekiel responding to him one month, "Nope, that's not it. Was to egg-scape the chicken coop."

Will walked back up alongside Isaiah.

A while later, Alwin slowed the wagon and turned around in his seat. "At this pace, I reckon the farm's about a half hour away. Might as well get the last two of you up in the wagon." Owen and Elmer leaped over the sides of the wagon and Roy climbed in to take his turn. Moses remained well behind the wagon, still singing, and apparently not hearing that it was his turn.

Isaiah didn't turn around but yelled straight ahead. "Moses! Git up here! Git youself into the wagon. Now!"

With that, Moses ran toward them, dashed around Isaiah, and jumped into the tilted wagon. He scrambled toward his seat but turned and wagged his finger at his brother with a laugh. "You's just the dickens, you's is, Isaiah!"

Moses plopped himself in the seat, his shoulder banging into Roy, who pushed him aside. "Get away from me! Don't touch me again. You get it?" he barked at Moses. Moses scooched to the side and started humming.

Alwin turned to the two boys seated just behind him. "Hey, Roy. Not gettin' along is one of the main reasons we send people home. The way you're startin' out, you'll be headin' home tomorrow morning. You understand?"

Roy just stared out into the fields.

Alwin shook the reins and the wagon set off for the last few miles to Helgeveld Farm. Two or three workers appeared along the road or in the fields, turning toward Alwin with a wave or a yell.

"Almost there," Alwin said to the boys. Off to the left was a red barn and fenced pasture surrounding black dairy cows, bigger and bulkier than the boys had ever seen, each circled by a wide white stripe.

"Never seen cows that look like that," Elmer said out loud.

Up ahead was the farmhouse.

* * *

The main farmhouse sat on a rise, bright, white, and at attention, wrapped by sycamores, poplars, and white oaks. As the boys got closer, they saw wagons, both empty and full, alongside people walking and working. Out-buildings, silos, fenced-in hogs and sheep, and chickens everywhere. The day shifted from wondering to seeing, and it caught their breaths.

Rolling to the front of the house on three wheels, the wagon drew over two of Alwin's younger brothers who were loading a pull-cart near the house.

"Now, that's some trick, Alwin. Can't you go to town without one thing or another happenin'?" said Gerwin Helgeveld, his arms folded in front of him as he examined the three-wheeled wagon.

"Bet those Peoria ladies took a second look at that," Jakob Helgeveld added.

Alwin turned around to look at the barely together transport and joined in. "Tough enough getting Peoria ladies' attention without a motorcar these days. Lucky for me, it happened on the way back." Alwin turned to the six summer workers in the wagon but said to his brothers, "I'm gonna get these boys some lunch, then drop them at their bunkhouse. Then I'll leave this wagon at the back barn and head up to the house after that."

Alwin eased the wagon along the path to the right side of the main farmhouse, pulling on the reins and stopping the wagon near the rear kitchen door. "Ya'll wait here. I'll be right back." Alwin jumped from the wagon and met a tall, young blonde lady who'd come out of the kitchen. From her laugh, Alwin knew she had already heard about the three-wheeled wagon.

"Don't you start, Vlinder," said Alwin. "Gerwin and Jakob already had a go at me about the wagon, and besides, we made it from Peoria like this. Seems like a good trip."

Vlinder Helgeveld held in a laugh. "Gerwin told me to come out back if I wanted to see a sight." Still smiling, she bent around Alwin to view the wagon. "That there, that's a sight. Not sure if father's gonna be mad or proud, you makin' it from Peoria on three wheels."

"Laugh all you want," Alwin answered. "At least I never mixed up the soap and lard when I was cookin' eggs. But you go ahead, go check it out," he said pointing at the wagon. They shared a laugh, and Alwin turned and headed into the kitchen.

Will stood behind the wagon, next to Isaiah, and watched the young lady walk toward them. She was a startling copy of Alwin and his brothers, just a different size with different curves. She wore work jeans and work shoes and had a tucked-in checkered shirt. Her blonde hair fell and bounced out of place from a day of work. This had to be Alwin's sister.

Vlinder reached the wagon and walked to the back, putting a hand on her hip and shaking her head. "Now, I gotta say, it's been a while since I've seen anything like that." She got down on one knee, looked underneath, shook the axle, and poked a finger up through the floorboard. "That's a mess, that is. No wonder the spring and axle went out. Mostly rot under there. Doesn't seem worth saving." She stood up and clapped the dirt off her hands. "Welcome to the farm, boys." She gave the group a welcoming smile and headed back along the short path and into the farmhouse.

Will watched Vlinder Helgeveld disappear into the white farmhouse. He breathed deeply through his nose, shaking at how everything had just changed. Women in Pittsburgh didn't wear pants and they didn't get down on one knee to figure out problems with a wagon.

But mostly, Will Parlor knew that there was no woman in Pittsburgh, Pennsylvania, or anywhere else, as pretty as Vlinder Helgeveld.

CHAPTER 3

Will wasn't sure how long he stared at the door after Vlinder Helgeveld walked back into the farmhouse, but at some point, Alwin came through that same door with pieces of bread and chunks of ham. He handed them out to the boys. "Lunch was all cleaned up, but I found this in the ice box. Should hold you 'til dinner." Alwin hopped into the wagon and the boys scoffed down the welcome, late lunch. "Let's get you boys settled." Roy and Moses stayed up in the wagon, keeping the three remaining wheels balanced for the rest of the journey. The others walked behind.

Alwin finessed the wagon away from the farmhouse and down between two clean, white rectangular bunkhouses and then to another one at the back. There was a small porch out front with two benches, one on each side of the screen door. Alwin stopped the wagon and jumped off. "This is home for you boys. Bunkhouse 3," he said and motioned for the group to follow him inside. He turned to Will and Isaiah. "You two hop back up in the wagon. I need to take it down to the back barn where I can use your help. Then we'll head back here."

Elmer, Owen, Moses, and Roy followed Alwin into the bunkhouse where the beds were lined up, ten on a side. The boys who had arrived earlier in the month had taken the beds at the far end of the bunkhouse, and, as Alwin told them, were now repairing fences. Roy pushed Elmer aside and grabbed the first bed next to the door on the right. Elmer put his bundle of clothes on the next bed and Moses took the third. Owen claimed the first bed on the left, saving the other two beds next to him for Will and Isaiah.

"I'll be back in a bit and tell you the rules for the summer," Alwin said. "Get yourselves settled. There's a privy out back when you need it. Bucket of water over there if you need a drink."

Alwin returned to the wagon, jumped into the seat, and pulled out his pocket watch. He sighed at how much of the day was gone and then shook the reins. Will and Isaiah twisted their heads in the wagon, taking in the farm, the barns, the fields, the cows, the sheep, and the land. When they passed it, Will kept his stare to the back door of the main house.

Isaiah noticed Will's gaze and said, "You won't likely see her again the rest of the summer."

Will was more surprised than embarrassed at Isaiah's comment and he smiled back at him, both boys settling into the ride.

The back barn wasn't far off, but the short path to it was weed-covered. It was the only building without a fresh coat of paint, and it was missing several side boards. Alwin whoa'd Lily to a stop at the front barn door and hopped off the wagon.

"Come on, boys," said Alwin. "This wagon's got to be repaired or scrapped. We'll leave it here for now, but we need to make some space for it inside the barn. Too much other junk outside already." Will and Isaiah jumped out of their seats and onto the path. Alwin went in front, unstrapped the reins, and led Lily forward, taking time to knuckle-rub her between her eyes. Lily was a family favorite, smart, willing, and steady, with a bit of Morgan in her. "You don't ever complain about anything, do ya girl?" He bent in and put the side of his head against her snout. "Let's get you fed and rested up. Mother wants to take you to the Van der Beek farm tomorrow." He turned to Will and Isaiah and said, "I'll be right back."

While Alwin took Lily to the stable, Will and Isaiah stared at a jumble of dented or split plows, wagon axles, wheels, table tops, chairs, and sinks, all spread outside the barn. When Alwin returned from the stable and yanked the barn door open, Will and Isaiah stared at a further shebang of broken wagons, grain binders, cultivators, pipes, chains, windows, cabinets, random boards, yokes, and even more plows.

Alwin bent down and lifted up one end of a plow in front, then nodded toward another. "If we toss these two plows over against the wall and somehow push that wagon to the side, seems to me we can finagle our wagon over on the other side." Isaiah and Will nodded and picked up the sides of a plow, took it over, and laid it next to the barn wall.

Isaiah stood back and scanned the wreckage. "I has to declare, Mr. Alwin. My Granddaddy woulda thought he died and went to heaven above if he saw all of this stuff that needs fixin'."

"Well, Isaiah," Alwin said, "I think most of this stuff won't get fixed. Some of it's rotted and others, we can't get parts. Mostly though, we just don't have time to fix it all. We even got a busted down Dodge we hauled behind the barn for now. None of us can bear to look at it anymore." Alwin paused and nodded. "This used to be the main barn I was told, but that was long before I was born. Nowadays, we just try to keep my brothers and sisters from playin' in here. Seems each summer, someone of 'em sprains an ankle or something playin' around all this junk."

The three of them tossed the other broken plow to the side and then lifted a long metal counter onto the top of a cast iron sink. They still needed to push a collapsed Murphy wagon two or three feet to the right to make room. Using a few boards, they lifted and slid that wagon more than enough. A few minutes later, the three-wheeled wagon was backed into its spot, perhaps for the last time. "We got more stuff around the farm that should go in here, but this'll do for now."

Alwin and Will walked toward the door, but Isaiah lingered in the barn, examining a broken plow and a split axle. "You don't got a welding tool, do you, Mr. Alwin?"

Alwin turned and stared at Isaiah and then at the menagerie of scrap. He looked back at Isaiah and paused. "No, no we don't."

Alwin closed up the barn and the three walked down the path. "Let's get you boys back to the bunkhouse."

It took no more than three minutes to walk to their new summer home, and once there, Alwin followed Will and Isaiah inside. Owen, Elmer, and Roy had claimed their spots and were lying on their beds, but Moses was nowhere to be seen. Alwin looked around. "Who's missing? Is it Moses? Where's Moses?"

Isaiah stood looking down the bunkhouse. "I think I know," he said. With that, Isaiah got on his knees, bent down, and looked under the beds. "There he is." Isaiah stayed on his knees but looked up at Alwin. "Don't know what to say, Mr. Alwin, but Moses don't sleep in no bed. Sleeps right on the floor. Back home, Gramma and Granddaddy would pull him out sound asleep from underneath. They'd put him in his bed, but at some point, he'd just crawl right back under. Finally, they just gave up." Isaiah stood up and hollered, "Moses! Get yo'self up outta there!" With that, Moses crawled out between two beds and popped to his knees with a face-wide grin.

"That true, Moses?" asked Alwin, "You gonna sleep on the floor, under the bed all the while you're here?"

Moses stood to his feet. "If you don't mind, Mr. Alwin. Slept on the floor my whole life. Just need the pillow," his grin never ending.

"Well," said Alwin trying to keep his smile to himself, "Haven't had anybody sleep on the floor when they're here, but can't see it doing any harm. Alright, Moses. You go ahead and sleep on the floor."

Roy lay on his bed, legs crossed, and hat pulled down over his eyes. "Pretty stupid if you ask me, sleepin' on the floor."

"Well, you don't have to worry, Roy," said Alwin, "'cause the way you're starting out, nobody's gonna ask you anything all summer." Alwin turned to Will and Isaiah and pointed to the two beds just across from Elmer and Moses. "Looks like those beds are yours."

* * *

Alwin waited until Will and Isaiah got to their spots and then addressed all six boys. He'd repeated these words more than a dozen times this spring and he was glad this would be the last. "Alright, this is how it'll work this summer. There's altogether twenty of you in here. The other two bunkhouses aren't quite full, but this one is.

"This is Bunkhouse 3. Remember that. Sometimes we give you your daily work by the bunkhouse number.

"There's a privy for two people just behind the bunkhouse. It's up to you to keep it clean. There's a bucket hangin' on the side and you can get water from the well if you need to splash anything down. Be a good idea to wash yourselves a few times a week, too. Had some fellas come here and never wash themselves all summer."

Everyone was looking at Alwin except Roy who was lying on his bed, hat over his eyes, and his legs crossed over each other. Alwin shook his head at seeing him and continued.

"We ring the morning bell at 5:45. That gets you up and ready for 6:15 breakfast. The wagons head out to the fields at 7 a.m. sharp. If you miss them, you miss a day's pay.

Alwin looked over at Roy. "I'm just sayin' this once, so you all better get it." Roy didn't move and Alwin continued. "At lunch time, my brothers, sisters, and some kitchen workers bring lunch out to the road next to the fields. It's hard to say what time that will be. Depends on where your field is."

"Everyone gettin' this?" Alwin asked. All the boys nodded except Roy. "Wagons will bring you back at the end of the day unless you're close enough to walk. We ring the bell for dinner at 6:15. There's always plenty to eat. And we got dessert every night, too. Cookies, apples, sometimes pie. "We get you back a little earlier on Saturdays. That's tomorrow. It's washing day so you can wash your clothes for church and for the next week."

Alwin took a deep breath and continued. "After dinner, your time is your own up until nine o'clock. Then someone comes around to turn off the lamps. There's a flashlight on the shelf at the front of each bunkhouse for emergencies. After the lamps are out, it's quiet 'til morning. We got rules, but they're mostly common sense. Each summer, there's always a few who get sent home for one thing or another. Usually it's for being lazy, noisy, not gettin' along, or not listenin'." Alwin glanced over at Roy. "Already seen a coupla fellas who might not make it through the summer."

Roy stayed silent, still lying on his bed. He bit one of his fingernails, lifted his hat slightly to view it, then flicked it onto the floor.

"Day off is Sunday," Alwin said. "There's a pastor comes out to the Van der Beek Farm for church services. We passed it on our trip from town today. Most everyone goes and we leave just after breakfast. We're back before lunch and the afternoon is free. Free time. That's usually when people get into trouble. That's the day after tomorrow." Alwin, and the group of boys all glanced over at Roy, wondering how long he'd last. Alwin walked over and stood in front of Roy's bed. "Roy, you getting' all of this?"

"Maybe," said Roy.

"Well, you're lyin' there with your hat over your eyes so it doesn't look like you're paying attention," Alwin said.

"Don't need my eyes. Just my ears," Roy said.

"Here's something for your ears, Roy," Alwin said. "Like I said, each Saturday there's hot water and soap for washin' clothes. It's beside the chow hall and there's a dryin' line by the bunkhouse. From the smell and look of those clothes, you best consider washin' those. Does that sound good, Roy?"

"Nope."

"And why's that Roy?"

"Ain't got no other clothes," Roy answered.

Alwin moved down along Roy's bed, kneeled down and put his head about six inches from him. "You listen with those ears, Roy. I'm gonna fix that for you. Tomorrow, I'll bring a clean pair of pants and a clean shirt and put em' on your bed. We got some extra work boots in the house, too. I'll bring those down. Then, if you want dinner, these clothes you're wearing will be washed and hanging' on the dryin' line tomorrow afternoon. That way you'll have something clean to wear for church. You understand, Roy?"

"Nope. Ain't goin' to church. It's Sunday. Ain't supposed to do nothin' on Sundays."

"What? That doesn't include church, Roy," said Alwin.

"Does to me," said Roy, his hat still over his eyes.

"Really, Roy?" Alwin said. "Well, cleanliness is next to godliness and sounds like you're havin' a little trouble with both."

Alwin rose and walked back between the six workers. He sighed, but liked telling the boys the next part of the summer plan. "Paydays are every two months, the last Friday of May, July, September, and whatever day you leave. $25 a month. That's $50 each payday. And my father wants to teach you more than just planting and fixing, so we pack you all into wagons on those paydays and bring you to Peoria to open a bank account and deposit your pay. My father says a bank account is a sign of growin' up. Then you can walk around the town. Maybe buy somethin' for yourself." Alwin paused. "And, if you're wonderin', it's a day off from the fields, but we pay you for it."

The boys turned and smiled at each other over this unexpected, good news. Even Roy smiled from under his hat, but they weren't sure if it was for the same reason.

Alwin continued. "Mail truck comes to the house Monday, Wednesday, and Friday. If you write any letters, give them to us and we'll send them off for you." Alwin looked out through the screen door and looked back at the group. "I figure the other boys will be back from the fields shortly. It'll be a good time for you to get acquainted. The dinner bell comes along a little after that. Any questions?" They all shook their heads. "Okay, then. I'll see you all in the chow hall."

Alwin headed out the door and up toward the main house.

As soon as Alwin was gone, Roy popped off his bed and walked down the aisle toward the back of the bunkhouse, stopping and looking at each boy's bed. He went alongside one bed, sat on it, and pulled an old worn case from underneath.

The boys gazed at him and Owen yelled. "Hey, Roy. Put that back. It ain't yours."

"Shut up. I'm just lookin' at stuff." Roy pulled a few shirts and pants out of the case, held them up and laughed. "Look at this. This bugger brought enough clothes for everybody."

Owen jumped off his bed and headed down the aisle toward Roy. Roy shoved the clothes back in the case and pushed it under the bed. Then he stood up, passed Owen in the aisle, and threw himself on his bed.

Soon after, the other boys in the bunkhouse returned, walking and talking down the aisle to their beds and belongings. They turned their heads toward their new roommates and each group grunted a friendly greeting to the other. A few of them headed out the back door to the privy, while others flopped onto their beds, hungry, and glad their day was over.

Roy pushed himself onto his elbows, turned and stared at Elmer in the bed next to him. "Elmer! Keep that hand under your blanket or I'll have nightmares all summer!"

With that, Owen hopped off his bed and said, "Elmer, take my bed. I think I'll sleep next to Roy." Owen moved over and stood just above Roy. "You're gettin' real close to the third fight I ever had. First two fights went pretty good for me. Lookin' at you, I think the third fight would go good too. You keep that mouth of yours goin' and we'll find out."

"Okay, farmer boy," Roy replied and laid back down.

Owen stared at Roy and then lay down on his own new bed next to him.

*   *   *

The twenty boys in Bunkhouse 3 were ready to eat when the dinner bell rang. Roy jumped up first, headed out the door, and sprinted toward the chow hall. The others hustled close behind, not only from hunger, but also from the welcome commotion that dinner offered.

Workers from the other two bunkhouses merged into one path that wove around the back of the farmhouse to a large, white, rectangular building. The chow hall sat on a slope, across a path from the main farmhouse. Smoke rose from two chimneys and as the army of hungry workers approached, the boys ran headlong into aromas that smelled like family and home.

Once inside, the boys saw two rows of long tables, long enough to hold all the diners. The kitchen was open and sat at the end of the chow hall, the ovens and gas-fired stoves filled with baking or bubbling dinner. The kitchen workers were mostly young girls who, like the boys, had come to Helgeveld Farm for summer work. They stirred pots, filled trays, and scooped dinner, creating an orchestra of food frenzy.

There were two lines, one on each side of the hall. As they reached the front, each boy grabbed a plate, fork, spoon, and knife from wooden tables and moved slowly toward the steam and the smells. Will, Isaiah, Moses, Elmer, and Owen followed at the end of one line and Elmer noticed that Roy already had dinner and was sitting at the front of one table.

The girls scooped roasted chicken, mashed potatoes, gravy, and carrots onto the boys' plates. Lemonade, milk, and water sat at a separate table.

A young girl at the end of a serving table put a near plate-sized carve of bread on each dish, spread with butter and topped with strawberry jam. Then she slid two gingerbread cookies under the side of the dinner. Will looked at her and figured she had to be another Helgeveld sister, a little younger but still blonde, with suspendered blue jeans and bright eyes like Vlinder. With that, Will leaned out of the line and looked hard at the kitchen, searching for Vlinder Helgeveld, who looks under wagons. He made a second scan, but she wasn't part of this group of kitchen workers.

Alwin came through the side kitchen door and stood looking over the tables, smiling at the orderly commotion. "Remember," he yelled across the chow hall. "Take all you want, but eat what you take. We don't like wastin' food here."

Owen was the first of the five through the line. He waited for the others and nodded toward the end of the hall. "Looks like the only seats left are down the end of this table."

Heading there, the boys glanced at the other workers and their plates of food. No one was shy. Chicken and mashed potatoes formed small mountains on their plates. Carrots were there but pushed to the side. Moses' pile was the highest of the five and gravy covered everything. His slab of bread sat on the top like a raft on a brown ocean. He had a fork, spoon, and knife in the other hand and wore the grin of someone whose prayers had been answered. Owen looked over at Moses and shook his head. Moses could never eat all of that, he thought.

All five sat and focused on their plates, eating quicker than they should, and occasionally looking around at those they'd spend the summer with. The hum of conversation suggested friendships had begun to sprout, yet some sat alone, still searching to find a connection.

Owen, Elmer, Will, and Isaiah waited until their group of five all finished. That meant waiting for Moses, who, when he finished his plate, leaned over and scooped the leftover mashed potatoes off of Isaiah's plate. Not quite satisfied, he turned to his brother, "You eat both your dessert cookies, Isaiah?"

"Of course! I ate them first!" said Isaiah. "When you gonna be done? We're waitin' on you."

Moses finished his mouthful, jumped up to join the others, and the five of them stacked their dirty plates in tall piles on a table close to the front. Will scanned the chow hall one last time. Vlinder Helgeveld wasn't there.

Rather than head straight back to their bunkhouse, the boys took another route, past the stables, past an outbuilding, ending up on a rise just behind and above the main farmhouse. There was an open area and to the side, a tree pushed higher and wider than any tree the boys had ever seen.

Elmer bent back, almost falling over examining it. "That there is the biggest tree I ever saw. And look at the branches; they reach out almost halfway over the farmhouse."

Isaiah looked up. "Yup. You could build a whole house from the wood in this tree."

"What is it?" asked Will.

"Sycamore, I believe," said Moses. "Got 'em all over Alabama, but never saw one this big."

The five sat with their backs against the sycamore and viewed pastures of cows and sheep, plowed fields, and the straight road to Peoria. Through the western clouds, the sun sent out a final crimson surge. From the farmhouse, someone was playing *Let Me Call You Sweetheart* on a piano.

Owen leaned forward and picked up a stick, dragging it across some short grass in front of him. He kept his head down, wondering what his father would think of him sitting and talking with Isaiah and Moses. "Alwin was right about the food," said Owen. "If breakfast and lunch are like that dinner, that's reason enough to stay."

"Sure is," said Isaiah. "We don't get plates 'a food like that 'cept when we do repairin' for Miss Wilkins. Last fall, we finished rebuildin' and repairin' all four wheels and one of the springs on her wagon. When we brought it back to her house, me, Moses, and Granddaddy got our pay and a pile of collards, cornbread, potatoes, and pork chops. I swear, it brought tears to my Granddaddy. We always hoped Miss Wilkins would need more repairin'."

The horizon eased into an evening maroon and when there was more dark than light, the boys made their way back to the bunkhouse. Going through the door, Elmer walked behind Owen followed by Isaiah, Will, and Moses. There were four gas lights spread throughout the bunkhouse, but only three were lit. Roy lay on his bed, his hat over his eyes, twisting a hay stem in his mouth.

Everyone made a last trip to the privy. Coming out, Will caught the eye of a bulky fellow who looked a few years older. Will nodded and spoke first. "Hi. I'm Will Parlor. How long you guys been here?"

"Hi. I'm Lucas Miller." Lucas was friendly and welcomed the conversation. "Got here three days ago with four other guys. Only me and Robert Clark came to this bunkhouse. He's right there," Lucas pointed at Robert and continued the exchange. "The work's not bad here. It's all day, but they don't expect more out of you than you can do." Lucas paused, happy to share his summer work history. "I gotta say. Last two summers I worked at a farm in Ohio. Couldn't take it anymore. Nothin' you did was right, and both years I didn't get all the money they promised. This place, this farm, looks good and they treat you like people."

Lucas paused. "You friends with those two?" he asked, nodding toward Isaiah and Moses.

"Yeah, I guess," said Will. "We rode out from town with them."

"Keep an eye out for things," Lucas said, "there's a few fellas down in Bunkhouse 1 who want to make trouble."

"Okay," said Will. "Thanks." He looked over at Isaiah and Moses wondering what their crime was.

Once inside the bunkhouse, Will nodded to Lucas and both headed to their bunks. After a time, Jakob Helgeveld, Alwin's younger brother, came in with a tin of kerosene, filled the one empty lamp, and then turned off the others.

"We'll see you all in the morning," Jakob announced. He left through the back side door putting an end to the boys first day at Helgeveld Farm. It was a good one.

Other than Roy screaming, "Shut Up!" once or twice to snorers at the end of the bunkhouse, everyone slept hard and deep.

CHAPTER 4

Vlinder Helgeveld rose early the following morning. She was generally the first one up in the farmhouse, and she lit the oil lamp next to her bed, made her way down the hall, down the stairs, and across the big room where she would always look out the front window, even when there was no hint of light. She turned from the window and the oil lamp knocked over the only photo of her great-great grandfather and great-great grandmother, Henry and Arabella Helgeveld.

Vlinder picked up the photo, wondering if Henry and Arabella ever thought of the family legacy they would create. Vlinder certainly did. More than once, she wondered where she fit into it all. Would her children in future years love the farm as much as she does? Get married in the side yard like so many others had?

Vlinder reached past the photo to the family Bible, always open to a verse her mother had picked out for the week. She flipped through the Bible, noting a few pressed flowers and important documents. Then she moved to the front pages of the Bible, to the dates of family history: births, deaths, marriages. She saw her brother's name: *Alwin Peter Helgeveld, b. August 6, 1893*. Next was her sister: *Arenda Elsbeth Helgeveld b. February 19, 1895-d. February 27, 1895*. Then her older brother: *Gerwin Pieter Helgeveld b. October 2, 1896*. She followed next: *Vlinder Mae Helgeveld, b. November 27, 1897*. After that came her other brothers and sisters. She flipped further back, to the first entry in the Bible, *Henry Helgeveld, b. July 30, 1815*, followed by *Arabella Alders, b. October 2, 1817. Married June 23, 1837*. Under that was, *Journey to America, April 12, 1838*, written by her great-great grandmother Arabella, and signaling her and Henry's journey, the journey from Holland to America.

Everyone in the family knew the story.

*   *   *

In 1837, twenty-two-year-old Henry Helgeveld learned that a Dutch man, Martin Van Buren, had been elected president of the United States of America. Henry gathered up his belongings and he and his new wife, Arabella, left Rotterdam, Holland on April 12, 1838. Six weeks later they landed at the Port of New York and made their way into one of the many communities where Dutch people, Dutch language, and Holland handshakes were common.

Over the following year, they managed to save $148 and on April 3, 1839, they joined several other wagons full of German, French, Norwegian, and Swedish immigrants heading west from New York City. Henry and Arabella ended up in the small Dutch community in central Illinois that would later be called New Holland, and with the help of neighbors, they got their small farm up and running. Within eight years, they had five children and a profitable farm.

But slavery was dividing the nation. Although Illinois was a free state, Missouri plantation owners were allowed to recapture their "property" throughout Illinois. Many of the Dutch farming settlers remembered the rigid hierarchies and religious constraints back in Holland and were sympathetic to the plight of the slaves. Most saw echoes of their own desire for freedom and dignity and did all they could to frustrate the furious Missouri landowners. Their strongest strategy was to appear confused and to speak only Dutch when confronted with any questions from the southern slave owners. The Missourians would generally erupt into a chorus of English curse words that many of the Dutch had never heard, but were happy to add to their English vocabulary.

The Dutch children were in on it, too. They knew the best routes and best hiding spots for the escapees, taking them through New Holland to other helpers nearer Chicago and eventually to Canada.

However, when 1860 arrived, war appeared closer than ever. There was some hope and pride when a fellow Illinoisan, Abraham

Lincoln, was elected President of the United States. He promised an end to slavery, but this position proved too much for southern states and in mid-April 1861, news reached the New Holland settlement that shots had been fired in the state of South Carolina.

The Civil War had begun.

Recruitment centers sprung up throughout Illinois, and young Dutch men in the New Holland Community were among the first to volunteer. Henry and Arabella's sons, Peter and Otto, joined seventy-eight Dutchmen in an artillery regiment heading south from Chicago. With little training, they fought in several skirmishes and battles in Missouri.

Peter wrote home often. In August of 1861, he informed the family that Otto had been wounded in the leg but continued marching with a crutch. Peter told his parents not to worry; he'd look after Otto. But his letters also spoke of blistered feet, constant sickness, and hunger. Peter longed for home and his letters ended with memories of Christmas, getting the fields ready, and the happy mealtimes when father and mother would tell stories of life back in Holland.

In early October 1861, the family received a letter from Isaac Braam, a neighbor's son, a friend, who fought alongside Peter and Otto. At the kitchen table, Arabella opened the letter, glanced at its contents, and dropped it to the floor. Henry picked up the letter and read to the family that during the Battle of Lexington, Peter was pulling Otto away from the main attack when both were shot and killed by Confederate forces.

Arabella slumped in her chair and then leaned forward. She clamped her hands together and pounded them onto the kitchen table, wailing at a God, her God, who could allow this. The three other Helgeveld children surrounded their mother, crying hysterically that their two older brothers, those who meant everything to them, were gone.

Henry Helgeveld sat emotionless. He got up from the table and walked out the front door, grabbing a shovel on the porch and heading to the fields. But he collapsed next to the barn, face down, beating the ground. From the kitchen, the children heard their father cry for the first time.

When the Civil War ended, the farm profited, but the deaths of Peter and Otto hung over it and never left. By the fall of 1867, daughters Angelien and Beatrix found Dutch farmer husbands leaving Bartel, the youngest of the clan, still at the farm.

Bartel, in his mid-twenties, wanted to build his own future. In late 1869, a 350-acre farm became available twenty miles north of the Helgeveld Farm, and Henry helped Bartel purchase it.

In early spring 1870, the Helgevelds accompanied Bartel on his move north. When they left him a month later, Bartel had a rebuilt three-room house, a small barn, a few fields ready to be planted, and cow paddocks well-repaired. That summer, he hired a traveling Meskwaki family, members of a local Fox tribe, who were searching for summer work.

Fall saw a successful harvest.

All that was missing was a wife.

Bartel felt the need to re-center himself in his faith and used that as a reason to make the two-hour Sunday trip to the Dutch Reformed Church in Peoria. However, while churchgoers were bowed in prayer, Bartel sometimes found himself scanning the congregation for a future Mrs. Helgeveld. On his third Sunday pilgrimage, he focused on a young lady in the pew just in front of him who was far prettier than what he could ever have imagined. Two weeks later, after the service, he gathered the courage to tip his hat at her. Her return smile kept him sleepless all week. When church finally arrived the following Sunday, his nervous hat tip was met with a "Pleased to see you again, sir."

Five months later, Luna Hofman and Bartel Helgeveld were married. Throughout the next year, Bartel found himself staring at his new wife, figuring he was luckier than he deserved. She listened to his problems and got him to slow down and look at options. Over time, she put curtains on the windows, doilies under the oil lamps, and planted lavender forget-me-nots across the front of the house.

February 1872 brought their first child, Joren, followed by Hendrick in 1873. In 1876, twins Elisabeth and Wilhelmina, along with half-sister Olivia, joined the family. In 1877, despite the financial uncertainty of the *Long Depression*, Bartel seized the opportunity to purchase an adjoining 500 acres with a sizeable loan, believing that expanding his holdings was worth the risk. Bartel hired eight, then twelve workers to farm the land, including several Indians from local tribes and a number of colored workers who had come north after the Civil War. In the years since, Helgeveld Farm continued to hire anyone who was willing to work hard.

During the late 1880s and early 1890s, the Dutch community grew and modern life brought more changes and more social connections. Soon, young Dutch men and young Dutch women were meeting on their own, occasionally dancing together. This left many parents to consider returning to Holland for the good of their children's Christian souls.

In 1892, Bartel and Luna's first child, Joren, took Anika Nouwen as his bride. A few eyebrows were raised when several Catholic friends attended the ceremony at the Dutch Reformed Church.

But times were changing, and a new generation had arrived at Helgeveld Farm.

*   *   *

Vlinder flipped ahead in the family Bible, viewing the empty pages waiting for future Helgeveld names, birthdays, and life events. Finally, she turned the pages and left the Bible open to the verse her mother had chosen for the week.

Vlinder's sister, Corrie, had come down the stairs and stood next to her. "Morning, Corrie," said Vlinder and she put her arm around her younger sister's shoulder. "Come on," Vlinder said. "Let's start breakfast."

CHAPTER 5

Minutes after the wake-up bell, Isaiah knelt at the end of Moses' bed, pulling him out from underneath, still asleep. "This ain't home Moses, and I ain't gonna go through this every mornin'!" With that, Isaiah lifted up both of Moses' feet and let them drop to the floor. Moses opened one eye and yawned. He tried to crawl back under his bed, but Isaiah was ready and pulled him part way down the aisle between the beds.

Moses stretched and lifted his head, then rose up on his elbows and smiled at his brother. "Mornin', Isaiah."

Isaiah shook his head, got up, and then sat on the side of his bed facing Will. "Wonder what we'll be doin' today?"

"Bustin' clods," said a voice on the other side of Will's bunk.

Isaiah looked at the speaker. "What's that?"

"We're gonna take most of the week goin' through the fields, bustin' up the big clods of dirt left by the plows," Nathan Carey told the six new arrivals. "Planting's gotta start in a coupla weeks, so the field's gotta be smoothed out."

Will and Isaiah both nodded at the prospect.

Everyone filed out of the bunkhouse and up toward breakfast, the chow hall as lively and noisy as the night before. Eggs, grits, toast, and apple juice filled their stomachs and lifted their moods. Will looked through the kitchen. He saw several Helgeveld family members, but not the one he had hoped.

At 7 a.m., three flatbed farm wagons gathered in front of the farmhouse, each pulled by a pair of draft horses. The wagons had space for up to twenty-five workers and the young laborers gathered around them. Soon, Alwin appeared from the main house and marched down the path toward the gathered crowd. On the way, he put a quick hand on the shoulder of several boys, along with a "Good morning." Gerwin and Jakob were already up front and they shared a laugh with their brother when he arrived.

At the wagons, Alwin turned to address the group of workers. "Okay, everyone has arrived and over the next several days, you'll be walking the fields and breaking up dirt clumps, flattening plow grooves, and leveling things out for the seed. Planting starts right after." Just then, Roy ambled up the path from the bunkhouse and leaned against the first wagon he came to. Alwin stopped his instructions and stared at Roy. "Roy, you show up late again and you've got the day off with no pay. You got that?" Alwin waited. "You got that Roy? I gotta hear it."

"I got it, boss," Roy said, arms crossed and looking down.

Alwin turned back to the workers and held up a long-handled tool. "We've got these harrowers. You'll drag these across the clumps and flatten things out. And you've got two other tools, your two feet. Keep dragging the harrow and kicking the soil 'til it's level. You got any questions, ask your man in charge." Alwin looked across the group. "Okay, let's go."

The five friends jumped and pulled themselves onto the closest wagon, and it sagged and bounced when it was lined with workers.

Elmer turned toward Owen. "That doesn't sound too bad, walkin' and kickin'." Owen agreed.

Their wagon driver was the man in charge. He was short and stocky and didn't appear to be a family member. He stood up in the front of the wagon and looked back at the group. "I'm Carlton Wallace. Call me Carl. I'll get you into your fields and you can get to work." Carl sat down, readying the reins. Seconds later they were off, passing fields the boys remembered from yesterday's ride in from Peoria.

After a fifteen-minute ride, the wagon turned right and followed a narrow path between field after field of plowed land. The boys could now see the breadth of the Helgeveld Farm and it appeared even bigger than when they came in from Peoria. They continued to pass fields, each bordered by a narrow wagon path. Moses, who sat next to Isaiah, bounced along with the others, matching the rhythm with a song:

I came from ole Virginy from the county Acomac,
I have no wealth to speak of 'cept de clothes upon my back,
I can do the country hoe-down I can buck and wing to show down,
And while I'm in the notion, just step back and watch my motion.

Will looked over at Moses. Isaiah spoke up. "That's one of my Granddaddy's favorite jigs. We sing it all the time back home," and Isaiah joined in, swaying with his brother and with the lyrics.

The path was tight and the wagon wheels rolled straight, finally stopping a few fields before a slight climb and a border of trees.

The sun had risen sharp, but a quick night rain had left the fields damp and smelling sweet and earthy, a promise of the harvest ahead. Everyone hopped off the wagon and waited for further directions.

Carl motioned to the boys to grab a harrow and follow him. He positioned each boy at the far end of a field and they stared at land that was rich, brown, and jagged. Head-sized clods sat aside grooves of plowed soil. Leveling each field looked like a week's work.

When it was his turn, Carl put Will in front of an unending field of lumpy and ragged work. Beyond that, Will could barely see the next field, his afternoon task. Will jumped in and started dragging the harrow and stomping through long lines of damp dirt. Soon, his feet and harrow settled into a rhythm, and at the end of the first row he looked back on his effort. Yes, he thought, they could plant seed in that.

Two fields over, Moses jumped, kicked, smoothed, and flattened the damp clods, easing into a rhythm that matched whatever song he was singing. Owen pulled his harrow and his two feet rose and fell like pistons, leaving the ground as smooth as a prairie. Elmer crossed his field side to side, kicking and pulling clumps of damp soil into plowed grooves. Isaiah and Will looked across their fields at each other, smiling at their equal progress. Carl walked alongside Roy's field, hurrying him along and hopping into his field to even out the job.

The sun climbed quick and steady, and before they knew it, the lunch whistle called them in. The boys stood and stared at their fields, now wavy sod canvases, ready for nature to generate its annual masterwork.

The workers filed off the fields and headed to their wagon, dirt and mud caked to their hands, pants, and shoes. Wiping the sweat from their brows spread the dirt from head to toe. Carl had turned the wagon around and then addressed the laborers. "Lunch is out at the main road. Hop onto the wagon and we'll get you out there in a few minutes."

Before they jumped onto the wagon, Owen brought his harrow over to Carl, broken in half. "This just broke, Mr. Carl. Must have pulled it too hard."

Carl held both pieces up and examined them. "Yeah, too bad. They do break from time to time. We don't have any extras. You'll have to use your feet, I guess."

Moses stepped in. "Owen, here. Use mine. I use my feet mostly anyways."

Owen stared at Moses. "You sure?"

Moses shrugged his shoulders. "Sure." And he handed Owen his harrow.

Owen looked at the harrow and nodded at Moses. He wondered how his father would have twisted this scene to make Moses look like the problem.

Everyone jumped onto the flatbed, sharing their morning strategies and anxious for a belly of lunch. They all agreed. Smashing, kicking, and leveling mounds of dirt was more fun than they had thought.

At the main road, there were already thirty or so workers stirring around the two lunch wagons that came out from the farm. The boys jumped off their wagon and headed toward the far lunch wagon which had fewer eaters. Each wagon had three or four girls organizing trays of sliced brown bread, cold carved ham, cooked potatoes with mayonnaise, and sweet pickles. Each boy took a provided towel to wipe their hands as clean as they could. Then they loaded their plates and slathered the ham with mustard.

After the food trays, and at the end of the wagon, a spoon dropped down to ladle potatoes onto Will's plate. Will followed the spoon up to Vlinder Helgeveld, who was wearing the same smile she had yesterday.

"Well, now. Just look at you," Vlinder started. "I thought you boys were using your feet to break apart these fields. Looks like you're using your faces, too. As much dirt there as anywhere else."

Will was too surprised to say anything and just looked up at Vlinder, his two white eyes peering from behind sweat and dirt. He gathered himself and finally said, "Gotta earn my pay and my lunch, don't I?"

"Learned that on your first day?" said Vlinder. "That's a good start."

Isaiah stood behind Will and pushed him forward. "Let's go, Will. We ain't got time for talkin'. Gotta eat."

Will grinned at Isaiah, took his plate, and they sat down at the edge of the road, next to Elmer and Owen. Isaiah sat next to Will who kept staring back at Vlinder, still ladling potatoes onto worker plates. "Don't know whatchu thinkin'," said Isaiah. "She's Alwin's sister, and she's part of the family."

Will nodded, lifted his mustard slathered ham sandwich, and took a bite. He wasn't sure what he was thinking either.

Roy wandered over and stood between the four boys and the lunch wagon. He put his apple juice on the ground and scooped ham and potato up with his spoon. He cocked his head back toward the lunch wagons. "Didja see those ladies up there? I'd take a flyer at any of 'em."

Will peered around Roy and saw Vlinder and two other blonde girls on the wagon. "Roy, that one in front with the striped shirt? Her? She looks about twelve."

"So?" A few potato pieces fell from Roy's mouth, one bouncing onto Will's shoe. "Doesn't have to be her. Any of 'em would do just fine," Roy laughed and walked away.

Will looked at Isaiah and shook his head.

Alwin finished his lunch, moved to the center and addressed the group. "Finish up your lunches. We're heading out in a few minutes. If you want to take a piece of ham or bread back to the fields, now's the time to get it." He looked around and waited until everyone quieted down. "Somethin' else. We're moving too slow. We gotta move faster and get these fields flattened. To do that, each one of you has to finish at least two fields today. Most of you haven't finished one yet. Planting starts in another week and these fields have got to be ready."

Alwin paused and gave a quick glance at Moses. "But Carl and I noticed a few of you getting your work done nicely. So," continued Alwin, "the field bosses and I came up with a plan. I know it's Saturday and we finish a little early today, but anybody who finishes two fields can be done for the day. I figure two fields is a good Saturday's work, so if you finish, check with your supervisor, and if he says it's good, you can head over to your wagon, sit down, whatever you want." Alwin paused and looked out at the fields. "Alright, get to work."

Wanting one last look at Vlinder, Will pulled Isaiah behind her wagon on their way back to the fields. She was kneeling down, pulling the trays toward the middle of the wagon when Will walked toward a pile of ham. Vlinder looked up, saw him coming, and put a slice of brown bread and two pieces of ham in a napkin and handed it to Will. "Never heard Alwin say anything like that before, about getting your work done early," she said. "Maybe you'll work hard and you'll get yourself some time off." She looked straight at him. "You know, even with all that dirt, you got the sharpest dimples I ever saw. I'll bet the young ladies back home take a liking to those."

"Haven't got a lady back home," Will said, smiling at Vlinder.

Vlinder smiled back and pushed her blonde hair off her brow. "Really? I'm surprised."

CHAPTER 6

Alll afternoon, there was whooping, jumping, and clod-smashing. Alwin's plan worked and some workers completed their two fields early and took their reward by lying next to their wagon.

When they got back to the farm, all the boys gathered their dirty clothes for Saturday washing. Will, Isaiah, Moses, Elmer, and Owen had worked just one day, but their dirt-caked shirt and pants needed the attention. A dozen tubs of warm sudsy water sat ready. Next to the tubs were clean water rinse tubs.

Roy was first at the tubs and he washed his shirt and pants, leaving him to wear the clean set that Alwin had lent him. He hung his damp clothes on the line outside the bunkhouse in full view assuring himself that he'd get dinner. Then he headed inside, laid on his bunk, and pulled his hat over his eyes.

Owen and Elmer weren't far behind Roy, carrying today's work clothes, washed and wet. They met Will and Isaiah on their way to the tubs. "Better get up there quick," Owen said, "It's getting crowded. We're going to hang these on the line and then walk around a little."

Will and Isaiah stepped up their pace. Isaiah and Moses made a deal to wash each other's clothes on alternate Saturdays. This week, Isaiah did the washing and Moses had stayed behind and headed under his bunk for a quick nap before dinner. Isaiah found a tub, dumped in his (and Moses') clothes and got to work.

For Will, his mother always did the washing, so the process was a little new to him. He looked around at others who kept plunging their clothes and sloshing them in the frothy water. Finally, he stepped up to a washtub, took his dirt-caked pants and shirt and swirled them around in the suds. At the far end of the tubs Will saw Vlinder, talking and laughing with a group of boys.

A voice to his left brought him back to his task. "You're not going to get those clean if you just drop them in the water like that." A blonde-haired girl reached over and pulled Will's pants out of the tub. Didn't his mother teach him anything, she wondered. "Look at them. Look at the knees." Will looked at them. Yes, more was needed.

"Okay," Will said looking over at her. "But I thought the soap cleaned them."

The young girl shook her head. "You must be from the city. Here, step back. I'll show you." Will stepped to the side of the worker, obviously a Helgeveld, who took his pants and pushed them under the suds, scrubbing one leg against the other, top to bottom, then again. She pulled them out and held them up to Will. "There. Look. It took work to get them dirty; it takes work to get them clean. Do the same with your shirt; give them a rinse and take another look."

The girl stood and watched Will wash his shirt and then toss it all into the rinse tub, plunging and rinsing next week's outfit. She nodded at the results and Will saw the same bright eyes and sure manner of Vlinder. He threw the pants and shirt over his shoulder and turned toward the washing helper. "With that blonde hair, you've got to be a Helgeveld." It was bold, but Will hoped to make himself known. Maybe she'd mention him to Vlinder. "Weren't you the one putting cookies on the plates at last night's dinner?"

She smiled and looked straight at him. "Yes, that was me. I'm Corrie. Corrie Helgeveld. I got a twin, Hans." She motioned toward her blond twin brother. "There he is. Actually, two sets of twins in the family. Lotta and Bram are the others. They're a little younger than us, but they're out here too." She gestured toward the pair helping other washers, as blond as the rest. "There they are." Corrie glanced at Will's cleaner clothes. "Those look a lot better." Then she turned and walked along the line of sudsy tubs, giving a quick twirl-around, and helping other city boys who knew little about washing clothes.

After the wash, Will met Isaiah on the path back to Bunkhouse 3. They headed to the drying line next to the bunkhouse and hung their clothes in the late afternoon sun. Isaiah walked inside the bunkhouse and Will left for the privy.

When Will finished, Isaiah ran out the door of the bunkhouse, saw Will, and dashed over. "They's gone! They's gone! My pennies! They's gone!" Isaiah reached Will and held up a shoe. "I put the pennies in my sock and pushed them in my church shoe, but now they's gone! They's our good luck!"

Will took the shoe and looked into the toe. "Maybe you put them someplace else?"

"No, no. Always put stuff in a sock and in my shoe. Never lost nothin'."

"They weren't in your pants pocket?" asked Will.

"Nah," said Isaiah. "Couldn't in my work pants. They's a hole in the pockets. Couldn't risk losin' 'em in the field. I swear, Will, when I held them three pennies it was like Granddaddy was right here with me and Moses. What am I gonna do?"

"We'll look around, Isaiah. Come on."

The boys hustled back into the bunkhouse. Will wondered if Roy, who was lying on his bed, might be at the bottom of this.

"Right there," Isaiah pointed. "Right under my bed, right there. That's where I put my shoes. I sat on the bed, put the pennies in my sock, stuffed the sock in the shoe, and put them both right there."

Will went to the other side of the bed, got down on his stomach, and wiggled underneath. He rubbed his hand back and forth but found nothing but dust and a nail.

"Lose somethin'?" asked Roy, hat over his eyes, arms behind his head, and feet crossed on his cot.

"Yes, I did," Isaiah answered, beginning to suspect Roy. "I'm missin' three pennies my Granddaddy gave me. I need 'em back real bad. You seen 'em? "

Roy didn't move. "Nope. Don't know nothin' about that. But I'll keep a sharp eye out for them."

That confirmed it to Will and Isaiah. Roy took them.

"Got any pennies in your pockets, Roy?" Will asked.

Roy thrust his hands into his pockets. "Nope. Nothin' there."

"Why don't you pull those pockets out so we can see for ourselves," Will said.

Roy reached down and pulled his pockets inside out. Nothing.

Will turned toward Isaiah, pointed at Roy and mouthed, "He did it. We'll find them."

"Told you I didn't have them," Roy said. "It's a real shame. Whaddya bothering me for, anyways? Why don't you look around? Maybe somebody else took 'em."

Will winked at Isaiah and said, "Let's check Owen's bed first." They lifted the pillow, pulled back the covers, and even searched a pair of his shoes. Nothing.

They moved to Elmer's bed and did the same, but this time they found two pennies sitting on top of the blanket under his pillow. Isaiah picked them up. The 1912 and 1916 Lincoln Cents. "Here's two of 'em," Isaiah said and he showed them to Will.

Roy rolled over and pushed himself up on his elbows. "Pretty lucky, I'd say. Didn't think that guy was a robber, but now we know, I guess."

"Where's the other one, Roy?" asked Will.

"Yeah, Roy. That other one. I need that one too." Isaiah said. "The 1909 penny with President Lincoln on it. We gotta get that one back to have 'em all together."

"Guess you better ask Elmer. But watch out. He might take a swing at ya with that hand of his." Roy started to laugh. "Probably poke you in the eye with that finger!"

With the commotion, Moses rolled out from under his bed, rubbed his eyes, and sat on his knees. He looked at Isaiah and said,

"Granddaddy's pennies? You put 'em in your sock and shoe? Yeah, I saw Roy pick up yo' shoes a while back, then he put 'em back down. Didn't think nothin' of it."

Roy exploded. "What the hell you doin' sleepin' under your bed! You're spying on me, that's what you doin'. And you're lyin' too!"

Moses shrugged. "I ain't lyin', Roy. I saw ya."

Will walked over to Roy's bed. "There's one penny still missing, Roy. You give us that one and maybe we don't make you sorry you came here."

"Go ahead! Do what you want! If you do, you ain't never gettin' that last penny back." He turned to Moses. "You saw I went outside, too? Well, I did. Go look for it. It's somewhere on the farm."

"That'd be true," Moses said. "He went outside for a bit."

"Leave me alone and maybe you'll get it back," Roy yelled. "You tell Alwin and you'll never get it."

Owen and Elmer walked through the door and saw Will and Isaiah standing over Roy.

"Something going on here?" asked Owen.

"Yeah," said Will. "Roy here, took some pennies out of Isaiah's sock and slid two of 'em under Elmer's pillow. Wanted us to think he took 'em, but Moses saw him do it. Still one penny missing and Roy ain't saying where it is."

"Maybe we should just make him tell us," Owen said moving toward Roy.

Isaiah looked over. "Wait, Owen. He said he's gonna give it back. Might ruin the good luck if we end up fightin' over it."

"I swear, Roy," said Owen, "you've caused more trouble in two days than I've seen anybody cause in their whole life. One of these times, Isaiah, or somebody else, ain't going to be around and stop you from getting' what you deserve."

"Why you stickin' up for the coloreds?" asked Roy. "They ain't worth nothin'."

Owen stepped back, looked over at Moses and Isaiah, and then back at Roy. "Hate to say it, Roy, but you sound just like my father. Best you keep your thoughts to yourself." Owen paused then added.

"One good thing. Looks like you washed your clothes and got on the new set Alwin gave you. But I declare, Roy, you still stink!"

Roy shrugged his shoulders and looked up at Owen. "Good," he said.

*　*　*

The next morning after breakfast, the boys and house girls wandered to the front of the farmhouse and waited for the wagons to ferry them to morning church services. From Bunkhouse 3, all the boys had shown up, except Roy. Before they'd left the bunkhouse, the boys told Roy that if anything was missing when they got back from church, they'd use his mattress to clean the privy.

Alwin came out of the farmhouse and strode to the center of the group. "We got most of you here now, and these Sunday services will be regular through the season. We're heading back to the Van der Beek Farm. They've got a flat piece of land behind their farmhouse where we'll have the church service. Like most churches, it lasts a couple of hours. We'll get back here in time for lunch. The Van der Beek's have a pastor come up from Peoria the night before." Alwin paused, took off his hat and rubbed his hand across his head. "Now, this pastor, Pastor Jannsen, he's new here. Just came over from Holland and he's helping out Pastor Kuyper in town. He speaks pretty good English and he's trying hard and learnin' new words, but you gotta stick with him to get it all."

Alwin scanned the group and sighed. "It's fine this time, this being the first week for church. But from now on, wear the clothes you washed on Saturday for Sunday church. Some of you have on clothes you wore in the fields. That ain't respectful to the Van der Beek place, to Pastor Jannsen, or to God. Everyone understand?" Alwin waited until everyone nodded. He hopped into the front wagon and started the caravan to church.

Will noticed the wagon in front of his had Vlinder as the driver. He wished he had seen that earlier. He glanced over at Isaiah and saw his clean, leather, Sunday shoes had some buff on them. He recognized them as the ones Isaiah wore from Peoria. "Isaiah, you brought these other shoes just for church?"

"Sure did. Granddaddy said we'd probably be going to church services here and he told me, 'Isaiah, you got clothes for work and clothes for the Lord.,' and he gave me these shoes." Isaiah held up a foot for Will to get a good look. "These was my Granddaddy's before, but he said God already knows his good and bad parts, but I'm just beginnin' my impression on Him. Granddaddy said clean shoes is a good start."

*   *   *

The Van der Beek farm sat on the main road to Peoria. It was surrounded by brown fields, large and lonely. The Helgeveld workers were the first to arrive and Pastor Jannsen stood out front, shaking their hands and greeting them with, "Hallo youngen mans and womans," and then directing them toward the field and the chairs. Pastor Jannsen was medium height and wore a white collar and a black robe over a white shirt and dark tie. His smile never left as he greeted each summer worker.

Several other Van der Beek sons motioned for everyone to move toward the front of the chairs. The Helgeveld Farm workers took up most of the rows on the right and Moses motioned for Will, Isaiah, Owen, and Elmer to follow him to the front row. Within fifteen minutes, the other farm workers arrived and were seated.

Pastor Jannsen walked down the center aisle to a wooden table with a small stand that was holding a Bible. He waited until all was quiet, held his arms apart, and beamed at the workers. "Welkom! Welkom! Welkomen to da hoose of God." And for the next hour and a half, everyone struggled through an unrecognizable message of unfamiliar words. The occasional hymn barely moved the morning along any quicker. There were several snores from boys in the back.

The only other diversion was Moses, who'd sporadically burst into a laugh at something Pastor Jannsen said. The pastor smiled back at Moses, suggesting that he was the only person who understood the pastor's message and his jokes.

When Pastor Jannsen concluded his comments, the worker congregation yawned and rose from their seats, joyful that it was finally over.

As everyone headed to the aisles, a voice blared from behind the rows of chairs. A tall, older man with a cane, stood and said, "Boys and girls, thank you for coming to the Sunday service at Van der Beek Farm. My name is Arend Van der Beek and I'm the owner of this farm." He pointed to a woman standing next to him wearing a lemon yellow dress and an apron. "This is my wife, Elise. We know you found the words of Pastor Jannsen inspiring and you will bring that message into your lives. We look forward to seeing you every Sunday to hear the pastor's words of encouragement." Pastor Jannsen stood next to both of them, nodding and holding one hand in the other, smiling at his congregation.

Arend Van der Beek continued, "Before you head back to your farms, please join us for punch and apple cake, just to the side of the farmhouse. Again, we thank you for coming and we will see you next Sunday." He pointed to his right and everyone headed to an open area, shaded from the noonday sun and back-bordered with a row of tables covered with punch and apple cake. The food and drink drew everyone into a well-ordered line that offered some reward for the past hour and a half. The boys and girls stood with their treats, speaking with workers from two or three area farms.

Elmer, standing next to his friends, looked at something green floating on the top of his punch. "What's this green stuff floating in the punch?" he asked.

"It's peppermint," Will said. "They grow it around here."

Owen raised his punch and sniffed it. "Smells a little like Christmas."

Will took a bite of apple cake and began to look around the gathering. Soon, he found and wove his way toward Vlinder Helgeveld, who also stood with a cup of punch and a piece of cake. She was listening to a young man explain how corn germinates and breaks through the sod. Vlinder's nods suggested both good manners and boredom. Will inched forward until Vlinder saw him. She looked up, pleased, and excused herself from the corn sermon and walked over to Will.

"Well, look here," Vlinder said, turning toward Will and putting a hand on her hip. "Gettin' that dirt off your face makes those dimples stand out even more. That one there," she pointed, "that one's a little sharper than the other," and even though Will was three or four inches taller, Vlinder's pluck and confidence left Will struggling to respond. Vlinder continued, "You don't talk too much, do you?" Still trying to urge some conversation, she said, "Where you from?"

"Pittsburgh. Pittsburgh, Pennsylvania."

Vlinder waited for more and finally said, "So, what do you do out there in Pittsburgh, Pennsylvania?"

"I go to school and work in my father's store."

"Well, okay," Vlinder said, pausing and looking into him. "I'm trying, but you just got a word here and there. What's your name, anyways?"

"William Parlor, Will Parlor," he finally said. "Well, I live with my mother and father, brother and sister. Go to school. Turned seventeen a while back and my mother and father thought it was time for me to get away and work hard. My father saw your ad for farm workers in the Pittsburgh paper."

"Seventeen?" said Vlinder. "Yeah, I thought you looked a little young."

Will's heart sunk, but he gathered courage. "Well, how old are you?"

"Me? I'm nineteen and I'll tell you, there's a lot of growing up between seventeen and nineteen." Vlinder paused a moment and nodded to herself. "I remember seventeen. I knew everything about everything back then. Now, I'm not so sure." She paused and waited. "Okay, Will Parlor. You gonna be a farmer or what are you gonna do with your life?"

Will knew this wasn't a question about his future, but about who he is. "Well, I might take over my father's business. But might go to a college out near Philadelphia. Villanova. Be the first in the family to go to college." Will wasn't sure if he wanted to go to college, but not having a plan didn't fit the response he wanted right then.

"Off to college, huh? Not for me," Vlinder said. "I finished school last year and that's enough. Working at the farm, it's home, it's good work, and I like it. But I'm thinking of doing other things."

The conversation felt like it was ending, but Will wouldn't let it. "You want to leave the farm someday? It looks like a good place."

"It is," said Vlinder. "The farm's my family. It was my grandfather Bartel who bought it back in 1869. He died when I was still little. Gramma Luna, she died just last year. We're still not over that."

"1869?" Will said. "You're lucky. You've got some good family history and stories. We just live in four rooms over my father's store. I never even knew my grandparents."

Vlinder reflected and nodded. "I do have family stories. Mostly good."

Workers were heading to their wagons and as Vlinder moved toward hers, she said to Will. "You'll probably end up with a business, a fine house, a smart wife, and four or five children."

Vlinder's conclusions smarted, but Will didn't push back. Instead, he said, "Well, I don't know about that. We'll see what happens when I'm nineteen. Someone told me there's a lot of growing up between now and then."

Vlinder stopped, turned to look at Will, and smiled. "Then maybe I'll find out if you come back to the farm over the next few summers."

Will walked to his wagon and found Isaiah at his side.

"Looks like you got to talk to your girl," Isaiah said.

"Yeah, I talked to her, but she ain't thinkin' what I'm thinkin'." Will shook his head. "She's looking for a man and I'm not there yet."

They reached the farm in time for lunch.

*   *   *

Sunday afternoon saw the boys spending time at the stables, the outbuildings, and walking around the farm. A warmer than usual April day kept the chill down and the five wandered to the back barn where Will and Isaiah had earlier stored the wagon with Alwin. They lay in the grass, but Isaiah and Moses soon hopped up and looked through the spread of broken farm equipment laying outside the barn, commenting to each other what it would take to get it back in working order.

After a while, Will pushed himself up on his elbows and looked toward the barn. "Got those two other pennies safe, Isaiah? You never know what Roy's up to, especially if he's walking around here all day."

Isaiah patted his pocket. "Yes, indeed. Right here in my church pants. And I hate to admit it on a Sunday, but there's part of me that'd like to see Roy get a whoopin'."

Moses added, "You see Roy's eyes? He's fulla hate. And he was lookin' right at you, Owen. Best be careful around him."

"Thanks," said Owen, who looked at Moses and paused. "But I can take care of Roy."

"Well, one good thing," Isaiah said lifting up a broken wagon wheel, "can't imagine Roy trying to steal anything else for a while. Wouldn't be smart. Everyone's watchin' him."

"Yes, indeed," said Moses. "That'd be ludicrous."

Isaiah turned around and looked at his brother. "What'd you say? Luda what? What's that word?"

"Ludicrous! Ludicrous! It means stupid!" said Moses.

"Where'd you learn a word like that?" asked Isaiah.

"Church this mornin'. Wasn't you listenin'? Pastor was tellin' stories about the *ludicrous* people in the Old Testament not listening to God. Sounded like a good word so I put it right up here," Moses said pointing to the side of his head.

Isaiah shook his head. "I swear, I didn't understand hardly nothin' that Pastor said. I don't know how you picked that word out. What was it again? Lucridous? Luricrus?"

"Ludicrous! Ludicrous! Don't be *ludicrous*, Isaiah!" and Moses bent over laughing at his joke. Will, Owen, and Elmer wanted to laugh too, but they hadn't understood the Pastor either, and they certainly never heard the word *ludicrous* that morning.

*   *   *

At dinner, Will overflowed his plate with sausages, sweet potatoes, biscuits and gravy. Vlinder was in the back kitchen and Will positioned himself at the table to watch her fill pans, take dirty plates back to the washing sink, and share a word with a number of workers.

Halfway through dinner, Alwin walked to the area just in front of the food and banged a spoon on a metal plate. The boys quieted and turned toward Alwin. "My father wants to greet all of you and he has some news he wants you to hear."

Into the chow hall walked the tall, sandy haired owner of Helgeveld Farm. He was broader than Alwin and wore a string tie that hung in front of a pressed white shirt. He stopped in front of the food tables, scanning the workers.

"Hello, boys. I believe all the workers have arrived and I want to welcome you to Helgeveld Farm. My name is Joren Helgeveld, the owner of the farm. Over there," he said pointing at a woman working in the chow hall kitchen, "is my wife, Anika." His Dutch accent was sturdier than Alwin's and Vlinder's, but easy enough to understand. "We have eight children, all of them out there working with you. You'll know them all soon enough." He paused, then continued. "We've been having summer workers like you come to the farm for years, starting with my father who hired a traveling Indian family in 1870, his first summer at the farm. It's been good for everybody. Many workers come back summer after summer. And if you like it here, maybe you'll come back too." He looked across the room, noticing a few boys talking among themselves.

Joren Helgeveld waited until they were silent and then took a deep breath. "And there's some news you should know about. I'm not sure if it's going to affect us here on the farm, but it might. Maybe you heard that there's a war going on across the ocean in Europe. It's been going on for a few years and they say over a million people have died already. They're calling it the *Great War*. Well, last Friday, the United States decided to enter that war. The feeling is that with America in there, it'll be over quicker. Some people say by Christmas. We hope so."

The boys looked at each other. Most had heard of a distant war but knew little else.

"As for all of you, the work will be the same," continued Joren Helgeveld. "The government might want to send some of our crops over there, but that's just a guess and a rumor. We're going to increase our dairy cattle and sheep numbers anyway. Even if the war is over soon, there could be shortages. Best to be ready."

There was murmuring in the hall at the news and Joren Helgeveld waited until it quieted. "This news is difficult for the Dutch community. This war is happening just south of our homeland. In many ways, Holland is still home to us and it hurts to see loud men with big guns sending boys off to die." He paused and then continued. "Three times a week, we get the newspaper from Chicago in the mail truck. If there's anything you should know, we'll tell you at dinner." Joren Helgeveld was more concerned than he let on. He worried that wars were beginning to pull in countries from all around the world. Where would this all end, he wondered.

The owner of the farm looked across the hall and stayed serious. "One other thing. I've heard some talk over the last few days about a couple of our workers up from Alabama." Joren Helgeveld looked across all the boys, but everyone knew he was talking about Isaiah and Moses. "Over the years, we've had white and colored workers come through here. Had several Indians: Shawnee, Meskwaki, a few from the Peoria tribes. A couple of Chinese fellas, too." Joren Helgeveld paused, looked across at the boys, and continued. "On this farm, you work, you get paid, and everybody's the same. If that doesn't sit right with you, best that you head back home. Does everyone understand?" The chow hall quieted.

"Good. Good," Joren Helgeveld said and he clapped his hands together. "Alright, boys, I'm looking forward to a good summer here on the farm and I hope I get to know all of you." Joren nodded at the boys and left the chow hall through the side door.

Alwin walked to the front. "Alright, everyone. Tomorrow begins the first full week of work for many of you. We'll keep leveling the fields and getting them ready for seed next week. First crop is corn. That takes a little longer to mature. Soybeans go in just after that, but most everything should be planted in the next several weeks."

Alwin looked out and across at the boys. Overall, this group of workers looked good to him, but he smiled and remembered. They always look good the first week of each season.

CHAPTER 7

Leveling two fields each day kept the boys on schedule for seeding, but the weather turned wet and cold, and the next couple of days they returned to the bunkhouse wet and muddy. This routine continued until the middle of the following week when the sun shone and the wet fields steamed dry.

At dinner, Alwin announced the schedule. "Boys, it's been a wet few weeks, but the fields are drying and we need to get the corn in the ground. Tomorrow, most of you will switch to planting. We've had seed drills ordered for the last two years, but they haven't come in, so we'll plant by hand again this year. There'll be two of you working together, one of you planting, the other just behind, hoeing over the soil. We'll show you how when we get out there."

Alwin looked at the silent assembly. "One more thing. My father says there's no recent news about the war. Looks like the United States is deciding what, and who, to send over there. Growing crops is about the best thing we can do for the country right now."

* * *

The next morning, Alwin came to the table at breakfast and asked Isaiah to follow him. Isaiah shot Moses a panicked look as he exited the chow hall and headed down the path toward the back barn with Alwin.

With the barn in view, Alwin said pointing ahead, "The day you got here, you saw this barn full of busted stuff that needs fixing. Carl usually fixes what's broken, but we need him in the fields now." They reached the barn and Alwin stood in front of piles of busted-up farm equipment. "Hasn't been anybody down here working on this for weeks, maybe more. But after I saw what you did with the wagon on the trip from town, I thought maybe you'd like to switch from working in the fields to back here, fixing what you can."

Isaiah glanced over at Alwin, trying to hide his excitement. "Fixin' plows and such back here? Yes, Mr. Alwin, I believe I'd enjoy that a great deal."

"Okay," said Alwin. "We'll give it a try." Alwin saw Carl up near the farmhouse and yelled to him. When Carl arrived, Alwin said, "Isaiah here, he's pretty handy with repairs and since you're busy out in the fields, I'm gonna have him work up here for now, repairin' what he can. Can you get him acquainted with things? You know the tools and what needs to be done better than I do."

"Sure thing, Alwin," said Carl, feeling much more at home in the fields than trying to fix anything back here. Carl pointed to a few plows on the outside of the barn. "I'd start with those two plows," he said. "Their hitches need fixing. Those other two are cracked, so just leave them for now."

Isaiah walked around the four plows, kneeling at the spots that needed attention. He stood up, looking down at a cracked plow. "Mr. Alwin, you said you don't got a welding tool?"

"No," said Alwin. "You used a welding tool before?"

"Yes, sah. Soon as they was in town, my Granddaddy got one. Fixed things that couldn't be fixed before." Isaiah kneeled down behind another plow. "Looks like the coulter of this one is bent pretty bad. With a weldin' tool, I could add some braces on each side to keep it strong. Add some bolts if you got 'em. Might try to lower the hitch, too. That'd send it straighter through the fields."

"Alright, Isaiah," said Alwin. "Next time I'm in Peoria, I'll ask around about a welding tool."

"That'd be good, Mr. Alwin," said Isaiah.

Alwin opened the door to the barn exposing the broken chaos. He pointed to the back. "Got a steam tractor back there that won't fire up. You worked on those before?"

"Yes, sah," Isaiah said. "Me and Moses worked on a few of them over the last coupla years. I'll see what I can do," said Isaiah.

Carl took Isaiah to the tool bench. "This is what we've got for tools. Some of them are broken, too. Got an anvil here. A few sledgehammers. Crowbar's right there. Vices. Got some different size bolts there. Screws, nails, hammer, saws, files, drill is right there."

The three of them stood back and stared at the unending tasks. "I don't expect you to finish all of this, Isaiah," said Alwin.

"That's alright, Mr. Alwin," Isaiah said. "Rather have too much to do than not enough."

"Okay, Isaiah," Alwin said. "We're just gonna leave you to it back here. I'll check in later, see if you need anything, and I'll make sure you get some lunch."

"I'll do my best, Mr. Alwin."

* * *

The boys were gathered in front of the farmhouse when Carl and Alwin appeared without Isaiah. Carl hopped onto his wagon and, when he was sure he had everyone, he headed out.

Moses was just behind Carl and spoke up. "Mr. Carl, sah. Is Isaiah comin' with us?"

"He's gonna be working down at the back barn," said Carl, "See if he can get some of the plows and anything else repaired."

That satisfied Moses and the boys hung on as the morning wagons moved from farm to fields.

Wagons stopped or pulled off at their familiar spots. Carl's wagon emptied at the edge of the farm where everyone mulled around waiting for instructions. Alwin's younger brother, Gerwin, walked over from another field and stepped in front of the boys. Gerwin had an easy manner and, like Alwin, was just as familiar with the daily tasks.

"Okay, listen here, everyone," Gerwin started. "We'll start planting the corn now and switch to soybeans, probably the end of next week. Takes two of you to plant a field, whether corn or beans. First thing," continued Gerwin, "you'll measure out the rows with spikes and strings we give you." He held them up and showed them to the boys. "The strings have a knot every forty inches. You'll line those at the ends of each field and use that as a guide to drag the rows. That leaves enough room for a horse to pull a cultivator through to keep the weeds down. But to get the best yields, you gotta keep the rows straight." Gerwin pointed his index finger out straight to stress the point.

"After measuring and stringing the field," Gerwin said, "drag the hoe handle along the soil about two inches down to make the rows. When that's done, one of you will have a bag of seed hanging off your shoulder." Carl stepped up and showed the boys a full seed bag. Gerwin held out a seed and continued. "Drop a seed down every four inches or so in the row. That's about the length of your first finger. The other one of you is right behind, pulling the dirt over the rows with a hoe."

With Isaiah gone, Will moved over next to Moses. "Hey, Moses. How about you and me work together?"

"Sure thing, Will," Moses said.

"This first day," Gerwin continued, "you'll get about one field done. After that, you should finish one field and measure out another for the next day. Alwin, Jakob, Vlinder, the supervisors, and I will be out in the fields to make sure you're getting it right." Gerwin looked across the workers. "Okay, pair up."

Will and Moses, Owen and Elmer, stood as pairs, but Roy stood alone. Carl saw this and he caught the eye of Jackson, another supervisor. Soon, George Griffith, a chunky fellow, medium height with a flannel work shirt, arrived at the wagon. Carl pointed to Roy and said, "You're working with him."

Roy looked George Griffith up and down and turned away. Roy must have said something because George walked up behind him and said loud enough for Roy and everyone else to hear, "You got a problem? You don't pull your weight, I swear, I'll sit on you 'til you can't breathe. You got that?" Roy didn't move, but Carl and Gerwin smiled at the development.

Will and Moses were the last pair and Carl placed them in a field near the edge of the farmland, abutting a rocky outcrop surrounded by trees.

"Okay," said Carl. "You saw what I did with the others. Measure the field and get the rows lined up and stringed out. Open the rows and get the seed in."

Carl stood at the end of the field and watched Will and Moses get started. After a time, he yelled to the boys, "Looks like you've got it. We'll come by to check on you from time to time."

As they laid out the string and began dragging the rows open, Will stood and watched Moses. Moses didn't appear to be working that much faster, but he was far ahead. "Moses!" Will yelled out. "Slow down! I can't keep up with ya."

Moses stood up, took a breath and smiled at Will. He slowed his pace but kept his rhythm to a song.

> *I hear the train a'comin'*
> *She's comin' round the curve*
> *She's loosened all her steam and brakes*
> *And strainin' ev'ry nerve*
> *The fare is cheap and all can go*
> *The rich and poor are there*
> *No second class aboard this train*
> *No difference in the fare*

Moses found a way to swap work for a vision. Will yelled ahead, "Moses, you got all kinds of songs. You learn them from your Granddaddy?"

Moses stopped and put both hands on the top of the hoe handle and rested his chin on them. "Yup. Learned 'em from Granddaddy. This here's one of my favorites. Granddaddy sings it all the time. He told us they's from when times was tough for us. But now, the law says we's free."

"Sure you're free. Civil War says so," said Will

"Yeah, law says we's free, but still lots of places we can't go, things we can't do." He looked at Will and across the fields. "But out here, making my own money just like you, I feel the sun and this hard work as a free person, my own person. That's freedom. I don't think they's no better feelin'." Moses paused and then began to drag the hoe handle along the row, and sang.

No second class in this train,
No difference in the fare.

Back to work and the two boys knew they were making good time. The sun raced up the sky and the morning passed quickly. Will removed his hat, closed his eyes, and faced the sun. The hard work brought its own reward and, like Moses, he felt free and lucky to be here. Carl or Gerwin would occasionally show up, look out at their efforts, and nod their heads.

Carl came by and called the boys to lunch. He examined their field. "Had a feelin' you boys would be movin' along." He looked from Moses to Will. "Good job."

The boys filed out to the lunch wagons and as Will hoped, Vlinder was on one of them, doing double duty of supervising the fields and serving lunch.

Will waited at the end of the line, keeping his eyes fixed on Vlinder, who looked out and met his eyes. He stood in front of her with his plate and a smile. "Well, Will Parlor from Pittsburgh," Vlinder said. "You look a little more respectable without dirt all over you. Dimples are standin' out too."

Will pointed to the dimple on his left cheek. "I like this one better. What do you think?"

Vlinder put a hand on her hip, tipped her head to the right and gave the matter some thought. "Tough to tell," she said. "Tilt your head to the other side so I can get a good look at the other one." Will obliged and after more time than dimples deserved, she concluded, "Good balance, but that one there, the one on the right. That's a first-class dimple."

Will stood straight and nodded. "Good. First time I've had a dimple expert take a good look at them."

Vlinder scooped lunch onto his plate. "Use 'em for all you can, Will Parlor."

"Okay, but takes more than dimples to make a man," Will said.

Vlinder stopped working, looked at Will, and smiled. "Maybe you're a little further along than seventeen." She turned and reached into a tray at the back of the lunch wagon. "Here's a couple of extra cookies, one for each dimple." She shoved them under the beans on his lunch plate. "We don't have many. You say I gave them to you and they're the last ones you'll get all summer," said Vlinder. "Now, go on, Will Parlor."

Will nodded at Vlinder and put the cookies into his shirt pocket. And after lunch, when the sweet scent of oatmeal and raisin occasionally drifted to his nose out in the fields, Vlinder was alongside. Will and Moses managed to finish one field and started measuring out the next. At the end of the day, Carl's, "Good work, you two," made the muddy shoes and tired shoulders worth it all.

CHAPTER 8

Back at the farm, Will and Moses walked to the back barn to collect Isaiah and head to dinner. They found him with a ball-peen hammer, sitting under a plow brace and pounding away. Moses examined the work. "You poundin' out them bolts?"

"Yup," said Isaiah. "I gotta get this plow by itself. I'm fixin' to use that brace over there. Took most of the morning to take it all apart."

Moses glanced at the pile of broken farm equipment strewn about and nodded. "This here's some sweet work, Isaiah."

"Sure is," Isaiah said. He scooched out from under the plow, washed his hands and face in the water barrel, and the three of them followed the path to dinner.

*　*　*

The next morning at breakfast, Alwin came over to Isaiah. "Let's take a look at what you're working on Isaiah," and the two headed to the back barn. Alwin looked ahead and saw that Isaiah had also replaced the missing boards on the side of the barn. They stopped in front of a plow, one end hoisted up on a rusted bucket for easier access. Tools and metal braces sat to the side. Alwin walked around a plow to examine the main brace. "Looks like you're changing the angle there."

"Yes, sah. Somewhere along, this here got repaired wrong. Look right there," said Isaiah, pointing to the brace holding the plow. "Got angled up at some point. Not gonna pull through the soil too good with that. And it's gonna break again before you know it."

Alwin lowered his head and gave a quick laugh. "Might have you work back here all summer, Isaiah. You could get more done with that welding tool you mentioned?"

"Work'd go about twice as fast, sah," Isaiah said. "Not just puttin' stuff together, but cuttin' stuff apart."

Alwin looked around the barn. "Some of this stuff's been sittin' here for years." He paused. "After we get everyone out to the fields today, I'll head into Peoria. See if I can pick up a welding tool for you. You don't mind workin' back here rather than out in the fields?"

"I like it just fine back here, Mr. Alwin," Isaiah said, hesitating before his next suggestion. "One thing, though. Lot of this, especially that tractor back there, is hard for me to move around and work on. For a time, if my brother Moses could work here with me, we'd get a lot more fixed."

"Yes, Moses," Alwin nodded, "he worked with you and your Granddaddy, you said?"

"Yes, sah," Isaiah said. "I'd fix things like plows and wagons while Moses and Granddaddy worked on buildin' and fixin' motors, engines, and such."

"Engines?" asked Alwin. "He can fix engines? Tractors? Motorcars?"

"I believe he could, Mr. Alwin. Lots of people back home brought their machines to us. Moses and Granddaddy would take 'em apart, fix 'em up, and get 'em runnin'."

Alwin rubbed the back of his neck, thinking. "My father wouldn't like losing two workers from the fields, especially at plantin' time. But gettin' all of this fixed and in working order might be worth it. You think you've got enough work if I send Moses over?"

Isaiah turned and looked around the barn "I believe we could pull a lot of what's in the barn outside and get a idea of what needs to be done. It'd take both of us to move those heavier pieces." Isaiah looked at the mess of metal, anxious to have his brother join him in the tasks. "And I think we could take enough from these three broken wagons to make two sturdy ones. Some wagon wheels need attention, too. Yes, sah, I believe there's plenty Moses and me could do back here. And Moses, he'd be better at fixin' that steam tractor.'"

"You keep talkin' like that, Isaiah, and you and Moses might find year-round work here," Alwin said.

"That's kind of you, Mr. Alwin," said Isaiah, "but we couldn't leave Granddaddy and Gramma. They's our only family now. I know it hurts 'em that we's even here for the summer."

"I know, Isaiah," said Alwin. "I'm just thinkin' that with the farm growing, we could use someone steady back here." Alwin turned to head to the wagons. "I'll send Moses back here to work with you. Then, I'll head to Peoria for that welding tool."

"That'd be just fine," Isaiah said. "Oh, and Mr. Alwin, you'll have to gets a tank of oxygen and a tank of gas with it. Weldin' rods, too. They'll know what you need, but all of that might cost a bit."

"I'll look into all of that, Isaiah. I'll be sure to get what you need." Alwin turned to leave then looked back at Isaiah. "Good to have you and your brother here."

"Good to be here, sah."

Alwin reached the assembly of wagons and workers gathered in front of the farmhouse. He found Moses, put his hand on his shoulder, and told him the plan. Moses' eyes spread wide. "Go on, now," said Alwin. "Plenty of work back there." Moses took off running down the path toward the back barn.

Will heard the conversation and knew he had lost his partner. On the wagon, Elmer leaned over and asked Will, "Where'd Moses go?"

"He's working with Isaiah down at the back barn," Will said.

"Who you going to work with?" asked Elmer.

"Not sure," said Will. "I think everyone has a partner. I guess they'll figure somethin' out."

Another mile or so and they reached the fields. Will jumped off the wagon and headed over to the buckboard where Alwin was giving a few final instructions to his brother, Gerwin. Alwin looked up when

Will approached him. "Mr. Alwin," said Will. "Moses was my field partner. Not sure what I'm supposed to do now."

"That's right," Alwin said. "Never crossed my mind." He hopped off the wagon and looked around. "Hold on. Wait here. I'll get someone." Alwin wove his way through workers until Will lost sight of him. A few minutes later he returned, Vlinder at his side.

Will stared at his new partner.

Vlinder saw him and smiled. "Well, Will Parlor. Alwin says you need some help out there in the fields."

Alwin looked at Vlinder. "You know him?"

"Sure do," said Vlinder. "Mr. Parlor here, he keeps managing to get extra cookies from me when I'm on the lunch wagon."

"Well, okay," said Alwin and he turned toward Will. "Vlinder, she's usually walking the fields and supervising when we're seeding, but with no other workers, she'll work with you today." Alwin looked at both of them. "You set?"

Vlinder, happy to be working in the fields again, looked at Will. "Let's get to work."

Will grabbed a bucket of corn and a seed sling. Vlinder tossed two hoes over her shoulder and she and Will headed off.

Alwin watched them and then hopped into his wagon. He shook the reins and headed to Peoria for supplies and a welding tool. He hoped to be back by mid-afternoon.

Once they reached the field, Will adjusted his stance, trying to appear more interested in planting than Vlinder. "Right there at the stick," Will said, "Moses and I stopped seeding there yesterday. We can finish this and get that next field measured out." Will and Vlinder stepped into the field, carefully stepping across yesterday's work to the empty rows waiting for seed.

Vlinder leaned the hoe against her shoulder, put a hand on her hip, and surveyed the field. She turned and looked behind her. "You get those two fields done yesterday?" She didn't wait for an answer. "Some only finished half that."

"Moses keeps singin' and we keep workin'," said Will. He looked to the trees in the distance, marking the end of their field. He adjusted the seed bag on his shoulder, filled his right hand with seed, and started the rhythm of seed to ground, four inches apart. Vlinder picked up the hoe, following Will, pulling dirt over the seed.

Halfway down their third row, Vlinder said, "Will Parlor, I swear you got farmer blood in you."

"Maybe," Will said and continued down the row. Maybe I do, he thought.

The work was steady, but it was never more than a minute before Will looked back, or over, to see Vlinder's progress and watch her. Since seeing her that first day, he thought of little else, and he'd measure the time each day until he'd see her again.

Will thought he knew women. In Pittsburgh, they were gentle, shy, usually bent their heads down, and shifted their eyes up at him. But with Vlinder, there was no shyness, no future that wasn't her own. Back home, girls talked about marriage, children, a big house, and Will wasn't interested. Here, Vlinder never mentioned those things, and he ached at their exclusion. He was helpless.

That May day had July heat and when Carl brought over a jug of water, Will and Vlinder headed toward it. Will nodded to Vlinder to take the first drink and she put her finger through the hole in the neck of the jug and raised it to her mouth. After the drink, she lowered it, breathed deep, and raised it again, water escaping the sides of her mouth and dripping down her shirt. Vlinder lifted the jug and splashed water over her head and across her face. She lowered the jug, wiped her mouth with her left sleeve, and held the jug out for Will. "Here ya go."

Will took the jug with both hands and raised it to his mouth, his lips around the opening where Vlinder's mouth had just been. He took three long swigs, lowered the jug, and looked into Vlinder's eyes. She looked back, her mouth almost a smile.

Vlinder grabbed the hoe. "Back to work," she said. Will watched her step and jump across opened rows.

Will picked up his seed bag and threw it across his shoulder and continued seeding. A full sling would make it down and back two rows. Vlinder walked just behind him, pulling the damp earth over the seed.

As they were finishing the field, Vlinder said, "You've got the spacing down here. That saves seeds. Last year we ran out of seed and had to order a hundred more pounds from Chicago. Double the price of pre-ordered seed, and it took five days to get here."

Will nodded. "Never been out in a field doing anything like this before. Never planted corn." He paused. "But not the first time I've handled it. We sell it in my father's store. Sometimes my brother, sister, and I would grab a handful, hide in the store, and flick seeds at each other. Didn't figure that learning how to flick them with my thumb would come in handy."

Vlinder laughed. "You're an honest man, Will Parlor. You sound like my father, not afraid to say what he hasn't done."

"There's plenty I haven't done." Not wanting it to end there, Will continued. "What about you? What haven't you done? What would you do if you leave the farm?" He kept up his rhythm with the seeding.

Vlinder continued to drag her hoe across the rows, covering and smoothing. "My father said he'd send me to college. He knows I want to see what else is in the world. He thinks I'd be a good secretary, but I don't want that." Vlinder paused and squashed a leftover lump of soil flat. "I might open a store in Peoria, maybe Chicago. I want to sell things that ladies like, clothes, make-up. Their men will come in, too. Buy things for birthdays or maybe after an argument." She and Will laughed. "They're even talking about giving women the right to vote. Things are changing. I want to be ready."

A distant bell announced lunch. They brought the hoe and seed to the field's edge and walked toward the lunch wagons. "What does Alwin think about that? And does your father think that's a good idea?"

Vlinder didn't hesitate. "Doesn't really matter what Alwin thinks, and my father…he always says, 'Vlinder, I never know what's gonna come out of you next.'" She stopped and thought. "But it's not just me. A lot of women are opening businesses in Peoria, Chicago, even New York. Clothes stores, hat stores. I even heard about one woman in Chicago who's like *Sears and Roebuck*. She sends catalogues all across the country with clothes, jewelry, undergarments, cosmetics, all sorts of things women are looking for. I want to do something like that."

It was such a new idea to Will. Some women in Pittsburgh took in sewing or gave music lessons, but to be in charge of a store? Be the boss? "If anybody could do it," Will said to Vlinder, "you probably could."

"I even bought a book on how to open a business," Vlinder added. "Keeping the books, finding suppliers, hiring workers, paying the rent and wages. I'm saving some money and I'll be ready in a few years." She paused and looked across the fields. "But I have to admit. There's a lot to fill a person up right here on the farm."

They reached the lunch wagons. Other workers were sitting to the sides, plates of lunch balanced on their laps.

Vlinder pointed to the second lunch wagon. "Come on," she said and Will followed.

Will pointed ahead to the wagon workers. "These are your brothers and sisters? All twins I think."

"Yes, all twins," said Vlinder. "There's Lotta. That's her twin, Bram. They're twelve. Corrie and Hans, they're fifteen. Twins. Having twins was a surprise each time. Look at 'em. I love 'em all." All the twins returned Vlinder's smile.

Corrie stood with Lotta in the wagon and looked down at Vlinder, then at Will. "Is that the dimple worker?" Corrie asked and laughed. "He's the one who couldn't wash his pants the other day. I had to show him. And lookee there," Corrie said pointing to Will's pants. "They're a mess again." All four laughed.

Lotta handed plates to Vlinder and Will and then scooped cheesy beans over biscuits. Hans added half a jam sandwich to the plates.

Vlinder nodded to Will and went over to Gerwin and Jakob to discuss the morning's progress. Will found Owen and Elmer and sat down next to them.

Elmer looked up. "You working with Vlinder?"

Will settled himself and put his lunch on his lap. "Yeah. She works hard, hard as anybody out there." Will switched topics. "Where are you two working?"

Elmer pointed back over his shoulder. "About a 10-minute walk back thataway." Elmer finished his lunch and put his plate on the ground. "We'll get one more field done this afternoon."

Vlinder came over to where the three boys were finishing their lunch and said to Will, "I'll be at the lunch wagon with the twins. Come by when the bell rings and we'll get back to work." Vlinder turned to the group. "See you later, boys."

Owen shook his head as she walked away. "She ain't silly like girls back home. Real pretty, too." Owen looked over at Will. "Right, Will?" and the three laughed.

The lunch bell clanged ending lunch and drawing workers to the wagons with their empty plates and cups. Will was facing the fields, waiting for Vlinder when he heard, "Will. Is that your name?" said Corrie Helgeveld. "Doesn't seem right to call you *dimples*." He turned and saw Corrie and Lotta smiling in the back of the wagon.

"Right. That's me." Then he pointed at each of them. "And you're Lotta and you're Corrie?"

They nodded and smiled.

Vlinder walked past him and said, "Let's go, Will Parlor. The fields won't plant themselves."

The seeding worked itself into a rhythm for Will, walking slowly, and dropping out seven seeds per step. Vlinder followed him, covering the seed, her pace in the fields long established. Will remembered Moses' field song about freedom. He hummed it and it added ease and timing to his task.

None of the supervisors came by; they were alone. There was unmemorable talk of the work, the fields, the farm, but it was the talk they'd have with anybody. Words to move the day along.

Their field was finished and Vlinder looked around at Will and then turned back toward the horizon. "From the look of the sun," Vlinder said, "I'd say they're about to call us in."

Will stood just behind her, the afternoon sun shining over one of Vlinder's shoulders. Her blonde hair had fallen from its morning form, one shirt sleeve rolled up and the other dropped to her wrist. Her work shoes were caked with mud and her beltless jeans were smudged with dirt from the fields.

Vlinder turned back around, only to catch Will staring straight into her. Already close, Will took a step closer and stared deeper.

Vlinder smiled and stepped back. "You got summer eyes, Will Parlor. Last three or four seasons, someone always ends up looking at me like that. But you've got your life and I've got plans stronger than anything my heart can catch up with."

Just then, the afternoon bell rang ending the day's work. Vlinder again tossed the hoes over her shoulder and Will carried the leftover bag of seeds back to the wagon. Vlinder glanced back and saw Will, head down, about ten steps behind her. She turned and put a hand on her hip. "Mr. Will Parlor. We're working together. Might as well walk together." Vlinder waited until he caught up and they walked side-by-side to the wagons.

The transport wagons were waiting for the workers when Elmer saw Will and came running over. Out of breath, Elmer said, "Alwin just left with Owen for the doctor in Peoria. He stepped in some hole when he was seeding, maybe a pocket gopher hole Alwin said. Owen's foot was bent all wrong and he was in real pain. Not sure if he broke it, but Alwin said best to take him to town right away. Said they might stay the night if they have to." Elmer paused and looked down the road to Peoria. "You shoulda seen it. Looked something like this, but way worse." Elmer held up his foot and tried to bend it to the side to give Will an idea. "Almost made me sick lookin' at it. Lucky that Alwin was just back from Peoria."

Elmer held up a package. "Alwin gave me this. Said it's a welding tool and rods he got for Isaiah. He left a tank of oxygen and a tank of gas over there. Kinda heavy."

"I'll give you a hand," Will said, and when they got to their wagon, Elmer carried the package and Will lifted the two tanks onto his lap.

They were set to go when they heard a commotion and saw Jakob waving his hands and yelling at Roy, who was just coming onto the road. "Haven't you got any sense at all? You knock over the bag of seed, then you pick it up like this?" Jakob held up the bag in front of Roy. "Here, look in here. You just scrape up the seeds along with the dirt and put it back in? That's gonna rot the seed! Tonight we're, I mean *you're*, gonna empty this all out and pick the seeds from the dirt."

"I didn't do it. He did!" Roy said, pointing at his partner, George.

"Roy! I was standing on the side of your field," Jakob snapped. "I watched you. In fact, I think you kicked the bag over on purpose!" Jakob pointed at Roy's wagon. "Get up on the wagon, Roy, but you stick around after dinner. You'll be cleaning this up on one of the tables where someone can watch you." Roy walked away while Jakob was still talking.

"Too bad Alwin wasn't here to see that," Elmer said. "Might have got Roy sent home."

The wagon jerked forward and Will thought of the day. Working with Vlinder both filled and emptied him. He cradled the tanks in his lap and gazed at the horizon, barely hearing Elmer relive the story of Owen's ankle.

* * *

At the farm, Will and Elmer headed to the back barn with the welding equipment. Isaiah was out front and Moses was clanging away in the back of the barn. Elmer told Isaiah about Owen, and then reached out and gave Isaiah the welding tool and welding rods. "Here ya go," said Elmer as Will placed the two tanks alongside.

Isaiah opened the package and a pair of safety glasses tumbled onto the ground. Isaiah glanced at them, and then held the welding tool in front of him. "OoohWee! This here's a good one." He looked at the tip. "Yup. Should be able to get a lot done with this. And those tanks, those'll last most of the summer."

Moses came out of the barn and looked at the new tanks and new tools. He pointed to the safety goggles. "What are them? Eye goggles or somethin'?" Moses tried them on. "Can't see nothin' through these." Then he looked toward the sun. "No, wait. These must be special for weldin'. No wonder Granddaddy don't see so good."

The boys moved the welding equipment inside the barn and headed off to dinner.

*   *   *

After dinner, Vlinder came over to their table. "Who's Elmer?" Elmer raised a hand. "You're Elmer Duggan? You worked with Owen?"

"Yes, ma'am," Elmer replied.

"Well, Elmer, you need a partner and I need to keep an eye on the fields. Think it's best if you team up with Will Parlor tomorrow. He'll show you what we've been working on."

The words drained Will and he stared at his empty dinner plate.

"How does that sound, Will Parlor? Mr. Parlor?" Vlinder asked.

Will looked up. "What? Work with Elmer? Yes, be good to work with him tomorrow."

"Okay," Vlinder nodded and smiled at Will. "It was Gerwin's idea. Good working with you out there today." Vlinder turned and walked back toward the kitchen area where Hans, Corrie, Bram, Lotta, and other girls from the house were scraping off dinner plates and stacking them next to the sinks.

Isaiah looked at Will and shook his head. "You might be walkin' down a dead-end road there."

Will took a deep breath. "Maybe I am." Will got up from the table. "Let's go."

Isaiah, Moses, Elmer, and Will left through the chow hall backdoor and headed to their spot by the sycamore behind the farmhouse. It felt lonely without Owen, but the shaded area greeted them like a friend. The buildings, fields, and animals spread out below them and the road to Peoria split the land. The evening was cool and the piano sounded from the farmhouse.

Below them, Corrie and Hans were in the stables, opening hay bales and grooming the eighteen draft, Morgan, and riding horses.

Lotta hung late-day washing on the back drying line. Gerwin was at the hog pen, pouring dinner scraps over the fence. The dairy cows headed into their barn, Jakob leading their way. Vlinder walked back and forth between the house and chow hall.

The boys were quiet. Twilight settled them.

CHAPTER 9

Turned out that Elmer and Will worked well together. Elmer worked as fast and as hard as anyone, and the two boys swapped hoeing and seeding tasks.

Elmer shared what life was like with just a thumb and finger on one hand. Back home, he told Will, he kept it mostly in his pocket. The bullies were there so Elmer put up a brave face and joked along with them. But at night he wondered about his future.

"Never had a girlfriend," Elmer shared. "Can't imagine I ever will. Even heard my mother and father say I might live my whole life alone. That'd be worse than the bullies." The two workers seeded and hoed another row. "There's a doctor in Chicago who makes plastic parts for people missing something, like legs and arms. My mother took me down to see him a while back. He said he could make three fingers for me, but I saw some pictures and it still looks fake. I don't know. Maybe I'll try it. It's just for looks. They don't help holding or nothin'."

Lunch came and Will saw Vlinder, in from the fields, ladling out rice with chicken to a long line of workers. Elmer headed to the other lunch wagon and Will followed. In the afternoon, Jakob came by and hopped into their field. He bent down to measure the spacing of the seeds. He stood up and yelled across to Elmer and Will. "Good job."

The boys finished their fields with a half hour left in the day. Carl said that if they finished their two fields early and he checked them, the workers could bring the tools and seed to the road and relax until the transport wagons showed up. Elmer and Will hustled back to find two other teams who'd also finished early. They found a dry, grassy spot, slid seed bags under their heads, and fell fast asleep in the warm and the cool of late afternoon.

* * *

Back at the farm, Will and Elmer saw Alwin's wagon had returned from Peoria. They hoped Owen was back, and the two hurried from the wagon to the bunkhouse. Out front, Roy sat on one of the benches, legs crossed in front of him. He stared straight and gave no hint whether Owen was there or not.

The two boys pushed through the screen door and saw Owen lying on his bed, his foot in a cast, crutches leaning against the wall. Owen pushed himself up on his elbows. "Hey, Elmer. Hey, Will. How you guys doin'?"

"Owen," Elmer said. "What happened? What did the doctor say? Is it broken?"

"Nope," Owen said. "Not broken. Just a real bad sprain. Gotta wear this brace for a few weeks, then use the crutches for a while."

"But you can stay at the farm? You can work? What did Alwin say?" Elmer asked.

"Yeah," Owen said. "I was afraid they'd send me home, but Alwin said if I can manage on the crutches, he'd find things for me to do. Maybe help with meals, or with the sheep and hogs." Owen lifted his leg to display the brace. "Not much pain, really. Doc gave me some pills if it gets bad."

For Elmer, hearing that Owen would be staying was a relief. Will's first thought was that when Owen was back in the fields, Owen would work with Elmer and maybe he could work with Vlinder again.

Roy walked through the door and looked at Owen and the cast. "They didn't send you home after that?"

"Sorry, Roy," said Owen. "Just a sprain."

"And you layin' around doing nothin'?" asked Roy. "Think I'll sprain my ankle, too."

"I'll be working, Roy," said Owen. "Here at the farm. I'll still be workin'."

"Ha! You been lickin' their backsides since you got here. Course they'll let you stay." Roy thought for a moment. "Lots of lady-work here on the farm. You'll be good at that." Roy turned and threw himself on his bed, the day's dirt tumbling off his boots onto his blanket. He gazed at Elmer from his pillow. "And good news for you, two fingers. You'll still have your bodyguard."

Owen pushed himself up and stared at Roy. "If I was you, I'd sleep with one eye open. Wouldn't want an accident to happen to you with one of these crutches, Roy."

"Yeah, go ahead," said Roy. "I'll just tell them you hit me with a crutch. Who do you think they'd blame?"

"They'd blame me. And then they'd thank me," said Owen.

*   *   *

The mid-May sun eased the corn plants from the soil. Each morning on the way to the fields, the boys would evaluate yesterday's growth, pointing to the fields they'd planted, claiming victory for the greenest areas.

Owen stayed working at the farm, usually at the hog pen and sheep pastures. He was able to maneuver the silage cutter on one foot, loading and grinding grasses, hay, and other house and yard scraps for the 45 hogs and the 150 head of sheep. Toward the end of May, Owen took the brace off and hopped around with just one crutch.

"How's it feeling?" Will asked Owen each day. Owen's answer swayed Will's mood. A good report convinced Will that he'd soon be back in the fields working with Vlinder. But as the days wore on, it was apparent that even the soybean fields would be planted soon and the teams would end.

Will still saw Vlinder most days, either driving the wagons to the fields, working the lunch wagons, or helping at dinner. They'd sometimes share a quick comment or laugh, but for Will, there was too much distance.

Isaiah and Moses kept fixing. Next to the back barn was a line of restored metal parts, tools and machinery, much of it with a fresh welding line and a brace. Four draft horses had pulled the steam tractor onto the grass, ready for Moses to bring it to life. Alwin walked down to the back barn often, talking to Moses and Isaiah and reporting the successes to his father.

Isaiah thought back to his Granddaddy's decision to fix things on Sweetwater Plantation in 1858. "Hated workin' in the fields," Granddaddy told Isaiah. "Had to find somethin' else, so learned to fix things." More than once, Isaiah reflected on that one hard choice in 1858 which was still shaping his and Moses' purpose to this day.

* * *

Whether mandated from God or not, Sunday afternoons were a welcome time of rest for Will, Elmer, and Owen. After church and lunch, the boys headed to the back barn where Moses and Isaiah saved certain repairs for Sundays. "Fun fixin'," they called it, claiming it wasn't really working on the Sabbath, but a time that reminded them of home, being alongside their Granddaddy.

The calming commotion eased Will, Elmer, and Owen back onto the grass and when Moses launched into a ballad, they were lost to sleep.

Swing low, sweet chariot
Comin' for to carry me home
Swing low, sweet chariot
Comin' for to carry me home,
I looked over Jordan and what did I see
Comin' for to carry me home
A band of angels coming after me
Comin' for to carry me home,

But not everyone napped. On most Sundays, the back barn drew Bram, Lotta, Hans and Corrie, who would jump and hide, on and behind, the maze of broken and repaired. Behind the barn, the four of them sometimes climbed ladders next to the stored away Dodge and jumped into well-positioned hay bales below. The screeches and yells usually brought Alwin from the farmhouse who'd scurry them off to the stables or to a nearby grove of poplars.

Back at the bunkhouse, Roy stayed to himself, eyeing everyone who came and went.

*   *   *

On Tuesday night, when the farm was asleep, the boys woke to a scream. Dashing outside, Elmer and Will saw shadows of Owen, swaying, shrieking. Will raced back into the bunkhouse and grabbed the flashlight and shined it on Owen. He was holding his right wrist close to his chest and he rocked back and forth. Will could tell from the bend of his wrist that it was most likely broken.

"Owen!" Elmer hollered. "What happened? Where are your crutches? "

"Left them inside. Tripped over that bench on my way back from the privy." Owen took his good hand and pointed to the small bench that was usually on the front porch. "Wasn't there when I went down."

Will shined the flashlight on a small bench near Owen's feet, then back at Owen. "Let me see it, Owen," Will said. "Lift off your good hand." Owen raised his left hand and the twisted bend in his right wrist confirmed the break, but Will saw what he wanted. No blood. No bone piercing through the skin.

Will had seen blood back home when his friend, Bobby Davis, fell out a second story window. The fall shattered his thigh, the upper bone slicing through the skin along with pulsing blood. In the neighborhood, Will's mother was the closest thing to a doctor and she grabbed her bag and raced to the commotion. Will watched over her shoulder as she set a splint on Bobby's leg and raised it up, higher than his heart as she later explained to him. She shouted for a towel and gently wrapped the injury, adding some string above the wound to slow the blood loss. "Somebody get an ambulance, quick," she yelled. "This needs to be operated on right away." Bobby Davis got to the hospital in time, his leg and life saved. But with no x-ray machine in that hospital, the bones were not set right, and he'd spend his life with a slight limp.

"I'll go to the house and get Alwin," Will said. "You need to get to the doctor. We'll get help."

Owen was rocking, his good hand over his bent wrist. "It's bad though, isn't it?"

"Don't worry. I've seen worse," Will told Owen. Actually, Will had never seen a broken wrist, but whenever his mother treated someone who was scared, she'd say, "Don't worry. I've seen worse." Now he knew why.

Will turned to Elmer. "You stay here with Owen. Isaiah, come on." Isaiah and Will rushed to the farmhouse, banged on the kitchen door, and yelled to the second floor.

Lamps were lit, and soon, Alwin appeared at the door in his night clothes. "What is it? What happened?"

"It's Owen," Will said. "He broke his wrist going to the privy. Looks like he tripped on a bench on the way back. It's bent all wrong. I can tell it's broken. He's in a lot of pain." Will looked at Alwin. "He needs to get to the hospital. A doctor needs to set the bone."

Alwin nodded. "We'll get him to the doctor." He turned to Isaiah. "Isaiah, hook Lily up to the small wagon and bring it out."

"Right away, Mr. Alwin," and Isaiah hustled to the stables.

"Will, get Owen and bring him out front," Alwin said. "I'll meet you there."

"Yes, sir." Will hurried back and he could hear Owen's moans as he neared the bunkhouse. He remembered Owen had some pain pills for his ankle and he found the bottle on the floor, next to Owen's bed. The directions said take one, but Will grabbed two pills and poured a glass of water from the bunkhouse water pitcher.

"Take these, Owen," said Will when he went outside. "They'll help the pain."

Owen took the water and swallowed down the pills.

"Can you stand?" asked Will. "We're gonna get you to the doc. Alwin's gonna take you right now."

Owen got to his feet, held between Will and Elmer, but he winced when his healing ankle touched the ground. They shuffled along the path in the moonless night, Moses walking just behind them. Isaiah had the wagon out front and the boys helped Owen onto the front seat.

Alwin, followed by Vlinder in her night clothes, hurried out the front door of the farmhouse. Alwin jumped onto the wagon seat and turned to Owen, "This could be a little bumpy, especially in the dark, but Lily knows most of the bad spots. We'll rely on her." Alwin rubbed a hand across Owen's shoulder. "We'll get you to the doctor, son. You'll be alright."

Elmer put his hand on Owen's side as they were ready to go. "How does it feel, Owen?"

"Hurts bad. Real bad," Owen said. But Owen's bigger concern was that he'd be sent home.

Will reached up and eased Owen's good hand away from his wrist and saw the injury had begun to swell. He turned to Vlinder. "Vlinder, is there any ice in the house, in the icebox?"

The ice truck came two days earlier so Vlinder said she was sure there was. "Yes. I'll get some."

"And bring a towel we can wrap it in," Will yelled to Vlinder as she headed toward the farmhouse. He turned to Owen. "We'll get you some ice. That'll bring down the swelling and those pills will kick in soon. You'll be okay."

Vlinder returned with three good-sized chunks of ice wrapped in a towel. Making sure the ice was secure in the towel, Will swung it and smashed the ice inside into manageable sizes. He took the towel with ice pieces and laid it over Owen's wrist. "Here, hold this. It'll feel better soon."

Owen was rocking back and forth in the wagon. "Yeah, this feels good. It feels a little better."

"Okay, then," Will said. "Get going. The doc will fix you right up."

The others offered their good lucks and with that, Alwin shook the reins and Lily, Owen, and Alwin were off to Peoria. Will watched the wagon disappear into the dark.

Vlinder turned to Will. "You did some good doctoring there."

"Just from watching my mother," Will said. "Never thought much about it. Never figured I'd ever use it."

Vlinder nodded at Will and headed toward the farmhouse. She stopped when she reached the porch steps, turning to watch Will's silhouette walk through the dark, down the path to the bunkhouse.

CHAPTER 10

The night was cool and full of stars, but the horizon signaled the upcoming day. Once the boys reached the bunkhouse, Will took the flashlight and shined it on the spot Owen tripped and on the bench to the side. How did it get alongside the bunkhouse in the middle of the night? His thoughts were the same as everyone else.

Will brought the flashlight inside and Roy appeared asleep in his bed. Not surprisingly, Roy never went outside after Owen tripped. Will put both hands over Roy's ankles and shook him. "You did it! I know you did it! You put the bench out there after Owen went to pee. You wanted him to trip!"

Roy sat up and pulled his legs back. "Get away from me! Don't touch me! I didn't do nothin'! You got no proof! Them benches are all over. People move 'em all the time. Did you see me? Did Owen see me? How could I do it?"

"Is that right?" asked Will. "Moses! Hey, Moses! Did you see Roy get up at all? You see him get up when Owen went to the privy?"

Moses was sitting on his bed, figuring sleep was done for the night. "No. I was asleep. Roy's up a lot though. Seen him leaving the bunkhouse on a lot of nights."

Will yelled down the bunkhouse. "Any of you see anything? Any of you see Roy getting up?" Everyone shook their heads. He turned to Roy. "Just 'cause nobody saw you, Roy, doesn't mean you didn't do it."

"Nobody saw me 'cause I didn't do it!" Roy turned to Will. "All of you shut up and leave me alone!"

Everyone thought Roy was behind this, but Roy was right. People move the benches all the time. And it was dark. Maybe Owen stepped to the side on his way, but tripped on the way back. There was no proof.

Sleep was done for the night and the bunkhouse hummed with theories of what happened to Owen.

Later, in the fields, Elmer and Will spent the day planting soybeans and speculating on Roy, Owen, and the rest of the summer. Turns out, it's easy to find someone guilty when you don't like them. More troubling was that a sprained ankle and broken wrist suggested that Owen might be finished at the farm for the summer.

*   *   *

The boys were at dinner when Alwin, just back from Peoria, came to their table. "You were right, Will. Owen's wrist is broken in a few places. Doc took an x-ray and even I could see it wasn't good. He set the bones and it's in a cast now. Could take two, maybe three months to heal. Even then, it'd be weak, too weak to work. Might take six months to get back to normal."

Alwin took a deep breath. "He'll stay at the hospital tonight and we'll put him up in a hotel tomorrow. We'll check on him when we go to town for the first payday this Friday. You can all see him if you want to." He shook his head. "But I don't know about the rest of the summer. I don't think he can work. Be a shame for him to go home. He's a good worker."

Elmer slumped at the thought of his good friend going home. Will leaned toward him, "You don't know for sure, Elmer," but Will thought the same as Alwin. A broken wrist probably meant Owen would be going home.

They'd see Owen in a few days. First payday and a trip to Peoria.

CHAPTER 11

On the last Friday in May, the boys first payday, they gathered in front of the farmhouse, giddy, sharing their shopping goals and plans for a free day in Peoria. Chewing gum to baseballs, playing cards to spin tops, magnets to Hershey Chocolate kisses.

Money and stores. An unknown combination for most of them.

They were using the larger Murphy wagons without the tops for the trip. Each had two draft horse out in front and Gerwin, Jakob, Carl, and Vlinder were watering, feeding, and knuckle-rubbing the horses' heads. Will eased toward Vlinder's wagon, pulling Isaiah, Moses, and Elmer with him. Roy was nowhere to be seen, but it was payday, so he'd be along.

Alwin was off to the side of the wagons, waiting. Soon, Joren Helgeveld and his wife Anika, came out of the front door of the farmhouse and walked toward the group. Joren Helgeveld looked clad for town in crisply pressed black pants and a clean white shirt, his string tie completing his outfit. Next to him stood Anika, long-skirted and tightly bonneted. Her knee-length apron suggested that she was staying at the farm.

The owners of the Helgeveld Farm walked through the crowd of boys, occasionally patting a boy on the shoulder, then another, along with a "Good job, son," or "Good to have you here." Joren stood taller than anyone, and the group fell silent as he and Anika reached the wagons, turning to address the boys.

Anika stepped in front of her husband and spoke first, her smile reaching into each worker. "Good morning, boys. It's so good to have you all here! I've spoken with some of you, but I wanted to come out with my husband today and thank you all for your hard work. You add more to Helgeveld Farm than just your work. You bring life and joy to the summers here." Anika paused for a moment, and that gave Will time to consider how Vlinder would look in the years ahead.

Anika continued. "It's an exciting day for all of you. You'll be in Peoria getting your pay and opening your own bank account. I wish I could be there with you, but Mr. Helgeveld will take you to the bank and give you some ideas of where to shop for a few things. And please, if we can do anything for you throughout the summer, let us know." Anika lowered her head, and then stepped to the side.

"*Goed gedaan*," Joren Helgeveld said to his wife. Then he turned toward the boys. "Well, boys," he began. "I've spoken to you a few times in the chow hall but, and as my wife said, we want to formally welcome you to Helgeveld Farm for the summer. With your hard work, the crops are up and, if the weather holds out, we're going to have a good harvest."

Joren Helgeveld paused and looked down, then back at the boys. "Before we head to town, Alwin tells me some of you have asked about the war. What they're saying in the newspapers is that our country will soon send soldiers to fight over there. They say that if we send enough men, this business will be over soon. Honestly, I'm not even sure what this war's all about, but somehow we got in the middle of it, so it's best if we can finish it early."

His expression changed. "Alright, I've got your pay here and we'll head to Peoria in a few minutes. You'll be able to open a bank account and then have a free day in Peoria. From past summers, I warn you to keep only about fifty cents for in-town shopping. Deposit the rest in the bank. You'll be glad you did once the summer is over. We've had boys who spend almost half their pay on candy, cakes, and other things that make no sense. Fifty cents for shopping will give you all you need."

Good advice, maybe, but the boys looked at each other and smiled, knowing that nobody would follow it. Having a few dollar bills in a front pocket was a joy none of them would surrender.

Joren Helgeveld turned and looked at the wagons. "We're taking the bigger wagons, but we only have three that are in working order. It'll be a little tight; some of you might be on the floor, but we'll make it. These wagons are pretty slow for Peoria streets, so we'll leave the horses and wagons just outside of town and take a trolley car. We could walk from there, but I know most of you have never been on a trolley, and I'm happy to pay your fare."

Snowball, one of the two draft horses in front of Gerwin's wagon, reared up. Gerwin held the reins tight, but the morning activity was making Snowball nervous. Anika stepped over to Snowball, putting a hand on her side, calming her. She took another moment to walk in front, giving her a carrot, and rubbing her snout.

Joren nodded toward his wife and then returned to the boys. "That's Snowball. Looks like she's as anxious as all of you to get to town. Where was I? Oh, yes. We'll get off the trolley in front of the Northern Illinois Bank and Depository. That's where I'll hand out your pay and you'll head inside. They know we're coming; you can set up your account. It's a good lesson. That's how you build wealth, a little at a time."

Joren Helgeveld turned serious. "And one other thing. I'm sure you all heard. One of our summer workers, Owen Whitcomb, down in Bunkhouse 3. He had an accident the other night. Alwin and I are gonna check up on him, see how he's doing. He's at Hotel Fey, I understand." Joren spoke a little slower. "Be real fine if some of you boys who know him could drop by and say hello. I'm sure he'd appreciate it. The hotel's just a few blocks from the bank. We'll show you."

After a pause, Joren clapped his hands together and smiled at the boys. "Alright! Let's go to Peoria!"

With that, the boys headed to the wagons.

Isaiah pointed at Vlinder's wagon and said to Will, "I'm supposin' you want to get on that wagon?"

"Yup," Will said and he marched toward it. Isaiah, Elmer, and Moses followed.

Vlinder stood in front of her wagon, rubbing Bessie's nose, one of the two draft horses in front of her wagon. It was the first time Will had seen her in a dress. It was white and tight around the middle with light purple flowers dancing across it. Will hopped into the wagon followed by his friends. He took the front seat, and Corrie, Hans, Lotta and Bram hopped onto seats across from them. Several other boys tumbled in after.

Hans saw Will across from him and said, "Will, you going to see Owen?"

"Yes," said Will. "We all are," he said looking over at Isaiah, Moses, and Elmer.

"We're going, too," Lotta and Corrie chimed in.

Lotta added, "After that, Alwin said if we went to see Owen, we could go to Talbot's Drug Store for lunch and he'd pay."

The four boys looked at each other and nodded. Isaiah added, "This is turnin' into a real, fine day."

"And with only two of them pennies," Moses added. "Seems as though they's doing their job. You got 'em with you, Isaiah?"

"Yup. Wearin' my church pants without the holes. Got 'em right here," Isaiah said, tapping his pocket.

Vlinder pulled herself up onto the driver's seat and saw Will just behind her. "I swear, Will Parlor, you seem to show up a lot. Just as well. I can use some company on the trip." She tossed the rucksack full of carrots back to Will. "Here, hold these until we get to town."

Will thought maybe those pennies were working for him too, but that ended when Joren Helgeveld hopped onto the seat next to Vlinder, tossing a sack of pay envelopes in front of him. The wagons began to move, and Joren Helgeveld started a conversation with Vlinder in Dutch that lasted all the way to Peoria.

The wagons approached Hollandse Winkel, a Dutch general store on the outskirts of Peoria. A young boy in suspenders hopped out the back door and ran up to Alwin. Alwin pointed at the horses and gave the boy some money for hay and care while they were in town.

Joren Helgeveld walked toward the street, motioning the boys to follow. Several of them skipped or hopped, barely able to hold the excitement of their first trolley ride and a day of adventure. Since there were over fifty boys, it took a second trolley trip to transport them all to the center of Peoria but, once there, they gathered in front of The Northern Illinois Bank and Depository.

After the boys spread across the sidewalk, Joren Helgeveld addressed them. "Alright, boys. I've been inside the bank and talked to the Vice President Hampstead. There are four bank tellers ready to take your deposits. Because most of you are under twenty-one, I vouched that all of you are working at Helgeveld Farm this summer. There's a card you have to fill out with your name and address to start your account. If you have trouble with your writing, the teller will help you."

Joren continued. "I've got a meeting with some government officials from Washington, D.C. who've come out here to talk to farmers in the area. After that, I've got to buy a few things for the farm. I'll meet you back here at the end of the day."

While the owner of Helgeveld Farm was speaking, Roy eased through the crowd of boys and soon stood close enough to the pay envelopes for Joren Helgeveld to stop and look down at him. "Anxious for your pay, young man?" Roy just looked up at him. Joren Helgeveld nodded and said, "You'll get it soon enough." His smile turned to a frown and he took a step to the side. "Son, you might consider washing yourself down from time to time."

Joren Helgeveld turned back and continued to address the boys. "Alright. If you'd like to visit Owen at the hotel, wait in front of the bank after you open your account. Alwin, Vlinder, and a few others are going over. I'll drop by to see him later this afternoon." He scanned the crowd of boys. "When I call your name, come forward and take your pay into the bank. Everyone's pay is a little different this first time since you arrived on different dates. Remember, keep fifty cents for spending around town. That's enough to get your lunch and buy something for yourself."

Vlinder said something to her father who was ready to hand out the pay. "Oh, yes, *Bedankt, Vlinder.* Most important. We're going to meet back here at 4 o'clock and take the trolleys to the wagons. There are clocks around town and it's up to you to be here on time. Otherwise, you'll have to hire a taxicab or pay for a wagon and driver to get you back to the farm. That'll eat up some of your pay."

Vlinder stood next to her father and handed him about a dozen pay envelopes at a time.

"Marcus Barnstead…Nathan Carey…Raymond Brookstone." Joren handed each boy an envelope with an added, "Here you go, son," or "Thanks for your work." The pay amount was written on the front of their envelopes and they opened them quickly, pulling out bills and staring at more money in one place than many of them had ever seen.

Will, Isaiah, Moses, and Elmer all agreed to wait until they all got their pay before heading inside.

Moses got his pay first and rushed to show the others. "Looka this! We gettin' $43 in dollar bills. Looka this one! It's a $20 bill that says right down at the bottom I can get $20 worth of gold for it if I want."

"No, sah, Moses! Let me see that," said Isaiah. Moses passed him the bill. Isaiah took it, held it up, turned it over, and nodded. "Looks like you're right. Not sure what Granddaddy would do if he saw one of these. Sometimes people pay him with a gold coin, maybe worth $2.50 or $5, but nothin' like this. I heard they's $20 gold pieces, but I ain't never seen one. Guess you could buy one with this here bill."

Once the four boys got their pay envelopes, they headed into The Northern Illinois Bank and Depository, past the uniformed guard who held the door for them all. They stood in different lines, excited, waiting for the tellers. Will planned on depositing $40 and keeping $3 spending money. You never know what you might see and need in Peoria, Illinois.

Roy was one of the first out of the bank and they never saw him again until 4 o'clock.

*   *   *

Once they deposited their pay, most of the boys scattered throughout Peoria. But outside the bank, Will, Elmer, Moses, and Isaiah gathered with the eight Helgevelds, ready to visit Owen.

"After we visit Owen," Alwin said, "we can eat lunch at a drug store Lotta knows about. We'll pay." Alwin looked around at those who were coming. "Let's go."

Alwin hurried along the sidewalk, everyone else just behind. Occasionally, Vlinder and Corrie would stop to look in a clothes store while Will and Elmer fell further behind, taking in the streets, the sites, the stores, and the motorcars. Further back were Moses and Isaiah. At one store, their faces were inches from the window when Isaiah put his arm around Moses' shoulder and pointed. They burst into a run to reach the others.

"Find something you want in that store?" Will asked them when they arrived.

"Ain't never seen nothin' like it, nothin' at all," said Isaiah, out of breath and shaking his head.

"Nothin' like what?" asked Elmer.

"Back home, we don't have no stores where black folks and white folks shop together. We each gots our own stores." Isaiah pointed back down the street, slapped his thigh and laughed. "I declare. That bakery right there, the one with the round sign, it had a white lady waitin' on a colored lady at the counter!"

"Granddaddy told us things is changin' some places," said Moses. "Well, they's sure changin' here!"

Alwin stood outside the hotel until everyone arrived. He turned and headed through two large glass doors, *Hotel Fey* written on them in gold lettering. Inside, Will looked at the shiny floors, shiny tables, and shiny counter. Four large vases were spread through the lobby filled with red, yellow, and orange flowers. Two men with brimless hats stood by the front desk, waiting to carry the suitcases of newly registered hotel guests.

Behind the counter a bespectacled man scanned a large guest register, ticking and circling items down a page. As Alwin approached, the man raised his eyes above his glasses rim and smiled. "Welcome to Hotel Fey," he said. "How can I help you today?"

"We're here," said Alwin turning to glance at the others. "All of us are here to visit Owen Whitcomb. We think he checked into the hotel yesterday from the hospital."

"Ah, yes," said the hotel representative. "A young man from the hospital helped Mr. Whitcomb check in yesterday. We've brought up a few meals for him. He's in room 331. Actually, the doctor is up checking on him now." He leaned out and over the counter and pointed down the hall. "You can take the elevator just there on the right to the third floor. How many of you will be going up?"

"All of us," Alwin turned again to give a quick count. "Wait! Where are Isaiah and Moses? They were just here."

Elmer walked back and peered through the front doors and onto the sidewalk. "There they are."

Alwin hustled outside. "Isaiah, Moses, don't you want to see Owen?"

"Yes we do, Mr. Alwin," said Moses. "We want to see him, but you mean it'd be alright if we come inside this hotel with all of you?"

"Of course it's alright. Come on," Alwin said, walking back through the front doors, Moses and Isaiah just behind him.

Moses turned to Isaiah, shaking his head. "Granddaddy ain't *never* gonna believe this!"

* * *

After Alwin's knock, the doctor greeted them at Room 331.

Owen was lying on the bed and he waved with his good hand when he saw everyone. "You all came to see me?" said Owen.

"I told you we'd be here," Alwin said.

Holding his wrist and cast up in the air, Owen waved at everyone, his exposed fingers slightly blue. Also troubling was a small cast on his sprained foot.

Alwin turned toward the doctor. "How's he doing?"

The doctor breathed deep. "Well, the good news is that he'll recover. He re-sprained that ankle. X-ray says it might be a slight fracture so we put it in a cast." The doctor paused and rubbed his chin. "But the wrist. That's broken in a few places. I was able to reset it, and everything is in place, but he absolutely can't use that hand for a few, maybe several months."

The room was silent. Alwin spoke up and said what everyone wondered. "So, he really can't work back at the farm?"

"Not unless you want to pay him to lie in bed all day," the doctor replied.

That sealed it. Alwin nodded and Owen knew.

"Owen," said Alwin. "I'll have Gerwin stay in town with you tonight. He'll help get you on the train to Chicago. Someone there can help you switch to the Cleveland train."

"Okay, Mr. Alwin," Owen said. "I understand."

"We'll miss you at the farm," Alwin continued. "If you're all healed and want to come back next summer, write to us after the first of the year. We'll put you on the list."

"I already thought of that, sir," Owen said. "That's my plan. Be good to be back and work here another summer. Just hold my things till then." His mood lifted, giving hope to this harsh ending.

The doctor addressed the group. "Not much else I can do here today. I'll check in on him tomorrow morning." He nodded goodbye to Owen and to the others and left.

"Alright, Owen. I'll wire your parents from the hotel desk and tell them you're coming. They can wire back to the hotel to confirm. We'll get you home either tomorrow or the day after. My father said he'd come by later this afternoon to see how you're doing, too. Best of luck. You're a good worker and I hope we see you next summer." Alwin reached in his pocket and pulled out Owen's pay. "Here you go, Owen."

Owen took the envelope and nodded, fighting back tears.

Everyone came to Owen's bedside and shook his good hand with a "get better Owen," or "see you next year." Owen reached his hand over to Isaiah, then Moses. "Good working with you guys," he told them. "Hope you're back next summer." Isaiah and Moses both nodded and shook Owen's hand.

Elmer came by last, shook Owen's good hand and looked down. "I'll miss you, Owen."

Owen looked straight at Elmer. "You take care of Roy and tell him I'll see him next summer. He's all talk." Elmer looked down and nodded.

Once in the lobby, Alwin sent a telegram to Owen's parents and then Lotta led the group to Talbot's Drugstore, two blocks over.

*   *   *

In Talbot's Drug Store, the eight Helgevelds and four workers sat on wobbly red stools in front of a polished, stainless steel counter. Talbot's was the first lunch counter in Peoria to serve hot dogs and that, along with baked beans and a slice of bread, sat in front of each eater except Alwin, who opted for roasted chicken and mashed potatoes. Ice cream sodas sat alongside each platter.

Another group of boys from Bunkhouse 2 were also in Talbot's. Elmer knew several of them and he moved over to their table when they asked about Owen.

Alwin ate quickly, and he, Jakob, and Gerwin left to order fence wire for the sheep paddocks. Before he left, Alwin gave Vlinder $4 to pay for everyone's lunch. "Take the change and get the flowers and anything else you need," Alwin told her. "We'll meet you back at the bank at 4 o'clock."

Vlinder knew it was time to leave when her brothers and sisters tried to see how many times they could spin around on the stools. She paid the bill and everyone spun back to their ice cream sodas, sucking up the last slurry of flavors through their straws, much louder than necessary.

Moses stood up and walked toward the door. "Me and Isaiah, we's heading back to where we stayed when we first came to Peoria. They's some stores out that way. Told them we'd come back if we got to Peoria again."

"Moses, Isaiah," yelled Vlinder after them. "Do you know how to get there? What's it near?"

"Near a lake or somethin'," Moses said. "River maybe. Right near a big bridge."

Vlinder gave them directions toward the bridge and turned back to her brothers and sisters. "I'm going to put flowers on Grampa Bartel's and Gramma Luna's graves for the summer service. I know you want to go to the moving pictures, but I swear, if you aren't back to the bank at 4, we'll leave without you and you'll have to figure out how to get home."

"Hey, Will," called Elmer from the other table. "Ephram bought a baseball. There's a field near here where we can throw it around. You want to come?"

Will looked at Vlinder who was sitting next to him. "You're going to the family graves?"

"I am," said Vlinder. "I have to buy some flowers first. Come if you'd like."

Will nodded at Vlinder and turned to Elmer. "I'm all set, Elmer. I'm going to walk around Peoria, but I'll see you back at the bank." Elmer nodded with a grin stronger than Will expected.

Elmer and the other boys waved and headed to the baseball field off of Spring Street.

CHAPTER 12

O nce outside Talbot's Drug Store, Corrie, Hans, Lotta, and Bram ran down Jefferson Avenue toward the Princess Theater on Fulton Street, anxious for a few hours of Charlie Chaplin short films. Each had five cents for the theater and another ten cents to buy things that Vlinder assured Will they didn't need.

"Come on," Vlinder said to Will. "We turn right on Adams Street, just up there." Peoria was lively with Friday traffic and once they turned onto Adams, Vlinder pointed into stores and shared stories about past shopping trips and the newest trends and prices. She also let Will into the family, the journey from Holland, her granduncles killed in the Civil War, and the good and bad harvests.

Vlinder stopped in front of Goodhue's Variety Store, a double-sized retailer that Vlinder said carried almost everything. "This was Gramma Luna's favorite store. They'd order things special for her, all lavender if it was for the house." Vlinder laughed. "When you come into the house, you'll see what I mean. Lavender drapes, lavender paint, lavender lamp bases. Christmas dishes too." She pointed to her dress. "Gramma Luna even ordered this dress for my eighteenth birthday. Lavender flowers everywhere."

"Lavender? Those look purple," Will said, looking at the dress.

Vlinder laughed. "It's like purple, but don't call it purple around Gramma Luna. She says that purple turns into lavender once it decides to calm down." She peered through the front window of Goodhue's Variety. "They've got flowers here. Plants, too." She pointed to flowers off to the side. "Look," Vlinder said to Will. "Lavender forget-me-nots, Gramma Luna's favorite."

Will followed Vlinder inside. He watched as she kneeled and picked up different pots of forget-me-nots, judging each, brushing up the sides of the flowers and comparing them again. She chose one pot and held it out for Will to approve. "I think she'd like this one," she said.

"Yes, those are pretty," Will said, looking around at the others. He bent over and picked up one that was to the side. "This one has three plants in the pot. I think it's the only one." Will pointed at the base of the others on the floor and the one Vlinder was holding. "These others just have two plants. With this one, you get an extra."

Vlinder put her choice down and examined Will's suggestion. "Maybe you're right. I didn't see this one." Vlinder smiled at Will. "All set. We'll take this one."

Will nodded at the forget-me-nots and at Vlinder.

Outside, Will volunteered to carry the forget-me-nots along Adams Street where there were more shops and more family stories. They traveled down several streets until the shops turned into oversized homes with wraparound porches built mostly, Vlinder told Will, from Rye Whiskey profits. Then there were open spaces signaling the outer edges of Peoria. "We're going to the cemetery? Your grandmother's grave?" Will asked.

"Yes, Gramma Luna died last fall and she's buried in Springdale Cemetery with my Grampa Bartel," said Vlinder. "We haven't been to her grave since she was buried last September. I wanted to plant some flowers since there's a service for her there this summer. The whole family is coming out."

The sidewalk was gone and they walked along the road while wagons and motorcars passed them by, turning right on Prospect Road.

Vlinder told Will stories about Gramma Luna, how she taught her to ride, taught her how to fix fences, taught her that hard work was a gift not a burden, and she taught her how to dance. The stories further welcomed Will into a hidden part of Vlinder's life.

"You've got a good life," said Will. "It sounds…big, lots of people, happy people."

Vlinder laughed. "I suppose that's how it sounds, and I do feel lucky, but that doesn't mean it's been perfect. We've had our problems." Vlinder pointed to a rise ahead. "There it is, up past this field."

Springdale Cemetery swept upwards across several small hills where commanding spruce and poplar trees stood guard over the now silent residents. Vlinder and Will hiked to the front gate where *Springdale Cemetery* was spelled out across the top in metal letters. When they entered the gate, they weren't alone. Several motorcars and wagons were parked at the edges of rows, signaling a family member or friend who was visiting a gravesite and talking to a name chiseled into stone.

Will walked alongside Vlinder, traveling past one row, then another. Occasionally, she stopped and declared, "Look at this one, Bertha Chipman, Died 1849, 8 months old," and further along, "George Whitford, 1768-1861, 93 years old."

They reached the top of a slope and wound down a lane on the other side. "They're right over there," said Vlinder pointing to a sunny neighborhood of granite memorials. They stepped off the roadway and moved gently between those recent and those long deceased.

The forget-me-nots were tucked into Will's right elbow and Vlinder motioned ahead. "There they are," she said. A few more steps and they stopped in front of a headstone that read: **Bartel Helgeveld, 1847-1903** and below that **His Beloved Wife, Luna Helgeveld, 1850-1916**. "Good," Vlinder said, pointing at the stone. "They added 1916 to Gramma Luna's name over the winter."

They were silent. Finally, Vlinder said, "She died right during the harvest last year. It was a tough time for everyone, but we had to keep the farm going."

Vlinder turned to Will, took the forget-me-nots, and grabbed the burlap pay satchel she had tucked into her belt. She laid it on the ground and kneeled on it in front of the stone monument. She pulled out a trowel she brought from the farm and dug a hole larger than needed, centered perfectly under the names. She freed the forget-me-nots from the pot and lowered the lavender tribute into the hole and pushed soil around it. She straightened up on her knees and looked at the grave. "Look. The flowers come up just under Gramma's name, like they're holding both of them up." She breathed deeply. "I miss you, Gramma Luna. I miss you, too, Grampa Bartel."

Vlinder got up and stood next to Will, nature's silence and sounds bringing balance.

Vlinder looked at the headstone. "Grampa said he wanted to be buried on the farm, but Gramma said no. She thought it would be too lonely there. Looking around here, maybe she was right. She's got a lot of neighbors." Then, Vlinder pointed to some open space to the right of the headstones. "Gramma Luna bought all these other plots in case anybody from the family wanted to join them here. Guess she hoped she'd have more company someday."

They stood for a moment.

"And that's one of the problems," continued Vlinder. "Gramma Luna said she couldn't have her son, my Uncle Hendrick, exhumed and brought here, especially since my Aunt Olivia wants to be buried here." Vlinder breathed deeply. "But Gramma Luna said she wouldn't be around to decide, and maybe we'd have more forgiveness in our hearts than she did." Vlinder turned serious. "We struggle over it, pray over it, but bringing him here still feels like something we can't bring ourselves to do."

A moment later Vlinder said, "Oh, no. One thing I forgot was water. That plant's pretty dry. Some water would help it settle in." She looked around. "I don't see any. We'll look for some on the way out."

They wandered down different roads and rows, past a 100-year history of local citizens. They arrived at the south entrance and Will saw two large water cisterns with several buckets to the side. "Here's some water," he said. They filled two buckets and walked back to the grave. There was no urgency in Will. He thought that if the grave was in Chicago, he'd gladly carry the water and listen to Vlinder's family history. They soaked the forget-me-nots and poured the extra water on some thirsty plants of close-by neighbors.

They returned the buckets and then curled back along the paths and rows without any real direction. Soon, the cemetery gave way to open fields, and finally, over a mound, Vlinder pointed to elk and deer, tucked behind a fence and feeding on bales of hay.

"It's not much, but that's our zoo. The Peoria Zoo," Vlinder said. "On the other side, there are two bears. Or at least there were last year." They drew near and tucked their fingers through the fence, watching the elk feed. Two calves pushed under their mother for their own share.

After too long a time, Will turned to Vlinder and said, "I'm glad you asked me to come. Why did you?"

Vlinder looked over at him. "Well, earlier you seemed interested in the family. In the stories." Vlinder paused a minute and looked in toward the elk. "Maybe because you saved me from that farmer boy at the Sunday church service." Another minute passed and Vlinder turned her head to look at Will. "Maybe you're just easy to be around."

Will let go of the fence and looked straight into Vlinder. She kept her eyes on him as he bent his head toward hers. Inches from her, she turned away. "I can't. Not now. I told you before." A moment passed and she continued. "It feels right being here with you. I can't deny it." Then she shook her head. "But every summer, workers like you come to Helgeveld. They say things, and then they go away. You'll do the same. I have my plans, life plans. You do, too."

Will stepped back, looked toward the ground, then back at Vlinder. "Okay. We should probably get back."

Their wandering route through Peoria seemed more planned than random. Dress and clothes shops kept appearing and Vlinder would go inside after pointing to a close-by General Store or someplace else she thought Will would enjoy.

Will went into several stores, flipping through copies of *Boy's Life,* looking at the candy, and walking up and down the aisles. In one store, he picked up an edition of the *Chicago Daily News.* He stared at the front page headline. *Woodrow Wilson Authorizes Draft.*

The war was coming closer but Will didn't know what that would mean.

In the end, Will broke one of his dollar bills and purchased fifteen cents of Beech Nut Spearmint Gum, Tootsie Rolls, and four Clark Bars. He headed out to meet Vlinder.

*　　*　　*

Will and Vlinder arrived at the bank just before 4 p.m. Vlinder left Will and walked over to her brothers and her father who were standing next to a trolley. As she approached them, Alwin pulled a newspaper from under his arm and pointed to the headline. She looked from the paper to her brother and then back at the newspaper. Vlinder looked at her father who gave her a solemn nod.

More boys arrived carrying large or small parcels, their reward and proof of hard work. Will saw Roy leaning against the bank. He held a large bag with string handles and with the other hand, yanked red licorice sticks from his clenched teeth.

Isaiah and Moses came up the sidewalk. "Where'd you go, Will? What's in the bag?" asked Isaiah, pointing to the small paper bag Will was holding.

"Just bought some candy," Will said, holding up the bag. "Walked around town with Vlinder."

Isaiah shook his head. "I swear. Youse just like Moses with the ladies. When we was buyin' things down in the general store, Moses got a flock of girls gigglin' and pointin' at him." Isaiah turned toward his brother. "Just like home. The girls is over you like gravy over biscuits."

"Whatchu talkin' about?" Moses replied. "Didn't see no girls there."

"Oh, really?" said Isaiah. "Saw you askin' one of 'em her name. What was it, Celia or somethin'?"

"Just bein' friendly. That's all," said Moses.

"Hah! Just bein' friendly," Isaiah laughed, "and telling her you'd be back in a couple of months and come see her?"

"Just bein' friendly. That's all."

Isaiah shook his head while Moses and Will shrugged their shoulders.

"What's in your bags?" Will asked.

"I got me some candy and some marbles," said Isaiah, "but Moses got some other stuff."

"Sure did. Lookee here." Moses held up two small bags. He reached in one bag and pulled out a round, wooden yo-yo. "Watch." He put the string around his middle finger and let the disc drop toward the ground only to see it wind halfway back up the string. "You gotta practice a little, but you can get it to keep going up and down." Nobody else had tried one and they nodded that it was a good purchase. Moses put the yo-yo back in the bag and pulled out a small book and two decks of playing cards. "Got a book here on doin' magic tricks and some playin' cards. Always liked magic."

"What's in the other bag?" Will asked, noticing it was wet on the bottom.

"Bought me and Isaiah's favorites," Moses said. "Got us four sour pickles here. One for you, me, Isaiah, and Elmer." Moses lifted up the bag of sour pickles and took a sniff. His eyes started watering and he shook his head. "Whew! That's serious sour!"

Moses reached in the bag and handed a pickle to Will and another to Isaiah. Will held his up, looked at it, and smelled it. He shook his head and closed his eyes. No way he's eating this, he thought. Moses and Isaiah held theirs in front of them, took a cautious bite off the top, squeezed their eyes together, trembled, and chewed with their mouths open. Tears streamed down their cheeks.

Elmer arrived and watched Isaiah and Moses. "What you got? What you eatin'?"

Through half-chewed pickle and tears, Moses said, "Got us a sour pickle...got yours right here." He reached in the bag and gave the final pickle to Elmer.

"Sour pickles!" Elmer exclaimed. "I love sour pickles!" Elmer examined the green cylinder and chomped off the top quarter. Like Isaiah and Moses, tears flowed from Elmer. He closed his eyes tight then opened them wide. Finally, he stomped his left foot up and down. "Whoooeeeeee! That's about the sourest thing I ever tasted!" Elmer pointed at the pickle and said, "that's worth the whole trip to Peoria!" Isaiah and Moses nodded in agreement.

Each took a second bite and yelled out their own version of joy and pain, turning the heads of others, and bringing Corrie Helgeveld over.

"What's the matter? What happened? What's wrong?" Corrie asked.

"Nothin'," said Moses between breaths and chews. "Got us…some…sour pickles…here."

"Sour pickles!" exclaimed Corrie. "You got sour pickles?! I love sour pickles!"

Will didn't miss his chance. He stepped over and handed his to Corrie.

"You sure?" she asked.

"Never been more sure of anything," Will said.

Corrie smiled at Will and stared at the sour pickle. She sniffed at it, closed her eyes and crunched off a small mouthful. She opened her mouth wide and breathed in and out around the half-chewed pickle. Corrie took another bite, waited a second, and then swallowed it all down. She squeezed her eyes together, held her hands in fists in front of her, and twirled twice. She opened her eyes and tears poured down, dripping off her chin. "Jiminy Cripes! That's about the sourest one I ever had!"

Moses nodded his head between deep breaths. "Yes, indeed.…These here must be… Illinois sour pickles. Ain't nothin' that sour in Alabama!"

The four sour pickle eaters agreed to finish theirs on the wagon trip back to the farm, their hoots and foot stomping providing entertainment for the first part of the trip.

∗   ∗   ∗

The sun sat at the top of the trees when the wagons rolled into Helgeveld Farm. Anika met her husband, children, and the workers at the front of the farmhouse and told everyone to drop off their packages and come right back to the chow hall. Dinner was waiting for them.

The boys ran to the bunkhouse and inside was Roy, walking down the aisle with his bag of candy, sizing up what everybody bought and checking where they were keeping it.

At each bunk, he'd look and laugh. "That's all you got? Look. I got five times that, right here. Got even more back home."

Roy walked toward the front of the bunkhouse and lay down on his bunk. "So, where's the farmer? He didn't come back in the wagon good as new?"

"He's going home, Roy," said Will. "Looks like you got your way. Oh yeah, Owen said he'd see you next summer."

"Got my way? Don't know what you're talkin' about." Roy paused. "Next summer? You think I'm comin' back to this cussed place? Can't wait 'til summer's over. Gonna work in a swanky place next year. Might work in a hotel in Philadelphia." He bit off a fingernail and examined it before flicking it onto the floor.

Roy was tiresome.

* * *

At the dinner bell, the workers headed out of the bunkhouse and up toward the chow hall, Moses practicing his yo-yo along the path. The chow hall hosted exaggerated stories of Peoria, pay, and too much candy. Alwin wandered along the tables, asking the boys about their trip to town and reminding them that tomorrow was a workday. The late dinner was over, and since it was getting close to 9 p.m., the boys all headed back to their bunkhouses.

Before leaving, Isaiah and Moses walked over to Alwin who was just about to leave the chow hall.

"Mr. Alwin, sah," said Isaiah.

Alwin turned. "You boys have a good time in town today? Get to look around and buy a few things?"

"Yes, we did, Mr. Alwin. It was a good day," said Moses. "But we got a favor to ask you." Each boy reached into their front pants pocket and pulled out their pay envelopes.

Alwin looked at them, surprised. "Is that your pay? Didn't you open an account?"

"No, sah," Moses said. "Bank said it didn't make no accounts for coloreds. Said some people in town don't want their money mixin' with ours. Said they's other banks in town for us but we don't know none of them."

Isaiah spoke up, "So, Moses and me, we was wonderin' if you could hold our pay for the summer and then give it to us when we go back to Alabama?"

Alwin looked at both of them. "They wouldn't take your money?"

"No, sah," they both said.

Alwin thought for a moment, turned, looked toward the farmhouse, then back. "Alright, I'll hold your pay for now," and he put both envelopes in his pocket.

Isaiah and Moses got back to the bunkhouse just before lights out and everyone quieted down onto their bunk.

When it was dark, each boy relived the day. It was a good one.

CHAPTER 13

That Sunday after church, and after lunch, the routine took hold.

At the back barn, Isaiah and Moses continued working on the undercarriage rot in one of the wagons. A week earlier, Isaiah gave Alwin a list of parts, including some lumber and a spring. The lumber arrived from Peoria in three days. Two days later, the spring came directly from Chicago on the mail truck.

Will and Elmer wandered to the back barn and climbed into the loft. From below, Isaiah would talk the work, Moses sang the songs, and the sawing and hammering led to a welcome nap.

But the nap didn't last.

A parade of Helgevelds: Bram, Lotta, Hans, and Corrie scuffed and skipped down the path from the farmhouse to the back barn. They went inside to oversee Moses' and Isaiah's progress, but soon headed outside, climbing and jumping from broken and repaired plows, tables, cabinets, and wagon parts. Hans got a bale of hay from the stable to allow higher jumps with softer landings.

Corrie discovered she could step from a plow to a windowsill and she launched herself over it and landed on the hay, rolling into a somersault. Hans was not willing to let his twin sister better him, so he ran to the other side of the barn and brought back a ladder, positioning it next to a barn window. He climbed two rungs higher than Corrie and spread both arms ensuring an attentive audience. Then he jumped, twisted, and landed backside on the hay, claiming victory.

Lotta looked at her twin and yelled, "Come on, Bram. We can beat that!" She ran into the barn and pointed to Will and Elmer, looking down from the loft. "We can jump out the loft door!" and the two of them scrambled up the stairs.

Alwin heard the chaos and came running down the path. "Hey!" he roared. "Are you jumping off this junk again?" Then he looked to the second floor loft door. "You think you're gonna jump outta the loft??!! *Stop het nu!* You get hurt and it'll fall on me for not keeping an eye on you. Bram, Lotta, get out here!"

The four siblings gathered at the front of the barn, asking for forgiveness and blaming each other. When Alwin shooed them away, they burst into a run, off toward the stables.

Alwin turned and looked at Moses and Isaiah. Will and Elmer had come down from the loft. "They've been told over and over to stay outta this barn." Alwin rubbed the side of his face and gave a small laugh. "But a few years ago, Vlinder and me, we did the same."

Gerwin walked up and around the side of the farmhouse and stopped at the assembled group. "Got Owen on the train at 7 this morning. He'll switch in Chicago and be home tonight. He told me about the accident. Said he was sure there was nothing alongside the bunkhouse when he went to the privy. Somebody had to put that bench there. Owen figures it was Roy."

"We figure it was Roy, too," Will added. "Just don't have any proof. Those benches get moved all the time."

Alwin nodded and looked at the others. "What do you all think? Any of you see anything that night?"

"No sah, Mr. Alwin. I didn't see nothin'," said Isaiah. "But Moses says Roy gets up and goes outside sometimes at night. Real quiet."

"That right, Moses?" Alwin said. "What do you think? Think Roy did it?"

"Tough to tell, Mr. Alwin," Moses said, "Roy being so bombastic and all."

Alwin straightened up. "What? Bomb what? What did you say?"

"Said Roy's really bombastic, all the time."

Everyone looked at each other. "Moses," asked Alwin. "What does that mean? What does bom...bastic mean?"

Moses shrugged his shoulders. "Means Roy says a lot of words, but don't really say nothin' at all."

Isaiah interrupted, anticipating Alwin's next question. "He learns them words at church, Mr. Alwin." He turned to Moses. "You learn that bomb word at church?"

"Sure did," Moses exclaimed. "Pastor Jannsen, his message a few weeks back was about high-talkin' folk, and how they's always goin' on about one thing or another."

"I swear, Moses," said Alwin. "I'm Dutch and I hardly understand anything Pastor Jannsen says." Alwin turned back toward everyone. "Yeah, I guess Roy is... bombastic...tough to tell what's truth and not. With no proof, nothing we can do right now."

* * *

The next morning, breakfast was over and everyone agreed it was tough getting used to Owen being gone.

As the boys rose from the tables to bring their empty plates and cups to the front, Joren Helgeveld strode through the side door of the chow hall sporting a string tie and ironed shirt, looking more ready for business than a day at the farm. He moved quickly across the hall, heading straight toward the four boys.

Elmer whispered to Will, "Will. It looks like he's coming over here. He's coming over here! Oh no! What did we do? Will, what does he want?"

Instead, Mr. Helgeveld stopped in front of Moses and Isaiah. Both boys faced forward, afraid to meet Joren Helgeveld's eyes.

"Isaiah, Moses," Joren Helgeveld said. "I need you boys to come with me. You won't be working down at the barn today."

They looked at each other, wondering if this was their last day on the farm. "Yes, sah." They followed behind him, out the side door, and down the path to a ready buckboard hitched to Lily. Mr. Helgeveld motioned for Isaiah and Moses to hop up on the seat next to him.

Alwin was rubbing Lily's head and then came up alongside. He nodded to his father and offered good luck. "*Veel geluk in de stad.*"

His father mixed his Dutch with English, "*Bedankt zoon.* We'll be back for dinner." And with that, Joren Helgeveld snapped the reins and the three of them jolted toward Peoria.

Isaiah sat straight in the seat, afraid to speak for more than a mile. Finally, he asked, "Sah, Mr. Joren, sah. We headin' into town today?"

Joren Helgeveld looked straight ahead. "Yes, we are, Isaiah. We're going to The Northern Illinois Bank and Depository. We need to straighten a few things out." Joren Helgeveld had taken the news personally that Northern Illinois wouldn't make bank accounts for Isaiah and Moses. Over the last several weeks, their names were mentioned almost daily in the farmhouse when Alwin reported on what was being worked on, what parts needed to be ordered, and on what was newly repaired. Before Isaiah and Moses started working in the back barn, broken equipment and slowdowns were woven into the daily plan. Now, the daily plan assumed those tasks being completed. Joren Helgeveld noticed the change.

Lily trotted past fields and around road holes while Joren Helgeveld pointed to one area of the farm, then another.

"Right here," he told Isaiah and Moses, "that's where the farm ended when my father bought it back in 1869. Planted just corn and a little tobacco then. Nowadays, soybeans are becoming more popular than tobacco and most of the tobacco's grown further south." Mr. Helgeveld paused, then continued, "Had a fella from some company out east, think it was American Tobacco or something. They make those Bull Durham cigarettes. Made us an offer if we switched to growing all tobacco. Bad business deal, though. But we keep our options open."

At first, Isaiah and Moses didn't know if going to the bank meant they were in trouble, but the ease of Mr. Helgeveld suggested otherwise.

The three of them pulled into downtown Peoria a little before 10 a.m. But, the first stop was not The Northern Illinois Bank and Depository. Instead, Joren Helgeveld eased Lily to the sidewalk in front of The Illinois Mutual Bank. He turned to Isaiah and Moses. "Alright, boys. We're going to get you two a bank account here, or somewhere else, and then head over to Northern Illinois." He reached into his right front pocket and pulled out two folded $5 bills. "I know you boys are fixing things down at the back barn every Sunday after church." He paused. "Can't say Mrs. Helgeveld and I approve of you workin' on the Lord's Day, but...I'm in no position to judge. Not me." Joren Helgeveld looked toward the ground then back toward Isaiah. "But Alwin tells me it doesn't feel like work? Is that true?"

"That's true, Mr. Joren," said Isaiah. "Moses and me, we just like fixin' stuff, even on Sundays. Makes us feel like we're back in Alabama, right alongside our Granddaddy."

Joren nodded and said, "Well, work or not, we'll let God figure that out, but either way, you're not going to fix things on your own time without getting wages."

He handed one $5 bill to Isaiah and the other to Moses. "These are yours for the fixin' you've done on Sundays. You keep doing extra and there'll be more." He pointed to the bank. "For now, I want you to go into this bank and try to open an account in your own names with these bills. Tell the bank you're working at Helgeveld Farm, and if they need someone to vouch for you, come get me."

He looked at the boys. "And if they won't take your money, we'll go to every last bank in Peoria until we find one that will." Mr. Helgeveld reached into his shirt pocket and pulled out their pay envelopes. "Alwin gave these to me. If they open your account, you tell them you want to add the rest of your pay to it."

Moses and Isaiah put their pay envelopes in their pockets and held open the $5 bills. Isaiah noticed that Abraham Lincoln was on the $5 bill, just like on their lucky pennies. They smiled at each other, not just at the money, but that they weren't in trouble.

"Yes, sah, Mr. Joren," and they jumped from the wagon and ran into The Illinois Mutual Bank. A few minutes later, they were ushered out the door by a guard who seemed surprised when they walked to a wagon driven by Joren Helgeveld.

Moses hopped into the seat next to Joren Helgeveld and said, "No, Mr. Joren, that bank said no deposits from colored folk."

When the boys were settled, Mr. Helgeveld eased Lily into the Peoria traffic. "Don't worry," he said. "I got a list of banks we can go to." As they pulled into the street, a black Model T clipped the front left corner of the wagon and sped away. Joren Helgeveld shot up from his seat, shook his fist, and screamed *Verdomme! Klootzak!* at the driver who disappeared into a cluster of black autos.

Joren Helgeveld sat back down and stared up Wisconsin Avenue. "Each time I come to town, there's more motorcars and fewer wagons." He paused and shook his head. "But, you can't fight progress. Automobiles are the future, I suppose. Gonna have to fix that Dodge behind the barn at some point." He turned to Moses. "Moses, Alwin said you work on engines. See if you can get the Dodge behind the barn running. Probably need it at some time or another."

"Yes, sah, Mr. Helgeveld," Moses said. "I'll see what I can do."

"Good." Joren Helgeveld said shaking the reins. "Heeya, Lily."

But it was the same at the next bank.

Then, at the Community Bank of Northern Illinois, Isaiah and Moses stayed inside almost half an hour before running out the door holding passbooks high above their heads. "Got 'em Mr. Joren!" Isaiah said.

Moses turned to Isaiah. "Yeah, and did you see, even had a colored man pushin' a broom in there! Never saw such a thing before."

Joren Helgeveld looked at the sign over the bank door. *Community Bank of Northern Illinois.* "That's a Chicago bank. Heard they got locations as far south as Springfield. A few other Dutch farmers bank there. Yeah, that should work out just fine." He waited until Isaiah and Moses were settled into their seats and eased Lily into the traffic. He looked straight ahead and said, "Okay, let's get over to the Northern Illinois Bank. Your money isn't good enough for them? Well, then their bank isn't good enough for mine."

When the doorman at Northern Illinois Bank and Depository saw Joren Helgeveld searching for a space in front of the bank, he shooed away another wagon and took Lily by the reins and eased the wagon into a space. He tipped his hat. "Good morning, Mr. Helgeveld. It's a pleasure to see you, sir."

Joren Helgeveld hopped off the wagon. "Same to you, Walter. I'll be in the bank for a few minutes. Can you keep an eye on the wagon for me?"

The doorman glanced at Isaiah and Moses, paused, and said, "Certainly, Mr. Helgeveld. My pleasure."

Joren Helgeveld looked up and said to Isaiah and Moses, "I'll just be a few minutes. You boys wait here."

Walter ran to the door and, with a slight bow, opened it for Joren Helgeveld who walked inside. He scanned the lobby and saw Vice President Hampstead just finishing up with a customer. Alan Hampstead soon raised his hand and gestured to Joren Helgeveld to come to his desk.

"Indeed!" said Mr. Hampstead. "This is a pleasure, indeed, Mr. Helgeveld. I certainly didn't expect to see you again this soon. Please sit down. How is Mrs. Helgeveld?"

"Why, thank you, Alan," Joren Helgeveld said, easing into his seat. "Mrs. Helgeveld is fine. Up to her neck in work with the summer season underway."

"Certainly, certainly. How can I help you today?" Alan Hampstead asked.

"Well, Alan, I'd like you to make out a cashier's check for my entire balance. I'm closing my account here."

Alan Hampstead sat speechless. He looked across at Joren Helgeveld. "Excuse me? You want to close your account here? Whatever for?"

Joren Helgeveld leaned forward. "Seems that the pay for two of my workers isn't good enough for your bank. Isaiah and Moses Butler, two of my best workers this summer. They couldn't open an account here last Friday."

Alan Hampstead thought for a minute. "Were they colored boys? You have to understand Mr. Helgeveld, that we hold to the highest community standards in Peoria. People who bank with us want assurance that their money is combined with others who are like them, who want the same things." Alan Hampstead was getting nervous. "You understand that if it was up to me, of course, if it was up to me, I'd be willing. After all, we're all equal in God's eyes, don't you feel? I certainly do, but in these times, there are certain realities, other business considerations we must adhere to, Mr. Helgeveld. You understand, don't you?"

"Well, Alan," said Joren Helgeveld leaning in. "Seems their money was good enough to open accounts at the Community Bank of Northern Illinois. If that bank is good enough to take their money, it's good enough to take mine." Joren Helgeveld reached down, pulled out his pocket watch, and checked the time. "The day's moving along, Alan. Can you get me that draft?"

Fumbling for words, Alan Hampstead said, "Joren, Mr. Helgeveld. It's not quite as easy as that. You're our second largest depositor. We'd need some time. It's not that easy."

Joren Helgeveld stared into Alan Hampstead. "You wire Chicago, you wire whoever you want, but if I don't have my draft within half an hour, I'll make sure I'm not the only one who'll be taking money out of your bank. Seems to me you've got several other Dutch farmers in the area. Am I right?"

Alan Hampstead nodded, mouth open.

Joren Helgeveld continued. "You probably wouldn't want me to tell them I couldn't get my money out of your bank, would you?"

Mr. Hampstead shook his head from side to side.

"And for this season," Joren added. "I don't mind if the other boys at the farm keep their accounts here. Probably cause quite a stir in town if fifty or so boys were seen taking their money out of your bank and walking it to another bank."

There was fear in Alan Hampstead's eyes. "Wait right here, Mr. Helgeveld. I'm sure something can be arranged," and he dashed from his desk to a room at the back of the bank.

Joren Helgeveld crossed his legs and tapped his fingers across his knee. He waved at two tellers he knew, and he waited.

Twenty minutes later, Alan Hampstead returned with a cashier's check for $27,257.39 made out in the name of *Joren Helgeveld/Helgeveld Farm*.

Mr. Helgeveld took the check and examined it. He stood up and reached his hand out to Alan Hampstead. "Why, thank you, Alan. You might revisit your policies at your next meeting."

Alan Hampstead shook his hand and nodded.

Walter held the door on his way out. "Good to see you, Mr. Helgeveld. Hope to see you again soon."

"I think not, Walter, but best of luck to you."

Joren Helgeveld walked to the wagon, pulled himself into the seat and shook the reins. Looking straight ahead, he said to Isaiah and Moses, "One more stop. Let's go back to the Community Bank of Northern Illinois. I need to make a deposit. After that, I'm getting a little hungry. You find any good places to eat in town the other day?"

Moses looked at Isaiah, eyes wide and said braver than he imagined, "Yes, Mr. Joren, sah, we could try Talbot's Drug Store. We ate there last Friday."

And after a welcome stop at the Community Bank of Northern Illinois, where the Helgeveld Farm became the third largest depositor in the Peoria, Illinois branch, Joren Helgeveld treated Isaiah and Moses to frankfurters, baked beans, and ice cream sodas at Talbot's Drug Store.

CHAPTER 14

The next Thursday after dinner, Alwin found Will, Isaiah, Moses, and Elmer still at their table.

"Looks like we've got another job for you tomorrow," Alwin said. "My mother is taking the working girls from the house to Peoria. They'll open bank accounts and get a free day in Peoria just like all of you did. But that leaves us a little short for breakfast, lunch, and dinner helpers." Alwin paused, then got to the point. "I don't know if this is good news or bad news for you, but tomorrow you'll be working in the farmhouse kitchen, cleaning up and helping with the meals." He looked at the boys. "Vlinder and Corrie suggested you four. After breakfast tomorrow, come on up to the farmhouse. They'll show you what to do."

Alwin continued. "I won't be here. I'm going to Peoria with my father tomorrow. I don't want to say much, but we might be making a business deal with the government for the crops and some livestock. We'll tell you more later."

The boys nodded and Alwin headed out the chow hall door and into the farmhouse. Minutes later, the four found themselves on the rise behind the farmhouse, under the sycamore, trying to decide whether working in the kitchen was good news or not.

"Be good to have a day away from the barn," Isaiah said. "We're waiting for parts from Chicago, anyways."

Will added, "and I wouldn't mind seeing what the farmhouse is like on the inside."

All good points and the boys were happy at the prospect.

There were a few moments of silence and then Moses asked the group, "Any you done any cookin' or worked in a kitchen?"

The mood switched.

* * *

Just after breakfast the next morning, four house and four kitchen girls, along with Alwin, Anika, and Joren Helgeveld headed off to Peoria in a Murphy wagon. Anika had promised them the same trolley ride as the boys, a trip to the Community Bank of Northern Illinois to open a bank account, and a free day to explore the city.

The early departure allowed Alwin and his father to make a 10 a.m. meeting at the Peoria Town Hall where they, and several other farmers in the area, would meet with two U.S. officials from the Department of Agriculture. The Great War was intensifying and the country was making offers to farms for their corn and soybeans, as well as encouraging them to raise beef cattle, all for the war effort.

Joren Helgeveld had listened to dozens of business proposals over the years, but those offers included several restrictions, making the deals unattractive. While the farmers were anxious to help the country, they would need to hear the details. Regardless of the outcome, Joren Helgeveld promised Anika that he and Alwin would be at the bank by 4 o'clock to take the trolley back to the wagon and head back to the farm.

* * *

Will, Moses, Isaiah, and Elmer wiped a little more dirt than usual from their clothes for their day in the kitchen. Their knowledge on cooking ranged from mistaken to absurd. Elmer even wondered if some potatoes grew already half-mashed.

As the boys headed to the farmhouse, Vlinder and her younger brothers and sisters were in the farmhouse kitchen, kneading bread dough and washing the endless cycle of dishes, cups, pots, and pans. Anticipating the unskilled kitchen helpers, much of the lunch and dinner preparation was already completed. However, the boys were still in for a morning and afternoon of peeling, cutting, organizing, washing, and carrying food to the hungry workers.

But the first chore would be the annual initiation of boys who had never worked on a farm.

When Vlinder came into the kitchen, she saw the two buckets labeled *Cow Paint* and smiled at Lotta. "Are you sure none of them have been down to the cows or the barn?"

"Yes, I'm sure," Lotta said. "Elmer and Will have been out in the fields and Isaiah and Moses have been working at the back barn all season. And none of them ever worked on a farm before." The buckets were filled with a mixture of milk and flour, giving the white liquid a paint thickness. On the floor next to the buckets sat four paint brushes.

Corrie stood at the side window. "Here they come!"

A knock at the farmhouse door brought Vlinder over and she escorted the four boys into the kitchen. With a hand on her hip, she sized up the unlikely kitchen crew. "Alright, all of you will be helping with lunch and dinner today. Ready?"

The boys nodded and shrugged their shoulders indicating confused enthusiasm. "Alright. Here's what we'll be doing today. For lunch, we'll be carving cold ham, packing biscuits, cutting wedges of cheese, and loading up apples and pickles. Bread for dinner is going in the ovens shortly and Lotta is making cookies. And you'll be washing. There's always plenty to wash."

Vlinder paused to let the tasks settle in them. "Once all of that's done, we'll load it onto the wagons along with the dishes, cups, forks, and knives for lunch. Drinks too. You'll be getting the punch ready in those containers there. Then we'll head out to the fields and get everyone fed. Sound good?" The boys stood frozen. Vlinder laughed. "Then we've got dinner."

"First, though," Vlinder said, "we've been so busy in here, we haven't got to the cows yet." The boys stood, confused. "So, before we do anything else," continued Vlinder, "I want you four to head down to the barn and get those cows painted for the season." She pointed to the buckets. "We've got the paint here and Lotta, Corrie, and I will follow you down and you can give their stripes a fresh coat of white paint. It won't take long. How does that sound?" She waited for one of the boys to challenge the proposal, to see through the joke.

But instead, Will said he thought it was a great idea and Moses asked, "How come you paint the cows, anyways?"

These were city boys. The plan was in motion.

"Well," said Vlinder, "that's how we can tell them apart from a distance." She held up binoculars to add to the story. "And from the different stripes, we know which cow is which, right here from the farmhouse. Could be a sick cow or maybe a pregnant one. This might save us a trip to the barn."

The boys nodded at the reasonable answer, but Lotta left the kitchen to hide a laugh.

"It won't take long," said Vlinder. "Some cows just need a touch up on a few faded spots. If you need more paint, we'll get it for you."

To Will, painting the cows sounded like a much better way to start the day than working in the kitchen. And they'd finally get to visit the cows they'd been watching from above the farmhouse.

"Okay, let's go," said Vlinder.

Elmer grabbed the handle of one bucket, Isaiah took the other, and Moses grabbed the four brushes. Will walked just behind them, Vlinder to his side and making sure the story continued.

"Never heard of painting cows before," Will stated.

"It's easier to tell them apart and easier on the cows than branding," Vlinder said. "It's a new trend in this area. A few farms around here are trying it. You probably saw some other painted cows on the way from Peoria."

She was right. The striped cows were on a couple of hills between here and Peoria. Will couldn't wait to tell the people back in Pittsburgh about this new trend.

Trailing behind were Corrie and Lotta, slapping each other and doubling over at each new story Vlinder invented. Hans and Bram stayed at the farmhouse, swapping the binoculars to follow the event.

As they reached the barn, about half of the fifty dairy cows grazed in the fenced pasture, the others still in the barn. Vlinder stepped ahead and opened the gate, letting the four boys in among the cows. Matt Gorman, supervisor of the dairy business, was in on the prank and had unbundled some hay bales by the fence to keep the cows steady. Vlinder spied him peering out from the side of the barn door as she moved four of the cows toward a separate hay bale. Corrie and Lotta ran alongside the fence until they were next to the cows on the other side. They stood on the bottom rung, hanging over the fence top.

"Alright, boys," Vlinder said. "Put the paint buckets right there and grab a brush. Load up the brush with some paint and pick a cow. Walk up to them slowly; they need to get used to you. Then, just start painting, following the pattern already on the cow."

Moses handed out the brushes and he and Will shared a bucket of cow paint. Elmer and Isaiah did the same and the four boys stood with brushes loaded and ready.

Vlinder surveyed the four. "Good, and make sure you paint up and down, like this." Vlinder walked over to Will, covering his brush hand with hers and giving a persuasive cow painting demonstration. "Up and down. Up and down," she demonstrated. "Never sideways like this." The boys mimicked the lesson.

Lotta pointed from the fence. "Moses, take that cow right there. The one with the fat stripe."

Corrie pointed across. "Elmer, paint Brandy. She's there. She'll need a lot of paint. That stripe goes from her front legs to her back legs."

Will walked up to the closest cow who was grinding and chewing a mouthful of hay. She lifted her head, viewed Will, and returned to her favorite feed. Will peered closer. "Vlinder, I don't see where to paint. It looks like it was just painted." Corrie fell off the fence at that, straight on her back, her hand over her mouth to keep from giving it all away.

"Well," said Vlinder. "That's true. This is your first time so we didn't want to make it too tough for you. This is more of a touch up for summer. But you wait, the summer sun fades them fast. We'll have you out here in the fall for the winter painting."

Will nodded at the reasoning and started considering the fall painting project.

Each boy approached a cow and Isaiah gently brushed the "paint" up and down the side of a husky one near the fence.

"She's pregnant, Isaiah," yelled Corrie. "You're going to need a lot of paint to cover her." Isaiah kept painting her side but he didn't see any benefit to his effort. He loaded the brush again, but the mixture just rolled off the hide. He looked at his brush and then across to the other boys, each of them puzzled.

Will held up his brush and looked across to the girls. "I don't think it's working. Maybe we need thicker paint."

Vlinder, Corrie, and Lotta couldn't keep it going any longer. Vlinder held herself up on a fence post while Corrie and Lotta bent in half, their laughs heard back at the farmhouse where Hans and Bram watched with binoculars. The four boys still didn't get the joke.

Vlinder yelled from the fence. "These are Dutch dairy cows, Lakenvelder. They're born with those stripes."

Elmer paused and asked, "you mean they come out already painted?"

Corrie and Lotta buckled over once again.

The walk back to the farmhouse gave them time to digest the hoax, but cows and kitchens would remain foreign to these city boys.

* * *

As the morning moved ahead, the boys proved little better in the kitchen than with the cows. Will mixed five dirty dishes in with the clean dishes; Isaiah let a sink overflow; Elmer used a knife instead of a peeler on the potatoes, cutting his thumb; and Moses slathered mustard on the ham before it was sliced. Vlinder changed strategies and gave the boys easier tasks, including cleaning the floor underneath the sinks and stoves, washing the kitchen windows, and scouring the pots that had baked-on food. Later, and to the relief of everyone, the four boys successfully loaded the lunch wagons.

Being familiar with the routine, lunch out in the fields went smoothly. Will, Isaiah, Elmer, and Moses handed plates and cups to the other lunch crew who filled the workers' plates. Roy wandered between each wagon asking why the lunch boys weren't wearing aprons.

In the afternoon, and as expected, Will, Isaiah, Moses, and Elmer were no more productive in preparing dinner than they had been for lunch. Watching their kitchen efforts, Corrie commented that cow painting was their most successful task of the day.

However, when Isaiah and Moses told Vlinder they could weld two broken legs back onto a kitchen stove, she pointed to a crack in an unused metal sink. "Could you fix that, too?" she asked.

Isaiah and Moses smiled and nodded. They went to the barn and brought back the welding tool, rods, tanks, and eye-goggles.

With the help of Will and Elmer, the four boys lifted the cast iron stove onto blocks. Then, Isaiah and Moses rolled the two tanks alongside and welded the stove legs back into place. Next, Isaiah welded the split in the back of the metal sink, and as soon as the bead was down, Moses and Elmer leaned in against the side of the sink to hold the seam tight while it cooled.

"Can we use it right away?" asked Vlinder.

"Yes, ma'am. You can fill it right up," said Moses.

Corrie cranked the pump lever and the kitchen staff watched the side sink fill and return to duty after more than four months.

Lotta reminded Vlinder of the four broken chairs in the main room and the damaged table that had been moved to a closet on the second floor.

"Do you want to fix a few more things in the house, chairs and such?" Vlinder asked.

Their uniform nods suggested that any work outside of kitchen work was welcome. Isaiah and Moses brought the welding equipment to the back barn, returning with a bucketful of screws, screwdrivers, nails, glue, chisels, saws, files, hammers, and a hand drill.

"Come on," said Corrie. "We'll show you what needs to be fixed." With that, Isaiah and Moses followed her and Lotta into the main house. Will watched the door swing open, catching a glimpse of a large window across a big room before closing off this secret world.

Will's thoughts wandered through the door right alongside Moses and Isaiah. He pictured grand rooms, ornate hallways, proud furniture, and upstairs, her room, her bed, smartly made, a table to the side with a lamp, a book. What book? The Bible? A book on running a business? Or perhaps a book like Will's mother read, a book about love. The one called *The Rosary*. By Florence somebody. Why hadn't he taken time to scan the pages to see how women fall in love?

Will tried to refocus on the kitchen chores. He and Elmer carried plates, cups, trays of chicken, and pots of vegetables to the chow hall. Will glanced at the upstairs windows each time he returned to the main house. Where were Isaiah and Moses now? What were they hammering? Which window was hers?

After almost two hours, Isaiah, Moses, Corrie, and Lotta reappeared in the kitchen, Isaiah carrying a chair that needed a new leg. Vlinder looked up from a sudsy sink. "How did the repairs go?"

"Everything's fixed," said Corrie. "Just this chair is left. Isaiah said he'd make a new leg for it in the back barn. Oh, and they fixed our door upstairs. Now it closes."

Vlinder turned and shook the suds from her hands. "Really? I'd almost gotten used to that door never closing. Good job, Moses, Isaiah."

Corrie took eight warm raisin cookies, fresh from the oven, and gave two each to Will, Elmer, Isaiah, and Moses. All four boys were hoping that the repairs would be remembered more than the kitchen work.

Six-fifteen arrived and dinner was ready. The workers filed through the two back doors of the chow hall into well-rehearsed lines. The Helgevelds cooked and served, while the four boys carried what they were told. Roy still asked where their aprons were.

After dinner and cleanup, Will, Moses, Isaiah, and Elmer sat down with the Helgeveld workers and shared the same chicken, biscuits, and vegetable dinner. Afterwards, Corrie brought over a serving platter piled high with raisin cookies.

"Too many cookies here," said Vlinder. "You boys can head to your bunkhouse. But take a handful of cookies back for the other boys. We're all set here." The boys nodded, took several cookies, and moved toward the back door.

"Oh," Vlinder yelled after the boys, "and good job all of you, for the most part. So good a job that we might not tell anybody about the cow painting."

The words could have stung, but keeping that secret, especially from Roy, earned a sigh and a thanks from the boys.

Evening crept over the farm and the four headed to the bunkhouse feeling as weary as a day in the fields. Elmer pointed back toward the road. "Here come the girls."

The boys turned and could hear the wagon returning from Peoria, the riders clapping and singing.

> *What's the use of worrying*
> *It never was worth while*
> *So, pack up your troubles in your old kit bag*
> *And smile, smile, smile.*

Will waited as long as he could. Halfway back to the bunkhouse, he asked Isaiah, "so what was the main house like? What's in there? What are the rooms like?"

"Theys got big rooms with big windows everywhere," Isaiah said. "Chairs spread all around, soft chairs looked like. A long divan, too, against the back window. We fixed some chairs in there that go around the big table. Looked like that's where they do their Sunday eatin'. The piano was in there, near a wall."

"What about upstairs? Did you see inside any of the rooms?" asked Will.

"Just one," said Isaiah. "We fixed the door to it. Straightened the hinge and chiseled the frame to make the door swing shut."

Will knew that one more question would tip off Isaiah.

But Isaiah was already tipped off. "Had three beds in it. Corrie said that Lotta, her, and Vlinder sleep in there. It's the room right over the kitchen." He gave Will a quick smile.

A few steps further, Moses added, "One thing, though, everything's purple. Purple coverings for the windows. Purple tablecloths. Purple on the chairs. Purple rugs."

"It's not purple," Will said. "It's lavender."

"Lavender? What's lavender? Sure looked purple to me," Moses wondered.

"It's like purple but not as purply," said Will.

"Yeah," said Moses. "Seemed a little friendlier than purple. Lavender, huh? Sounds like a good word. I'll remember it."

CHAPTER 15

Pastor Jannsen's message on Sunday was that God was in charge, but it's up to us to make good decisions. Or at least that's what Moses said the message was. Nobody else knew.

Back at the farm, Will, Moses, Elmer, and Isaiah settled into a Sunday afternoon at the back barn, planning, wondering, and fixing.

"Isaiah," said Moses, looking at Isaiah's task. "This here wagon, be better if we took it out back and set a match to it. I bet that's what Granddaddy would do."

"Gotta fix it. Have to order some boards and braces," said Isaiah. "Got some spokes around here someplace. We can get the wheels fixed up today."

Word had gotten out that Moses and Isaiah were able to fix just about anything and as a favor, Alwin began taking in broken items from neighbors who couldn't afford a proper repair. Every Sunday, Alwin came to the back barn, examined the work, and handed Moses and Isaiah $1 each for the afternoon work. Occasionally, Alwin even passed on a compliment from an area farmer, causing Isaiah or Moses to stop working and nod at the unaccustomed approval.

This Sunday was cool, bright, and the clouds raced east. While Isaiah and Moses worked, Will and Elmer lay in the grass, a footlong hay stem twisting in their mouths.

"You all think you'll come back here next summer? I want to," Elmer started. "More than ever when I heard Roy didn't want to come back."

"Nothin' Moses and me'd like better than to come back next summer, but Granddaddy, he's getting older," Isaiah said, while still focusing on his work. "He can't do a lot of the work by hisself no more. And Gramma, she ain't well. Next year? Not sure." Isaiah went into the barn and carried out more than a dozen spokes from broken wheels. "But this is good work here at the farm, for sure."

"I'm coming back," said Will. "I have to say, working here is good. The people are good. The work's good."

Isaiah added, "And maybe there's a lady that's good?"

There was no hiding it. Everyone laughed.

Moses added, "Workin' here and makin' my own money? Feels real good." Moses stood up and considered his future. "Granddaddy, he's a businessman, I figure. His name's on the barn in town. But he don't own the barn. He gotta pay rent. Me? I want my own place, a business. Don't want to pay no rent to nobody else. Have a wife, kids. Everything's my own." Moses looked up at his brother. "Hey, Isaiah, if you work hard, maybe you can work for me!"

"You ain't *never* gonna be my boss, Moses Jeremiah!" Isaiah shot back.

It was Sunday, so Corrie, Lotta, Hans, and Bram harnessed Lily to a wagon and lined up bales of hay along the path in front of the back barn. The wagon raced past the four boys, each Helgeveld taking a turn, jumping from the moving wagon onto a hay bale.

Will and Elmer sat up, raised their arms, and hooted approval, which led to faster rides and higher jumps. After one jump, Hans bent over, holding his wrist and shrieking. Alwin ran out the back door of the main house and down the path. "Every Sunday! It's the same with you! *Doe dat niet!*" yelled Alwin. Hans stood up and shook his wrist. He hopped back into the wagon with the other three who promised Alwin they would just go for a ride along the Peoria road.

When the wagon eased around the side of the main house, Will continued sharing his plans. "Before I came here, everyone figured I'd take over my father's business. Now, I don't know."

Elmer jumped in. "I don't care what I do. I just want to find a wife and have a job. Just be happy. Where nobody cares about my hand. Where I'm just like everyone else."

"Yeah, just like everybody else," Moses said. "There's freedom in that."

And once Moses started pounding metal and singing, Will and Elmer drifted off to sleep.

Oh, I'm gonna take a little journey,
Lord remember me.
I'm gonna take a little journey,
Lord remember me.
Oh, I'm gonna take a little journey,
Lord remember me,
Oh, do, Lord, remember me.

* * *

On Monday, dinner was baked egg, ham, cheese, and potato, but the rumored piece of apple pie for dessert was the only thing the boys considered. Moses had earlier smelled the pies, skipped dinner, and offered other workers two cents each for their piece. Several accepted, and Moses wound up with nine slices of apple pie for dinner.

Halfway through dinner, Alwin came into the chow hall and asked everyone to stay after dessert. Joren Helgeveld had something to say.

Other than Moses, everyone was finished eating when Joren Helgeveld walked through the side door of the chow hall. The house and kitchen workers followed him and stood against the side wall. Alwin, Jakob, Gerwin, and Vlinder joined their father, all standing in front of the serving tables and facing the boys.

When they settled, Joren Helgeveld looked out at the boys and over to the girls. The room quieted.

"I invited the girls from the house to come over because I have some news that will affect the farm and affect all of you," Joren Helgeveld said. "As many of you know, Alwin and I met with government officials in Peoria last Friday. Seems the war isn't going as quickly as they had hoped. The country's sending United States soldiers over there and they'll be needing provisions: food, clothing, medical supplies. Turns out that because of our high crop yields and access to the railroad, farms in this area are being asked to help. I want to help the country as much as anybody, but any deal has to pay your salary and keep the farm running, so I wasn't expecting much from the meeting."

Joren Helgeveld paused, looking out over the summer workers who were anxious for his news. "But I was wrong. They need our fall crops and their offer was more than I expected. I agreed to it and it's all but final. We've been given the go-ahead and the government is already putting up some money. I go up to Chicago next week with Arend Van der Beek and a few other farmers from around here to sign the final papers."

"This won't change your jobs much," he continued, "but it's important for you to know our purpose now. Your work is helping the war effort. Helping the country."

There was a low buzz at the news and Joren Helgeveld waited for the room to quiet. "There will be a few changes. We've got 175 acres of open field out to the right on the road to Peoria. You've seen it, past the corn and next to the hill with the grove of trees. I thought the government would want us to plant those acres, but instead, they want us to raise beef cattle. In about two weeks, the U.S. government is sending, and paying for, 100 head of Hereford beef cattle, a few bulls, and fencing for it all. The cattle arrive in Peoria by train and we'll drive them along the road into a fenced pasture which isn't built yet.

"The sawmill in Peoria is cutting up the fencing now, and they'll start sending it out toward the end of next week," continued Joren Helgeveld. "The timing will be tight but that should give us several days to get those post holes dug and the fencing up."

The summer workers looked around at each other, now feeling part of the war effort.

"Jakob and Gerwin have been measuring the acres and putting sticks where fence posts need to be dug," continued Joren Helgeveld. "We'll fence off about 100 acres for now and we'll send out fifteen or twenty of you each day to start digging the holes. If we're lucky, we'll be done with the fence when the cattle arrive."

Joren Helgeveld paused and took a deep breath.

"It's a good opportunity for the farm, but these cattle won't be ready until next fall, more than a year away. Makes me think this war might last longer than we expected." He shook his head. "And even after asking the people from the government, I still don't know what this whole fool war is all about."

The owner of Helgeveld Farm looked at his sons and daughters who were standing next to him. "Okay, everyone. Again, Mrs. Helgeveld and I are happy we got to meet so many of you when we went to Peoria. We'll take another trip there next payday, the end of July."

The workers stood up, silent, thinking of their role in all of this. When they moved toward the door, Mr. Helgeveld spoke again. "Oh, yes, one more thing. With this new agreement, we're able to pay you all an extra $2 per month. That works out to $4 extra each pay period."

Both the field and house workers stared at each other and broke into a cheer, fists punching into the air.

"Off you go!" Joren Helgeveld yelled, smiling and waving everyone out the doors.

*   *   *

The next morning after breakfast, the boys buzzed in front of the farmhouse, ready to dig holes and win the war. The farm wagons stood ready, along with an extra Murphy wagon loaded with shovels and crowbars. Lily was usually out front of one of the wagons, but today, she was saddled and tied up to one of the wagons.

Alwin came out of the house and marched over to Lily, sliding a set of papers into the saddle. He walked back to where the boys were gathered and announced that digging post holes would be staggered and done by bunkhouse. Today, Bunkhouse 2 would head to the empty pasture with Jakob. Sandwiches, punch, and cookies were already on board for lunch.

"I think a few of you from Bunkhouse 1 are still working in the vegetable garden," Alwin said, "and if you're not digging posts, you'll be out in the soybeans looking for bugs. Two to a field. One of you'll spray each plant to hit as many bugs as you can. Don't soak 'em, just a quick spray. Your supervisors'll show you." Alwin hesitated, weighing his trip to Peoria along with the duties of the farm.

"The other one of you," Alwin continued, "will be walking down the rows, thinning, looking for sick plants, pulling weeds, shaking plants, and looking for more bugs. The spray doesn't get them all. You need to squish beetles, grasshoppers, or any other bugs you see. Grasshoppers'll strip a field if you let 'em. With the corn, there's the cornworm. You'll get to those fields in a few days."

Alwin paused again and looked out across the workers. "Okay, get to work. I'm going to Peoria today, but I'll be back with all of you tomorrow." Alwin walked over, hopped on Lily, and galloped down the road toward Peoria.

* * *

Out in their field, Elmer sprayed each plant with a mixture of vinegar and soap. Will followed behind, mostly on his knees, easing down each row, pulling weeds that were close to the plants, and squishing bugs. Each team had to do three fields a day. A day or two later, the draft horses would drag cultivators down the center of the rows to keep other weeds down. The workers would be back in ten days to do it all again.

At the sound of the lunch bell, Elmer, Will, and the other workers funneled out of their fields. They walked past Roy, propped against a rock with no lunch again, probably for sleeping between the rows.

Elmer followed Will to the wagon, where today, Vlinder handed out cheese sandwiches with potato salad. Corrie stood alongside her sister, both of them serious and silent. As Will got to the wagon, he saw Vlinder's eyes were red. She looked away and Will followed her alongside the wagon to where she hid herself, working between the pans and the plates.

Will waited for her to look up, but finally said, "Vlinder. Vlinder. What's wrong?"

Still kneeling, she turned toward Will. "It's nothing. No, it's something. It's Alwin. He went to Peoria today to sign up for the draft. For the war. The government is drafting men over twenty-one to go fight in Europe."

Will paused and considered his response. "Maybe they won't call him up. Maybe they won't need everybody."

"It doesn't matter." Vlinder shook her head and wiped her sleeve across her eyes. "He told my father that if they don't draft him, he'll volunteer once the harvest is in. He's going to go, now or later."

The two shared the silence.

Until then, the war had been newspaper headlines. The dead were strangers. Vlinder's news brought the war to the farm. Will's closeness to Alwin had seeped in unnoticed. In front of the house, in the fields, at dinner, Will looked for him. Alwin created order on the farm with a kind word and a nod. He gave directions that everyone wanted to follow. But soon, Alwin would take a horse, then a train, then a ship, and be given a gun to shoot at people who would shoot back.

Will met Alwin just two months ago, but he shared, in some small part, the emptiness and fear that Vlinder felt.

*   *   *

Will told nobody about Alwin's plan to go to war. He wondered if his silence was to keep Alwin closer or was a secret he could keep with Vlinder.

Back from Peoria, Alwin's routine and demeanor didn't change. He oversaw the post digging and spent afternoons in the fields, inspecting plants, and considering rows. Most days, Joren Helgeveld went out to the fields, standing and talking with Alwin. Will watched them when he could, wondering if they were talking about corn, fence posts, or war. Joren ended his talks with a hand on Alwin's shoulder and a wave to workers before heading back to the farmhouse.

As June settled in, the daylight lingered, and after dinner, Will, Isaiah, Elmer, and Moses spent their evenings on the rise behind the farmhouse, lying in the grass or leaning against the sycamore.

"Hey, Isaiah," Elmer said. "You still got those other two pennies?"

"Always," Isaiah replied. "Got 'em in my sock today." And he patted the side of his foot.

"Be good to get that other one back, the one Roy took," Will said. "With this war, be good to have all three together."

Isaiah nodded, "Just being patient, hopin' Roy will give it back like he said."

"Maybe," Will said, "but I don't think Roy does anything for anybody but himself."

The first star appeared and the boys sauntered back to the bunkhouse. Moses pulled out his yo-yo, sending it down then up, matching the rhythm to a song.

The bunkhouse was lit. Some of the boys were settled, others were settling.

Roy lay on his bunk, arms and legs crossed, his oily hat pulled down over his face. He seldom talked to anyone and everyone was surprised he worked hard enough to stay at the farm, or maybe he'd figured out how not to get caught enough.

Will stood in front of Roy's bunk. "Roy. Roy. It's time you give Isaiah his penny back. It doesn't mean anything to you now."

"Leave me alone," Roy said from under his hat. "I don't know what you're talkin' about."

"You know full well what I'm talkin' about!" said Will. "The penny you hid outside after you tried to blame Elmer for taking it."

"Oh yeah. I remember," said Roy. "That stupid lucky penny. Don't seem so lucky now, Owen being gone and all. Thing is, I do need it. I need it so all of you leave me alone. Like I said, maybe you'll get it back at the end of the summer."

"That a promise, Roy?" Isaiah asked. "We get it back at the end of the summer?"

"I don't make no promises. Leave me alone."

"Well, Roy. I make promises," Will said. "If we don't get that penny back, I promise there's about half a dozen guys in here who'd be happy to give you a dollar's worth of payback."

"Count me in." "I'll hold him down." "Just tell me when," echoed from workers at the other end of the bunkhouse.

With that support, Will wondered whether he hoped Roy would give the penny back or not.

* * *

The next day, Bunkhouse 3 joined Bunkhouse 2 to dig holes. More than 250 fence post holes were finished, but Jakob and Gerwin took new measurements and reported they'd need almost 1,000 posts. The cattle would arrive soon and they were falling behind on the fence.

The boys hopped into the Murphy wagon, pulled by Snowball and Patch, and driven by Alwin. Will walked to the front. "Mind if I sit up there with you?"

"Sure. Hop on up, Will," said Alwin sliding to the right. Will pulled himself up and alongside. "Heya, Lily." Alwin snapped the reins, easing into a line of wagons heading to the fields.

"You been out to the new pasture yet?" Alwin asked.

"No," Will said.

"Well, it'll be something once we get the cattle in there. First beef cattle we've had."

"They going to take much work?" asked Will. "Or do they just eat and get fatter?"

Alwin laughed. "That's about it. We've got to keep them fed, though. The government is gonna pay for some hay and we got that silage cutter. We can grind up quite a bit of feed with it, soybean plants, mix it with hay and some corn stalks. A few of you might be workin' on that at some point. This fence though, we gotta get that done."

Will wanted to bring up the war, ask Alwin about the draft, ask why he wanted to go and fight. But he didn't.

"Beef cattle. It's quite an investment'" Alwin said. "We talked about it in the past but never could afford it. Even now, it'd be tough to pay for all of this fencing, the cattle, the feed, and then have to wait a year or more 'til they're ready for market. But the government, they're spending money like crazy at farms all around Peoria. Might work out for us in the long run."

"Sure, if the war ends soon," Will said, easing into the topic.

"We're all just doing our part, praying it will be over soon."

Up ahead, where the wagon would veer off to the pasture, Will saw Joren Helgeveld sitting up in a Murphy wagon pulled by a team of draft horses. He hopped down from his seat and came over to Alwin who whoa'd Lily to a stop.

"*Hallo, Alwin,*" said Mr. Helgeveld raising his hand.

"*Hallo, vader. Ga je nu naar Chicago?*"

"*Ja,*" said Joren Helgeveld. "*Ik ben donderdag weer terug. Denk eraan, ik zal ongeveer 100 hekpalen in de wagen hebben om te beginnen. Zorg dat je genoeg jongens hebt.*"

"Yes, father. We'll be ready." Alwin responded. "Godspeed, and we'll see you on Thursday." He waved at his father who jumped back into his wagon and shook the reins.

Alwin turned off the main road and followed the wagon tracks toward the new cow pasture. "He's goin' to Chicago to sign some papers with the government about the crops," he told Will. "He'll be back on Thursday with around 100 fence posts. That'll get us started. Next week, there'll be other wagons coming out from Peoria with more posts and fencing. After that, the cattle arrive. Might have everybody out here for a few days to get this fence together on time. It's running a little behind."

The topic of war had passed and Will sat silent, happy to be sitting next to Alwin.

*   *   *

Most days, Will and Elmer envied Isaiah and Moses working in the back barn and fixing things. But not today. Today, they'd be digging holes and Elmer was proud to show that he could shovel just like the others, even missing three fingers and two toes.

The boys lined up in front of several fence post markers. Alwin wanted the holes two feet deep and he marked the depth with paint toward the bottom of each shovel handle. Few holes gave up their two feet easily. Most holes required the crowbar to yank and lift massive stones from their underground home. Since the hole spacing had to be consistent, no hole could be abandoned because of a large rock. About once an hour, Lily was hooked up to a chain that was laid around a stone. Half the bunkhouse lent a hand and offered a cheer when Lily pulled, and they lifted, the stubborn stone out of the way. The rock piles sat to the side. Alwin said they'd be back later to gather those up.

Will loved digging holes and he measured the progress with each shovelful. Stones were passive adversaries, a challenge, daring Will to dislodge them. Other post diggers felt the same and they joined each other to reach under, pull up, and pry the unwilling holdouts from beneath the ground.

With nowhere to hide, Roy was forced to shovel in full view. He even asked for help when a big stone challenged him, but he never joined others when they needed it. Not surprisingly, Will and Elmer were happy with that arrangement.

The June sun drained the boys. Much of Alwin's work was bringing jugs of water, bread, cheese, and nut paste to the sweaty laborers. Lunch was corned beef that the boys piled high onto bread, slathering it with mustard. For dessert, the girls handed out apples that had been stored over the winter. One of the larger milk churns filled with punch sat in the back of the wagon and Alwin encouraged everyone to drink their fill and pour a full bottle of water over their heads from a neighboring bucket.

Over the next few days, the boys managed to bring the total post holes to more than 700.

Alwin gathered the workers and they walked and surveyed the holes for the first 100 fence posts that Joren Helgeveld would be bringing back from Peoria the next day.

CHAPTER 16

After dinner on Thursday, a Model T Ford with a red lantern raced from the distance toward the farmhouse, the driver swerving around ruts, grooves, and holes. Will, Elmer, Moses, and Isaiah watched from the path just after they left the chow hall. They were surprised since the only vehicles they generally saw at the farm were the twice-weekly ice truck and the mail truck that came Mondays, Wednesdays, and Fridays.

The uniformed driver pulled up in front of the farmhouse and jumped out before the motorcar came to a complete stop. He bolted to the front door and within seconds there were screams from inside. The driver, Anika, Alwin, and Vlinder bolted out the front door and into the Peoria police auto.

Will, Isaiah, Moses, and Elmer hustled along the path that wound around to the front of the farmhouse, watching the Ford make a sharp circle and speed off. Corrie raced out the front door, her brothers and sisters just behind.

Reaching her, Will asked, "Corrie, what happened!?"

"It's my father," Corrie said, her hands clasped in front of her. "There's been an accident." Hans reached his twin and put an arm around her shoulder. The rest of the brothers and sisters arrived and stood silent, facing down the road to Peoria.

* * *

4 Hours Earlier

The train from Chicago pulled into the Peoria station at 3:15 p.m., 5 minutes early. Joren Helgeveld stepped off the train, the signed contract with the government sitting in his back pocket.

The meeting with the government took place a day earlier with the U.S. Secretary of Agriculture, David Houston, traveling in from Washington D.C. There were fourteen farmers from Illinois gathered and Joren Helgeveld knew five of them, including Arend Van der Beek. Secretary Houston indicated to Joren Helgeveld, and the other farmers, the importance of these agreements. The Secretary addressed the farmers. "This terrible war in Europe has reached into the very heart of our great nation. Soon, U.S. soldiers will be joining their counterparts overseas to beat back the German invaders. Your crops and your livestock are a critical part of this war effort."

He explained why the U.S. government choose Illinois farms and how modern-day transportation made the decision attractive and possible. At the signing, Secretary Houston went around and personally thanked and shook the hand of each farmer.

That night, the government paid for each farmer to stay at the Palmer House Hotel, one of Chicago's finest. Joren Helgeveld checked into room 502 and was anxious to tell his wife about the fluffy towels, the free bar of soap, and the telephone in his room. He took a bath, but was baffled at how hot water could make it all the way up to the fifth floor.

The next morning at 9:30, Joren Helgeveld and Arend Van der Beek stepped onto the train from Chicago to Peoria.

"That was quite an event, Joren," said Arend Van der Beek once they settled into their seats.

Joren Helgeveld laughed. "I think they tried to make us feel a little more important than we really are."

"How's the fence coming along?" asked Arend Van der Beek. "The way the government is pushing this, those beef cattle will be here before you know it."

"I know. I've got to get right on that fence. We still have a number of holes to dig and with the posts and railings coming out soon, we still have a lot to do," said Mr. Helgeveld. "You know the field. It's on the left as you head toward our farm."

"I know the field. It's a good spot for them. This could work out very well for all of us, Joren," said Arend Van der Beek.

The two men settled in for the nearly six hour train ride to Peoria.

Once in Peoria, the two men parted, Arend Van der Beek walking to the Dutch Reformed Church where he had left his horse.

For Joren Helgeveld, his wagon would be at the Peoria sawmill where Pastor Jannsen would leave it to be loaded with 100 fence posts, ready for his ride back to the farm. The sawmill was on the outskirts of Peoria, a 30-minute walk from the train station. But after he arrived, Joren Helgeveld took another route and stopped at Weiser Jewelry and Optical to purchase the gold necklace Anika had pointed to when they walked through Peoria last fall after his mother's funeral service.

Afterwards, Joren Helgeveld arrived at the sawmill and the Murphy wagon stood at the front gate, loaded and ready with the 100 fence posts. While he examined the load, John Martin, the owner of the sawmill, came over. He was short, but strong-armed, and his dark red shirt was rolled up at the sleeves.

"Hello. You must be Joren Helgeveld. Good to meet you. I'm John Martin. I understand you're just back from Chicago?"

Joren Helgeveld shook the owner's hand. "Good to meet you. Yes, just off the train. Good to see Chicago, but good to be back home."

"Well," John Martin said, "The pastor brought your wagon over around noon. Said you'd be here about now. I know you're anxious to get home, but here, let me show you the fencing we're working on for you." John Martin guided Joren Helgeveld to a field behind the sawmill. There sat hundreds of fenceposts and more than 1,500 fence railings, all in ordered piles. "That's what we've got so far. The fence posts are done and the railings should be finished soon. I expect we can start sending it all out your way within a few days."

Joren Helgeveld considered the mountain of fencing. "I have to say, when the government says it's going to do something, they do it." He and John Martin returned to the loaded Murphy wagon at the front gate. "You know where the farm is. My sons, or somebody, will be along the road next week and they'll direct you where to drop the fencing. You're sending out the posts first?"

"Yes, those will go first, then the rails. Government paid for the transportation, too." John Martin paused as Joren Helgeveld hopped up into the wagon seat. "And I have to say, it feels good knowing this is all supporting the war. We're just a small part, but still a part."

"I feel the same, John. Quicker this whole business is over with the better." Joren Helgeveld checked his pocket watch. He'd be home by seven, in time for some leftover dinner. He tipped his hat to John Martin and snapped the reins. The draft horses struggled with the heavy load of fencing and the Murphy wagon jerked and pulled onto Darst Street.

Joren Helgeveld never saw the Packard Twin Six motorcar that didn't brake and smashed into the front of the Murphy wagon, hurling him, the wagon, and the 100 fence posts into the air, all crashing to the ground. The auto then careened into the draft horses, killing one immediately. John Martin and other sawmill workers ran to the chaos, lifting off fence posts and shattered wagon pieces. An ambulance was called, but nothing could be done.

Joren Helgeveld, the owner of Helgeveld Farm, was dead.

CHAPTER 17

B ack at the farm, no one slept that night. Will went outside his bunkhouse several times, hoping to see or hear a late night rider or driver from Peoria. There was none, only dim lights shining from the second floor of the farmhouse the entire night. In the morning, the boys headed to the chow hall as usual. The doors were open, but there was no breakfast.

Will and Isaiah walked across to the farmhouse kitchen and went inside. Four of the summer girls were there, as confused and fearful as everyone else. This morning, they had arranged platters of scrambled eggs, sausage, and biscuits with butter and jam on the serving tables.

Betty Granger, sixteen-years-old and one of the kitchen workers, looked at the boys who came into the kitchen. "We didn't know what to do. We don't usually use the ovens without Vlinder or Corrie here. Did you hear anything? What happened?"

"We just know what we heard yesterday from Corrie," said Will. "There was some kind of accident. The lights were on all night upstairs. I don't know if someone is coming down this morning or not."

Gerwin heard the voices from the second floor and came downstairs. He walked into the kitchen and looked at the platters of food, the kitchen girls, the hungry boys, and he ran his hand across his head. "Is this breakfast? Maybe everyone can eat this."

Betty added, "there's milk in the icebox we can put out, too."

Gerwin looked across the platters to Betty. "You got this ready?"

"Yes," she said and nodded.

"Good. Good," said Gerwin giving Betty a weak smile.

Gerwin was about to leave the kitchen when Will asked, "Gerwin, do you want us all out front like usual after breakfast?"

Gerwin stopped but didn't turn around. "I don't know. Maybe just stay at your bunkhouses." He left through the swinging kitchen door and went into the main farmhouse.

Will, Isaiah, Moses, and Elmer were familiar with the kitchen and volunteered to help the girls do the best they could with breakfast. They pulled out plates, cups, forks, and knives and Will went outside to direct the summer workers into the kitchen, around the center table for breakfast, and out the door.

The workers found spots to eat their breakfast, either outside, or in the chow hall. But there was no hurry, only guesses on what would happened next.

With breakfast over, the four boys gathered dirty plates and cups while the others returned to their bunkhouses. Will washed the plates in the sink that Isaiah had fixed just days earlier. He examined the beaded repair on the back of the sink and thought how everything had changed since then.

"Maybe they're with him in Peoria, at the hospital, or some-where," Betty Granger suggested from across the kitchen. "That's why nobody came back yet."

"If he was in the hospital, I think somebody woulda come back and told us," Elmer added.

Moses and Isaiah washed dishes and pots, saying little, fearful for the health of the man who took them to town for bank accounts and ice cream sodas.

Corrie pushed the swinging door open and came into the kitchen. Everyone turned to her, silent, hoping for news.

"Oh," Corrie said. "I heard the noise, but I didn't know who was down here."

"We made some breakfast if you want some, Corrie," said Betty.

Corrie looked around the kitchen, her eyes red from tears and a sleepless night. "No. I'm not hungry. I don't know why I came down.

Lotta and Bram fell asleep and I wanted to go someplace." She covered her face with both hands. "I don't know what's happening. I don't know how my father is."

A single horse rode up the path behind the farmhouse and stopped outside the kitchen door. Alwin jumped off a horse that Pastor Jannsen had lent him and came into the kitchen. He spied Corrie who was looking at him, her hands in front of her face, trembling. Alwin stood at the door, giving no hint. He walked toward his sister and then shook his head. "No, Corrie. He's gone. Father's gone." Corrie began to fall and Alwin caught her and held her close. Corrie wailed, Alwin's cheek resting on the top of his sister's head. Isaiah and Moses leaned on a table and then on each other, drenched in tears and disbelief. Will and Elmer shocked, empty, surrounded Isaiah and Moses. The kitchen girls covered their mouths and looked at each other, shaking.

The kitchen cries brought Gerwin, Jakob, Lotta, Bram, and Hans downstairs, through the swinging door, and into the kitchen. Seeing Alwin holding Corrie showed them the news they had feared. The siblings held each other, broken, sad beyond sadness. They circled each other. Life stopped.

Will, Elmer, Isaiah, and Moses looked across the kitchen at a scene nobody should see, especially not summer workers who weren't family. They ached as much for them as for the loss of Joren Helgeveld. How could they go on? How could the farm go on?

Alwin pulled back and wiped his eyes. He went around to each brother and sister, kissing them on the head, two hands on their shoulders. He breathed deep and told them what happened.

"A motorcar hit father's wagon just as he left the sawmill to come home," Alwin said. "The owner of the sawmill saw the accident, but said there was nothing anybody could do. The driver told the police that the brakes had failed." Alwin breathed deep and continued. "The doctor said it was sudden. No pain. No suffering. Mother wanted to stay with him in Peoria, and Vlinder wouldn't leave her there alone. They'll be along; I don't know when."

Alwin looked around the kitchen. "Mother said I should go back to the farm. Get the fence finished. Tell everyone what happened.

Keep things going like after Gramma Luna died last year. That's what father would want. So, I left the hospital and stopped by the sawmill earlier this morning to be sure the fencing was coming."

Jakob looked at his brother, crying. "But what do we do, Alwin? Father is dead!"

His mother's advice to keep the farm going seemed right back in Peoria, but now at the farm, without his father, that's not how things worked.

It was Joren Helgeveld who put the days together. Each night, after surveying the day's progress, Alwin and his father sat at the big table, organizing a plan for the next day. They'd wait until Anika sat and played the piano, sometimes adding her voice to a song. Alwin would offer plans and strategies, but Joren Helgeveld thought deeper than Alwin. He'd nod at Alwin's ideas and offer changes that smoothed out the complications that Alwin hadn't considered. Each day was Alwin's design, but it was Joren Helgeveld who made the plan work.

Today, there was no plan. No order from the night before. "Today," said Alwin and he paused. "Today, we need to finish the post holes." Alwin walked to the kitchen door and looked through the window toward the chow hall. "Yes, we need to finish those post holes. The cattle will be here soon." Alwin sighed and looked at the floor. "And we aren't ready. We won't be ready."

Gerwin spoke up. "Jakob and me, we can get the Murphy wagons ready. We can put the tools in there to take to the fields. At least we can work on the post holes."

Alwin looked at his brothers. "Alright. Yes. Bram and Hans, you help too." He could come up with nothing more.

Finally, Betty Granger said, "Do you want lunch out in the fields?"

Alwin looked across at Betty and stared. "I don't know. Maybe have lunch here. A little early. Then we'll go out."

"Okay," Betty said. "We'll have it ready."

"Good. Let's do that." Alwin turned and looked at his sisters, his eyes vacant, empty. "Corrie, Lotta, you be in here too. Help with lunch."

There was a knock at the kitchen door and Alwin went to it. Carl and the two other supervisors, Jackson and Clifford, stood just outside. Alwin stepped out and closed the door. His news brought muffled cries from the three supervisors who were almost family. Moments passed and Will saw Carl point down toward the dairy barn and Alwin nodded. The three supervisors headed off to a task they all agreed to.

Alwin came back into the kitchen, not sure where he left off. He looked at Bram and Hans. "What are you doing?"

Hans, still shaking said, "You said we should help get the wagons ready. Should we still do that?"

"Oh, yes," said Alwin. "Do that. Get the wagons ready." Alwin looked around the kitchen and focused on Will, Isaiah, Elmer, and Moses. "All of you, could you go around to the bunkhouses and tell them to be here for lunch." Alwin looked at Betty Granger. "When can you have it ready?"

"We could have lunch ready around, I think probably around 11:30?" said Betty.

"Good. 11:30," said Alwin. "Then we go to the pasture."

"We'll tell the workers, Alwin," said Will, but Alwin gave no response.

The boys nodded and headed to the three bunkhouses to give the news about Joren Helgeveld and the plan for the day.

Will went to Bunkhouse 1 and told them what happened to Joren Helgeveld. The bunkhouse chatter hushed and the boys looked at each other. Joren Helgeveld was the reason for the summer. How could he be dead? The workers looked to Will for answers he didn't have. "All I know is that Alwin wants us back to work," Will said. "They'll ring the bell for lunch at 11:30, and afterwards we're heading to the pasture to work on the post holes."

After Will left the bunkhouse, his walk brought him alongside Bunkhouse 2 and then up a rise, past the stables. He was surprised to see the horses loose and the Murphy wagons still standing behind the stables. Jakob and Gerwin weren't there, but Will spied Alwin, his back against the stable wall and his head in his hands. Will stopped. He longed to talk to Alwin, but death put a line between family and workers. Perhaps he could help with the horses, he thought. Maybe get the Murphy wagons loaded. So he stepped through the fence and strode to Alwin.

Alwin looked up at Will and then back down, arms crossed on his knees, staring at the muddy dirt of the stable.

"Alwin," said Will. "Do you need help with the wagons? I could get Isaiah, Moses, and Elmer. We could get the horses ready and bring the wagons out front."

"He held us up, he and my mother," Alwin said, looking straight ahead. "We never even noticed." He leaned down, picked up a piece of hay and dragged it back and forth across the mud in front of him. "Lotta caught diphtheria when she was around six or seven. She could hardly breathe and was burning up. The doctor came out to the farm and stayed for two days, putting hot compresses on her chest and ice on her head. But she didn't get better. The doctor finally said that if the fever didn't break one particular night, we might lose her. That night, my mother and father took turns holding her against them in the rocking chair. The next morning, when my father was holding her, he saw that she was sound asleep. Her fever broke."

Will was silent.

The hay stem broke and Alwin jabbed the tip into muddy clumps in front of him. "Last night, Vlinder and I were standing in the hospital with my father. My mother was sitting next to him. Her head was on his chest and her arms around him." Alwin paused between each thought. "They weren't just a husband and a wife. They were one thing. He was the head of the family. She's the heart."

They were silent together. Finally, Will said, "Alwin, want us to get the wagons and horses ready?"

Alwin turned around and looked at the horses and thought for a minute. "No, not today." Alwin looked over at Will, knowing he needed some direction. "Maybe you can help with lunch and dinner, but no work in the fields. Maybe Gerwin and Jakob…no. They left.

They said there was no purpose, no reason. I don't know where they went. No work today. Can you tell everyone?"

"Okay," said Will. "I'll get word out to the bunkhouses." Will wanted to ask if there would be work tomorrow, but he knew Alwin didn't want that question.

*　*　*

Before lunch, all the Helgeveld children went to the second floor of the farmhouse and, other than Corrie, weren't seen the rest of the day. After lunch, some workers slept in their bunks while others wandered out from their bunkhouses, doing routine chores to stay busy.

Will envied the kitchen girls who kept their routine, lunch, dinner, cleanup. Betty decided to use the ovens on her own and put together a baked ham, cheese, and potato evening meal.

Corrie came downstairs in the afternoon and baked cookies. Something to do.

Will, Isaiah, Moses, and Elmer were in the kitchen, happy to follow Betty's instructions, still unsure of what it took to make a meal.

After dinner and cleanup, the four boys wove their way along the path to the rise behind the farmhouse. Backs against the sycamore, they watched the supervisors taking over the evening tasks and Matt at the dairy barn tending to the cows. There were no Helgeveld children running or yelling. The piano sat silent.

"Wonder what's gonna to happen tomorrow?" asked Elmer.

"Me and Moses," said Isaiah. "We got stuff we can work on in the barn."

"Don't really feel like it though, not with Mr. Joren gone," said Moses.

Will stared down the road to Peoria. Was this how the summer would end, he wondered.

The four boys watched the kitchen door to the farmhouse, hoping someone would come out to pull the summer back together, but no one did. They waited until almost dark before heading to the bunkhouse. The lamps were on and the boys sat on their bunks, unsure about tomorrow and the rest of the summer. From the end of the bunkhouse, someone said there probably wouldn't be any work until after Joren Helgeveld was buried.

Roy shot up in his bunk. "And they better pay us for all this time, even if we aren't doin' nothin'. It's not my fault he's dead."

"Yeah, that sounds about right for you, Roy," Nathan Carey said. "You've been getting paid all summer for doing nothin'."

CHAPTER 18

The next morning, familiar smells drifted from the chow hall and the workers were greeted with platters of flapjacks, maple syrup, and bacon. Betty Granger stood behind the tables of food and directed the workers. The boys took their fill but watched the door as they ate. No one from the family came into the chow hall.

Will and Moses brought their plates up for more flapjacks and Will asked Betty, "Any news? What's happening in the house?"

Betty shook her head. "We haven't seen anybody, not since Corrie came down yesterday."

Because Will had delivered the news of Joren Helgeveld's death to Bunkhouse 1 the day before, several boys asked him about today. Will walked to the front of the chow hall, and to his surprise, everyone quieted. "I know you're wondering about today. We haven't heard anything. For now, we can just wait." He thought for a moment. "Maybe we can do our usual Saturday washing today?" Will looked over at Betty, who nodded and said they'd get the tubs ready right away. "Tomorrow, we'll go to church. We can get the horses and wagons ready in the morning. Maybe we'll know something by then."

The workers nodded.

* * *

The boys welcomed the washing task and gathered their dirty clothes. It was Isaiah's turn to wash Moses' clothes, and Moses stripped to his underwear, piling everything dirty onto Isaiah's bed.

Isaiah stared at his brother.

"Whatchu lookin' at?" said Moses. "Need clean clothes for church tomorrow, don't I? Make sure you get them knees clean. Give 'em a good scrub. Figure I'll take a nap until they're dry." Moses held back a laugh and crawled underneath his bed.

Isaiah, Will, and Elmer gathered their clothes and headed for the washing tubs. The three stopped along the path and Isaiah pointed to a rider who rode half-speed to the farmhouse. He tied his horse to the gate and walked up the path to the house.

"Who's that?" asked Isaiah. The boys all shrugged. They took the path to the front of the farmhouse to see if there was any news.

The stocky, red-shirted man knocked on the door, and soon Betty Granger appeared.

"Hello, I'm John Martin. I own the sawmill in town. Are you one of the Helgeveld daughters?"

Betty lowered her head. "No, no, sir. I'm one of the help. I work in the kitchen."

"Oh, I see. Is Alwin here? I need to talk to him about the fence posts."

Betty knew Alwin was upstairs, but to disturb him? "I don't know," she said nervously. "He's been upstairs for a while. I'm not sure."

"Well, if you could let him know I have the fence posts and most of the railings. He stopped by the sawmill yesterday morning and asked us to bring them out. We wanted to get them here as soon as we could." John Martin paused and looked at Betty. "Horrible what happened. We're all so upset about this. But we wanted to be sure that the farm got what it needed since the cattle are coming soon."

Betty looked toward the stairs and back at John Martin. "Wait here. I'll tell him." She left and returned a few minutes later, Alwin just behind her.

"Hello, Alwin," John Martin said reaching out and shaking his hand. "I know this is a bad time for the family, but we wanted to do what we could. We finished cutting the posts and most of the rails yesterday and last evening. The rest of the rails will be here on Monday." John Martin pointed his thumb back over his shoulder toward the road. "The wagons with all of that are back there, about a mile or so. We can deliver them wherever you want."

Corrie came down the stairs and went to her brother. She put her arm around Alwin's waist.

Alwin looked at John Martin, expressionless. "The fence posts and rails? They're here?" He looked down and shook his head. "We haven't even finished the holes. Nothing's ready. The cattle will be here next week and nothing's ready." Alwin stepped back, sat down, and slumped in the chair.

Corrie knelt down in front of her brother, sobbing right alongside him. She faced out through the front window and saw a commotion of wagons pulling and advancing toward the farmhouse. Corrie stepped away from her brother and moved out onto the porch.

"What's that? Who's that?" she asked John Martin. "Are those the fence posts?" Corrie asked.

John Martin smiled. "No, the fence posts are about a mile out. These are the people who are going to build the fences."

Corrie stepped past John Martin and down the porch stairs. Ahead of her were twelve wagons, full with almost 200 workers from neighboring farms. Pastor Jannsen was riding a horse out in front. Corrie put her hands alongside her cheeks and walked down the path where she met the pastor.

"Hallo, Corrie," Pastor Jannsen said. "We are heer te helpen."

Corrie ran in the house and pulled Alwin onto the porch. "Look!" said Corrie. "Look! They're going to help with the fences." She held Alwin's arm and they walked down the front path, staring at the parade of wagons. Alwin looked down at Corrie who looked back at her brother, smiling and sniffling through tears.

"Maybe we can help them, too," said Corrie.

"No, Corrie," said Pastor Jannsen. "We knowen the tragedee. You stayen in da hoose. We doen the werken."

Alwin breathed deep and turned to Pastor Jannsen. "No. We can't just stay in the house. We'll go out there with you. I'll get our workers." He looked at Corrie. "Tell the girls to plan for lunch out at the pasture. Can you get that ready?"

Corrie nodded at her brother, realizing that she had about three hours to make lunch for the 200 helpers and their own 56 workers.

Alwin turned to Will, Isaiah, and Elmer, who were standing just to the side. "Tell the other bunkhouses to meet out front as soon as they can. Isaiah, I want you and Moses to come with us today so I can show you where the gates will go. We'll need two gates and I want you to build them." Isaiah nodded.

Gerwin and Jakob came down from upstairs and went out front. "Look," Alwin said to his brothers. "The fencing is here and all these workers are going to help us. Get into that first wagon and take them out to where we're working." He turned to John Martin. "Mr. Martin, follow that wagon out and you'll see where to bring the posts and rails." Alwin reached over and shook John Martin's hand. "And thank you."

Will loaded Elmer with his dirty clothes and told him and Isaiah to give all the clothes a quick wash and hang them to dry. He'd run to each bunkhouse to get everyone ready.

Less than an hour later, the boys were sitting on the farm wagons, driven by Alwin, Gerwin, and the supervisors. A Murphy wagon left fifteen minutes earlier, loaded with shovels and crowbars.

Heading to the pasture, Moses sat between Isaiah and Will, his shirt, pants, and socks still soaking wet from the morning wash. Moses held his hands out in front of him. "Look! Look! You hadda wash it all? Couldn't leave me a dry shirt and pants after you knew we was workin' today?"

"Just doin' what ya told me. Gave 'em all a good scrub!" Isaiah laughed. "Whatchu complainin' about? They'll be dry by the end of the day." Isaiah slapped his thigh at his joke and began to sing.

How dry I am, How dry I am!
God only knows How dry I am

Most of the wagon joined in.

*   *   *

The Helgeveld workers and the other helpers arrived at the pasture. Arend Van der Beek, walking with his cane, saw Alwin and came over, shaking his hand.

"You didn't have to come out, Alwin," said Arend Van der Beek. "But I'm glad to see you. We're all so sorry about this. It's hard on everyone. We looked up to your father." Alwin and Mr. Van der Beek looked around the pasture. Most of the workers were in groups, some pulling posts and railings off the wagons, some setting posts in finished holes, and others spreading fence railings around the pasture to put it all together.

"I was in Chicago with your father when we signed those contracts. We rode back on the train together," Arend Van der Beek said. "My land is more suited for the crops, but you've got this space here. That's why your father agreed to the cattle. We talked about the fence he'd need. I never thought I'd be out here working on it."

Alwin nodded and looked back at his workers. He pointed down the pasture. "If I could ask a favor of you, Mr. Van der Beek. I'll take my workers down there to finish the holes if you could help coordinate the work up here."

"My pleasure, Alwin," said Arend Van der Beek. "I see what we need to do."

Alwin nodded at his neighbor and shook his hand. Soon, the Helgeveld workers were attacking the final post holes, some digging, some prying and pulling stones. Others were carrying fence posts and railings from the wagons to the newly dug holes. Alwin watched it all.

*   *   *

An hour earlier, after Corrie told Alwin she'd arrange lunch for all the workers, she ran through the house and into the pantry that opened into the kitchen. She took three jars of sourdough yeast and told Lotta and Betty to drag out two bags of flour. Soon, Corrie, Lotta, Betty, and the three other kitchen workers were kneading together flour, warm water, sourdough yeast, salt, butter, just enough vinegar, and a little sugar. Two other girls pulled out all twenty-eight bread pans.

"That won't be enough," Corrie said and she pointed to the pantry. "Get the five Dutch ovens and as many cast iron pans with covers that you can find. We'll have to bake some of this on top of the stoves."

Between extra yeast and kitchen prayers, the dough rose twice, and after an hour and twenty minutes, baking began. At 12:25, thirty-nine loaves, still hot and of assorted sizes, were being shuttled to the wagons. Twenty jars of apple jam, twelve jars of honey, five platters of cheese, and nine trays of baked beans also made the journey, and at 1:10 p.m., two lunch wagons pulled alongside the pasture. Rolling in just behind them was a half-repaired wagon that Corrie discovered in the back barn. She had filled it with four churns and nine covered buckets of sloshing red punch. Over 250 workers got baked beans, cheese, a sandwich and a half of jam with honey, and two cups of punch. Four bushel baskets of apples provided dessert for the workers.

After lunch, Will came over to Corrie who was kneeling in a wagon, collecting dirty punch cups. She saw him and stood up, her face still.

"None of us expected lunch today, Corrie," said Will. "I know there was nothing ready in the kitchen." He looked at the workers returning to the fence and then back at Corrie. "I don't know how you did it."

"Me neither," said Corrie, offering a weak smile.

*   *   *

Just after lunch, John Martin came up to Alwin. "We're heading back to the sawmill to get started on the rest of the railings. We'll send those out early on Monday." He pointed to some boards and hinges to the side. "There's the lumber and hardware for the gates." Alwin shot Isaiah and Moses a look and a nod. They nodded back.

Alwin shook John Martin's hand. "I saw you yesterday morning in Peoria, Mr. Martin." Alwin gazed across the pasture. "Now, look at this. Look at what's been done. It's hard to believe."

"Pastor Jannsen put the plan together," John Martin said. "He came to see me yesterday and then he went around to the farms. Didn't take much convincing to get everyone out here. We're glad to do it."

The boys were heading toward their wagons and Alwin searched for Pastor Jannsen. The Pastor was leaning against one of the settled fence posts, talking with Moses. Pastor Jannsen had a hand over his mouth and nodded occasionally.

Pastor Jannsen saw Alwin coming and turned to Moses. "Taank yu Moses. I vill seen you tomorgan at de cherch." Moses nodded and hustled to join the others at the wagon.

Alwin shook the Pastor's hand and put his other hand on his shoulder. "This is all because of you. I know. Thank you from all of us. We'll be at church tomorrow."

"Ik hope we helpen," Pastor Jannsen said.

"More than you know, Pastor," said Alwin.

$$*\quad*\quad*$$

The wagons and the workers bounced their way back to the farm, a day in the fields bringing some measure of order.

"See, I told you," Isaiah said to Moses. "Clothes are all dry now. But you got them knees a mess again." Even Moses had to laugh.

"Hey, Moses," said Elmer. "Saw you talkin' to Pastor Jannsen out there today. Did he teach you some new words?"

"Nah," said Moses. "Fact is, I hadda teach him some words."

"Whatchu talkin' about, Moses?" asked Isaiah. "You don't know no words."

"Well, Pastor Jannsen thinks I do. He asked me about some words he heard in the field today, words he ain't never heard before."

Moses paused. "Truth is, I didn't want to tell him, him being a pastor and all. But he said God would forgive me since there was no meanness in my heart." Moses shrugged. "So, I told him. And I gotta say, the pastor, he turned bright red and covered his mouth when I told him each one."

CHAPTER 19

The Sunday message the next day was as obscure as all the others, but Pastor Jannsen's warmth toward the Helgeveld family, along with the embrace of the entire community, was more comforting than any words.

Like most Sundays, until Moses stood up, no one was ever sure when the service was over. On this Sunday, the group of worshippers followed Moses' lead and they funneled to the center aisle and toward the back, the reward of sweet punch and something homemade foremost on their minds.

Lotta was the first to see her mother, Anika, standing at the back of the chairs, the loss of her husband and the comfort of her family both visible in her face. Her children ran to her and Alwin saw her crying. He wondered if she had ever stopped crying since he left her and Vlinder two days ago.

Anika reached out and kissed the forehead of each of her children and put a hand on Alwin's cheek.

"Moeder, how did you get here?" asked Alwin.

"Agatha Wilton," said Anika. "Her husband owns the Wilton Mortuary. That's where your father is now." She looked around at her children. "I hoped you would all be here. She kindly offered to drive me."

"Where's Vlinder?" asked Corrie.

"She stayed in Peoria," Anika said. "She didn't want to leave your father by himself. And there are things she can do at city hall tomorrow about the farm and your father. I could do them, but I had to come home to see all of you."

On the trip back from church, Alwin drove the front wagon and Anika sat next to him, her head laying on his shoulder the entire trip.

*   *   *

Sunday afternoon eased back to normal on the outside. Will and Elmer headed to the back barn to connect with Isaiah and Moses. From the path, Will saw Anika in the stable, brushing down Lily.

At the back barn, Elmer pointed at one of the wagons. "Is that the wagon Corrie brought out to lunch with the drinks?" he asked. "Didn't think it was fixed."

"It's not," said Isaiah. "If I was here, woulda told her not to take it. Looka here." Isaiah stuck his finger through a sideboard. "Rot. Good thing the drinks was on the floor. You put people in them seats, they'da been on their backsides right there on the road." Isaiah began pulling off the rotted boards. "Told Mr. Alwin about the boards we need for this, but not gonna ask him again, not right now."

Moses was at the side of the barn, staring at the stripped-down steam tractor and proud that he was in charge of getting it in working order. He reckoned it had seized up from sitting too long, and just needed a good cleaning and lubrication. One by one, he cleaned the piston rods, valve gears, and flywheel, then wiped them down with oil. Then he walked around the tractor and began putting it all back in place.

Something got into the tractor seat, too, leaving only the metal frame. Rats? Squirrels? Mice? So, the last time Moses was in Peoria, he ripped some seat covers from the busted-down Dodge that he and Isaiah slept in when they first came to Peoria. He fashioned those into a seat cover, shaped it around the metal tractor seat, and stuffed it with horse hair. For a few minutes, Moses bounced in the seat and turned the wheel. Not bad, not bad at all, he thought.

Will and Elmer sat to the side and watched Moses and Isaiah. There still wasn't enough ease in the farm for a Sunday nap. But Moses was bringing the calm closer.

Oh, freedom, Oh, freedom
Oh freedom over me
And before I'd be a slave
I'd be buried in my grave
And go home to my Lord and be free
Oh, freedom

The boys were surprised to see Alwin heading down the path toward them. He walked the usual speed, head down, then up, looking across at the bunkhouses, the stable, and the outbuildings. When he reached the boys, he stopped in front of the tractor Moses was working on.

"Whaddya think, Moses?" asked Alwin. "Think you can get this tractor working? We'll need it to bring the crops to town once they're in."

"Yes, sah. I think I can get it running," Moses said. "Haven't seen one just like this." Moses shrugged. "But like a lot of things, they's all different and they's all the same."

Alwin looked at the wagon that Isaiah was ripping apart. "John Martin's delivering the rest of the fence railings tomorrow. I'll remind him of the boards we need for this wagon. We'll have them soon."

"That'd be fine, Mr. Alwin.," said Isaiah.

Alwin stepped back and nodded. Then he reached into his pocket. "And here. Here's your Sunday pay." He went to hand Moses and Isaiah $1 each, but they backed away.

"No, sah," said Isaiah. "We can't take that, not today. Don't feel right. We're doing this here for Mr. Joren. It's our pleasure."

Alwin reached into his other pocket and pulled out an envelope. "See what this says?" and he showed it to the boys.

"Yes, sah," said Moses. "Says, *Isaiah and Moses.*"

"Paying you for Sundays was my father's idea," Alwin said. "He'd put the money in this envelope each week and leave it in the desk for me to bring down on Sundays. I checked this morning. Your money was there for today. He must have put it in the envelope before he left for Chicago." Alwin held the bills out to the boys. "This is from my father. I'm sure he'd be honored if you took it."

The boys reached over and took the bills, Isaiah's head lowered and Moses lower lip shaking.

"We'll see all you boys later." Alwin left and walked up toward the stables.

Will turned and saw Anika, still in the stable, now brushing down Snowball.

*   *   *

On Monday, breakfast was on time and the workers met in front of the farmhouse at 7 a.m. Gerwin, Jakob, and the supervisors were waiting at the wagons, the boys gathered haphazardly around them. The routine was the same, if not the mood.

All eyes were on the farmhouse door when Anika emerged, Alwin just behind her. They were stern, but with purpose, and they made their way to the front wagon. The workers quieted. Alwin spoke first.

"Good morning, everyone." Alwin looked out at the boys. "Last night, my mother, brothers, and sisters, sat together and tried to plan for the rest of the summer. Each time we weren't sure what to do, we asked ourselves, what would our father do? When we said that, the decisions were easier."

Alwin lifted his hat and ran his other hand across his head. "My father made an agreement with the government; it was a good agreement. And we're going to fulfill that. There's still some fence to finish. We've got cattle comin'." Alwin paused. "The help we got with the fence on Saturday made things a lot easier. I'm taking John Martin at his word that the rest of the railings will be comin' this morning. We might not need all of you out there today, but I want to finish the fence so we're all going to the pasture."

Alwin pointed at two extra wagons. "We're bringing out these Murphy wagons. If we finish early, we'll start collecting the rocks we dug out for the fence posts. We'll use them to build a wall at the edge of the farm." Alwin looked at the group. Roy had his back turned and was peeing in the side field. Normally, Alwin would have said something, but it didn't seem as important today. "Alright, let's load up, but before we leave, my mother wants to say a few things to all of you." Alwin moved to the side and Anika stepped in front.

The silence was even deeper for Anika.

"Good morning, everyone," said Anika, stepping up onto the back step of a wagon. "Alwin told me that some of you were wondering if you would be sent home, if this was the end of your summer. It is not. My husband went to Chicago to sign a contract to help the country. That's what we're going to do."

She looked across the workers and offered a shaking smile. They were mostly strangers to her, but these summer workers brought a responsibility, a purpose to continue on at the farm. Would she have had the same strength if they weren't here, she wondered.

"The death of my husband," Anika continued, "is the most difficult thing I've ever gone through. The most difficult thing we, as a family, have ever gone through. We will never be the same. But together we'll all keep the farm and the summer moving forward." She waved at the workers and stepped off the wagon.

Some boys wiped tears while others silently clapped their hands. Joren Helgeveld was at the farm as much as ever.

*   *   *

The remaining fence posts were dug and set in the morning. John Martin sent out the remaining rails and Isaiah and Moses sawed, hammered, screwed together, and sanded the two gates smooth. The rails were in place by 3:30 p.m. and by 5 p.m., the gates were hung and they opened or closed with the push of a finger. The fence was complete.

Alwin walked the pasture inside the fence. He reached down and passed his palm over the grass. When the cattle arrived, they'd have food. Alwin stood up, breathed deep, and felt the late afternoon sun on his face.

His father would be proud.

*   *   *

The following morning, Alwin's instructions brought some order back to the farm. Will and Elmer were with most of the workers, back to spraying, picking weeds, and squishing bugs. Bunkhouse 1 picked fifteen baskets of lettuce, early peas, and radishes and by late afternoon, the vegetables were on their way to Peoria, alongside Matt in his daily milk run.

At breakfast, Alwin had asked for a few volunteers to help with the stone wall and Roy's hand shot up. Gerwin took Bunkhouse 2, the few volunteers, and two Murphy Wagons to collect the rest of the rocks from the fenced pasture, and begin the stone wall.

Isaiah and Moses were at the back barn, working on the wagon and steam tractor.

At lunch, Will found Corrie's wagon. He filled his plate with ham, baked beans, and cornbread, and walked to the side of the wagon where she gathered plates.

"Corrie, where's Vlinder?" Will asked.

Corrie looked over at him and offered a weak smile. "We don't know. My mother said she had things to do in town about the farm."

"Oh, okay," Will said. "And just to let you know. All of the workers, everyone, we really liked your father. It was good to hear your mother this morning. That we'd still be here."

Corrie couldn't hold in her cry. She nodded a thank you at Will.

*   *   *

Later that afternoon, Bunkhouse 2 and the volunteers had finished the rock wall. It was no taller than three or four stones, but it reached across the back of the pasture and it marked the border of the farm. With a job well done, they hopped into their wagon only to notice that Roy wasn't there. Looking across the pasture, they saw no one.

The wagon was ready to leave without him when one of the workers, Fred MacDonald, told Gerwin to hold on. Fred jumped off the wagon and ran to the beginning of the rock wall. He stepped over the stones, and there was Roy, fast asleep, twigs and moss for a pillow. Gerwin took a half day's pay from him.

CHAPTER 20

The next day, after breakfast, Anika left on Lily, riding to Peoria. She dreaded this day, the day she'd go to Wilton Mortuary and make arrangements to bury her husband.

She and Joren never talked of death. Her only hint was last fall when his mother, Luna, was buried at Springdale Cemetery. After the service, Joren Helgeveld looked around the cemetery and down at the headstone. "It's pretty here. I think she's happy. Lots of people around." It tore her heart, but she'd make sure her husband was buried next to his parents, in town, away from the farm. On the headstone, she'd have the stonemason chisel her name under his with just her birth year for now-1873. That way he'd be waiting for her.

* * *

On Thursday, Alwin came into the chow hall during dinner. "Any of you want to see what that pasture is for, come with me. The cattle are almost here." He pointed toward Peoria. "You can see the dust above the road."

The workers spooned down their pudding and ran to the farm wagons, just arriving at the front of the farmhouse. The drivers hustled the boys and the house girls along the road until they reached the turn-off for the pasture where they stopped. The workers saw nothing, but heard a chorus of moos and bellows.

Out in front of the commotion, Anika appeared, riding Lily. The cattle were just behind her, heads bobbing. To the side of the herd walked Vlinder, holding a switch and keeping the cattle moving forward. Just behind and to the sides were twelve Dutch farmers and four dogs, herding the young Hereford cattle to their new home.

The workers all jumped off the wagons and formed a line on the road, turning the cows left toward the pasture. Isaiah and Moses ran to the gates and threw them open. Vlinder smiled when she saw Will. What wouldn't he do for her, he wondered.

The cattle followed orders, funneling through the gates and measuring out their section of pasture. Anika rode Lily up next to Alwin and hopped off.

"Looks like there's enough grass for now," said Anika. "They'll start sending out hay in about a week."

"Father would be happy with this," said Alwin.

"I know," said Anika, "I'd give anything for him to be here."

Everyone marveled at the accomplishment, the fence, the cattle, the agreement.

When the cattle were settled, Vlinder walked over to Alwin. Will moved past other workers, longing to hear her news, hear about her week away. Vlinder saw Will easing toward them and her eyes encouraged his arrival.

"When did you leave Peoria?" Alwin asked.

"The cattle came in late last night and we left this morning, early," said Vlinder. "I was surprised that they all came in at once." She turned around and pointed to her helpers on the drive. "Pastor Jannsen got some farmers to help us. And every farm on the way let us rest and feed them in their pastures."

"It's good to see you. It's not right at the farm when you're away," Alwin said. "How's mother? How are you?"

The 13-hour cattle drive had held Vlinder's mind, but Alwin's question brought back the emptiness. Vlinder stared at him, silent, then she started to cry. He pulled her toward him, her head against his shoulder.

Will stepped back and turned away. He imagined his own father gone, something he'd never done. He imagined himself, his mother, brother, and sister, broken beyond fixing. The thought scared him and he walked over to Isaiah and Moses who were hanging over a gate, watching the cows graze.

"Coupla days ago," Isaiah said, "was just a field here. Now, look at this."

"Yeah," said Moses. "A lot's changed in a coupla days."

*　*　*

Saturday work. Sunday church. Monday, Tuesday, field work, routine.

The Helgevelds were back to doing what they always did, but everything had not returned to normal. On Tuesday, after dinner, the boys heard the piano from the farmhouse but only for a short time. Soon after, Anika emerged from the farmhouse kitchen door and headed to the stables where she leaned her head against Lily and then brushed her down.

*　*　*

After the evening meal the next day, Alwin came into the chow hall. "Hello. Good evening, everyone. The cattle are here and the crops are on schedule. We've been lucky with the rain." Alwin paused. "This Saturday, there's a funeral for my father at the church. Then, the family will go to the Springdale Cemetery where he'll be buried next to my grandfather and grandmother. We have a family plot there."

The reality of it was too harsh. Alwin stopped and dropped his head. The chow hall was silent, watching, wondering what would happen. Vlinder hustled around the food table to her brother. She stood next to him, her hand resting on his shoulder. Alwin lifted his head up and looked at his sister. He smiled at her and then continued. "All of the family is going on Saturday and we'll be gone all day. It'll be a day off from the fields for you." Alwin lifted his hat and ran his hand across his head. "Carl, Jackson, Clifford, and Matt, they'll be around. There are things to do, like always. Milking, cleaning the stables, checking on the new cattle."

Vlinder stepped up. "Don't forget the girls in the kitchen. They'll be working all day like always, getting your meals. Some of you've been in the kitchen before. Lending a hand in there would be a real help. We'll be back late and here for church and a usual day on Sunday." Vlinder paused and looked at Alwin. "Anything else?"

Alwin looked at Vlinder. "Fourth of July?" he said. "I don't think we've talked about that." Vlinder nodded.

Alwin looked out at the workers. "Fourth of July is a big celebration for us each summer, for the whole community here. It's next Wednesday and we want all of you to join us. It'll be at the Van der Beek Farm. There'll be food, games, running races, some music, fireworks. It's always a good time. We'll be in the fields in the morning and go there after lunch."

Vlinder added, "And we'll pay you for the whole day. We know that's what my father would want."

It was welcome news, but this time there was no cheer in the chow hall.

* * *

As the workers headed to breakfast on Saturday morning, a wagon filled with Alwin, Gerwin, Jakob, Corrie, Hans, Lotta, and Bram left the front of the farmhouse heading toward Peoria to say goodbye to their father.

Needing to make a few final arrangements, Anika and Vlinder left a day earlier on

Friday. They stopped first at Goodhue's Variety Store to order flowers for the cemetery and were told that more than thirty floral arrangements had already been ordered by friends and neighbors, and that Goodhue's would assemble them all at the gravesite.

Anika also wanted to visit her husband by herself at Wilton Mortuary, to talk with him one last time. Vlinder walked through town.

* * *

Will, Isaiah, Moses, and Elmer agreed they'd help in the kitchen and that started with breakfast. Afterwards, the four boys helped the kitchen girls get the washing and rinsing tubs ready for Saturday clothes washing.

Throughout the morning, Roy wandered around the farmhouse, the stables, the back barn, and the bunkhouses. Midmorning, from Bunkhouse 1, then Bunkhouse 2, everyone heard, "Get outta here Roy! Go back to your own bunkhouse!"

After lunch, Will was washing dishes in the kitchen when he looked up and saw Roy staring at him through the window. He shook the soap off his hands and went out the door to find Roy peering into other windows in the farmhouse. "Roy, what are you doing? Get away from there."

"Shut up," said Roy. "I ain't doin' nothin'. Besides, you're in the house, aren't you? Workin' next to them kitchen worker girls, all of 'em ripe for pickin'."

Will took a step toward Roy and he ran along the back of the farmhouse, taking a quick look into each window. Before he reached the end of the house, Roy turned to see Will striding toward him. Roy called back, "Where's your apron?" and he disappeared around the corner of the farmhouse.

* * *

In the afternoon, Will told Elmer he was going to the bunkhouse, but instead he followed a weed-covered wagon path to an area of the farm he'd never seen. The noise of the farm had faded when he stepped off the path and over a hump covered with fir trees. On the other side, the land was flat and stretched out wide, full of saplings and brush, none taller than he was. Will figured the land was once clear, but was now overgrown. He looked ahead and then back over his shoulder. Just land. He was alone.

He sat on the rise and scanned the wild overgrowth, letting it blur into a vision of Springdale Cemetery. He imagined the Helgeveld family gathered. Neighbors and friends. Anika stood at the grave, holding Pastor Jannsen's arm. Will closed his eyes and Vlinder's image appeared. She stood next to her mother, pointing at the forget-me-nots planted in front of Grampa Bartel and Gramma Luna's headstone, the ones he had picked out. Will noticed that his own sadness had moved on from the death of Joren Helgeveld to Vlinder, to the purpose that was taken from her, to her emptiness with no relief, and it pulled at him.

Will opened his eyes and looked across the land. He sat for some minutes, then stood up and took a different route back, coming across a forgotten path that ended at the back barn. Moses was there, standing on a ladder and reinstalling one of the flywheels on the side of the steam tractor.

"Hey, Will," said Moses looking around. "Where'd you come from?"

"Just took a walk around. There's an old field out there. A big one."

Moses nodded and said, "See that wrench there next to the sink? Can ya pass it up here? Brought up four wrenches, but not the one I need," Moses said.

Will handed him the wrench. "I'm going up to the kitchen. They're probably getting dinner ready."

"Okay," said Moses, and Will headed up the path.

*   *   *

The June sun had set when the clatter of horses signaled the return of the Helgeveld family from Peoria. Will and Isaiah went to the bunkhouse porch and saw several silhouettes advancing to the stables, or the farmhouse, putting an end to the day and starting life on the farm without Joren Helgeveld.

*   *   *

After church and after lunch the next day, Isaiah and Moses settled into their afternoon at the back barn. The wood came in for the wagon and Isaiah measured, cut, and hammered the floors, seats, and sides. On Monday, planing and sanding would smooth it out to finished.

Moses had overhauled the steam tractor during the last week. Today, he'd re-check and tighten the whole repair and try to fire it up.

When Will woke from his nap, Elmer was next to him, up on his elbows and watching Isaiah and Moses. Will hoisted himself onto his elbows, too.

"Anybody been around?" Will asked.

"Nope," Elmer said. "Just Alwin. He came down to give Isaiah and Moses their Sunday pay." They watched Moses grease the tractor wheels and Elmer added, "I thought we might see Corrie, Hans, and the others come down. They usually do."

"I thought so, too," said Will. "Probably too soon to have fun."

CHAPTER 21

After lunch on Wednesday, the Fourth of July, the field and kitchen workers gathered in front of the farmhouse, as excited as on a Christmas morning. The Helgevelds were there, too, Anika to the side, her hands clasped, watching the assembled summer workers. A Murphy wagon stood near the farmhouse gate, filled with trays of food, drinks, and an eight-foot Fourth of July cake carried out on a board.

The transport and other Murphy wagons stood ready, and once loaded with workers, they jerked forward, the riders a little noisier than on the weekly ride to church.

"You all seen fireworks? We got 'em each year back in Pittsburgh," Will said to Elmer, Isaiah, and Moses.

"Yeah," said Elmer. "Back home, they got 'em down by the lake each year. Games and things. Food. My cousins are there."

"We got 'em in Alabama, too," said Moses. "Mr. Halyard, 'bout the richest man in the state, he gets a bunch of fireworks. It's the whole day along the river. Best food all year." Moses nodded. "They's got corn. Short ribs. Grillin' chicken. Cakes and pies. Must be about a million people there."

"A million people??" said Isaiah. "Ain't no million people. Whatchu talkin' about?"

"Okay, half a million," Moses replied.

Isaiah just shook his head, then added, "But you right. Best food of the year. Granddaddy brings his whiskey barrel smoker and smokes up a barrel full of chicken. Don't know what he puts on 'em, but even the white folk come by each year for that chicken. And Gramma, she cooks a bunch of pecan pies. Best along the river."

Arend Van der Beek had cleared out an area for the wagons, double the size for Sunday services. Three of the Van der Beek sons directed the wagons and two of the sons remained, feeding, watering, and keeping the horses happy.

Maybe there weren't a million people, but hundreds had already gathered from several farms in the area. The Sunday church chairs now circled the area with people, games, drinks, and food spread around inside them. Lunch was only a few hours ago, but the platters of food brought everyone over and Pastor Jannsen offered a blessing. Moses covered his chicken, gravy, and cornbread with some salted fried potato slices they called potato chips. The boys all tried one and returned for their own share.

Will spied Vlinder next to the punch table, corralled by the same worker who weeks earlier told her about the miracle of corn germination. Will took his opportunity and left his three friends. This day, the worker had switched topics from corn to the miracle of the wagon, and how it would always be superior to the motorcar. Vlinder nodded at his talk, but looked from side to side. She saw Will and gave him a smile he hadn't seen since her father died. "Oh, Will," she said, "I've been meaning to talk to you," and she excused herself. They walked a short distance and she took his elbow. "I was hoping you'd come by. That was painful. Somehow, he always finds me."

"Who is he?" asked Will.

"That's Cornelius Van der Beek," Vlinder said. "He's the second oldest son here and he's been following me around since first grade."

"Well, you never know," said Will. "Someone might ask you about corn or wagons sometime."

Vlinder squeezed Will's elbow. "This is good. It's good for all of us to be here." She pointed to the back of the farmhouse where Anika was being greeted by well-wishers and supporters. "See my mother there? She didn't want to come today, but I told her that if we're all coming, she needed to come, too." They walked a little further. "We talked last night. She was worried she'd never get over losing my father. I told her she was right. You don't ever get over it. You learn to live with it. Gramma Luna told me that after Grampa Bartel died." Vlinder pointed at her mother again. "See. See her? It's the most I've seen her smile since he died." Vlinder shook her head and looked down. "I can't even say it. I can't say his name. I can hardly say 'my father.' I need to learn to live with it, too."

They walked toward the edge of the crowd.

"I thought about you at the cemetery on Saturday," Will said. "Did it go alright?"

"Yes, it was very nice," said Vlinder. "There were more people there than I imagined. Aunt Elisabeth and Aunt Mina came on. Aunt Olivia was there, too. Seeing all the people helped my mother." Vlinder paused. "It helped all of us. Pastor Jannsen said the service in Dutch and then in English. He brought up things I had forgotten about my father or never really noticed. It was wonderful to hear. And so difficult."

Will kept silent, feeling she had more to say.

Vlinder continued. "Almost everyone came to the cemetery from the church. You remember the empty plot next to my grandmother and grandfather? He's buried there."

"Yes, I remember," said Will. They walked past the tables to an empty area that backed up to a grove of poplar trees.

"And there were flowers stacked on top of each other," Vlinder said. "I'm not sure, but the headstone might be ready in a few weeks. I want to have it finished for the memorial service for Gramma Luna and Grampa Bartel. Now, it's for my father, too."

They wandered together without a direction.

"Oh," said Vlinder. "At the cemetery, I showed my mother the forget-me-nots in front of Grampa Bartel and Gramma Luna's headstone. She said how pretty they were and I told her you picked them out. It was the only time I saw her smile that day."

A crowd had formed in an open area to the left of the food tables.

"What's going on?" Vlinder asked.

"I don't know. Let's see," said Will.

They moved toward the crowd and saw Moses at the center and Isaiah at his side. By now they could hear Moses.

"Ladies and gentlemen. For my next magic trick, I'm gonna slip this solid metal ring off of this here solid rope." He pointed to Corrie who was right in front. "Corrie, could you take this ring here and this rope to see if they's solid and look okay?"

Corrie stepped forward and took the items. She examined them and showed them to the crowd. "Yes, they look good. Just a metal ring and rope."

"Good. Now please watch while I put this ring down onto the rope." Moses slid the ring along the rope letting it hang from the bottom, holding each end of the rope between his other fingers. "Now, watch closely." Moses held up the rope in one hand and the ring in the other. "Hocus Pocus!" And the ring was now separate in his left hand, the rope in his right.

The crowd looked at each other, amazed. "Do another one!" they yelled.

Alwin stood to the side, near a group of boys from Helgeveld Farm who were milling around the food table. One boy said, "Look at that there. Magic tricks. Not surprised. You know the coloreds are all workin' with the devil." Alwin turned back to the magic show. Now wasn't the time.

"My assistant here, Isaiah," Moses continued, "would you please get me a plate and a cup from that table over there?"

When Isaiah agreed to help Moses with the magic tricks, he didn't realize that Moses would be telling him what to do. Isaiah glared at Moses but went over and picked up a plate and cup from one of the tables. He brought them back to Moses.

Moses held them up. "You can see this here is just a regular cup and plate. Now watch. I'm gonna balance this cup on the top edge of the plate." He gripped the plate with his fingers curled over the top and his thumb pressed behind it, holding it upright with the bottom edge pointing toward the ground. Then, he carefully placed the cup on the upper edge of the plate and it stayed there.

The show continued for two more tricks until Isaiah dropped a cup of punch that Moses tried to make disappear.

~ 174 ~

Will and Vlinder both clapped. "Those two. I swear it's good to have them at the farm this summer. My mother was so pleased when she saw the chairs and the door they fixed in the farmhouse."

"The day we painted the cows?" said Will.

Vlinder laughed and said, "I'm going to find Alwin and Corrie. I'll talk to you later and I'm glad you saved me from the wagon talk." She was off.

Will headed over to Moses and Isaiah. They were still arguing about the final trick, but they stopped when Arend Van der Beek told the crowd that games were starting in the field just below the farmhouse.

The next two hours saw four running races, a three-legged race, a carry-the-egg race, and finally, a tug of war with at least fifty pullers on each side. Turns out, Elmer is really fast and he came in second in the 100-yard dash, and first in the run-around-the-farmhouse race. The whole crowd cheered the runners and Will saw that Elmer kept his right hand in a tight fist while he ran.

"You run like the wind!" Moses said to Elmer when he came over after the race.

"Don't know why," Elmer shrugged. "Just always liked runnin'."

It was time to eat again and more plates of food and pitchers of punch were brought to the tables. The chairs were full when Arend Van der Beek walked to the center. He led the crowd in one song after another: *For Me and My Gal, My Old Kentucky Home, Way Down Upon the Swanee River,* and several others.

While everyone was singing, Corrie and Vlinder carried the eight-foot cake to a table and cut it into pieces. There were other pies and cakes and everyone ended up with at least two desserts.

Twilight eased into the day and Mr. Van der Beek stepped back to the center.

"Welcome! Welcome! I think this is our biggest crowd ever and we are so happy everyone came. Did everyone have enough to eat?"

"YES!" the crowd roared.

Mr. Van der Beek raised both hands, holding his cane up with one. "Good! Good! We'll start our fireworks in a few minutes. We don't want to keep you here too late. We know tomorrow is a workday. We'll leave dessert on the tables so when the fireworks are over, please take some for your ride back to your farms."

He paused for a moment and the crowd quieted. "This is a difficult time for all of us. Our hearts are broken along with those of the Helgeveld family. Joren Helgeveld was one of the most respected men in the area. We'll miss his leadership." He gestured over to Anika who was with Alwin. "This year, every year, please know that we are here with all of you. Anything we can do for you, let us know. Joren Helgeveld was a good man and he will always be missed."

There was a silence that no one wanted to break. Alwin sat next to his mother, his arm around her shoulder. He looked at her and stood up. "Thank you, Mr. Van der Beek, for your kind words and support. Yes, it's a difficult time for us, but it's wonderful to be here with all of you today. My father loved the fireworks each Fourth of July, so on with the show!"

The crowd cheered and moved to a large mound that overlooked the field for the fireworks.

The boys found a spot halfway up the mound and sat, sharing stories about fireworks back home. Isaiah looked over Elmer's shoulder and stood up. "Lookee there. Ain't that Roy?" The friends stood and stared at Roy who was holding the hand of a girl and leading her into the trees at the far end of a poplar grove.

"Wait here," Will said. "I don't like the way that looks," and he hustled off toward the couple. He went up a rise and through a grove of white oaks, hoping to head Roy off on the other side. There was enough light left to maneuver around the trees until he stood at the top of another rise. He peered below but couldn't see Roy or the girl. He crept down the rise, looking and listening, until he saw Roy kissing the girl, who was backed up to a tree. Will ran up to them.

"Roy, get away from her. Leave her alone!" said Will.

Roy backed off, but it was the girl who spoke. "Who are you? Why don't YOU leave US alone!"

"Yeah, bunkhouse boy," Roy said. "Mind your business. Or maybe you're just jealous."

With that, the girl put her arms around Roy's neck and brought him in for the longest kiss Will had ever seen. Will backed away from the kissers and banged into a tree, not sure if he felt nosy or foolish. But it was just Roy he figured, so those thoughts passed quickly.

The first firework exploded in colors above the field and ended with a boom. Will moved his way back through the trees to the crowd standing above the fireworks field. He saw Vlinder by the house, arm in arm with her mother. Will waved across at her and even in the dim light, she saw him and waved back.

Corrie, Hans, Lotta, and Bram were close by. Will watched them follow each firework skyward and cover their ears for the boom they knew would come. Will saw their smiles, the first since their father died. He edged over to their side.

"Will, come over here," said Corrie when she saw him. "Watch them with us," and she took his elbow and brought him into the group. The five of them stood and waited for the *poof* that sent the firework up, blasting into colors and light. Then they waited, dreading and hoping for the boom they'd feel to their core. A haze of sparks rained down after each blast and partygoers ran and stomped on the burning clusters.

Will spied the young girl who had been with Roy hustling from the woods, alone, and tucking in her shirt. She turned and pointed, yelling something into the woods, but Will couldn't hear what she said.

"Corrie," Will said and pointed. "Who's that? I saw her in the woods kissing Roy."

Corrie stared and recognized her as she got closer. "Her?" Corrie laughed. "That's Margaret Clark. She's kissed every boy from here to Peoria five times over."

Minutes later, Roy strolled out of the woods, easing through the crowd to the dessert table. He put a whole piece of cake into his mouth and slid a wedge of peach pie into his shirt pocket. He took another piece of cake and turned to watch the fireworks.

The evening ended in a flurry of colors, booms, and sparks. The crowd applauded and Mr. Van der Beek stood to one side, thanking everyone for coming and hoping to see them next year.

Will walked with the four Helgevelds toward the wagons. Lotta and Bram each took two pieces of cake when they passed the dessert table. They all reached the wagons and Corrie turned to Will. "Oh, Will, Vlinder told us that you picked out the forget-me-nots in front of my grandmother and grandfather's grave. They're my favorite flower. I told her we should put one of those flowers in front of my father the next time we go."

"Yes, they're real pretty. I think they're my favorite, too," said Will.

"Really?" said Corrie, smiling. "Okay, see you later," and she twirled once and headed to her wagon.

Will looked across and saw Vlinder standing with Anika and several well-wishers. He went over and Vlinder whispered to him, "Look at my mother. I think she actually enjoyed herself. And Corrie, Hans, Lotta, and Bram. All of us. I'm so glad we came."

"Yes, this was a lot of fun," Will said.

Will laid in his bed that night and reviewed the Fourth of July. It was another good day.

CHAPTER 22

The Fourth of July brought the summer back, the work, the meals, the jokes, the friendships. Even the Helgeveld family returned to the summer schedule, at least on the surface.

"There's a girl I kind of liked yesterday," Elmer said to Will heading out to the fields the next day on the wagon. "She's a kitchen helper at the Van der Beek farm. We talked a little while. She's from St. Louis and it's her first time away from home, too. Her name is Louise. She's so pretty."

"That's great, Elmer," Will said. "Are you going to talk to her again?"

"Maybe. I think so," said Elmer. "She has to stay in the kitchen during Sunday church to get the cakes and punch together, but she said she'd try to come out next Sunday after the service."

Will looked up toward the horizon and then at the ground passing underneath. "Did you keep your hand in your pocket?"

"Well, yes," said Elmer.

"You gotta tell her, Elmer," Will said. "You can't hide it forever. Maybe she won't care. And if it bothers her, you don't want her for a girlfriend anyways."

"Yeah, I know. You're right," Elmer said. "But she's so pretty. I never had a pretty girl talk to me like that back home."

"And don't be shy," said Will. "Show her and pretend it's not important. Better to find out now what she thinks."

Elmer looked down and nodded.

* * *

In the fields, it was a morning of spraying and hunting corn earworms, chinch bugs, and stalk borers. Dull work.

The corn field was next to the road and late morning, Will saw the mail truck arrive, delayed a day by the Fourth of July holiday. Usually, it drives right to the house, but today, it stopped next to the wagons where Alwin, Jakob, and Gerwin had gathered with the supervisors.

"Got the mail here, Alwin. Telegram, too," said the driver. "It's for you." The driver handed Alwin the telegram and he tore it open.

Alwin looked it over and nodded. "Well, looks like I've been drafted," he said to his brothers. "Got to report to Fort Sheridan outside Chicago."

Alwin, Jakob, and Gerwin stood together, looking over the fields.

"Really? When do you leave?" asked Jakob.

"Says I have thirty days to report," said Alwin. "That gives me some time to get things in order." He turned to the mail truck. "Mind if I catch a ride with you to the house? Best if I let everyone know I'll be leaving soon."

"Not at all," the driver said. "Hop in. Been givin' this news to a lot of fellas lately."

Will had forgotten about the draft, about Alwin wanting to defend his country. But that was before the death of Joren Helgeveld changed everything. Will hustled to the next field and told Elmer the news.

"Just when the summer and the work was coming back," said Elmer. "What's going to happen now? Who's going to run the farm?"

Will didn't know and Elmer didn't know.

* * *

The mail truck dropped Alwin off and returned back along the road, the driver waving at Jakob and Gerwin as he passed.

Within half an hour, Will saw a horse galloping up the road from the farmhouse. As it neared, Will saw Anika dressed in a work shirt and pants. She pulled her horse next to her other two sons.

"Where's Lily? I want to take Lily," Anika said to Jakob and Gerwin.

"Right there, next to Carl," said Jakob pointing at Lily.

Anika hopped off her horse and unstrapped the saddle. She carried it to Lily and threw it over her back, fastening the straps underneath.

Gerwin stood next to his mother when she jumped onto Lily's back. "Mother. Where are you going?"

She held Lily's reins and looked at Gerwin. "To Peoria. To Chicago. Maybe Washington D.C. This war, this damnable war. It took my husband. It's not taking my son." And she was off.

Gerwin and Jakob stood together watching her gallop toward Peoria. "Now that's something, that is," Gerwin said. "First time I ever heard mother cuss."

Alwin arrived shortly after, riding one of the draft horses. He hopped off in front of his brothers. "I tried to stop her. Told her my duty was to my country. But she said now my duty was to the family. To the farm. She said that father already gave his life for the war effort and that was enough." The three brothers stared down the road to Peoria, Anika long out of view. Alwin continued, "But I don't know what she can do. Does she think she can talk to the President of the United States?"

Nobody laughed at what might have been a joke at another time. Each of them headed out to the fields.

That night at dinner, there was no mention of the draft, or Anika. Vlinder was behind the food tables in the chow hall and when she spied Will in the dinner line, she gave him a weak smile. Will imagined she was nervous, and even though Vlinder never showed it, the Great War in Europe still hung over Helgeveld Farm.

* * *

Two days later, the mail truck arrived unexpectedly, just after breakfast. Alwin was in the farmhouse, but soon appeared at the chow hall door, motioning for Vlinder to come to the house. Ten minutes later, she walked back into the chow hall, crying. She scraped the pans, directed the workers, collected the dirty plates, and cried. She looked across the chow hall and found Will. She put her hand on her heart and smiled through her tears.

There had been a telegram.

128 South Clark Street Chicago, Illinois. Paid

Helgeveld Farm, Peoria

ALWIN STAYING AT FARM STOP HOME SATURDAY MOTHER

* * *

Two days earlier on Thursday, Anika arrived in Peoria and after leaving Lily with Pastor Jannsen at the Dutch Reformed Church, she walked to U.S. Congressman Clifford Ireland's offices, arriving at 1:45 p.m. The receptionist, Miss Agatha Hartshorne, told Anika she was fortunate that Representative Ireland was in his office and he would soon see her. "Please take a seat," she said. At 2:50 p.m., Miss Hartshorne escorted Anika into Representative Ireland's office.

"Mrs. Helgeveld to see you, congressman," Miss Hartshorne announced.

"Thank you, Agatha." Representative Ireland appeared stern and wore a tightly pressed, vested, grey suit. He rose and said to Anika, "Please, sit down Madam. How can I help you today?" The representative listened to Anika's situation, losing her husband just a few weeks earlier, and now her eldest son drafted. She showed Alwin's draft notice to the congressman.

"Yes, madam," Representative Ireland started. "Please accept my deepest condolences for your husband." Representative Ireland leaned forward and folded his hands in front of him on the desk. He patted his thumbs against each other. "This draft has created quite a stir here in Illinois, and around the nation. Almost all of my recent meetings with the good folks of Illinois are regarding this draft. You must understand, Mrs. Hegevel...."

"It's Helgeveld, sir," Anika corrected.

"Ah, yes, Helgeveld. You must understand, Mrs. Helgeveld, that I see mothers and fathers daily explaining why their sons can't be drafted. Yesterday, a father from up in Evanston came to my office. He brought his son who he said wasn't right in the head." The congressman pointed in front of his desk. "And at that, his son proceeded to roll on the floor right there and bark like a dog! A simple phone call to his former school indicated he graduated near the top of his class."

Anika sat straight in her chair and glared at the congressman. "Mr. Ireland! Are you suggesting that I'm lying about my husband's death, about my son being drafted, about the state our family would be in if my eldest son left the farm!?"

"Certainly not, Mrs. Hevelel." Congressman Ireland tapped his fingers on his desk. "Of course, there is the Agricultural Exemption. You're aware of that?"

"No, congressman," said Anika. "I'm not aware of that. What is it?"

"Well," Congressman Ireland continued. "Under some circumstances, the Agricultural Exemption would allow the eldest son to stay working on a farm if the head of that farm has passed away. Would that be something you might be interested in applying for?"

Anika's mood changed. "Yes! Yes, of course! That's exactly our situation. Can you give us that approval? I could sign some papers if that's what it would require."

The congressman sat back in his chair. "I'm afraid it's not as easy as that. You see, the family must apply when the applicant registers for the draft. Even then, it can take months to investigate and even longer to approve. You're welcome to apply, but for now, it's best that your son report to Fort Sheridan as the draft notice indicated." Congressman Ireland watched as Anika's eyes widened into distress. To soften the news, he added, "If the application is approved, your son could possibly be home by next spring, next summer at the latest."

Anika stood up in front of his desk. "Next summer!? No! My son must stay on the farm! You're our congressman, Mr. Ireland. We voted you into office to help the people of Illinois with problems just like this! Are you saying you are not willing to investigate the matter and help us now?!" Anika reached into her back pocket and raised a document. "I have my husband's death certificate right here. You can check the date! My son registered for the draft before he died! That's the investigation! What else do you need?!"

"Mrs. Helevel," the congressman replied. "I can tell you're upset. What I can do is get your address and send you the application. I'll tell Miss Hartshorne to get a copy and send it to you as soon as possible."

Anika put her hands on the congressman's desk. "Upset, Mr. Ireland? You think I'm upset!? My husband is dead and now you will do nothing to help keep my son at home and keep our farm running!?" She slapped the table. "This is not the end of the matter! And perhaps *you'll* be upset when you lose the Dutch vote in the next election!"

Anika hurried out of the congressman's office and headed straight to the Peoria train station where she caught the afternoon train to Chicago, arriving that evening at 8:45 p.m. Anika had dinner at The Windy City Cafeteria and then checked into room 719 at the Palmer House Hotel, the same hotel her husband had stayed in just weeks earlier. She left a wake-up call for 6:15 a.m., and at 7:00 a.m. on Friday, July 6, Anika Helgeveld was sitting in front of the offices of the U.S. Senator for Illinois, Lawrence Sherman. His office opened at 8.

At 8:15, Anika was ushered into Senator Sherman's office and sat in front of a tall, bow-tied government official who explained, like Congressman Ireland in Peoria, that the Agricultural Exemption was possible, but getting approval would take several months. It should also be applied for when registering for the draft. Again, Anika told him that applying for the Act before his father's death was impossible for her son. She then showed Joren's death certificate to Senator Sherman. The senator thanked Anika and said again, approval would take months.

Anika looked at the senator and said, "Fine, I'll wait," and she moved herself to a chair at the back of his office.

"Madam!" said the senator. "You can't wait here! I'll have you removed."

Anika sat upright in her chair. "Then you should have me removed, senator. And my first stop will be the Chicago Tribune, then the Chicago Daily News, and then the Chicago Daily Post. I'm sure one of them would be interested in the story of an Illinois mother who lost her husband less than a month ago, and was now losing her oldest son to the war. And they might also be interested in hearing about the U.S. Senator who was unwilling to help and had her removed from his office!"

The senator leaned forward, placed his hands flat on his desk and glared at Anika. Anika leaned forward and glared back. But soon, Senator Sherman eased back in his chair and smiled. "Perhaps your circumstances require more immediate attention. If you could leave your husband's death certificate and your son's draft notice with me and take a seat out in the waiting room. I'll wire Newton Baker, Secretary of War in Washington D.C. He and I are good friends and he has some influence. Perhaps we can come to an agreement."

Senator Sherman's offices closed at 5 p.m. but Anika and the senator stayed, waiting for a response from Washington. At 5:45 p.m., the senator received a wire. Alwin Helgeveld was approved under the Agricultural Exemption and could stay at Helgeveld Farm.

Anika thanked Senator Sherman and headed to the telegram office to give the family the news. Afterwards, she stopped at The Lake Michigan Diner for baked chicken and grilled tomatoes. Then she walked back to the Palmer House Hotel where she had kept her room. Satisfied with the day, she took a bath and soon drifted off to sleep, wondering how the hot water ever made it all the way up to the seventh floor.

* * *

The next day, Anika took the mid-morning train from Chicago, arriving at the Peoria station at 3:15 p.m. After a short walk to the Dutch Reformed Church, where she informed Pastor Jannsen of the recent events, she hopped onto Lily and headed home.

Anika arrived at the farm and rode around the farmhouse to the stables. She opened the gate and led Lily inside. Anika broke out a bale of hay and put her arms around Lily's neck. "I'll be back later to brush you down, girl."

CHAPTER 23

"AHHHHHHH! Get away from me! Don't touch me with that!" Louise Thomas backed away from Elmer the next week after church when he told her about, and then showed her, his hand.

Elmer had been waiting for her outside the Van der Beek kitchen hoping to see her when she brought after-church snacks to the back tables. Her scream brought several other kitchen workers out the back door of the farmhouse.

Elmer backed away and searched for his friends. They found him first.

"I just want to leave," Elmer said to Isaiah, Will, and Moses as he pulled away and hustled toward the wagons. Will and Isaiah followed him while Moses said he'd get some cake for everyone. Elmer reached the wagons and sat on the ground against a wagon wheel.

"Elmer, Elmer," said Will. "I told you to show her. Maybe that wasn't the right thing. I'm sorry. Really sorry,"

Elmer rocked back and forth against the wagon. "I had to show her sometime. Like you said, better to find out now. But, that's what always happens."

It was a quiet ride back, but by the time they reached the farm, everyone knew what had happened to Elmer.

That afternoon, Alwin strode to the back barn and found Will and Elmer inside, their backs against the far wall.

"Elmer," said Alwin. "I want to talk to you. That girl had no right to scream at you like that today. Even Arend Van der Beek came over and offered me his apologies and then had a word with that girl. He's thinking about not hiring her back next year. You're a good worker, Elmer. A good boy. You're going to have a good life."

"Thank you, Mr. Alwin. I hope you're right," said Elmer.

Alwin gave an encouraging nod to Elmer and stepped outside the barn. There he watched Isaiah weld braces onto two plows that, over the years, had been tossed in the grass behind the barn and forgotten.

"This one here," said Isaiah pointing to the back of one of the plows, "it already has about five repairs, Mr. Alwin. Not sure how long it's gonna last."

"I know, Isaiah," Alwin nodded. "But we need it to turnover some fields we're gonna clear soon. If we get a week or two of work out of them, it's still worth it. Just do the best you can."

Alwin turned and saw Moses, his hands on his hips and staring at the steam tractor. "How's it look, Moses?"

Moses shook his head. "I don't know, Mr. Alwin. Tried firing it up last week, but it wouldn't run. It wanted to, but it just locked up. I'm gonna take a few parts off today and take another look. Sorry, Mr. Alwin. Thought I'd have it runnin' by now."

Alwin lifted his hat and ran his hand across his head. "Okay, Moses. Let me know when you get it running. We'll need it soon." He turned to leave, but stopped and turned. "Moses, Isaiah. I heard some talk on the Fourth of July about you two that I didn't like. How's the summer going here? Anybody giving you any trouble?"

"No, sah, not really," said Isaiah.

"Yeah, no more than usual, Mr. Alwin," Moses added.

"What does that mean?" asked Alwin.

"Well," said Moses. "Some people, they say things here and there. Sometimes cause some trouble. We kinda used to it by now."

"It's the workers in Bunkhouse 1, isn't it?" Alwin asked.

"Rather not say, Mr. Alwin," Isaiah added.

"Right. I thought it was them. Well, like my father said. We're not going to have that going on here," Alwin said. "I'll take care of it."

"Mr. Alwin," said Moses. "We don't want to cause no trouble."

"They're causing the trouble, Moses. Not you." Alwin nodded and gave Moses and Isaiah their Sunday pay and then headed up toward the stables.

* * *

By the next morning, all the workers had found out about Anika going to Chicago and that Alwin could stay at the farm. It was good news.

But Alwin, Gerwin, and Jakob, weren't out front in the morning. Instead, Carl, Jackson, and Clifford got the workers organized and out into the fields.

At lunch, Will found Vlinder at the back of a lunch wagon lifting a small tub of oatmeal cookies to the front.

"Vlinder, where's Alwin?" Will asked.

"He left early for Peoria with Gerwin and Jakob. They're sending some workers home."

"Why? What happened?"

Vlinder turned toward Will. "Seems Alwin had a talk with Bunkhouse 1 about how they've been treating Moses and Isaiah. Four of them had a little too much to say about it, so bright and early, Alwin, Gerwin, and Jakob loaded them on the wagon to Peoria and they're sending them home."

Will nodded. Freedom wasn't as easy a word to figure out as he had thought.

* * *

Over the next few weeks, the rain joined the war effort, supplying several overnight showers, wedged between bright, cloudless days. The crops were healthy and ahead of schedule.

There was a new project. The contract with the government had already been extended another year, and more corn, more soybeans, and more of everything would be needed. Alwin told the workers at dinner that the overgrown field behind the back barn needed to be cleared. So, the next day, Bunkhouse 2 headed to those fields that Will discovered just weeks earlier. There were over 200 acres and Alwin said about half needed to be cleared and plowed for next season. Only Anika remembered when that field was last tilled in the early 1890s.

Three days later, Bunkhouse 1 joined Bunkhouse 2 to cut, pull up, and burn twenty-five years of growth from that field. Several draft horses stood ready, yanking out determined stumps. The workers dragged all the brush into piles, creating more than thirty bonfires and opening the fields.

*   *   *

At the back barn, Alwin asked Isaiah to set up the block and tackle on the beam above the second floor loft door. The plan was to start storing hay up there to help the winter feeding of the beef cattle. Isaiah found the block and tackle in the barn, but the block was warped and the rope had rotted. Alwin ordered both. The rope would come in from Peoria, but the block would come down from Chicago.

Two days before their July payday trip to Peoria, Alwin rode a wagon to the back barn. "I got the rope here," Alwin said. "Could be a while for the block." Alwin brought the rope over to Isaiah and pointed at the second floor loft door and the beam just above it. "That beam there. That hasn't been used in more than twenty years. When you get a chance, throw this rope over it and see if it will hold enough weight. Maybe both of you could hang from it down here to see if it holds."

"Yes, sah, Mr. Alwin," Isaiah said.

The boys looked at each other and grinned, seeing more potential to the task.

After Alwin drove off in the wagon, Moses carried the rope to the second floor loft door and managed to throw it over the beam and then lowered both ends of the rope to the ground. Moses tied up one end of the rope inside the barn leaving the other end hanging low. Isaiah tied a knot in it, allowing a loop at the end.

Isaiah went first, sliding his foot in the loop and grabbing the rope. He bounced a few times assuring that the beam would hold him.

"You ready?" asked Moses. Isaiah nodded and Moses began pulling the rope from side to side, sending Isaiah higher and higher until Isaiah was able to pump the rope himself. He swung across the front of the barn, reaching halfway to the roof edge on each back and forth.

"OoohWee!" hollered Isaiah with each swing.

"Come on, Isaiah," Moses yelled. "Yo' turn is over. It's my turn!"

A few more swings and Isaiah slowed himself, allowing Moses to grab him to a stop.

Moses slid his foot into the rope, but before Isaiah began swinging him, Moses pulled out his yo-yo. "Let's see how this works up there." He crooked his left elbow around the rope and held the yo-yo in his right hand. Isaiah smiled at the innovation.

But by the fifth swing, the yo-yo string was wound around the rope and around Moses's legs. That didn't stop the swinging. Moses continued until he was sure his swings were a little higher than his brother's.

*   *   *

For two Sundays in a row, Elmer told Alwin his stomach hurt and he didn't go to church.

But Will knew the real reason. "You know, Elmer, Roy's around here all day Sunday."

"I know, but like Owen said, I gotta deal with Roy." Elmer sighed. "And that's easier than seeing the people at church."

*   *   *

The final Friday of July, the workers gathered out front for their payday in Peoria, each imagining their new bank balances. For the Helgevelds, the first stop would be Springdale Cemetery. Pastor Jannsen said he would meet the family at the cemetery at 10:30 a.m. for a memorial service. Originally, this service was planned for just

Grampa Bartel and Gramma Luna, but now their son, Joren, lay next to them.

As the workers waited in front of the farmhouse, Anika came out the front door, wearing a ruffled bonnet and a long, pleated skirt. She held her head up and as she passed through the gathering of workers, finally reaching Vlinder. The two stood next to the road and Vlinder pointed at the final two wagons. Anika covered her mouth and looked out at the workers.

Earlier, the boys heard that the family would visit the gravesite of Mr. Helgeveld and almost half asked if they could also go to the cemetery to pay their respects. Those last two wagons would be rerouted to the cemetery. Anika, Vlinder, and Alwin thanked the boys as they piled in. Will, Isaiah, Moses, and Elmer chose to go to the cemetery, anxious like the others, to see the burial site of Mr. Helgeveld and reluctantly confirm the certainty of his death.

Since Carl and the supervisors would take the other boys straight to town, Alwin handed out all the pay envelopes at the farm so they'd each have it when they got to the bank.

*   *   *

The wagons reached the cemetery on a road below the gravesite. Anika led the way from the wagons, the family walking behind her, the workers following last. Anika stopped halfway to the gravesite and pointed ahead. "Is that the headstone?" Anika asked. "Is it already there?"

Alwin pointed at Vlinder. "You can thank Vlinder. She went back to the stonemason after you left Peoria and told him we'd be here the end of July. He knew father from school. He promised that the headstone would be ready."

Anika put her hands on Vlinder's cheeks. "What would I do without all of you? Thank you, dear Vlinder."

At Joren Helgeveld's grave, Pastor Jannsen reached out to Anika, taking her hand, and the two of them faced her husband's finished headstone. Anika reached out and put her fingers on the chiseled name of her husband and then on her own name under it. She offered a weak smile. Joren's sister, Olivia, had come on from

Indianapolis once again, and she stepped next to Anika. They fell into each other's arms.

After a time, the Pastor turned and faced the gathering. He opened his Bible. "Thar is a time fer everting, and a season for everting under da heavens: a tim fer to be born and a tim fer to die," started the Pastor. His remarks were brief, but he told stories about Grampa Bartel, Gramma Luna, and Joren Helgeveld, their strengths and kindness.

When Pastor Jannsen finished his words, Corrie stepped in front of her grandparents' headstone. She kneeled and pulled a trowel from her pocket, wrapped in paper. Corrie dug into the three forget-me-nots in front of Gramma Luna and Grandpa Bartel's headstone, the flowers that Will had picked out two months earlier. Corrie separated one of the plants from the other two and brought it over to a space in front of her father's headstone. She laid it on its side and pushed the trowel into the solid ground in front of her father's memorial. The hole complete, she eased the single forget-me-not into its new home, settling it in with the brown earth and connecting parents and son. Then she moved back over and pushed dirt around the two remaining forget-me-nots under her grandparents headstone.

Corrie stood up and faced the grave and the lavender tributes. She eased next to Vlinder who turned to look at the workers, to look for Will. He was just behind her and their smiles connected them.

"Wait!" said Will and he turned and ran down, then up and over, a nearby rise.

Vlinder knew where he was going and she motioned patience to the others.

Will returned minutes later with a bucket of water and handed it to Vlinder who gave it to Corrie. "Here, Corrie. You do it," said Vlinder. Corrie took the bucket and slowly poured water around the forget-me-nots in front of her father's, and then her grandparents' grave. The water soaked in and she poured more, helping life to grow above the dead.

Corrie emptied the bucket and reached over, handing it to Will and smiling. "Thanks, Will," she said.

Anika stared for a moment at her husband's grave and flowers. Then she turned and looked at the workers, gathered and silent. With her right hand, she reached toward her neck where she took the gold necklace between her fingers, the one Joren bought her and was found in his pocket the day he died.

"This morning," Anika said to the group, "I knew we would come to the cemetery with my children to honor my husband and his parents. I knew that Pastor Jannsen would speak comforting words from the Bible." She reached out her left hand toward the group. "But I didn't expect this. Look at all of you here when you could be in Peoria. You have made this day something I will always remember. Thank you so much for coming." She smiled across the workers. "Now, let's go to Peoria." She walked to the wagon next to Joren's sister, Olivia, who also accompanied them to Peoria.

As everyone headed toward the wagons, Alwin came over to Isaiah and Moses who were still standing with Will and Elmer. "The Community Bank is close by," Alwin told them. "We'll swing by there and you two can deposit your pay. We'll wait for you outside. Then we'll go to Northern Illinois Bank for the other workers and you can all walk around the town."

"We appreciate that, Mr. Alwin," said Moses. "But you can just leave us at the bank. We'll walk down to the lake after that where we know some people."

"Alright," said Alwin and he joined his family.

Will turned to Moses and asked him, "Celia down there?"

Isaiah almost fell over laughing. "Yeah, Moses, is that the *people?* Is that the people we gonna see? Celia?"

"Don't know what you talkin' about," said Moses. "Met some people there last time in Peoria. Gonna say hello, that's all. And we gotta see about sending some money back to Granddaddy." Moses thought for a moment. "And I'm gonna get some parts outta them junk cars down there. Might help with the tractor. Maybe the Dodge, too."

Will returned the water bucket and caught the wagons as they left the cemetery and headed to town. As they passed it, Will pointed out the Peoria Zoo to Isaiah, Moses, and Elmer where three elk grazed near the fence. He stared at the spot where he had stood next to Vlinder two months earlier.

At the Community Bank, Alwin stopped the wagon and Isaiah and Moses jumped out and headed to the bank. Alwin leaned over and yelled, "Hey, Isaiah, Moses. Four o'clock at the Dutch Reformed Church. That's where the wagons will be. You know where that is?"

"Yes, sah, Mr. Alwin," they both said. "We can see the steeple from half the town," added Moses.

"That's the one," Alwin said.

Elmer turned to Will in the wagon. "Can't believe they had to switch banks. Doesn't seem right."

"Yeah," said Will and he nodded. He hadn't noticed that Isaiah and Moses were the only colored customers in the bank when they tried to open bank accounts back in May. Will wondered what else he might not have noticed.

As Isaiah and Moses headed to their bank, Will saw Corrie jump out of her wagon and run to Isaiah and Moses. She said something to them, reached into her pocket, and handed them a coin. They nodded and went into the bank.

There were more motorcars in Peoria than when the workers arrived at the farm just months earlier. More horns targeted the wagons, some happy to scare the horses.

The boys landed in front of The Northern Illinois Bank. Next year, all the workers would use Community Bank for their accounts.

CHAPTER 24

For Will, there would be no walking around Peoria with Vlinder this day. Anika asked the family to be with her in town and Will was glad she was with her mother, and that the family was all together.

Will, Elmer, Nathan Carey, Lucas Miller, Robert Clark, and several other boys from Bunkhouse 3 got together for their day in Peoria. The boys' bank accounts eased to just under $90 and each kept several dollar bills in their pockets, ready for an unexpected purchase or just proof of their work in the fields. Lunch was at the Peoria Diner, frankfurters or bologna sandwiches, potato chips, and milkshakes.

"Getting' close to $100," said Elmer at the counter. "We got almost $100."

"Yeah," said Lucas. "At the farm I worked at last summer, they never paid us all of our wages. Here, it's in the bank and I ain't worried about it."

"Alwin told me," said Elmer, "that if you leave $100 in the bank for a year, they give you $3.50 extra. For nothin'. Just for leaving it there. That's what I'm gonna do when I get back home, put all this money in the bank and leave it."

Lunch was over and the boys reached into their pockets, took out some coins, and paid for their lunch. Adults pay their way, and now so did they.

Next, was Addison's Candy Store where the boys watched toffee, chocolate, gum drops, and candy corn being made. Each boy walked out biting a sticky candy apple and carrying a bag full of candy for the days ahead.

The boys from Bunkhouse 3 wandered through Peoria ending up on Monroe Street and then turning left on Spring Street. They shared their payday stories with other Helgeveld workers who passed by.

"Hey, there's Roy," pointed Robert Clark. The boys looked to the other side of Spring Street to see Roy running up the sidewalk, looking back over his shoulder, and turning left on Madison Avenue. Will and the others gazed down the sidewalk but saw nobody running after him. "You know he did somethin'," Robert said.

At Serve-Yourself General Store, four of the boys and Will pitched in for a wooden baseball bat and another baseball. Since the last payday, several boys had been throwing a baseball after dinner in an open area beside the stable that Alwin had suggested. Now, with a baseball bat, they could play games and Will looked forward to it.

Will liked baseball. In 1909, his father took him to watch the hometown Pittsburgh Pirates play the Detroit Tigers in the World Series. The stands were full that day, anxious to watch their local hero, Honus Wagner, battle the American League enemy, Ty Cobb. Wagner hit two singles, driving in the ultimate winning run. In the 9th inning, Cobb, furious at the looming defeat, tried to steal second base. He came in with spikes high and slammed into Wagner covering the bag. Wagner stumbled back and the two men nearly came to blows before the umpire and several players jumped in to separate them. The crowd erupted into a chorus of boos at Cobb's dirty play. Cobb was fined after the series for "unsportsmanlike conduct." Will's father said it was the best baseball game he'd ever seen. After that, Will began playing baseball with friends in a field behind the school.

As the boys continued through Peoria, Luke pointed through the window of Barclay's Toy Store. "I think my sister would like that." The red-haired, red-cheeks, red-nosed doll was called a Raggedy Ann Doll. With that, the boys began looking for something they could bring home to their brothers and sisters. What better way to show that they were grown up and had money to spend? The list ranged from Crayola Crayons to marbles to harmonicas. Seeing Moses with his yo-yo put that toy on each boy's list. But those purchases would wait until their final trip to Peoria in October, when they were heading home.

Will looked, but he never saw Vlinder, nor the family, that day in Peoria.

* * *

Toward 4 p.m., the boys arrived at the Dutch Reformed Church and were met by about half of the other workers. The Helgevelds were already there, at their wagons, tending to the horses.

Will left the others and walked toward Vlinder's wagon. She was standing with Corrie and Anika and they all smiled at Will as he approached. Anika voiced her appreciation of his choice of the three forget-me-nots at the graves. He nodded to her and considered how that casual choice had become so important.

"Have you seen Moses and Isaiah?" asked Corrie. "Are they here yet?"

Will turned and looked at the growing crowd of workers. "No, not yet. I haven't seen them."

From around the other side of the church, Moses and Isaiah strode toward the group. Moses held up a bag and beamed. Corrie ran to him and Will knew. She took the bag and brought it over to Vlinder and her mother. "Look what we got!" said Corrie opening the bag for Vlinder and Anika.

"Corrie, are those sour pickles?" asked Anika.

"Yup! I had Moses and Isaiah buy some for us all," said Corrie.

"Corrie! Sour pickles! I love sour pickles," said Vlinder.

Will closed his eyes and shook his head.

"I know. Nothin' like a Peoria sour pickle," said Moses. Corrie took the bag and handed a pickle to her mother, Aunt Olivia, Vlinder, Isaiah, and Moses. She went to the other wagons and gave one to Lotta and to her brothers. She stepped to the side and looked down the wagons. "Hey, Elmer! Come here! Look what we got!" Elmer came running.

Will heard the crunches and saw the pain. Corrie, okay. Vlinder, maybe. But Anika? What were these people thinking, Will wondered.

That night, when the stories ended and the bunkhouse lights were turned off, Robert Clark yelled loud enough for everyone to hear. "Hey, Roy. We saw you runnin' from someone in Peoria. What'd you steal?"

"Didn't steal anything. Just felt like runnin'," he asserted.

On Wednesday, Anika, Vlinder, Aunt Olivia, and Corrie took the kitchen girls to Peoria to deposit their pay and explore the town. At the end of the day, Olivia took the train back home to Indianapolis.

The night before, Isaiah jangled the two lucky pennies and the four boys had their prayers answered. A different group of workers would help in the kitchen this time.

* * *

Later that day, Alwin walked down to the back barn. He managed the farm now and he saw the workers, the family, the land, and the farm differently. When his father was in charge, the daily tasks were lists to be completed. Separate. First this, then that. Now, those parts were connected. Matt at the dairy barn. Lily and Snowball. A trip to Peoria. Corn borers. Anika playing the piano. The summer workers. His father used to say, "when you fix a fence, you help to bake the bread." All one thing. Now he understood.

Alwin stood in front of Isaiah, examining the work. "Isaiah, at some point, take a look at the binders. We got two of them and both were running a little rough last year. They've got to be right for cutting the soybeans this season. Can't risk them jamming when they hit the tougher patches." He pointed toward the horses. "They're up there behind the stables."

"Sure thing, Mr. Alwin," Isaiah said, "just after fixin' these yokes."

"Good," said Alwin. "Let me know if they need any parts. They'll have to come from Chicago."

Alwin turned to Moses. "How's the steam tractor coming, Moses?"

"Took some of it apart again, Mr. Alwin." Moses pointed to some tractor parts. "Got a few things in Peoria that might help, too."

"Peoria? I don't want you spending your own money on things for the farm, Moses," said Alwin.

"No, sah," said Moses. "Got these parts from the field me and Isaiah stayed in when we first came to Peoria. Big pile of junk there and a few busted cars. Some still had parts in 'em."

"Alright," said Alwin. "End of next month is when we really need this running, Moses."

"Yes, Mr. Alwin. I'll have it workin'."

* * *

Will, Elmer, and most of the other workers were in the fields, spraying for bugs, and pulling weeds. "Elmer," Will said, "you think you'll go to church again? Doesn't do any good staying here all the time. Pastor Jannsen even asked where you were."

Elmer breathed deep. "Maybe, probably. I'll go sometime."

"Other people asked about you, too," Will said. "Even the Van der Beek sons. They said it wasn't right for that girl to scream like that."

"Might not have been right," said Elmer, "but she did it. I've had people laugh at my hand, but never had anybody scream."

"Well, Elmer," said Will. "There's always people like that, but you got a lot of friends here."

Elmer paused and nodded. "I know. I wish we worked here all year."

After dinner on Thursday and Friday, the boys headed behind the stables where there was always a group of boys playing baseball.

CHAPTER 25

After lunch on a Sunday in mid-August, the four headed to the back barn. From the path, they heard, then saw, Hans swinging from the rope Moses and Isaiah had tied to the beam above the loft door.

"My turn!" yelled Lotta. "Come on. You've had it long enough!"

Hans slowed himself and stepped from the rope. Once Lotta had her foot secure and both arms around the rope, Hans pulled her from side to side until she was on her own, bending her knees and straightening, swinging ever higher above the grass on one side and broken farm equipment on the other.

Alwin came down the path and gave Isaiah and Moses their Sunday pay. He stood back and watched his brothers and sisters trying to outdo the swinger from before. Alwin thought of putting a stop to it, but his brothers and sisters swinging back and forth on a rope appeared a safer alternative than jumping out of the loft or jumping from a wagon.

"Alwin!" yelled Corrie. "You take a turn! Maybe you could reach the roof edge."

Alwin considered the offer. "Maybe another time," he told her. "And Corrie, Hans, when you're done here, remember to brush down the horses, all of them. Check their hooves, too." They nodded to Alwin who turned and followed the path back to the farmhouse.

Will and Elmer moved over and settled into the grass, watching a Sunday of play they hadn't witnessed for weeks.

After Lotta finished her turn, Bram managed to swing higher than the others, bringing nods of approval from Isaiah and Moses. He came within inches of the roof edge and that became the new challenge.

"My turn!" yelled Corrie. Hans held the rope as Corrie slipped her foot into the loop at the bottom. Hans ran from side to side, yanking Corrie higher each time until she swung within inches of the roof's edge. On the next swing, she bent her knees and threw herself toward the edge, finally touching it with a finger. Corrie turned to the crowd below to claim victory, and as she did, her foot slipped out of the loop. She grabbed for the rope but missed it as she fell toward the ground. She twisted to her side, but her left ankle slammed onto the top of a broken plow and her scream echoed across the farm.

Will jumped up and ran to Corrie who was reaching down to her ankle. And he saw something he hadn't seen since Bobby Davis fell from the second floor window back home. Bone and blood burst through the skin around Corrie's ankle.

Will went back to that day when his mother nursed Bobby. "Isaiah," he yelled. "Get me a piece of wood, about a foot long and a few inches wide. Get some twine too. Elmer, give me your shirt."

Isaiah ran into and out of the back barn with a collection of small boards and a ball of twine. Will choose one and had Corrie lay back on Lotta's lap so he could get to her ankle. He rolled up her pant leg, slid the board under her calf, and eased her shattered ankle onto it. Corrie's screams continued, bringing Vlinder, Alwin, and Anika running from the farmhouse.

"God have mercy, no," Vlinder said under her breath when she saw the wound. Alwin leaned over Corrie and watched Will wrap Elmer's shirt around the board and around Corrie's ankle, binding it with twine to keep it locked. Will took another piece of twine and tied it tight a little further up Corrie's leg, slowing the blood flow.

"Vlinder," said Will. "We have to lift Corrie's leg up higher than her heart." Lotta moved aside and gently laid Corrie's back and head on the ground while Vlinder positioned her own legs under Corrie's ankles. Corrie began shaking, shivering. "She needs a blanket," Will yelled. "Can somebody get Corrie a blanket?"

Will's actions suggested to everyone that he could do whatever Corrie needed. But back home, this was when Will's mother said Bobby Davis needed a doctor and a hospital fast.

Other workers were arriving, circling the turmoil.

"What do we do?" pleaded Anika, leaning over her daughter.

"Hans, get the wagon and bring it down. Quick," Alwin said.

"Wait," Will said, standing up next to Isaiah. "That would take hours to get to Peoria and she'd be bouncing in the wagon. She's losing too much blood too fast for that."

"What if I ride Lily to get the doctor?" said Vlinder. "He has a motorcar. He could drive back here."

Will was nervous with the lack of options. He remembered his mother on the sidewalk with Bobby Davis. He looked at Vlinder. "She needs an operation and an operating room to set the bone. An x-ray machine. She'll need blood. The doctor can't do that here. She needs to get to the hospital right away."

"Alwin! What are we going to do? What are we going to do!?" Anika pleaded.

Alwin looked at his mother and then down at his sister, the blood beginning to show through the shirt wrapped around Corrie's ankle. He looked at his family and the workers. He began to shake. A few short weeks ago he lost his father. Was he about to lose his sister?

Moses was standing behind Will and Isaiah. He stepped between them, just in front of Alwin. "Mr. Alwin, sah. You can take the Dodge."

Alwin shook his head. "Dodge doesn't run, Moses."

"But it does," Moses said. "Just needed to clean the carburetor and put in a different starter motor. Been fixin' the fender before bringing it around."

"Starter motor?" Alwin said.

"Yes, sah. When we was in Peoria, took it outta the busted Dodge that me and Isaiah first slept in. She fired right up."

Alwin put his hand on Moses' shoulder. "Good work, Moses. Bring it around."

Moses ran to the back of the barn and the Dodge rumbled to life. He drove it to the side of the barn, next to Corrie.

Will asked Lotta to go to the house and smash some ice in a towel. Elmer ran to the bunkhouse and brought back some pain pills left over from Owen.

The Dodge's four doors were open and Will and Elmer lifted Corrie off of Vlinder's lap and carried her toward the Dodge. Vlinder jumped into the back seat and the boys eased Corrie there, her legs raised onto Vlinder's lap again. Lotta brought down the icepack and Vlinder gently laid it across Corrie's ankle.

Will tucked the blanket around Corrie's shoulders, then lifted her slightly to take the pain pills with a glass of water. She laid back down on the seat, sweating, shivering. Corrie looked up at Will, chattering. "It's b-bad…isn't it? It's r-really bad."

Will put his hand on her forehead and smiled down at her. "Don't worry, Corrie. I've seen worse."

Alwin hopped into the driver's seat, but before Anika got into the seat beside him she turned to Moses and put her hands on the side of his face.

"Thank you, Moses. How lucky you fixed it."

"Thank you, ma'am, but really, it was Mr. Joren. He asked me to fix it if I could. Said you might need it sometime."

"Joren said that?!"

"Yes, ma'am."

Anika put her hand across her mouth and stared at Moses.

"Get in mother! Let's go!" Alwin yelled.

Anika got in next to Alwin and the Dodge sped off, around the side of the farmhouse, flying down the road to Peoria.

Thirty-nine minutes later, Corrie was on an operating table at Methodist Hospital of Central Illinois, a mask over her nose and mouth, drifting off under the anesthesia.

CHAPTER 26

Several hours after Corrie's fall, Carl came into the chow hall as the workers were finishing dessert. Next to him was a man dressed in a blue uniform.

"Wonder who that is?" said Elmer.

"I think he's from the hospital," said Will. "Those look like hospital clothes."

Carl motioned to Gerwin, Jakob, and Hans and they followed the man out the chow hall door.

"Not sure if that looks good or not," said Isaiah to the others.

A short time later, Carl came into the chow hall and stood in front of the serving tables.

"That man was from the hospital," said Carl, looking across the chow hall. "He's taking Gerwin, Jakob, and Hans back to the hospital to give more blood for Corrie. Anika, Alwin, and Vlinder gave all they could, but they need more." Carl took a deep breath. "They're operating on her right now. I asked him how she's doing and he said they're doing everything they can. Then he said that Dr. Browning is working on her and that's who he'd want working on him."

Monday and Tuesday there was work in the fields, but no news from Peoria.

The death of Joren Helgeveld brought the farm to the brink. If something happened to Corrie, the boys knew that the farm could break.

* * *

The August days baked the workers and the sun sat on them. The supervisors arranged the days, and the kitchen workers brought lunch and extra drinks out to the hot fields.

On Wednesday, as the boys ate a lunch of chicken sandwiches and pickles, a motorcar came down the road from Peoria. It was the Dodge, and Vlinder was behind the wheel. She stopped and got out in front of the wagons. Lotta and Hans ran to her. She looked tired, but Will read her face and the news was good.

Vlinder turned to the field and kitchen workers who circled her. "Corrie's doing well. The operation took more than six hours, but all of her bones are set and the doctor said now it's up to her. For now, he's worried about infection. He'll keep her in the hospital for a week, maybe two, to help it heal and watch for any problems."

"Where's everybody else?" Lotta asked.

"They're still in town. The doctor wants to x-ray her tomorrow to be sure everything is in place. If he has to operate again, Corrie might need a little more blood from us. I'll eat dinner here but I'll drive back to Peoria tonight."

"Is she awake?" asked Lotta. "Did you talk to her? What did she say?"

"She could only smile," Vlinder said. "She's taking a lot of pain pills."

Lunch was over and the workers headed back to the fields. Will took a route that brought him alongside Vlinder who was standing with Lotta at the lunch wagon.

"That's good news about Corrie," Will said to Vlinder.

"Yes. We're all happy, but still a little scared," said Vlinder. "Alwin keeps saying it was his fault, Corrie swinging on the rope. He said he should have stopped it."

"It wasn't his fault," said Will. "It was an accident. I was waiting to take a turn."

"Yes," said Vlinder nodding. "I probably would have taken a turn, too."

Will nodded and started to head to the fields.

"Oh," said Vlinder, and Will turned around. "Dr. Browning said the splint on Corrie's leg and getting her to the hospital in time. You and Moses, you saved my sister's life."

Will nodded. "I'll tell Moses," and he turned and headed to the fields. But he stopped and turned back toward Vlinder. "You know how to drive a motorcar?"

"I learned before Alwin," Vlinder smiled. "Are you surprised?"

"No. Not at all," Will chuckled and he turned again toward the fields.

As Vlinder walked to the Dodge, she wondered when this worker had become more than other workers from other summers, wondered how he'd begun to seep in and around her dreams. Was she risking everything she thought she wanted? Or maybe new dreams can hold onto pieces of old dreams. It all seemed worth the risk.

*   *   *

Two days later, just before dinner, the Dodge pulled up out front. Alwin, Vlinder, Gerwin, Jakob, and Hans got out and walked into the farmhouse. As the workers finished dessert, Alwin came into the chow hall and stood in front of the serving tables.

"Hello, everyone. We left my mother at the hospital to look after Corrie. The news isn't as good as we'd like. Corrie's ankle got infected and the doctor said if it continues, it could be bad. They could even amputate part of her leg." Alwin paused and took a deep breath. "I came back to check on the farm, but I'm going back to Peoria tomorrow with Vlinder. That's the news."

"That sounds pretty bad," Roy yelled from a front table. "Do we have to work tomorrow?"

Alwin glared at Roy. "I'll see you all out front in the morning."

The next day, Saturday, Alwin walked the corn fields. Long and full ears. It was a good crop and it kept his mind off Corrie.

As the workers ate lunch, Vlinder drove the Dodge out to the lunch wagons, stopping next to her brothers. Alwin, Gerwin, and Jakob jumped in and Vlinder told Carl, "I don't know when we'll be back."

Vlinder shared a quick look with Will. He smiled and she tried to.

*   *   *

Moses watched the Dodge speed off toward Peoria. He nodded to himself and walked to the lunch wagon where Lotta was putting dirty dishes into washing bins. "Lotta," he said.

Lotta turned and saw him. "Hi, Moses. You want another sandwich?"

"No, well yes, but that's not what I wanted to talk to you about," said Moses. "I need a favor. I'm wonderin' if you got any pennies back in the house?"

"Pennies? Probably. No, wait. There's a jar that my father would throw pennies in when he had extras. There's a bunch in there. Why?" said Lotta.

"I need one. I need a 1909 penny with Mr. Lincoln on it. See if you got a shiny one." Moses reached into his pocket and pulled out another penny. "Here," said Moses handing it to Lotta. "I got this penny here I can swap for it."

Lotta put the penny in her pocket. "I'll look when I get back to the house, Moses. I'll bring it to dinner tonight if I find one. What do you need a 1909 penny for?"

"Good luck. I think Corrie needs some good luck."

"Yeah," said Lotta. "Me, too."

"Keep it a secret, okay?" said Moses.

"Okay, Moses," Lotta said, reaching over and giving him another sandwich. "I love secrets!"

*   *   *

At dinner, Lotta looked down the line of hungry workers while spooning out shepherd's pie. She spied Moses and she couldn't hide her smile. She had the penny.

When Moses moved in front of Lotta, she kept the secret. "Hey, Moses. At lunch today, you dropped this when you left the lunch wagon." Lotta reached into her pocket, pulled out a penny, and handed it to Moses.

Moses examined it and smiled at Lotta. "Thanks." He slid the penny into his pocket. It had just the right amount of shine.

*   *   *

At the Sunday church service, Pastor Jannsen started the service and said, "I kaam from Peoria dis morgan. I sayed prayers wid Corrie and wid her moeder at da hospitaal." The pastor stopped and shook his head. "Mebee yoo knowd that Corrie Helgeveld haad a baad aka...aska...."

Moses put his hands around his mouth and leaned forward from the front row. "*Accident*, Pastor. *Accident*."

"Tank yoo, Moses," said the pastor. "Akseedent. Corrie haad a baad akseedent aand she need aar prayers. Pleese tink of her todaay. Tank you."

Pastor Jannsen raised both of his hands across the crowd. "Welkom! Welkom! Welkomen to da hoose of God!"

Almost two hours later, the worshippers gathered around tables of red punch and blueberry cake.

Elmer didn't go to church again.

*   *   *

That Sunday afternoon, Isaiah and Moses went behind the stables to check on the binders as Alwin had asked. They hadn't worked on binders before, but felt Granddaddy right beside them. He always told them to try to figure things out, so both of them climbed onto and around the cutter bars and knotters. They hooked each binder to a team of horses and pulled them a few feet. That taught them what they needed to know. Parts had to be ordered.

Will and Elmer hiked to the recently cleared back field and walked around piles of warm ash and spiky ground, nearly ready to be plowed and tumbled. They circled the field and took a different path back to the bunkhouse where they were surprised to find Isaiah, and even Moses, back from the barn and lying on top of their beds. Roy was on his bed with his legs crossed and his hat over his face. They never knew if Roy was asleep or listening. Moses hoped he was listening.

"Moses," said Elmer. "You sleepin' on top of the bed now?"

"Nope, not sleeping at all. Feeling real good about things," Moses said, "now that I got that other penny back. They work best when they's altogether. Just waitin' for the good fortune to come our way."

Isaiah jumped off his bed. "You found it? You got the penny?"

"Sure did. Right here," and Moses held the 1909 penny up for Isaiah to examine.

Isaiah took it and flipped it over. "Well, I'll be! Look at this!" He pulled the other two pennies out of his sock and held all three in his palm.

Roy lifted the hat off his face and shot up on his elbows. He glared over at Moses. "Where'd you get it? That's not it!" Roy yelled.

"Right outside, Roy," said Moses. "Told you I saw you go out the door that day. Only a couple of places you coulda hid it, so wasn't hard to find."

Roy jumped up and dashed through the bunkhouse door.

Moses hopped up. "Come on," he said and Isaiah, Will, and Elmer followed Moses through the door. They ran around the side of the bunkhouse to see Roy pulling something from underneath.

Roy held up the penny. "I knew you were a liar! You ain't never gonna find it now!" and he ran off, down and around the far end of the bunkhouse. Roy was skinny and fast and when the boys reached the privies, he was well down the path to the back barn. He turned and yelled, "What are you? A bunch of jokers? You run like my mother!"

Elmer looked at Roy and then at his friends. "I'll get him," and he sped ahead, closing the distance to Roy with each stride. Soon, Roy and Elmer were out of sight.

Then they heard the scream. "Ahhhh! Ahhhh! Get off me!" Roy yelled. "Don't touch me with that hand! Let me go! Ahhhhhh! Ahhhhhh!"

When Moses, Isaiah, and Will reached the pair, Elmer was sitting on Roy's chest with both of his hands wrapped around Roy's face.

Roy wriggled underneath him. "Get off me! Get that cussed hand off me! AHHHHH! AHHHHH!"

Moses saw his Granddaddy's 1909 penny to the side where Roy dropped it. He grabbed it and handed it to Isaiah. "Here. Put this one with those other two. I got that other 1909 penny from Lotta."

Isaiah swapped it with the real 1909 penny. Isaiah cupped the three original pennies and jangled them next to his ear. "Yup. The family is together again. I can feel Granddaddy right here with us."

When Elmer let Roy up, he ran off toward the stables yelling, "I'll get you for this! I'm gonna get all of you!"

Will turned to Elmer. "I gotta say Elmer, you runnin' after Roy was like seeing the sheriff going after an outlaw. It was one of the best things I've seen all summer." Moses and Isaiah agreed.

"Yeah," said Elmer. "Felt pretty good."

* * *

The next night, the boys were finishing cherry pie when Alwin, Anika, Gerwin, and Jacob arrived back from Peoria and walked through the side door of the chow hall. Lotta, Hans, and Bram ran around the serving tables and Anika motioned them to her side.

The room was silent. Anika and Alwin were smiling.

"Hello, everyone," said Alwin. "We just drove back from the hospital. Corrie's infection and fever broke late yesterday afternoon, and the doctor said her ankle is healing the way it should for now, but they need to keep an eye on it. We might be able to bring her home in a few days, but she'll need a long time to heal. Vlinder's at the hospital with her now. We just wanted to let you all know and we'll see you out front tomorrow morning."

"Dang," said Moses looking down at his half-finished cherry pie. "Didn't expect them pennies to work that fast."

CHAPTER 27

On Wednesday, Alwin walked to the back barn with a letter that arrived on the morning mail truck.

"Isaiah. This just came for you and Moses." He handed Isaiah the letter and Moses came over. Alwin walked into the back barn, but came to the door when Isaiah started reading it aloud.

Dear Isaiah and Moses,

Your Granddaddy asked me to write you a letter to tell you that your gramma died. Her breathing got really bad and she went to the Lord two nights ago. Your granddaddy said it was a blessing that her suffering was over but he's real sad about her being gone.

Esther Johnson and Martha Carpenter from church have been helping him, cooking some meals, and going through her things.

Your granddaddy says he is alright and he wants you to finish your time at the farm.

But I ask you, Isaiah and Moses. Your granddaddy still works every day, but he's behind on the rent more than $18. If you can send him a little money, that would help.

Yours in the Lord,
Pastor Matthews

Isaiah lowered the letter and looked at Moses, tears flowing down both their faces.

"That's real bad news, Isaiah, Moses," Alwin said. "I'm sorry. If you want to send your Granddaddy some money, I can send it for you when I go to Peoria in a couple of days."

"Thank you, sah," said Isaiah wiping his eyes. "Would you mind if Moses and me went down to the bunkhouse?"

"Sure, Isaiah," said Alwin. "I don't mind. You and Moses take the rest of the day off."

The two boys walked together down the path to Bunkhouse 3. Isaiah put his arm around his brother's shoulder and they sang together...

I can taste that milk and honey
From the wilderness, I am
Goin' down, down, down, to the promised land

* * *

Later in the afternoon, Anika knocked on the bunkhouse door and came in carrying chicken sandwiches with homemade mayonnaise. "Moses. Isaiah," she said. "I'm so sorry about your Gramma. Alwin told me about it. I brought some sandwiches in case you're hungry."

The boys sat up and each took half a sandwich.

"Thank you, Miss Anika," said Isaiah. He lowered his head, looking at the floor. "Moses and me, we been talkin'. Granddaddy, he's all alone now and we's all he got." Isaiah breathed deeply. "He done everything for us. He's our family. We know he's hurtin'. We gotta be there with him."

The changes death brings were still fresh with Anika. She wasn't expecting this news, but she wasn't surprised. "You'd like to leave then? Go back to Alabama to be with your Granddaddy?"

Moses spoke up. "Yes, ma'am. We was sayin', maybe when you and Mr. Alwin go to town to get Corrie, you could drop us at the bank to get our money and then we could make our way to the train station."

"Yes, of course. I understand," Anika said. "We'll miss both of you so much. You've been such a great help this summer. I'll tell

Alwin." Anika got up to leave. "If there's anything I can do for you before you leave, please let me know."

"If you got a prayer for my Gramma and Granddaddy," said Isaiah, "that'd be much appreciated, ma'am."

"Of course. We'll pray tonight and remember them both."

"Thank you, ma'am. We sure is gonna miss this place," Isaiah added.

After Anika left, Moses laid back on his bunk. "Guess them pennies just ran outta luck."

* * *

"Moses. Isaiah. Alwin told us your Gramma died and that you're goin' home," Will said when he and Elmer reached the bunkhouse. "That's real bad news." Moses and Isaiah just nodded on their cots, lost and empty.

A few moments later, Elmer said, "But you can come back next year? We're all coming back, right?"

Isaiah hadn't thought anything beyond getting back to Alabama, but the answer was still easy. "Can't imagine we can leave Granddaddy next year, him bein' alone now. It was tough enough leaving him and Gramma this year. Rest of the family's all moved away."

"He can't lift things like he used to," Moses said. "We gotta be there to help."

There had been enough death on the farm this summer, but having Isaiah and Moses leave the farm forever felt like two more to Will and Elmer.

* * *

Two days later after breakfast, Isaiah and Moses looked up when Alwin came into the chow hall and walked to their table. Today, they'd be going home. Alwin asked them to follow him and the three of them went through the farmhouse kitchen and into the big room.

"Sit down, Moses, Isaiah," Alwin said pointing to the large dining table. Anika was already sitting there.

Once seated, Anika began, "We know you're still hurting about your Gramma and you need to be with your Granddaddy, but we have an idea." Anika looked across at Alwin.

"What if you brought your Granddaddy back here?" Alwin said. "There's so much work to do right now and your Granddaddy could help us out."

Isaiah and Moses looked at each other and then Isaiah said, "Thank you, Mr. Alwin. Fact is, Moses even mentioned that. But by the time we get to Alabama and we get him back here, the summer's almost over. And he'd have to pay rent on his shop all the time he's here."

Alwin chuckled. "No, that's not what we're saying. What if you brought your Granddaddy back here permanent?"

Moses raised an eyebrow at his brother.

Alwin continued. "You know the farm is growing. We got beef cattle now. We're going to start farming those hundred acres out back. We got repairs and additions we want to make to the farmhouse. For all this, we're gonna need more tools, machines, and equipment. And we'll need people to build and fix all of that."

Isaiah and Moses didn't look convinced. "That's a kind offer, Mr. Alwin," Moses said, "but I believe Granddaddy would get a little lonely here workin' by hisself over the winter months."

Anika laughed. "No, we mean all of you. All year. All the time. We'd fix up the outbuilding behind the stables, the one next to the trees. Bring in some beds, tables, put in a sink, a wood burning stove. We'd still pay you, of course."

Moses glanced at Isaiah, then at Anika. "You mean live here on the farm? All three of us? All the time?"

"That's what we mean, Moses," said Anika. "You think about it and let us know."

"Nothing to think about ma'am," beamed Moses. "What do ya think, Isaiah? Think Granddaddy would wanna come and work here? No family left back in Florence, anyways."

"Sure would," said Isaiah. "This here is his kinda work. And all of us bein' together. We just needa get back there and take care of a few things."

Alwin reached into his pocket and pulled out some bills. "Here's $30 Isaiah. That should be enough for the train home, pay Granddaddy's back rent, and take the train here with all of your belongings. We can pick you up at the train station."

Isaiah took the money and unfolded the three $10 bills. He showed them to Moses and both boys shook their heads. "Not sure we deserve all of this," Isaiah said.

"Well, you do deserve it, both of you," said Anika. "And remember, you're helping us, too. Helping us to keep the farm going."

Moses took one of the $10 bills from Isaiah and said, "This money here, it'd get us back real quick and take care of the rent, but we don't need all of it. You can take back this $10 bill. We can drive back in Granddaddy's motorcar."

"Your Granddaddy has an automobile?" asked Alwin.

"Yes, sah," said Moses. "We can drive back in Granddaddy's Fodgabaker."

"What? Fodgawhat? Never heard of those before," said Alwin.

"Yes, sah," said Isaiah. "That's what Granddaddy calls it. He welded it together outta car parts he collected. Looks real funny. When people ask him about it, he tells 'em it's a little bit of Ford, a little bit of Dodge, and a little bit of Studebaker. A Fodgabaker. Runs real good too."

"Okay, Moses," said Anika. "But you keep that money. You'll have to buy gasoline and maybe stay in a hotel on the way back."

"Thank you, ma'am," said Moses and he thought a minute. "Pastor Jannsen always says, 'The Lord giveth and the Lord taketh away.' Maybe sometimes it's the other way around."

Isaiah pushed the bills into his sock and they sat right next to the 1916, the 1912, and the 1909 Lincoln pennies.

* * *

The next morning, the Dodge left for Peoria to bring Corrie home from the hospital. But first, Alwin dropped Moses and Isaiah at the Peoria train station for their two-day trip to Alabama. They looked at their bank as they rode past it, happy to leave their summer wages untouched.

In mid-afternoon, the Dodge arrived back at the farm with Corrie. Vlinder and Alwin eased her out and onto crutches, but Corrie looked up the path to the farmhouse and shook her head. Alwin, Jakob, and Gerwin lifted Corrie and brought her up the path and into the farmhouse where the divan in the big room had been made up with sheets and pillows, keeping her close to the family. She'd sleep and heal there for now.

*　　*　　*

"Think I'll go to church today," Elmer said as he walked with Will to breakfast.

Once there, Pastor Jannsen spied Elmer at the front gate. "Elmer! It ees so gud to see yuu at da serveeces today! Welkomen!"

After the service, everyone gathered for apple cake and punch. Will stood with Elmer who didn't seem too concerned about hiding his right hand.

*　　*　　*

On Monday, Gerwin brought Bunkhouse 3 to the back field to finish clearing the 100 acres. With the final piles of brush still smoldering, the workers walked the fields, breathing smoke, collecting leftover limbs, and tossing them onto the embers.

Each day, Vlinder drove a buckboard filled with lunches for the workers in the back field. She and Will talked easy.

"How's Corrie?" asked Will.

"She's going to be alright," Vlinder said. "But it'll take a while. Months the doctor said."

"Is she using crutches?" asked Will.

"Not yet. Soon, I hope," said Vlinder. "Oh! Alwin told me that Moses and Isaiah are bringing their Granddaddy back to live on the farm."

"Yeah," said Will. "They're pretty happy about it. Might be another week or so until they get here."

Vlinder pointed at Will. "All that soot on you. Looks like that day at the beginning of summer. Only way I knew it was you were the dimples. Even the dirt can't cover those." Vlinder raised her head and looked at the workers. "Go on now, Will Parlor," said Vlinder. "Gerwin's bringin' you all back to the field."

"Maybe see you tomorrow?" said Will.

Vlinder smiled. "Maybe."

* * *

At lunch on Thursday, Vlinder said Corrie wanted him to come visit her.

"Sure," said Will. "I'd like to see how she's doing."

"Good," said Vlinder. "Wash a little of that soot off yourself when you're done and come on up to the farmhouse."

Before the dinner bell, Will walked through the farmhouse kitchen and knocked on the swinging door. To Will, the swinging door was what separated him from a hidden world, from the family, from Vlinder. He knew where and how she worked. Now, he'd see where she lived. Vlinder pushed the door open and smiled at Will. "Come on in."

Will stepped in, wide-eyed. The big room had a large round table in the center with three oil lamps circling a lavender vase, tall with flowers. Around the walls of the room were soft chairs with small wooden tables to their sides. A floor-to-ceiling bookcase sat against a side wall, the piano and a pot of lavender forget-me-nots in front of it.

Corrie was on the divan against the back wall, under three windows that looked across to the chow hall. She was propped up onto pillows and there was a too-big quilt that hung over the back of the divan, across Corrie, and crumpled into a mound on the floor. On the table in front of her sat a half-eaten cheese and honey sandwich. Vlinder stepped back and to the side. Corrie smiled when she saw Will.

"Hi, Will," Corrie said trying to hoist herself up. "I'm glad you came."

"Yeah, good to see you at home, Corrie. We were worried for a while." Will walked over to the table in front of Corrie. "Does it hurt? Vlinder said it still hurts."

Corrie tried to pull herself up a little further on the pillows. "Yes, it still hurts. I take some pills after dinner and that helps me sleep."

"That's good. It's good you can sleep." Although she was in pajamas and lying on pillows, she held herself like Vlinder, her eyes linked to her smile.

"I hardly remember what happened," Corrie said. "I remember seeing blood and I remember you wrapping my ankle. And when I was in the car, you told me not to worry." Corrie pushed herself up a little further, but grimaced. "Vlinder said that Moses and Isaiah are getting their Granddaddy and coming here to live on the farm."

"Yes, they sure are," Will nodded. "They should be here in a few days."

"I hope they're back in time for the party." said Corrie. "It's for Hans and my sixteenth birthday and my mother said that you, Elmer, Moses, and Isaiah should come. All of you helped that day I fell. It's in a few weeks on Sunday."

The dinner bell rang.

"I better get going," said Will. "It's time for dinner."

"You think you can come to the birthday party?" asked Corrie.

"Sure, we'll all come," Will said. "You keep getting better, Corrie."

"Okay, bye," said Corrie.

"Bye, Corrie."

Vlinder followed Will through the kitchen and out the farmhouse door. "She's got a crush on you, you know," Vlinder said, smiling at Will.

"Really?" said Will. "How can you tell?"

"Honestly, Will Parlor, how can you *not* tell?"

Will laughed and shrugged his shoulders. "I hardly knew what a crush was before I came to the farm."

"Do you know now?" asked Vlinder.

Will looked at Vlinder. "I think I do." He turned toward the chow hall but stopped. He turned back toward Vlinder. "You know, there's a lot of lavender in there."

"Told you," smiled Vlinder.

*   *   *

As August ended, harvesting started and the farm buzzed. Isaiah had gotten one of the binders repaired before he left to get Granddaddy, but the other one was waiting for a new belt. Workers walked the rows, picking and packing corn ears into bushel baskets. Days lasted past dusk. Per the agreement with the government, Alwin sent the corn to the Peoria train yards by horse and wagon, a long job without the steam tractor. The soybean plants were about ready, too. Once harvested, those would be shipped off as forage to farms around the Midwest, providing feed to the government sponsored cattle.

Other than a quick wave, Will seldom saw Vlinder. She even stayed at the farm on Sundays. "I don't like missing church," she told Will, "but father used to say the farm still needs its shepherds on Sundays. We take some time to read from the Bible and say prayers," she told Will from the lunch wagon one Friday. "My father took care of so much that we didn't know about. And we don't want Corrie staying at the house alone."

Vlinder didn't have to give a reason to Will. He was sure that she could run the whole farm by herself if she had to.

CHAPTER 28

On the second Friday in September, Will and Elmer were heading to the morning wagons when first they heard, then they saw, Moses hanging out the side of Granddaddy's home-made motorcar. He had one hand cupped around his mouth and used both lungs...

The good times are coming, they're almost here,
The good times are coming, I hear 'em near;
The good times are coming,
The good times are near.

Granddaddy pulled the Fodgabaker to the front gate and it was surrounded by the workers. Alwin and Vlinder bounded out the front door of the farmhouse followed by Anika. Isaiah and Granddaddy stepped out of the car, but since the Fodgabaker had solid sides behind the front doors, Moses crawled out through a rear window.

Anika took a hand of Moses and of Isaiah in each of hers. "It's so good to see both of you. But it's early. Where did you drive from?"

Isaiah spoke up, "Well, Miss Anika, we gots to St. Louis sometime yesterday afternoon, but after having somethin' to eat, there wasn't no sleepin' for us. We was too excited, so we just left and drove through the night. Brought some extra gasoline and missed most of the road holes."

Granddaddy stood next to Moses with a wide grin and a top tooth. He had bits of short gray hair and he curved over slightly at the waist. One eye looked direct, but the other wandered left, and he wore brown suspenders over a dark blue shirt.

"You must be Granddaddy," Anika said. "We've heard so much about you, but I don't even know your real name."

Granddaddy grinned and nodded. "My name is Abraham, ma'am. Abraham Butler."

Anika shook Abraham's hand. "Well, Mr. Butler, I'm glad you made it. It's so good to have all of you here." Anika turned serious. "We know you recently lost your wife and I know that wasn't easy. I recently lost my husband. Things are never the same after that."

"No, ma'am, and thank you kindly," Abraham said. "But when Moses and Isaiah got home and told me about comin' here to work and live, I tell you ma'am, was like God hisself put his hand on my shoulder. Comin' here, I owe you a debt of gratitude, ma'am."

Anika smiled. "I'm afraid you've got that backwards, Mr. Butler." Anika moved behind Moses and put her hands on his shoulders. "I don't know if he told you, but Moses here, he helped save my daughter Corrie's life. He fixed our Dodge and we got her to the hospital in time. If he hadn't fixed it…I don't know what would have happened." Anika looked at Granddaddy. "And we know who taught Moses how to fix things. It's us who owe you the debt of gratitude."

Granddaddy put a wrist up to tear. "Thank you, ma'am. Moses done told me he fixed somethin' for ya, but he didn't tell me all the particulars."

Alwin stepped forward. "Moses, Isaiah, good to have you back on the farm. We've been afraid to break anything without you two around. Binder belt came in yesterday. Get that one working when you can."

Moses and Isaiah smiled full. "Sure thing, Mr. Alwin."

Alwin continued. "You can put Granddaddy's things into the outbuilding. We put a bed, table, a few chairs in there. No privy yet. Closest one down behind Bunkhouse 2." Alwin turned to

Granddaddy. "I can get you wood to build a privy. Just let me know what you need. Build one inside, if you like."

"That'd be all right, sir. I'll build one shortly," Granddaddy said. "And for now, if I find myself behind a tree from time to time, I don't mind. Figure if it was good enough for Adam and Eve, it's good enough for me."

"We'll get the stove and well-pump working up there," Alwin said, "but for now you can eat in the chow hall with the workers, or if you'd like, Moses and Isaiah can bring breakfast and dinner up to your place. We'll bring you lunch at the back barn, like for Moses and Isaiah."

"Yes, sah. That'd be just fine," Granddaddy said.

"Okay," Alwin said to Granddaddy. "Take a day or two to get settled. Look around the farm. Then you can head down to the back barn and work alongside Moses and Isaiah."

"Thank ya kindly. I'm fixin' to get to work real soon," Granddaddy said.

Alwin walked over to the Fodgabaker. "I gotta say. I've never seen anything that looks like this. The boys said you put it together yourself. That right?"

"Yes, I did, sah," said Granddaddy. "Got parts from all over and had to make a few."

"Granddaddy, tell 'em about the transmissions," said Moses.

"Well, now," Granddaddy said. "Couldn't find a transmission for it and couldn't afford a new one. The way life works, finally bought a used one for $14 from the junkyard, and at the same time, someone at church gave me one that needed fixin'. Didn't know what to do with two, so I fixed the second one and put 'em both in."

"Yeah," said Moses. "And now he got a low and high-speed goin' forwards and backwards!"

Isaiah started laughing and slapped his leg. "Yes indeed, and last summer, Granddaddy took the Fodgabaker to the auto races over in Huntsville. Came in second place going backwards the whole way! Got his picture in the paper standin' right next to the Fodgabaker.

Made everyone in Florence real proud, beatin' those highfalutin car-folk in Huntsville."

Everyone laughed and Alwin stuck his head into the Fodgabaker and saw the two gearshifts. "I swear, that's something right there, Mr. Butler," Alwin said. "You can park it behind the back barn. Show him where Isaiah, Moses. Then you can bring his things up to his house."

"Yes, Mr. Alwin," said Moses and Isaiah.

Granddaddy turned toward Anika, Alwin, and Vlinder and smiled. "Mighty fine to be here with you folks. Mighty fine."

Isaiah and Granddaddy got in the Fodgabaker and Moses crawled through the back window. Then they drove it along the side of the farmhouse, down the path, and behind the back barn.

* * *

The boys were part way through dinner when the floor of the chow hall trembled.

Kachug............

Kachug............Chug........Chug.......Chug......Chug....

Chug..Chug..Chug..Chug..Chug.

Will looked toward the serving tables and saw Vlinder smile. She hustled around the side and out the door followed by Will and several other boys.

Alwin was already at the back barn, his hands on his hips. From around the side of the barn, the steam tractor blew puffs and boom-chugs that shivered through each boy.

Granddaddy sat behind the wheel and Moses stood on the frame, one hand on Granddaddy's shoulder and the other waving at the gathering crowd. "OOOOOWEEE!" he yelled. The steam tractor rolled to the front of the back barn and stopped. Moses jumped to the ground and Granddaddy turned off the valve.

"All set, Mr. Alwin," Moses announced as Alwin walked to the tractor.

Alwin looked up at the massive engine. "Looks like Granddaddy went right to work."

"Yes, sah," said Moses. "Guess I kept puttin' a couple of the rods on backwards or somethin'. Granddaddy saw it first thing. She steamed right up after that."

"Well, that's gonna make a big difference, from threshin' to haulin'." Alwin looked up at Granddaddy. "Good job, Mr. Butler."

Everyone headed back to the chow hall to finish dinner and Granddaddy came in and sat alongside Moses and Isaiah. Afterwards, the four friends and Granddaddy headed to Granddaddy's House, as they began to call it. Once inside, there was plenty of advice on what should go where, but most attention was on where Granddaddy could build an indoor privy.

*   *   *

At 9 p.m., Gerwin came by Bunkhouse 3, shut off the gas lamps, and headed back up to the farmhouse.

From under his bed, Moses said to no one special, "Good to be back here on the farm."

"Why you here?" asked Roy. "Thought you'd be livin' up there with that granddaddy of yours."

"No beds up there yet, Roy," Isaiah said.

"I'll help you move 'em," said Roy. "And that other one of you, he just needs the floor."

"Roy, if you don't keep quiet," Elmer said. "I'm gonna put my hand right on your face when you're asleep."

Roy didn't say another thing, just bit off a nail and flicked it on the floor.

*   *   *

Almost a week later, lunch was over and Will walked to the lunch wagon where Vlinder was stacking dishes. "Is that a leftover cookie?" he asked.

"Might be," Vlinder said.

"Well, if you pass it over here," Will said. "I can keep it in my pocket. Might remind me of someone on the farm all afternoon."

"Will Parlor, if you think sweet talk is gonna work for you, you might be right." Vlinder passed the cookie to Will with a smile he hadn't seen in several weeks.

"Don't forget," said Vlinder. "After lunch on Sunday, come up to the house for Corrie and Hans' birthday party."

"Yeah, I'm lookin' forward to it," Will said.

Vlinder saw Moses, Isaiah, and Elmer sitting with their lunch plates and yelled to them. "Hey, Moses, hey, Isaiah, Elmer, you're coming to the birthday party on Sunday, right?"

Isaiah beamed. "Sure thing, Miss Vlinder." He paused. "Ain't got a birthday present, though. We could get somethin' next time in Peoria."

"No presents Isaiah, please," said Vlinder. "Corrie just wants to see you all. There'll be other friends, food, and a big cake. Mother'll play the piano and Pastor Jannsen is coming, too. Oh, and be sure to bring Granddaddy."

"Yes, ma'am. I'm sure he'd enjoy comin'," said Moses. He turned to Isaiah and whispered, "We gettin' her a present in Peoria. A lot of 'em."

"I know what ya thinkin'," Isaiah whispered back to his brother.

* * *

After church on Sunday, Moses brought Granddaddy over and introduced him to Pastor Jannsen.

"Welkom, Welkom, Mr. Butler," Pastor Jannsen said shaking Granddaddy's hand with both of his. "You have two fine grandsons heer."

"Thank ya kindly, Pastor," Granddaddy said. "It's good to be here with all you fine folks and I certainly enjoyed yo' message today." He turned to his grandson. "And Moses was right. You got some fine words you use in your talks. What was that one today? Digil...Digala."

"*Diligent,* Granddaddy," said Moses. "Means you gotta keep at it."

Pastor Jannsen put a hand on Moses' shoulder and smiled. "I'm glaad that at leest someone ees listening, Moses."

CHAPTER 29

After lunch, several wagons, two Ford Model T's, and a Chevrolet 490 sat outside the farmhouse and soon the four boys were knocking at the kitchen door. Down the path from his new home, Granddaddy met them, a paper bag under his arm.

"Whatchu got there?" Isaiah said, pointing to the bag.

"Present for Corrie and Hans. Checkerboard and checkers I made down in the barn," Granddaddy said.

"Told you, no presents," said Moses, tossing down his yo-yo again and again.

"Had to bring something," Granddaddy said. "Can't go to no birthday party without no present."

"Well, we got nothin'," Moses said.

"You said you was gonna get them a present in town later," Granddaddy said.

"Yeah, but that ain't today," Isaiah said. "You walkin' in with a present and we walkin' in with nothin'."

"Alright, then," Granddaddy said. "I'll just say this here is from all of us."

The matter seemed settled when Betty Granger heard the knock and opened the back door to the kitchen.

"Vlinder said you'd all be coming to the party," Betty said. "We're all going, too. This is so much fun!" They walked into the kitchen where house and kitchen workers were gathered around the center tables, finishing platters of ham, two carved turkeys, macaroni and cheese, sliced potatoes with Anika's homemade mayonnaise, cooked carrots, pickles, and bowls of cut fruit. Alongside were three loaves of bread, jars of honey, apple jelly, and a tin of peanut butter, a rare treat. A half-table sized cake with chocolate and buttercream icing sat in the middle. To its side, was a large oval platter, stacked high with Oreo biscuits, a recent arrival to local stores.

Granddaddy stared across the tables. "Ain't gonna go hungry with all this!"

"Come on," Betty said. "A lot of people are already here." She motioned the party guests to follow her and swung open the door to the big room. Inside, were the Helgevelds, the Van der Beeks, and a few other people from church, but many of the partygoers were unknown to the five. A brightly colored sign hung over the front window. *Happy Birthday Corrie and Hans!* And under it, *Get Well Soon Corrie!* Next to the window sat a table with several presents and Granddaddy dropped his there.

The platters of food followed them into the big room and everyone quieted and bowed their heads while Pastor Jannsen offered a blessing. "Deare Lord abuve. Plees bless dis wondeerful food and this hoppy time. Pleese bless Corrie and Hans on dis their sixteen beerthday. In da naam of or Lord, Amen."

Will looked around and saw Corrie standing with crutches next to the divan. Hans stood with her, keeping an eye on his twin. Even standing with her crutches, Will saw that Corrie was almost as tall as Vlinder. He gave her a wave and went over.

"Corrie," said Will pointing to the crutches. "That looks good. You must be getting better."

"I hope so," she said. "I got up with the crutches a few days ago. I'm taking a few steps. Watch." Corrie held her injured foot off the floor and moved herself forward with the crutches and good leg.

"You'll be twirling in no time," Will said.

"The doctor is coming next week to see how I'm doing," Corrie said.

"Good," Will said. There was a pause and smile between them. Will looked down and saw punch on the table in front of Corrie.

"You've got some punch. I'm going to get some, but I'll talk to you later, Corrie."

"Okay. Good," she said.

Will lingered for a moment. "I didn't expect to see you looking this good, walking and getting better."

"Thanks, Will," Corrie said.

The room was full and Will wove his way to the punch table.

Lotta and Bram, along with four or five friends, ran across the big room, out the front door, across the porch, and jumped off the railing. On the other side of the room, Will saw Moses give something to Corrie. She smiled and put it in her pocket.

Anika sat at the piano and played songs that everyone knew: *In the Good Old Summertime, Take Me Out to the Ballgame, Yankee Doodle, Put On Your Old Gray Bonnet, Won't You Come Home Bill Bailey* and others. About a dozen guests stood around Anika, holding plates of food and singing along.

Gerwin and Bram were to the side, talking with the Van der Beek sons, and in the group, Will spied Cornelius Van der Beek, Vlinder's church suitor. Will turned to see Vlinder smiling at him and then looking over at Cornelius. She looked back at Will, crossed her hands across her chest, and smiled. "Help!" she mouthed. Will laughed and went over.

"Just in time," said Vlinder. "I saw him looking around, but I guess he didn't see me yet."

"Good thing I came along," Will said. "I'd hate to find you on the floor, bored to death."

Vlinder laughed. "You're not far off with that." They turned and listened to the guests singing around Anika. Vlinder leaned over and whispered to Will. "We weren't sure if we could play music on Sunday, but Pastor Jannsen said that since it was a birthday, and it fell on Sunday, it would be alright."

Put on your old gray bonnet,
With the blue ribbons on it
While I hitch old Dobbins to the shay...

"Your mother's such a good piano player," Will said. "We listen to her after dinner when we go behind the farmhouse, up near the big sycamore tree."

"That piano is part of the family," Vlinder said. "I tried to play for a while, but it wasn't for me. Actually, Lotta is pretty good at it. I hope she keeps it up." Vlinder leaned forward and looked at the window behind Corrie. "Who's that?" she said to Will. "Is that Roy?" Will looked and saw Roy, his hands cupped around his eyes, peering in through the window. Will took a quick step toward the kitchen and Roy left. Vlinder looked at Will and shook her head. "Every summer, seems there's somebody like him who comes to the farm. He gives me the creeps."

Pastor Jannsen stood to the side with Granddaddy, Moses, Alwin, and Elmer. Moses pointed to two chairs that he and Isaiah had repaired when they worked that day in the kitchen. Alwin looked at Moses and Elmer and smiled. "Was that the day you tried painting the cows? Would that be true?"

Moses looked toward the ceiling. "Wouldn't know anything about that, Mr. Alwin," All five broke out laughing.

Alwin looked around. "Time for cake," he yelled. Betty and another kitchen worker brought the cake to a cleared area on the center table. Gerwin followed with the platter of Oreo biscuits.

As the crowd quieted, Anika got up from the piano and stepped in front of the cake. "Thank you all for coming today. As you're getting your cake, I want to introduce you to the workers who made this day a very happy one." Anika pointed around the room and called up Moses, Will, Isaiah, Elmer, and a reluctant Granddaddy. "I think you all know the story," Anika continued, "but here are the workers. Isaiah and Elmer, they helped get what was needed for Corrie from the barn and the bunkhouse the day she fell."

Anika moved over and behind Will and Moses, putting a hand on their shoulders. "And Will and Moses here. Will put a splint on Corrie's leg and slowed the bleeding. And Moses, thanks to his Granddaddy teaching him, fixed our Dodge that got Corrie to the hospital in time. We can never thank you all enough." Anika stepped back and clapped, the others in the room joining her. Corrie lifted her hands off the crutch handles and clapped along with everyone else.

Lotta, Bram, Vlinder, and Betty cut and passed out cake to all the guests and there was plenty left for seconds.

Moses stepped to a small table next to the front door, pulled a deck of playing cards from his pocket, and started shuffling them. He divided the cards into three piles which was supposed to draw an audience. It soon did. Pastor Jannsen saw the cards and was about to warn against card playing on Sundays until Isaiah told him they were just doing some card tricks for fun, no card playing.

Lotta and Bram, finished with their cake-cutting, came over. "You gonna do some more magic tricks, Moses?" asked Lotta. She turned to her friends and told them about the Fourth of July magic show that Moses put on.

"Gonna give it a try, Lotta," said Moses. "Here, I'll show you." Moses picked up the cards and shuffled them together. Then he spread the deck face down in front of Lotta and told her to pick a card, look at it, but don't tell anybody what it is.

"Okay," Lotta said. She chose a card toward the right of the spread and saw it was the Queen of Clubs.

"Remember your card, Lotta," Moses said.

"I will. I'll remember it," she said.

Moses held the deck of cards in the palm of his hand and told Lotta to push her card in any place she wanted.

Lotta nodded and pushed her card into the deck.

Moses took the deck and carefully shuffled it. "Now, Lotta, I'm gonna spread the cards out on the table and I'll show you your card." Moses spread the cards face up in front of her, but one card was face down. "I believe if you turn that card over, it'll be yours."

The crowd watched Lotta turn over the Queen of Clubs.

"Moses! That's it! The Queen of Clubs," said Lotta. The crowd clapped their approval.

Moses looked around, and spotted Alwin. "Mr. Alwin, maybe you'd like to try a card trick?"

"Sure, Moses," said Alwin stepping to the table. "But I think I know how you do them. They do these tricks down at Alfresco Park in Peoria. I just have to watch you carefully when you're shuffling the cards."

"Somethin' like that, Mr. Alwin. But I got a little different one for you." Moses shuffled the cards and spread the deck across the table, face down. "Here, pick a card from the deck. You look at it but keep it to yoself. Don't show nobody."

Alwin studied the cards and looked at Moses. "Alright, Moses. I'll take this one," and he choose a card just three from the end of the spread. He lifted the card to his chest, leaned it forward a little, and saw the eight of Diamonds.

Moses reassembled the deck, shuffled it, and held it out to Alwin. "Okay, Mr. Alwin. You put that card back wherever you want."

Alwin chose a spot in the middle of the deck and slid his card in. By now, most everyone at the party had circled the magician and the volunteer. Moses smiled at the crowd, paused, took a bite of cake, and then picked up the deck and shuffled it.

"Mr. Alwin," said Moses, "you tell me when to stop shuffling and I'll try to find your card."

Alwin nodded and waited for several shuffles. "Stop!" And Moses straightened the deck and put it on the table in front of Alwin.

"Now, Mr. Alwin," said Moses. "I believe that if you turn that top card over, it'll be your card."

"You think so, Moses?" Alwin said.

"I believe it is, sah."

Alwin reached down and turned over the four of Hearts. "Sorry, Moses. You sound like a real magician, though. Keep practicing."

Moses looked puzzled. "Wait, wait. That's right. Your card, it's on the bottom, Mr. Alwin."

Alwin turned the deck over only to find the nine of Clubs. He smiled. "Next time, Moses."

"I swear Mr. Alwin, I thought I had it." Moses picked up the deck and handed it to Alwin. "Could you flip through the deck here and show me where your card is?"

Will had moved over next to Elmer who whispered to him, "Moses is gonna get him. I saw him practicing this one."

Alwin took the deck and spread the cards in front of him, hunting for the eight of Diamonds. A quick look gave no results so Alwin spread the cards further apart examining them all. He looked at Moses. "It's not here."

"Not there?" asked Moses.

"I guess not," said Alwin, somewhat less confident.

"Well, Mr. Alwin," said Moses. "Maybe it's lost!" Moses looked across the crowd. "Anybody know where there's a playing card? Anybody seen one? We lost one."

Corrie picked up on her cue. "I have one right here!" and she reached into her pocket and pulled out a card, facing it backwards from Alwin.

"No! No! That can't be it!" said Alwin and he dashed across the room to Corrie and grabbed the card, turning it around to find the eight of Diamonds. His mouth open, Alwin turned to the crowd. "This is it! The eight of Diamonds! Moses! Moses! That's impossible! How did you do that?"

"Sorry, Mr. Alwin. A magician never tells how he does a trick."

The crowd cheered and laughed.

The presents were next, each family providing one gift for the twins. There was a bagful of beef jerky, a box of peanut brittle, a shirt with *Corrie* stitched onto it, and from another family, a shirt with *Hans* on it. Two books, *Anne of Green Gables* and *The Lost Prince*. There was stationary and handkerchiefs for Corrie and a fishing pole and jigsaw puzzle for Hans.

Vlinder and Anika thanked Granddaddy for the checkerboard and asked how he was settling in. Granddaddy assured them he was more than comfortable and welcomed the work.

"It's sure fine hearing you play that piano, Miss Anika," Granddaddy said.

"Why, thank you, Mr. Butler," Anika said. "I could play again if you'd like. Is there anything you'd enjoy hearing?"

"Well," Granddaddy said, thinking. "If you know a waltz, ma'am, I'd enjoy hearing that. Mrs. Butler and me, we'd always try to dance together when we heard one."

"Yes, of course," Anika said. "I haven't played one for a while, but I know a few." Anika sat in front of the keyboard and placed her hands on the keys. The waltz started slowly, softly, turning everyone in the room toward the piano. The music jumped faster, rising, falling. The crowd swayed, many humming the rhythm. Moses and Isaiah stood next to Granddaddy who was smiling, wiping a tear. Will searched for Vlinder and found her standing by herself, leaning against a wall, her hands behind her. He eased toward her, sliding between guests who were focused on Anika and the waltz.

Vlinder saw him and smiled. "That's Tchaikovsky," she said. "Mother plays these at Christmas, but it's good to hear them now."

Will listened and then gathered courage. "You said Gramma Luna taught you how to dance. Can you teach me?"

"Here!? Now?" Vlinder asked.

Will nodded.

Vlinder looked around and across the room. "Okay, come on." She took Will's hand and they went to a small area beneath the stairs. "I had to check first. Pastor Jannsen is across the room and he wouldn't like it if he saw us dancing on Sunday."

The music surrounded them and the two dancers faced each other. Vlinder looked at Will and said, "Put your hand here." Vlinder took Will's left hand and put it around her waist. She lifted his right hand with her left and held it out straight. "Now," she said, "count to three with the rhythm of the waltz. 1,2,3. 1,2,3. To that rhythm, step forward with your right foot, swing your left foot forward and across, and then bring your right foot over to it."

"What?!" said Will.

Vlinder smiled. "Just follow my lead and watch my feet." She pulled Will toward her and counted to the music. 1,2,3, 1,2,3. Vlinder moved the two dancers forward, across, then back, and soon they added a turn in the space under the stairs. "That's it. You've got it," she said.

The waltz finished, but the crowd wanted another. Anika obliged.

Vlinder listened. "That's Strauss. It's my favorite."

The two danced again, Will still watching his feet, but adding confidence to his steps. They spun, Vlinder still using her arm and hand to ease Will left, then right. "Mother told me that when she played this," Vlinder said, "Grampa Bartel and Gramma Luna would dance around the big room and then right under these stairs."

They spun and swayed, Will looking at Vlinder, holding stares and smiles. Then Vlinder looked over Will's shoulder. "I think someone else might want a dance."

Will turned to see Corrie standing behind him on her crutches. She smiled at them both. "Can I have a birthday dance, Will?" Corrie asked.

Will looked at Vlinder and back at Corrie. "Sure. But I'm not very good."

"Well, look at me!" Corrie said. "If I can stand up and not fall over, it'll be a good dance."

The three laughed and Vlinder stepped to the side. Will walked over and put his hands on Corrie's shoulders while she held the crutch handles. The two slightly swayed to Strauss, following Will's 1,2,3…1,2,3…. as best they could. Corrie took her hands off the crutch handles and put them on Will's waist. Vlinder watched them both, clapping to the rhythm.

Will looked at Corrie and then over at Vlinder. What was it about this summer, this farm, and this Helgeveld family, Will wondered.

CHAPTER 30

A
s September moved along, Granddaddy kept both binders working. He operated the older one himself, hopping off to fix one thing after another to keep it cutting and bundling the soybean stalks, low and clean. Most of those stalks were bundled for silage, while the beans were sent off as feed grain. Baskets of corn, followed by wagonloads of soybean stalks and beans, made their way to town, early and late.

An official from Washington came to Peoria to coordinate the collecting, loading, and shipping of all crops in the area. Extra trains were added, and on Saturdays, people from as far away as Bloomington came to the train yard to watch their state send food across the country, then across the ocean, to feed U.S. soldiers soon to arrive in Europe. Pastor Jannsen and several other clergy stood on platforms, blessing the shipments, and praying for an early end to the war.

On a Thursday late in September, the doctor came to the farm to check on Corrie. She was healing well. The doctor said she should continue walking with the crutches and keep taking the pain pills for sleep if she needed them. He'd be back at the end of October to check on her again.

* * *

"I can't go to Peoria for payday tomorrow," Vlinder told Will from the lunch wagon on Thursday. "I wish I could but with Corrie out, there's too much to do in the kitchen and in the house. Lotta,

Hans, and Bram are staying here. Mother too. We can't take the day off with this heavy harvest."

Will was disappointed. He'd imagined a final trip to Peoria with Vlinder, like the first. They'd walk together, Vlinder pointing into shops. He'd buy her lunch. They'd go to the outskirts of Peoria, walk roads without sidewalks, past fields and colossal sycamores. They'd stand under one and he'd look into her. So much time had passed since their walk to the cemetery. Perhaps this time, he had thought.

Instead, he came up with another idea.

*   *   *

On September 28, the final Friday payday of the season, the workers climbed into the wagons.

"Where's Granddaddy?" Elmer asked Moses.

"Not comin'," Moses said. "Said he didn't wanna walk around Peoria all day with a bunch of kids. Said he'd run one of the binders today and we can pack it all up tomorrow. Alwin's gonna hold his pay for now."

The workers bounced and swayed along the road to Peoria.

"What are you all doin' today?" asked Will in the wagon.

"Goin' to our bank," said Isaiah. "Then head down to the lake. Granddaddy wanted a few things."

"Celia down there, Moses?" asked Elmer.

Moses leaned over and looked at him. "Don't know. Don't know if she'll be there or not."

"Oh, she'll be there alright," Isaiah laughed. "Maybe wearin' that red dress she had on last time. And her hair put up all pretty again."

Moses looked at Isaiah. "Now, why you bein' like that?"

"And you can tell her you livin' 'round here now," Isaiah said. "You be able to see her all sorts of times."

Moses couldn't hold back a smile. "Yeah, I suppose I could mention that."

*   *   *

When they left the bank, Will and Elmer had $144 in their accounts. They'd be back to Peoria in another few weeks, collect their final pay, and head home with close to $170. They couldn't believe the fortune.

Will and Elmer found Nathan Carey and Lucas Miller and the four boys headed to the more familiar streets of Peoria. Lunch was at the Peoria Diner, but this time they proudly ordered blueberry pancakes with syrup and two eggs with bacon, feeling that having breakfast for lunch must be breaking some sort of rule.

Afterwards, they walked back to Block & Khul's department store. Will had visited department stores back in Pittsburgh, but Elmer, Nathan, and Lucas had never been in a store that sold almost everything: clothes, food in packages, hardware, medicines, furniture, farm supplies, toys, soaps, pillows, and blankets. Even Will hadn't seen all the new electric inventions that were in Block & Khul's.

"Looka this," said Lucas. "This here's one of those electric vacuum cleaners. Ladies push them over the floor and they pick up the dirt. Don't need a broom."

All four moved over and stood in front of an electric stove. "I suppose you turn those knobs there and you cook on it," said Will.

"So it makes the food electric? How does it get hot?" wondered Nathan. Nobody knew.

Outside Block & Khul's, the boys shared stories of electric irons, electric fans, electric coffee makers, and electric lamps. Elmer commented that probably nothing else ever needed to be invented.

Will announced, "I'm going to buy a few things for home. You guys go ahead and I'll meet you at the church."

"Now? Why don't you get them when you come to Peoria to go home?" Lucas said.

"I know," Will answered, "but they're small and I want to make sure they don't sell out before then," Will said.

That answer seemed reasonable to the others, so Will headed off. But he wasn't buying something for home. He was buying something for Vlinder.

Will wasn't sure where to head, but further down Main Street, he stood with his hands cupped around his eyes peering into the jewelry store window of L. E. McKown. Vlinder had told Will about the gold chain her father bought for his mother and there were several in the window. Even back in Pittsburgh, Will had never been in a jewelry store, but he imagined you buy things in there just like everywhere else. So, he opened the door and stood between two rows of jewelry cases, one on each side of the store.

Inside, an ample woman wearing a white blouse with a gray jacket and gray dress stood at the counter. There were several hatpins laid out in front of her on a black satin tray. The balding store clerk stood waiting for her decisions. Will looked around, but listened to the interaction, hoping it would help him know what to do in a jewelry store.

"These up here at the top," the woman pointed. "They're too big," she told the clerk. "They call attention to themselves, so I certainly don't want any of those."

"I agree, madam," the clerk said. Then he pointed to another selection. "Here are some of the newer designs you might like. They're in a variety of colors. What do you think of these?"

"Colored hat pins? Red? Green? I think not!"

The clerk chose another pin and picked it up. "These are becoming more popular, madam. They're just in from New York, items from nature. This one is a bird in flight."

"I *detest* birds," the women said.

That conversation didn't help Will, but he did spy a selection of gold jewelry and he stepped to the case. A woman, perhaps his mother's age, appeared from the back. She moved to where Will was standing and said, "How can I help you today, sir?"

Will had never been called *sir* before and he wondered if it was a mistake coming into this foreign territory. He smiled at the woman, but quickly looked back through the glass case at rings, charms, necklaces, bracelets, earrings, watches, and pins.

"Um...Um...I think maybe. I saw some necklaces in the window. They look a little like those," Will said pointing to a row of gold necklaces spread across a red satin tray.

The woman reached under the counter and pulled out the tray. "These?" she asked. Will nodded. "Yes, these are elegant," she said, "and all are 14-karat gold. Is there one you particularly like?"

Will studied the twenty or so necklaces in front of him. "Um…maybe that one?" Will pointed to a necklace right in the middle. "It's pretty," he said. "Do you think someone would like it?"

"This one?" asked the woman. "Oh, yes. It's a herringbone design. Ladies love these and they can be worn for formal occasions or for every day."

The woman handed it to Will and he felt its weight tumbling between his fingers. He imagined Vlinder hooking it together behind her neck. Wearing it all day. Remembering him and knowing he'd be back next summer. It was beautiful.

"How much is this?" he asked.

"This particular piece is $28.75," the woman replied.

Will didn't look up, but handed the necklace back to the woman. "Thank you. I think I'll look at some other things."

The woman smiled. "Silver is elegant, and beautiful as well. And it's much more reasonably priced." She pointed two cases further up. "Just there, we have an excellent selection if you're interested."

Will looked up at the silver alternatives but didn't move. He wanted gold and looked back down into the case. Surrounding the gold necklaces in the display case were gold bracelets, gold rings, and gold earrings. What do ladies like? What would Vlinder like? What wouldn't cost more than an entire month's wages? There were so many choices.

Sitting to the side was a tray of gold charms, and Will leaned over to examine them. There were dogs, the sun, babies, *Peoria* spelled out in gold, flowers, and many other designs. Toward the bottom of the tray was a charm with two people dancing. The woman wore a long dress and the man held her hand up and looked deep into her. Will's eyes widened. "That one. Could I see that one?" Will pointed. "The one with two people dancing,"

The woman reached into the case. "Yes, gold charms are also very popular. Ladies like these as well." She put the charm in Will's hand. He turned it over and saw the man's arm around the woman's waist. Both dancers were smiling. There was a small loop at the top where Vlinder could hang it from a necklace or pin it to a dress. Yes, this was the one.

"How much is this?" Will asked, flattening his hand and holding the charm in his palm.

"That piece is $9.85."

Will studied it again. He had kept out $15 from his pay and said, "I like this one. I think I'll take this one."

The woman nodded and said, "I like these charms because they often have a special meaning."

"Yes, we danced one time. I think she'll like it."

"I'm sure she will, sir," the woman said. "Would you like me to gift wrap it for you?"

"You can do that? Yes, that would be good. Thank you," said Will.

"Certainly, sir." The woman took the charm and wrapped it in white tissue paper before placing it in a small gift box. She moved to the back of the store to cut a piece of ribbon.

Will was pleased with his purchase and with his first journey into a jewelry store. He continued to scan the glass cases, stopping at the silver section. "Wait, Ma'am. Can I take a look at these, too?" Will said pointing at the silver necklaces.

The woman returned and pulled out the tray of silver necklaces and put it in front of Will. "Silver necklaces are perhaps our best sellers."

Will picked up a silver necklace at the edge of the tray. "This design looks like the gold one. How much is it?"

"Yes," said the woman. "It's also herringbone. Slender and elegant. This piece is $2.15."

Will held it up between his thumb and finger and turned it around. It was shiny and pretty. Will thought she'd like it. "Thank you," Will said to the woman. "I'll take this, too."

"I can wrap them together," the woman said, "However, I must tell you that ladies don't generally wear a gold charm on a silver necklace."

Will handed the necklace to the woman. "Oh, no. You can wrap it separately. It's for someone else."

CHAPTER 31

At 4 p.m., the crowd of workers had gathered outside the Dutch Reformed Church, ready to head back to the farm.

"Everybody here?" asked Alwin. "You know anybody missing?" Nobody spoke. "The wagons are a little full. We put food and supplies down the middle of each wagon so the sitting might be a little tight. We should be home near dinner time, maybe a little after."

The boys scrambled into the wagons, ready to tell their stories and show their purchases. Will put a jewelry box into each pocket and told the others that he'd buy gifts for home the next time in Peoria.

"What's in the bag," Elmer asked Moses.

Moses smiled and held up a large, soggy paper bag. "Got Corrie and Hans' birthday presents right here."

At the end of the wagon sat Roy, a small paper bag tucked under his arm. Everyone expected to hear about his purchase, but Roy never said a thing.

* * *

On the final Sunday of September, the only sound interrupting the hour and a half church sermon was the occasional laugh by Moses and Granddaddy at one of Pastor Jannsen's jokes.

Vlinder and Will sought each other out at the end of the service and stood to the side of the punch table. Only a few more weeks. Only a few more church services.

"You got a few letters over the summer," said Vlinder. "Guess they're from back home. Lookin' forward to seeing your family?"

"Yes...sure. I miss my mother and father. I miss them all. I'll work in the feed store afternoons and weekends until school is finished," said Will.

"That sounds good," said Vlinder. "Alwin told me that you're staying here an extra week."

"Yes," said Will. "He said I can leave with the last workers toward the end of October. I can start school late if I'm working on a farm."

"And back in April?" said Vlinder.

"Or sooner, I hope. I'll tell Alwin I can come sooner if he needs me."

"Yes, ask him," Vlinder said.

"How's Corrie?" asked Will.

"I think Moses and Isaiah's sour pickles were as good as any medicine," Vlinder laughed. "They brought her and Hans enough for a week. And she's doing well. She's getting up on her crutches. Still some pain though."

Three of the summer workers from the Van der Beek kitchen were bringing more punch and trays of peach cake to the tables. One of the girls in a yellow kitchen dress with red-haired pigtails, tripped on a root, sending her tray of peach cake everywhere. Much of it bounced off Elmer, who stood next to a table and managed to catch the young lady as she headed to the ground.

She righted herself, but Elmer knelt down, pushing split and tumbled pieces of cake back onto the tray.

The young lady knelt next to Elmer, almost crying. "I'm so sorry. This is such a mess! I can't believe I tripped! I hope Mr. Van der Beek isn't angry."

"He won't be angry," said Elmer looking at the girl. "He's a good man. It was an accident. I saw it."

The young girl looked at Elmer. The two stood up and Elmer put the tray of remnants on the table, his single finger bent over the tray.

"Thank you so much," said the young girl. She looked at Elmer. "I remember you. You ran really fast on the Fourth of July."

"Yes," said Elmer, lowering his head a bit. "Guess I just like to run."

"I'm Anna. Anna Wilton. Are you coming back to church next week?"

"Yes, I'm comin' back...and my name is Elmer Duggan."

"Pleased to meet you, Elmer. I hope I see you next week...at church, I mean." And Anna reached out and shook Elmer's hand.

* * *

After lunch, Will and Elmer wove their way to the back barn where they could hear the welding machine roaring from inside. As they got closer, they saw sparks and flashes bounce off the door and the sharp smell of burned metal filled their noses. Outside, Granddaddy was singing hymns and cutting lumber for the indoor privy. Earlier, Alwin agreed that if he bought two pull-chain flush toilets, Granddaddy could install one in his house and one in the main farmhouse.

"Yes, sah, I believe that would be a fine arrangement," said Granddaddy. Within three days, he'd finished digging the septic pits for both toilets, connecting a pipe into each house.

With Isaiah welding, Granddaddy sawing, and Moses hoisting soybean plants to the second floor of the barn, Will and Elmer fell fast asleep in the grass.

* * *

Monday during dinner, Alwin told the workers that more than 100,000 U.S. soldiers were arriving in Europe to fight alongside French, British, and Italian soldiers. He said that he still worried that the Dutch could be drawn into the war, but he felt that the efforts of Helgeveld Farm, and other farms across the nation, as some help needed for a speedy end to the Great War.

In the back field, Bunkhouse 2 and 3 finished plowing and flattening the newly cleared acres. Afterwards, they spread winter rye that soon sprouted, sending roots deep, holding and nourishing the soil for spring plowing and planting.

∗   ∗   ∗

On the first Saturday evening in October, most of the workers were back in Bunkhouse 3, some getting clothes ready for church, others laying on their beds talking about the end of summer and of going home.

Heads rose toward the front door, where outside, Alwin and Gerwin were shouting at someone. Alwin pulled open the bunkhouse door, and he and Gerwin held and lifted Roy under each of his arms. Once inside, they tossed him onto his bed.

"Monday, Monday first thing! You're on your way to Peoria! We're putting you on the train and we'll be done with you!" yelled Alwin, pointing at Roy. "You've gotten every chance here, but no more!"

Alwin and Gerwin stood over him for a minute and then moved to leave. Alwin stopped and turned, pointing to a set of binoculars hung over his own shoulder. "And don't think you're ever getting these back!" The Helgeveld brothers left the bunkhouse, their brisk footsteps heading toward the farmhouse.

A half hour earlier, Lotta and Vlinder were in their bedroom above the farmhouse kitchen. A crack and a snap brought Lotta to their window. She peered toward the stable, then higher where the sound came from. There was no breeze, but a close-by poplar tree wobbled, the branches shaking one at a time. Vlinder came over, looked out, and told Lotta to turn off the lamp.

The two girls stared out the window.

"Look," said Vlinder pointing. "There. About halfway up. There's somebody there." She peered closer. "And he's looking at us!"

Vlinder ran out of her room and down the stairs. She motioned to Alwin and Gerwin to follow her and in seconds, the three Helgevelds were at the base of the poplar, staring up.

"Get outta that tree! Now!" yelled Alwin.

"Bet it's Roy," said Gerwin and he was right.

~ 247 ~

Roy climbed down and about six feet from the ground, he jumped from a branch, rolled, and tried to run. Alwin and Gerwin were on him.

"Let me go!" yelled Roy. "Can't you see I was just climbin' a tree here?!"

"With these?!" Alwin grabbed the binoculars around Roy's neck.

*   *   *

On the way to church the next day, the news of Roy leaving the farm spread among the workers. Everyone agreed. They wished Roy had left earlier in the season.

When Bunkhouse 3 got back from church, Nathan Carey walked past Roy who was lying on his bunk. "Be good to walk in the bunkhouse tomorrow and not have to smell your stink, Roy."

"Be good to get outta here, away from all of you," said Roy.

CHAPTER 32

It was well past midnight and Will couldn't sleep. Everything at the farm had a chapter in his mind: the bunkhouse, the farmhouse, the jewelry store, the diner, church, his mother, his father's store, Vlinder, Corrie, Anika, Joren, Alwin, Isaiah, Elmer, Moses, Granddaddy, everyone, everything, and over again.

There was a rustle across from Will and he opened one eye to see Roy sitting up and looking down the bunkhouse. There were half a dozen snorers in Bunkhouse 3, and this night, Roy timed his movements to their noisy rhythm. Roy filled a small bag on his bed with his few belongings and stood on a snore. He eased his way through the screen and onto the porch.

Will sat up and watched Roy's figure as it headed onto the path that led to the farmhouse. To Will, it looked like Roy was planning to escape before being taken to Peoria in a few hours. Will pulled on his pants, slid on his shoes, and followed Roy. He couldn't see him, but heard his steps, confirming that Roy was just reaching the farmhouse. Will hustled closer but saw nothing other than Roy's bag of belongings sitting at the back door of the farmhouse kitchen.

Will waited outside. It made sense that Roy would take some food for his cross-country escape. When he came out, Will would grab him. The kitchen was dark and Will waited. More minutes passed. Will peered through the kitchen window beside the door but could make out no movement.

Then a sound, but not from the kitchen.

Will's eyes widened and he knew where Roy was. He shot through the kitchen, through the swinging door and into the big room where Roy was on top of Corrie, one hand across her mouth and the other ripping at her pajama top. Corrie moaned, but the pain pills kept her helpless.

Will was on him, one hand clutching his hair and the other grabbing his belt. Will pivoted and threw Roy across the room where he knocked into a side table, launching an oil lamp into the front window. Roy got up, but Will lowered his shoulder into Roy's stomach, hurtling him onto the floor. Will straddled him and anger filled his punches.

The commotion brought Alwin and Vlinder bounding down the stairs. Vlinder rushed to Corrie who was wailing, screaming. Alwin ran and pulled Will off of Roy, turning him over and putting his knee on his back. Blood oozed from Roy's mouth, his front tooth on the floor to the side. From a quick look, Alwin and Vlinder guessed what had happened.

By now, all the family had come downstairs. Alwin and Gerwin lifted and tossed Roy into a chair. Roy stood up and Alwin stared at him. "You sit back down there or we'll all have a go at you. You understand?"

Roy fell into the chair. "Look what he did to me!" Roy bawled pointing to his mouth. "Just came into the kitchen to get somethin' to eat and he starts punching me!"

Will went over to Corrie. She was shaking, swaying, and being held between Vlinder and Anika. Vlinder looked up at Will. She reached out her hand and took his. "What if you weren't here? How did you know?" asked Vlinder.

"I didn't know," Will said. "I saw Roy leave the bunkhouse and followed him. I thought he was going to run off. But he came in here first."

Anika reached out and took Will's other hand. "You seem to be around at just the right times."

Will brought Alwin to the bunkhouse and then back to the farmhouse, showing him what happened. Outside the kitchen door were Roy's few belongings, suggesting that Roy had a plan to run off when he finished with Corrie.

There was no waiting until dawn. Gerwin, Jakob, and Alwin tied Roy in a wagon, put an extra horse next to Lily, and they dashed off to the Peoria police station.

CHAPTER 33

Carl, the supervisors, and Vlinder brought the workers to the fields that morning. Granddaddy was already at work, finishing the last of the soybean cutting with the binder. A few more weeks and it would all be in.

Moses left early, driving the steam tractor to Peoria, six crop-filled wagons pulled behind. Farms along the way provided water for the steam. Isaiah sat to the side of Moses, keeping the firebox full, the steam steady, and the massive engine chuffing toward town.

Later that afternoon, Alwin and his brothers came back down the road from Peoria in the buckboard. They stopped and spoke with Vlinder, then headed back to the farm. Vlinder turned to look for Will who was working with Elmer, two fields over. She waved and met him at the edge of the field.

"That was Alwin," Vlinder said. "They left Roy at the jail. Alwin wired his guardian back in Philadelphia telling her what happened." Vlinder breathed deep. "Looks like there's a couple of choices. We could press criminal charges or they could send him up to St. Charles. There's a boys reformatory school there. We'll wait to see what his guardian says."

"How's Corrie?" Will asked.

"She doesn't remember exactly what happened, just that someone was on top of her and she couldn't move. She's still scared. We moved her upstairs and she'll sleep in my mother's room for now. She doesn't want to sleep downstairs anymore."

Vlinder licked the tip of her thumb and reached across to Will's cheek. "Looks like he scratched you here."

"Doesn't hurt," Will said and smiled. "But it feels better now."

"You're part of this farm," said Vlinder. "I wish you were staying."

"I'll be back next year." Will said.

"I hope so."

*   *   *

After dinner, Will saw Alwin standing near the door of the chow hall and he walked to him. "Alwin, Mr. Alwin."

"Yes, Will. What can I do for you?"

"Well," Will continued. "I wanted to talk to you about the work here, about next summer."

"Sure," said Alwin. "Let's go over to the house and talk."

Alwin brought Will through the kitchen and into the big room, where Gerwin and Jakob were seated at the main table.

"Will. Come on in. Here, sit here." Alwin brought a chair over to the table and Will glanced around the room. There was a board across the front window which must have broken during the fight. The divan where Corrie slept was made up, giving no hint of the earlier turmoil. Alwin saw Will scanning the room. "Corrie's upstairs with Vlinder and my mother. Afterwards, why don't you go up to see her."

Will nodded and looked across at the brothers. "I wanted to talk about next summer. I like it here and I'd really like to come back."

"You don't even have to ask, Will. You're a good worker and with everything that's gone on this summer, of course we want you back next year," said Alwin.

"That's good," said Will. "But what I'm wondering, I'll be all done with school soon and could come out here early, in March, even earlier if you needed someone."

"Well," said Alwin leaning forward at the table, "we're not really set up for workers until early April. We don't have supplies in. The chow hall isn't ready." Then he paused. "But we'll have more work next year. We'll have to think about it." Alwin looked at his brothers. "We'll get together in December or January. That's what we did with my father. We'll figure it out then." Alwin looked back at Will. "We've got your address. We'll let you know, Will. And you'd be the first on the list to come early."

Will nodded and stood up. "Okay. Thanks. I'll come back anytime."

"Good, go ahead upstairs," said Alwin. "Corrie would like to see you. It's the second room on the right."

Will turned and climbed the stairs. He held the banister, glancing below to where he had danced with Vlinder, then Corrie, just a few weeks earlier. He reached a landing halfway where the stairs reversed direction and continued up. At the top, he stepped off the stairs and into the hallway, doors leading into rooms on both sides. The hallway was bright, with two large windows at each end letting in light to the side tables, each with a lavender vase holding up bouquets of fresh autumn farm flowers.

The second door to the right was open and Will could hear people talking. He glanced left and saw another open door to a room that would have sat above the kitchen. That had to be Vlinder's room. He walked to the room with the voices where Anika saw him and rose from a chair.

"Oh, Will. Please come in." Anika went over, took Will's hand, and led him in. Vlinder and Corrie smiled at him. Corrie lay in a bed brought into the room and hoisted herself up a little further on the pillows. There was a round table to the side with three empty plates on it from dinner.

"We moved Corrie's bed in here," said Anika. "She thought she'd have a little trouble sleeping downstairs." Anika looked across at Corrie. "It's good for me, too, having another person in here again. Honestly, Will, we shiver when we think of what could have happened if you weren't there. Thank you just isn't enough."

"Well, thank you, Miss Anika. I'm glad I was there, too." Will smiled at Vlinder and turned to Corrie. "How you feeling Corrie?"

Corrie looked down. "Okay."

Vlinder sat on Corrie's bed holding her hand. "It'll take a little while. But he's gone and he's not coming back." Corrie started to cry, leaned forward on her bed, and hugged Vlinder.

"One good thing," said Anika, changing the discussion. "He didn't hurt Corrie's ankle. Come on Corrie, let's get up and walk around the room."

Vlinder helped Corrie turn and put her legs over the side of the bed. Anika got Corrie's crutches and they helped her to her feet, each staying close to her side. To Will, Corrie was moving even better than when they had danced.

"You look good walking, Corrie," said Will, waiting and watching while she took a few more steps. "You're brave," he finally said.

Corrie paused and gave him a small, grateful smile.

Will watched her take several steps around the room and then said, "Good job, Corrie. I'll be sure to see you again before I leave." He looked at all three and turned to leave.

"Thank you, Will," Corrie called after him.

Will looked back over his shoulder, smiled, and nodded at Corrie, then Anika, then Vlinder.

CHAPTER 34

It was the last week of church at the Van der Beek farm this season and Moses convinced Granddaddy to take them all in the Fodgabaker. Moses asked Granddaddy to drive to church backwards, but Granddaddy said it wasn't right to be foolish on the Lord's Day.

On the way, Moses said to Will and Elmer, "gonna be drivin' to Peoria for church each Sunday after this."

"Yes, indeed," said Granddaddy. "Gonna finally meet Moses' sweetie."

Everyone laughed except Moses. "Now, why you bein' like that, Granddaddy? Don't know if I'll see her there or not."

"Well," said Granddaddy. "Isaiah says you told her to try Pastor Jannsen's church in Peoria and she said she would."

Moses glared at his brother. "Your mouth flappin' again, Isaiah? I swear, if a bird flies over yo head, youse got to talk about it."

* * *

Whether everyone was getting used to Pastor Jannsen's accent, or his English was improving, his message this day was about endings, ending to the season and finding hope in that. "The preacher, wiise Old King Solomon saeid, 'Bettr ees the end of a ting thaan the beginning....'" The pastor ended his message with his arms wide, a broad smile, and a hope to see everyone next year.

At the punch table, Will spied Vlinder and went over to her. "After today, I won't be around if Cornelius Van der Beek comes by."

"I know," Vlinder said. "But his mother is German and the family goes to the Lutheran Church when they're in Peoria. I won't be seeing him much until next summer."

Over near the Van der Beek farm house, Will and Vlinder saw Elmer talking to Arend Van der Beek. Next to Elmer was the girl with red hair and pig tails.

"Wonder what Elmer is talking to Mr. Van der Beek about?" asked Will.

"I bet you find out soon enough," Vlinder smiled.

* * *

Back at the farm, Isaiah and Moses were moving up to Granddaddy's House, their new home. They carried their few belongings and Elmer and Will walked with them.

"You need a bed up there, Moses? You still gonna sleep on the floor?" asked Elmer.

"Yup. Still gonna sleep on the floor," Moses said, "but still like to have a bed over me. Don't know why."

Inside the house, Granddaddy had already made it look like home. There was a sink and a water pump, tables and chairs, a woodstove, an ice box, and the inside toilet was mostly finished. Granddaddy said it felt like they had a foot in heaven. Nailed to the back of the front door was a picture of Gramma and Granddaddy holding Moses when he was a baby, Isaiah standing to the side.

"So, you'll be livin' up here next year, Moses, Isaiah?" said Will looking around. "Not going to be in the bunkhouse?"

"Nope. This is home now," said Moses.

"That's okay," said Will. "Owen will probably be back and Roy won't be here. We can live with that, Elmer and me."

Elmer stayed silent for a moment, looking down. "Might not be here next year. Might be workin' over at the Van der Beek farm."

"What?" said Moses. "They's nice and all, but what you mean?"

Will remembered Vlinder's words. "Something to do with a young lady over there, Elmer?"

"Maybe," Elmer smiled.

"Maybe?!?" said Will. "Now you sound like Moses."

* * *

The next day, Alwin called Will into the farmhouse after dinner and they sat at the dining table.

"Got a message from the police chief today about Roy and thought you should know what's happening," Alwin said. "Roy's guardian, Mrs. Atwell, said she'd leave it to us to decide what to do with him. If we wanted to press charges, we could. But the chief made a suggestion. He said if Roy is convicted he wouldn't get much jail time. A year, maybe two. But there was enough cause to send him to the reformatory school up in St. Charles. They've got guards and fences. He'd be at St. Charles for at least two years. If he doesn't turn himself around, he could even go to prison after that. That seems like a better plan."

"Yeah, that sounds good," Vlinder said. "Corrie needs to know he's not going to be around."

"Yes. We'll let her know," said Alwin.

* * *

Work was light. Granddaddy hadn't seen the beef cattle, so on Tuesday, the four boys and Granddaddy piled into the Fodgabaker and headed to the pasture. The boys from Bunkhouse 1 were there, working with the cattle, spreading hay, collecting manure, and repositioning a few fence posts. In just a short time, the cattle had fattened.

The boys took Granddaddy around the pasture, sharing stories of Joren Helgeveld, the contract for the crops and cattle, and the fence building. Isaiah and Moses pulled Granddaddy over to show him the gates they had built.

Granddaddy looked across the field, the fence, and the gates. He looked at his grandsons and nodded. "Youse is men now."

Granddaddy teared up. "Oh, Lord above, if only Gramma could see you here, all growed up. She'd be so proud."

*   *   *

Lunches and dinners cleared out the summer stocks and the boys ate well. Lamb roasts, hot dogs, sugar breads, glazed carrots, a new treat of spaghetti with sauce, and pie upon pie. Vlinder and Will's smiles connected and lingered, both aware of the fast approaching departure date.

How would he say goodbye to her? How would he give her the gold charm? How could he even leave?

After dinner on Wednesday, Will saw Betty Granger just outside the farmhouse kitchen. "You coming back next year, Betty?" he asked.

"I want to," Betty said. "I already talked to Vlinder. She said I could. I'll write her after the first of the year. What about you, Will?"

"Yeah, I'm coming back, definitely. I already talked to Alwin about it."

"There's a rumor you might be sweet on Vlinder?" Betty said. "That might be a reason?"

"No secrets around here, I guess," Will laughed.

"Maybe just one," said Betty leaning over toward Will and talking low, "I been talkin' a little bit to Gerwin and he's been talkin' to me. Kind of anxious to come back next year and talk to him a little more."

"Good to know, Betty," Will smiled. "I'll see you next summer."

*   *   *

Most of Bunkhouse 1 and 2, along with a few workers from Bunkhouse 3, left for home on Thursday, October 18. The other workers stayed busy with short chores and cleanup for the upcoming week, but tomorrow, the remaining workers would head to Peoria and home.

At lunch, Will found Vlinder. "Let's meet after dinner," he said. "Outside the chow hall."

Vlinder nodded. "Okay. After dinner."

*   *   *

That afternoon, Elmer and Will wandered to the back barn, around the stables, and past Granddaddy's House. They roamed down to the dairy cows, both boys hanging on the fence watching a dozen nearby cows grazing on hay.

"I'll still see you all next summer," said Elmer, "every week, every Sunday at church." Elmer spoke differently, like someone who had his first girlfriend.

"Yeah," said Will. "It'll be alright, I think."

They agreed that home was just a place to wait out the winter.

Later, the two boys helped carry some of the late season vegetables to the root cellar and Will watched the afternoon sun slip toward the westerly trees. This time tomorrow he'd be in Chicago, in Pittsburgh the day after.

Only about a dozen workers were left at the farm and they gathered for dinner in the chow hall for their last evening meal.

Will wasn't hungry. He picked at his food, watching the others eat dinner, then dessert. As soon as the first workers left the chow hall, Will went outside.

Vlinder was waiting at the farmhouse kitchen door wearing the same dress she wore to Peoria so many months ago, lavender flowers dancing on the white background.

"You've got that dress on again." Will looked closer. "I didn't notice before, but those little flowers are forget-me-nots." Will stepped back and looked at Vlinder and the dress. "It's so pretty."

Vlinder held her arm out and turned her sleeve over. "I can't imagine how Gramma Luna found it, but she did." She smiled at Will, moved toward him and took his hand. "I'm glad you like it. Let's walk."

The two hiked to the back barn and then along the path to the acres out back that had just been cleared. They stood looking across the field, plowed and planted, the winter rye taller than before. The dusky light fading, Vlinder said, "I told Alwin you should come out early next year. I told him about this extra field, the new beef cattle, and anything else I could think of where you could help."

"What did he say?" asked Will.

Vlinder laughed and put her hand on her chest. "He said, 'you'd have him back here next month, Vlinder.' But then he said it might be a good idea. Father always waited until after Christmas to figure what we'd need next season. I'm guessing that's what Alwin's going to do."

They stepped through twilight shadows along a path that brought them past Bunkhouse 3. From inside, there were some laughs and goodbyes spilling from the few workers left. Vlinder took him to another path that wove behind the bunkhouse and the back barn, and then headed up toward the stables.

"This was the best and the worst summer we've ever had at the farm," Vlinder said. "Losing my father. Corrie getting hurt. Roy. But then you, all of you. The worst and the best."

They stepped over rocks and bent under low tree limbs, arriving at the stables. Lily walked to the fence, welcoming the head scratches she knew would come. "I'll see you next year, Lily," said Will.

Vlinder looked at Will. "Come on." She took his hand and hurried up past the chow hall, turned right, ending at the open area above the farmhouse, near the sycamore. They lay in the grass, the last hints of daylight gone.

"I remember when I was about twelve," Vlinder said. "My mother and father brought us out here to watch the big comet."

"Oh, yeah," said Will. "I remember that."

Vlinder pointed toward the horizon. "It was over there. So bright. We could see it for weeks. After that, Corrie and I used to come out here, usually in the winter, wrapped in jackets and blankets. The colder it was the brighter the stars were. I even got a book to learn about them." Vlinder pointed directly above them. "All of that white strip across the sky, the Milky Way, those are all stars."

"The Big Dipper," said Will. "Is that up there?"

Vlinder pointed a little to the left. "That's it. See the pot, those four stars, and then the handle up there?"

"Yes. There. I see it." Will looked back at the expanse overhead. "Space is so big."

"I know," said Vlinder. "I tried to compare it to other things to show Corrie how huge it all is. But she told me it's the stars, the sky. You can't compare it to anything. It's perfect the way it is and she was just grateful for it all." Vlinder paused. "She was right, of course. Now, I'm just grateful for all of it, too." They lay in the grass, hand in hand. "Wait," Vlinder said. "Watch." Will watched the sky, now dark and bright with stars. "Wait," Vlinder said again. A minute later, starting right above them, a streak of light blazed to the horizon.

"What was that? Was that a shooting star?" said Will.

"Yes," said Vlinder, "but wait. Watch."

Another streaked across the sky, followed by one slightly dimmer that passed above their heads.

"One night, Corrie and I counted forty-seven," Vlinder said.

The piano started playing in the farmhouse.

"Corrie's healing and my mother is doing better." Vlinder paused. "And it's strange. In some ways, Corrie's ankle and the troubles with Roy took my mother's mind off my father. Those problems gave her new purpose."

"That's the word I've been looking for. Purpose. There's purpose here at the farm. A reason. All of it. All of the family. You." Will rolled over, up onto his elbow, and looked at Vlinder. "That day in Peoria, at the zoo, you said you didn't want to get too close to anyone. You said that workers come and go. They say things and then they never come back. Do you still think that?"

"Yes," said Vlinder looking up at Will. "But maybe you're not that type of worker. Are you, Will? Are you coming back?"

"Just once I hope," said Will. "And never leave."

Vlinder looked into him. "If I knew that at the zoo, I would have kissed you then."

Will raised up on his elbow, looking over into Vlinder. He took his hand and cupped the side of her head. He leaned in and kissed her forehead, kissed her eyes, and moved down kissing her mouth, kissing her again.

Vlinder reached up and held his head to hers, guiding his next kisses to her cheek, neck, hair, lips. Will pushed himself onto his palms and looked down on Vlinder. She smiled at him and said, "I'll make this last until next summer."

"Good," said Will. "And maybe this will help." Will reached into his pocket and pulled out a small box, tied with a bow. "I saw this in Peoria and it reminded me of that night. The night you taught me to dance."

Vlinder undid the bow and opened the box. She caught her breath and took out the gold charm with the couple dancing. She turned it over in her palm and it shone in the dark. She looked up at Will. "It's beautiful. It's perfect. It looks like us."

"I'm not sure about that," said Will. "He looks like he knows how to dance."

They laughed and kissed again.

"Oh," said Will. "When I got this charm, I got something for Corrie, too. I thought she might like it if I got her something. It's not much. It's a silver necklace. But now I don't know. I don't know if it's a good idea."

Vlinder looked right at Will. "Of course it's a good idea! I'm sure she'll love it. You were so important to her this summer, Will. Bring it to the farmhouse tomorrow before you leave. She'll love that you thought of her."

"Okay," Will said. "And I'll see you tomorrow, too, right?"

"I'll be around," said Vlinder. "Right up until your wagon is out of sight."

They stood up and walked back to the farmhouse, silent, hand in hand. Will found himself glancing up at the sky, the stars. Perfect, just as it is. At the kitchen door they embraced and kissed again, Will holding his hand alongside her cheek. "I'll see you in the morning," he said and he walked backwards down the path, watching Vlinder blow him a kiss and then walk into the kitchen.

CHAPTER 35

The next morning, the bunkhouse was empty except for Will, Elmer, Nathan, and Lucas. Each had their travel bags packed and ready, sitting on their beds. The two wagons heading to Peoria wouldn't leave until around 11 a.m., giving the workers enough time to catch the afternoon train to Chicago. After breakfast, Will and Elmer headed up to Granddaddy's house to say goodbye.

"'Course we's comin' down to the wagons to say goodbye," said Moses when they came into the house. A quick fire in the woodstove took away the late October chill and it boiled the water for Granddaddy's coffee.

"Looks like home in here," Will said.

"Lookee here," said Isaiah and he opened two cupboards, one with dishes and coffee cups, the other with pots, pans, a baking tray, and a bowl full of knives, spoons, and flippers.

Granddaddy pointed to a corner of the kitchen. "Privy's right there. Behind that door." He slapped his knee. "Can ya believe it? A toilet right here inside the house!"

Will looked in the back room and saw three beds, a pillow and blanket underneath one.

"Alright," said Will. "We'll head back and get our things. We'll see you down at the wagons."

"We'll be there," said Moses.

As they walked back to the bunkhouse, Will asked Elmer, "What's the name of your lady friend at the Van der Beek farm?"

"Anna. Her name is Anna," said Elmer.

Will nodded. "Seems like most of us found someone or something this summer."

"Yeah, you're right," Elmer said. "I guess I still can't believe it. Anna Wilton. Talkin' to her is real easy. She says she's coming back next year and she's glad I'll be working over there."

"I bet she is, Elmer," said Will.

Gerwin was at the bunkhouse when they arrived and he was hauling bed frames out front. "What are you doin'?" asked Will.

"Most of the beds in your bunkhouse been around since the 1880's and they're broken, or almost broken," said Gerwin. "We're going to break them apart and have Isaiah and Moses make new ones over the winter."

Will looked at Elmer and then over at Nathan and Lucas "We'll give you a hand," and they began to pull bed frames out of the bunkhouse and drag them to the back barn.

Lotta came by while the boys were working and volunteered to bring their travel bags down to the wagons.

The workers made a few more trips to the back barn with the old bed frames and then went out front of the farmhouse, their travel bags sitting behind the wagon where Lotta had left them. The workers who were already there shared stories, joked and laughed.

Vlinder stood by the front fence and Will went over to her. She reached inside the top of her shirt, pulling out a gold necklace, the dancing gold charm swinging from the bottom.

Will opened his mouth and stared. "You have a gold necklace?" Will asked.

"No," Vlinder laughed. "This is the necklace my father bought for my mother the day he died. Last night, I showed my mother the charm and she said I should wear it on the necklace today to show you. Look. Isn't it beautiful?" Vlinder held the charm in her hand, the necklace tumbling off her palm.

"Yes, it's beautiful," said Will. "Next summer, I'll get you your own necklace."

"Now, you have to come back," Vlinder laughed. She put a hand on Will's shoulder and nodded toward the farmhouse. "There's someone who wants to see you."

Will turned and saw Corrie on the front porch, balanced between her crutches and smiling down the path at Will.

"Go on up, Will," said Vlinder.

Will smiled at Vlinder and walked toward the farmhouse. He took the stairs two at a time, landing just in front of Corrie. "Hey, Corrie. I was coming to see you before I left."

"I know. Vlinder said you'd come. And Lotta saw you and said you'd be out front in a little while." Corrie paused. "And I wanted to come downstairs and go outside. It's been so long since I've been out," she said.

"Well, you look better. How are you feeling?" Will asked.

"Better...not really," Corrie said, looking down. "I know you're sweet on Vlinder and I know she's going to miss you. But I'm going to miss you, too."

"Well, I'm going to miss everything here, everyone. You too, Corrie." Will reached in his pocket and pulled out the small jewelry box and handed it to her. "Here, I bought this for you."

"You did? You bought something for me?" Corrie took her hands off the crutch handles and untied the ribbon. She opened the box, looked inside, and looked at Will. "Is that a necklace? You bought that for me?"

"Yeah," said Will. "I bought it for you. I bought a charm for Vlinder, too. You're the two people I'll miss the most here."

Corrie held the box and lifted out the necklace. "Is this silver? A silver necklace? I don't have anything silver. I'll wear it every day." She held it out in front of her and looked at Will. "I can't put it on standing on just this leg. Can you put it on for me?"

"Sure," Will said. He took the necklace and examined it. "How do you take it apart? How do you undo this thing here?"

Corrie laughed. "See that little bump there?" She pointed at it. "Take your finger and push it back. That opens the loop and you can take it apart."

Will followed her directions and after unfastening the necklace, he moved behind Corrie, spreading apart the necklace in front of her, and snapping it closed behind her neck.

Corrie lifted the necklace to look at it. "It's beautiful. Thanks, Will. Vlinder said you promised you'd come back next year, right?"

"That's right. I promise. I don't even want to leave," Will said. "I just tell myself I'm going away for a few months, like on a trip. Then I'll come back."

There was a tear at the side of Corrie's eyes. "Yes. Come back. I'll miss you. I might wait right here on the porch until you do."

Will laughed. "Okay. I'll wave when I see you on the porch." Will looked at Corrie and said, "I have to go."

Corrie nodded and held her silver necklace between two fingers.

Will turned and waved at Corrie halfway down the path, then blended in with the other workers, soon heading to Peoria and home.

Moses, Isaiah, and Granddaddy were to the side talking with Elmer. "Hey, Will," Elmer said holding something up. "Look what Moses and Isaiah got us." As Will got closer he saw two yo-yos. Elmer had one and Moses handed the other one to Will.

"Hey, this is great! Thanks," Will said. "I gotta tell you, Moses, I always wanted to try yours, but I didn't think I could do it. Now, I can practice all winter."

"That's what I was thinking," Elmer said. "Look, here. The string fits right over my finger." Elmer held the yo-yo in his palm with the loop over his one finger. He tossed it down but it rebounded just a few inches. "Guess I need to practice, too. I'll show you how at church next summer at the Van der Beeks. I wonder if yo-yoing on Sundays is allowed?"

The boys and Granddaddy laughed, Granddaddy reaching over and shaking both boys' hands. "Mighty fine meeting you boys. Mighty fine, indeed."

Will and Elmer turned and looked at Isaiah and Moses, none of them knowing quite how to say goodbye to friends who had become like family. "Not gonna be the same around here with you guys gone," Moses said. With that, the boys shook hands and nodded, afraid their voices would crack if they tried to say anything more.

Finally, Will said, "I gotta go over there," and he headed to Vlinder who was leaning on the fence.

Will reached Vlinder and she smiled. She had picked up Will's travel bag and handed it to him. "Be sure you write, probably around the first of the year. That'll remind Alwin to keep you first on the list. I'll keep reminding him, too."

"Make sure you do," said Will.

Alwin yelled, "Let's go! Don't leave anything behind."

Anika came out of the farmhouse and down the path. She stood to the side of the wagon and the few remaining workers fell silent. "Hello, boys. We hope you had a wonderful summer at the farm." Anika paused. "As you know, this has been a very difficult summer. The most difficult summer of my life. But each time, all of you, you made the summer bearable. How can I forget when so many of you came to the cemetery to remember my husband? And with my daughter, Corrie. You've been so supportive through all of that. We'll talk about you all winter long."

Anika looked over at Alwin. "Alwin and I talked it over and with the government contract, there's an extra $10 for each of you in your pay. That's our thank you for your hard work and for being part of our family this summer. Please, if you would like to come back and work on the farm next summer, write to us over the winter. We'd love to see you again." Anika waved to the boys. "Have a safe trip home!"

The wagon was loading and Vlinder looked at Will. "I don't think I can kiss you goodbye here with everyone around," she said.

"Sure you can," Will said. "Close your eyes. I'll close mine." Will waited. "Are they closed?"

"Yes," said Vlinder.

"Mine, too. Okay, now imagine. I take your hand, and then I put my other hand on your cheek. Then, I lean in and kiss you goodbye. Do you see it?" Will waited. "Vlinder, do you see it?"

"How can I talk if I'm kissing you?" she said.

They laughed together.

It was time. Vlinder looked at the workers loading into the wagon and back at Will. "You have to go."

"I know." Will climbed into the wagon, standing and waving goodbye to Moses, Isaiah, and Granddaddy. Then he looked toward the farmhouse. Corrie was there, still on the porch, holding up her hand and waving. Will waved back. He sat down and thought of March, April, when he'd return.

Anika appeared next to Vlinder at the back of the wagon. She reached up and took Will's hand in both of hers. "Goodbye, Will. Again, I'll say it. Thank you. We're all looking forward to seeing you next summer. You're part of the family." Anika stepped back and Will nodded.

"Heeya!" yelled Alwin and the wagon heaved forward.

Vlinder walked behind the wagon, still holding Will's hand. "You're coming back? You promise?" she said.

The wagon moved faster and their hands parted.

"I promise," yelled Will, and Vlinder watched until the wagons were far down the road on their way to Peoria.

But in 1918, Will did not go back to Helgeveld Farm.

CHAPTER 36

Will got to Chicago, and the following day, he took the train to Cleveland, changing trains to Pittsburgh. Before he left Chicago, Will sent his parents a telegram and they were at the Pittsburgh station waiting for him.

Will's mother put a hand on her son's cheek. "You look different, older, happy, too."

"It was a good place, a good summer. I'm going back next year," Will said.

"Good, son," his father said. "My summer away, it changed my life back then. Maybe this will change your life, too."

Will smiled at his father and nodded.

*   *   *

The next morning, Will's mother came into his room holding a flower stem. "This was in one of your shirt pockets."

Will looked over. "It was?"

His mother examined it. "It looks like a forget-me-not. Lavender. Usually, they're blue. I guess she wants you to remember her."

"Who?" asked Will.

"The young lady who put it there," his mother said.

Will took the flower, and twirled it on its stem.

"I love forget-me-nots," Will's mother said. "They're so pretty."

"So is she," Will said.

"I'm sure she is," his mother said. "You could put it in the family Bible. That would press it and keep it. The rose your father gave me when he proposed is still in there, almost as good as new."

Will carried the flower until the next day, but when the leaves started to wilt, he opened the family Bible and pushed it flat between two pages.

Will started working in the South Sides Flats feed and supply store run by his Uncle Clive. Will's brother and father ran the main store across the river on Brighton Road. Will agreed to work there all winter after school, understanding that he would be returning to Helgeveld Farm next summer.

*   *   *

Toward the beginning of 1918, three wounded soldiers returned from the Great War to Mercy Hospital in Pittsburgh. A week later, reports of a serious illness, much worse than the annual flu, appeared first in the hospital, and days later throughout areas of Pittsburgh. Death followed for many, and soon similar reports began to arrive from around the nation. The city, the country, was scared. Rumors suggested the sickness originated in Spain and spread through Europe, returning with soldiers to England and the United States.

Will's brother, James, brought home a notice from his school principal stating that several students had come down with this new influenza. They were closing the school. The next day, James woke up with a high fever and dry cough. By evening, he had a sore throat and headache. Will's parents stayed up with him all night, putting cold cloths on his head, but James' cough and fever worsened. Will's mother became desperate. She even gave her son medicines she used for animals, but they had no effect.

By morning, James' coughing was non-stop. Will's mother said they should take him to the hospital and Will and his father wrapped him in a blanket. James' cough stopped. Will's mother looked at her husband with wide eyes and a smile. She put her hand on her chest. "Thank God, it stopped." She turned toward her son. "My dear Jimmy, thank God!" But Jimmy had died, wrapped in a blanket and held by his father.

Two days later, Will's father got a sore throat and started coughing. Will, his sister Annie, and his mother got him into their automobile and they drove to Mercy Hospital. Patients were in the hallways, laying on mattresses and blankets. A nurse told them, "Just find a place for him. We'll do what we can."

They found a spot on the floor next to another patient who Will's mother knew had died. She looked up at Will and Annie. "Get out of the hospital! Go home now! I'll stay with your father."

The next day, Will's mother walked up the stairs and stood in the doorway to their home over the store. She had no expression. Will and Annie came toward her and she held up her hand. "No, don't come over here. I shouldn't have come, but I had to see you." She lowered her head. "Your father is gone and this influenza is spreading. I'm going to stay in the back-office downstairs. I'll be alright." She looked up at them. "I love you both so much. I don't know what I'll do if I lose another one of you." She started to cry, turned, and walked downstairs to the back office of the supply store.

The sickness gripped Pittsburgh for weeks. Will's father and brother, along with hundreds of others who had died, were brought to the train yard to wait for caskets that were yet to be built. Will never caught the *Spanish flu,* but his sister and mother did and they recovered. Later, Will's Aunt Catherine, and her two children, moved into the back bedroom over the store. Her husband had died two weeks earlier.

The feed and supply stores stayed closed, along with most other shops throughout Pittsburgh. But the money was running out and people needed provisions. Later in the spring, despite the flu still ravaging some sections of Pittsburgh, Will and his mother decided to open the one store in the South Side Flats. Soon, his father's brother Clive opened the second location on Brighton Road.

That day, Will opened the front door of the store only to realize that he had not collected the mail from the postal box for several weeks. There was a letter from Vlinder dated January 29.

Dear Will,

I know I will hear from you, but I wanted to write anyways. The farm has been busier than most winters because of the new cattle. We lost six during a cold spell, but otherwise they are doing well.

Corrie is walking without crutches. She knows I'm writing to you and she says hi. We're all looking forward to seeing you again. I asked Alwin and he said you can come the first week of April.

I hope you are alright with this terrible sickness that is around. Many people have died in Peoria, but we are alright on the farm.

I'm holding the charm of us dancing in my other hand. I'll close my eyes now and kiss you goodbye.

Please write.

Vlinder

Will sat on the front stairs of the store and read the letter again. Throughout it all, Helgeveld Farm had never been far from his mind. Each day, he thought he'd find a way he could go back to the farm, to the flower, to her.

Will's mother walked up to him and saw him holding the letter. She knew her son and read his silence. She sat down next to him and put her hand on his shoulder. "Not once have you mentioned going back to the farm this summer, back to her, back to what you really want. But you're a man now. You need to make decisions that are right for you." His mother paused. "We'll be alright here. I can run the store; your sister can help. And your uncle Clive is here." She shrugged her shoulders. "Or maybe we'd sell it. It would work out the way it should."

"What about the loan that dad took out on the store?" Will asked. "It's over $1,800."

"We'll manage," said his mother.

Will knew his mother had no love for the store. Her heart was with healing animals and nursing others. His sister Annie wanted to go to college to be a teacher. His aunt and her children needed a place to live. And there was no money to pay back the loan.

JOHN BLOIS

Dear Vlinder,

I got your letter. I keep waiting for something to happen that would let me come back to the farm this summer. But the influenza took my father and brother. My mother says she will run our two stores, but she has too many other things that she needs to do. I have to stay here for now and make sure the stores stay open.

Corrie is walking? Maybe she's running now. Tell her I will see her twirl again.

I always think about you, Vlinder, when you came out of the farmhouse that first day, when we worked in the fields together, at the cemetery, and under the stars that last night. Each time you close your eyes, I'll be kissing you.

I promised that I would come back to the farm and I will.

Will

Say hey to Isaiah, Moses, and Granddaddy.

CHAPTER 37

31 Years: April 1918--October 1949

Each week settled Will further into the feed and supply stores and into Pittsburgh, Pennsylvania. He worked long hours, six days a week to keep the business running. School could wait.

There was no news from Helgeveld Farm other than a small parcel that arrived in July 1918. Will looked at the brown package and saw the return address:

Butler

Helgeveld Farm

Peoria, Illinois.

Inside was a letter and something wrapped in tissue paper.

Hey Will,

Vlinder told us about your father and your brother dying. Moses, me, and Granddaddy are real sad to hear that news. We know you got to stay there and take care of your family but we hope you'll come back someday.

The disease hit here too. Jakob passed on two months back and so did Carl. It's been real hard on everyone. Vlinder looks good but she says she misses you. She said you're coming back sometime. Corrie's all healed and working like before. She keeps saying it's cause of you.

Owen is back and Elmer looks real happy when we see him at church.

Moses and me, we talked and we think you need some good luck. We gonna keep the 1909 here just for insurance but we sending you two of the pennies in this package, the 1912 and the 1916. Make sure you carry them around with you. They's real powerful.

Isaiah and Moses. Granddaddy says hey.

Into the fall of 1918 and early 1919, the great influenza faded. The Great War officially ended in November 1918, but the draft continued, still recruiting men who were eighteen and above. Will's mother was relieved when the draft ended in March 1919 and Will could stay at the store.

With the influenza and the Great War over, both stores thrived. Will ran the South Side Flats store and Clive ran the other store on Brighton Road. During the 1920's, there was talk of hiring a manager for the Brighton Road store and sending Clive out to Chicago to open another feed and supply store as Will's father had planned.

Will held Helgeveld close, but at some point, he figured that Vlinder had probably gotten married and forgotten about him. Corrie and Lotta would have married, too, and moved away. That summer of 1917 had been just another season in the history of the farm.

In late 1924, Will met Emma Fall, who came into the store twice a week to buy grain and feed for her farm. Her father died young, and now she ran a small farm with her mother and two brothers just outside Pittsburgh. She wore pants, knew about grains, about tools, and about the Pittsburgh Pirates. Will cared for her, loved her.

In 1925, Will and Emma married. Emma left her farm and worked in the store alongside her new husband. He'd watch her now and then, thankful that he met someone who helped pull him from the past. But sometimes, Will's mother would come to him, put a hand along his cheek and give him a sad smile, knowing this wasn't quite what he had imagined.

There was a daughter Hillary in 1926, a son Tom in 1927, and then Julia in 1929. Will's sister, Annie, became a teacher just south of Pittsburgh in Bethel Park, and Will's Aunt Catherine worked in the Brighton Road store, living in two rooms above it with Will's cousins, Gracie and Michael. In April 1928, Will and Emma bought a four-bedroom Sears and Roebuck home and had it built on the outskirts of Pittsburgh. Then, in early 1929, Clive moved to Chicago with his family and opened their third supply store.

Later in 1929, the Depression hit Pittsburgh and the entire country hard. But Will had already paid off the store's debt and was able to keep both Pittsburgh stores, and the Chicago store, open throughout the 1930s. Will's mother still lived above the Carson Street store in South Side Flats, often traveling to farms and doctoring animals.

In 1933, Julia was playing with some tools in the store and cut her leg and foot. Three days later, she got a fever, headache, and her jaw hurt. They called the doctor. He saw that the cuts on her leg and foot weren't healing and that she couldn't open her mouth. It was tetanus. Julia spent three weeks in the hospital and Will and Emma were allowed to stay overnight when her condition became critical and the doctors told them to prepare for the worst. Whether it was a new anti-toxin from Philadelphia, or the strength of her body, her fever finally broke, and over the next few months, she recovered. The doctor said it was the worst case of tetanus he'd ever seen in a young person.

Will never told Emma about Helgeveld Farm, other than that he worked there one summer. Everyone has a past, he thought, probably even Emma. She was a good mother and Will was a good father. All three of the children did well in school, and during the late 1930s, they all worked in the store alongside their mother and father.

During World War II, Will and his family sacrificed like everyone else. His son, Tom, was too young to go to war, but as he approached seventeen in 1944, Will saw himself at that age, the joy of leaving home and working on a farm during the summer. Changing his life. But also being old enough to carry bits of emptiness that could resurface unannounced.

On May 8, 1945, the Germans surrendered, ending World War II in Europe and Pittsburgh celebrated along with the entire country. On May 9, Will woke up with Emma next to him, lying still. He shook her, got up, called an ambulance, and went back to bed to hold his wife. Emma's father had died at thirty-seven, her older brother two years ago at forty-three. Over the last three years, Emma had been tired, and finally, her heart just gave out. The ambulance left with

Emma's body and Hillary, Tom, and Julia got into their parents' bed with their father, held each other, and cried.

Over the next weeks and months, the two stores gave them purpose. Hillary and Tom finished high school and settled into working full-time between the Brighton Road and the South Sides Flats stores. Hillary had memorized all the merchandise and was doing the ordering for both stores. Will's mother came to their home, taking care of the house, having meals ready, giving a foundation for moving on from the death of a wife and a mother. Most evenings, Will sat on the porch until well after dark.

Helgeveld eased back into Will's mind. Sometimes he carried a cookie in his shirt pocket, the weight and drifting sweet smell bringing him back to the farm, back to Vlinder. When the roof on the store needed to be replaced, he envisioned Moses and Isaiah up there, pounding nails and singing Granddaddy's songs. And more than once, Will stopped and watched Hillary twirl in an aisle, and he imagined Corrie, twirling up a path.

Hillary and Tom embraced running the stores with much more purpose than Will. He thought both of them were a little young, but remembered that he was just eighteen when he took over the stores. Will's daughter, Julia, followed after her grandmother, tending to animals and healing. In 1946, Tom got married and Hillary followed in 1947. Both continued working in the store. In 1948, Tom and his wife had a baby girl, giving Will his first grandchild.

With a few more workers in the stores, Will took Wednesdays and every other weekend off. The stores almost ran themselves at this point.

"Dad," said Hillary one afternoon in the store, "why don't you take some time off, take a vacation. Tom and I can look after things."

But Will told her he needed to stay in Pittsburgh in case anything were to happen at the stores. Besides, where would he even go, he thought.

* * *

On October 4, 1949, Will's uncle Clive died. Clive opened the Chicago store in 1929 and Will had never gone there. He could have gone. He should have gone. But it was too close to Helgeveld. When needed, his mother went to Chicago, and over the last few years, Hillary or Tom made the occasional trip.

But someone had to go now. The deed to the Chicago store was in Will's mother's name and she, along with Will and Annie, decided to focus on the two Pittsburgh stores and sell the Chicago store to Clive's family for $1 since the success of that store was all due to them. And now, documents needed to be signed.

"You need to go to Chicago," Will's mother told him. "I'll give you Power of Attorney. You can sign the deed over to them."

"I can't go. There's too much to do here," said Will. "Hillary or Tom could go. You could go."

"And when you're there, you should go down to the farm," his mother said.

"What?? You mean Helgeveld? I haven't talked about that for years," Will said.

"You didn't have to," his mother smiled. "The flower she gave you kept moving between different pages in the Bible. It moved when your father and brother died. It moved when Julia was so sick. And it moved when you met Emma, and then again when you lost her."

Will looked at the floor and then back at his mother. "It held me up. She held me up, all these years."

"I know," his mother said.

"But it's been so long. Everything would have changed," said Will.

"*Everything* changes on the outside, but not always on the inside."

"She'd have gotten married, had a family. Probably moved away. I don't even know if the farm is still there."

"If you go there, you'll know."

Will looked at his mother. "Alright. I'll go to Chicago, but I might not go to the farm. I probably won't go."

Will's mother came over and held her son. "Good. Go to Chicago, Will."

*   *   *

Late Wednesday, Will arrived in Chicago by train and checked into the Palmer House Hotel, five trolley stops from the store. This would be a quick trip. He decided he didn't want another disappointment by going to the farm. Best to remember it as it was.

On Thursday, he met Clive's wife, Vera, at the store, along with two of his cousins, Elma and Joseph. He hadn't seen any of them for more than twenty years and he regretted it.

They went into a back room of the store where there was a table with a neatly piled stack of papers. "We did what you asked, Will," said Vera. "We got a lawyer to draw these up. But this is all more than we could have hoped for. You're really just giving us the store."

"It's only a success because of what you and Clive did here. Besides, we want to downsize," said Will. He looked up at Vera. "There are so many good ideas in the store. How to organize things. Signs. Specials. I'm taking some of these ideas back home."

"Well, you know Clive," she said. "He was a go-getter. He even managed to get the seed and supply business from many of the farms across Northern Illinois. But we're going to cut back on all of that now."

Will sat up and looked across at her. "You supplied farms from far away?"

"Lord, yes," she said. "One as far south as Springfield."

Will picked up the papers in front of him and tapped the bottom of them on the table. "You don't know if one of those farms was the Helgeveld Farm?"

"Oh, I don't know," Vera said. "There were several. Clive kept track of all that."

Will nodded and spread the papers apart. Everything looked in order and Will signed them on behalf of his mother. Vera smiled and handed Will a dollar. "Done!" said Will.

"When are you heading back to Pittsburgh, Will?" Vera asked.

"I'm taking the 3 o'clock train tomorrow afternoon," said Will. "I'll change trains in Cleveland the following day."

"Oh, good," she said. "I was hoping you could stay until tomorrow. I'd love to catch up on everything that's going on in the family. Tonight, my granddaughter is in a school play, but perhaps you could come by here for lunch tomorrow?"

"That's a good idea," said Will. "And I'd like to take another look at some of your ideas here in the store."

"Wonderful! Come by anytime in the morning," Vera said.

Will looked at his watch. "It's getting a little late. I'll just grab something to eat and head back to my hotel. Where's a good place to get a sandwich?"

"Oh! Milo's Delicatessen," Will's cousin Joe said. "Best sandwiches in Chicago, but they close soon." Joe walked outside with Will and gave him directions to Milo's on South Loomis Street. "If you get lost, ask anybody where Milo's is."

"Alright," said Will. "See you all tomorrow."

CHAPTER 38

Will hustled through the unfamiliar city, turned left instead of right on Ashland Avenue, recovered, and dashed across Vernon Park. He ended up on the wrong side of South Loomis Street, three blocks down from Milo's Deli which closed at 6 p.m. Traffic was thick. Will checked his watch and hurried along the sidewalk, scanning for a place to zig-zag through the rush hour to the other side of the street.

But he stopped and stood straight. Across South Loomis, between the parked cars, he saw a familiar stride, a silhouette that disappeared, then appeared, disappeared, then appeared, sparking a thirty-two year old memory, still fresh.

Holding up his left hand to stop traffic, Will stepped into the street and darted across South Loomis to another lifetime, to his summer of 1917.

Will hopped onto the sidewalk some steps behind the woman. He hurried around her side and found himself standing in front of a startled young lady, perhaps in her twenties, who Will had never seen before.

Will stepped back. "Oh, Miss! I'm so sorry. From across the street, you reminded me of someone I knew many years ago. But it's obvious I was mistaken. Again, I apologize and I'm truly sorry that I alarmed you."

The woman, still startled, looked at Will and half-smiled.

Will nodded and headed up the sidewalk, relieved and devastated.

But before he traveled far, the young lady yelled ahead to him. "Sir, Wait!"

Will turned to see her hurrying up the sidewalk toward him.

The young woman stopped in front of Will and the two shared an awkward smile. "Sir, I'm sure I'm mistaken as well, and I apologize for taking your time, but I feel I have to ask." She hesitated. "Did you ever by chance work on a farm south of here, actually south of Peoria? It would have been many years ago. It was the summer my grandfather died."

Will looked at her more confused than surprised. "Yes, yes I did, but why would you, why would you ever think...?"

"Well," continued the young woman, "my mother used to talk about a worker who came to the farm that summer and how much she cared for him."

Will just stared at her.

"She told me that they went to the cemetery to put flowers on my family's grave. That he saved my Aunt Corrie. That she taught him how to dance. And that they kissed the night before he left, just above the farmhouse."

The memory stirred Will and he stared at the young lady. "Yes, but why would you ever think that's me? We've never met."

The young woman smiled and pointed right at Will. "And she told me about his dimples, that one there, a little sharper than the other."

"Vlinder," said Will.

"Yes, Vlinder was my mother," the young woman said.

"Was?" Will asked.

The young woman put her head down. "Yes, my mother died four years ago. She had cancer here," holding a hand over her chest. "She died at the farm. We were all with her."

Will's mother told him to go to Chicago, go to the farm, then he'd know. He wished he'd never come. He stared at the ground.

"You must be Will," the young woman said.

Will nodded.

"I'm so sorry. Perhaps you thought that I was my mother from across the street. I wish I were, for both of us." The young woman pointed to a bench in front of a stationary store. "If you'd like to talk for a minute, we could sit there."

Talk about what, Will thought. What for? He knew all he needed to know. But he went to the bench and sat with the young woman.

"My name is Inga," the young woman began. "I was my mother's first child. I also have a brother, Jensen. He lives in Boston."

Will barely heard her. So many years. So many times he took the flower from the Bible, holding it, bringing him back to Helgeveld, lifting him up. For nothing. He sat, staring at the sidewalk under them.

Inga looked at Will. "I didn't mean to bring you any pain. I just want you to know how much my mother cared for you, even until the end."

Will looked across to the young woman.

"I'm sorry. Perhaps I should go," said Inga.

"No, no," said Will. "I'm glad you told me, and I'm surprised she would have mentioned me or told you about that summer."

"Yes, she spoke of you often." Inga said and laughed a bit. "Usually when she was having problems with my father."

"Your father? He didn't love her?" Will couldn't imagine anybody not caring deeply for Vlinder.

"Oh, he might have at some point," Inga said. "The problem was he "loved" so many other women at the same time." Will smiled and it encouraged Inga. "My mother would keep taking him back. They'd argue and he'd do it again. Finally, the arguing stopped and he left soon after. I asked my mother about it and she said, 'Once I stopped caring, there was nothing left to argue about.'" Inga continued, "He remarried. I still talk to him from time to time. He lives in Virginia now."

They sat in silence and then Inga said, "She mentioned you a lot. She was happy when she remembered you. I think you even tried to paint the cows?"

Will chuckled and then turned serious. "And she died at the farm?"

"Yes," said Inga. "When the doctors said there was nothing more they could do, my mother went to the farm." Inga thought for a moment. "It was four years ago. Aunt Corrie, Aunt Lotta, and I looked after her. My brother got there two days before she died. And my grandmother was there, of course."

"Anika?"

"Yes," Inga nodded. "Being at the farm during that time made my mother happy. She told us stories about the farm until the end." Inga paused. "We stayed with her in her old bedroom, staying up with her at night when she was in so much pain." Inga paused and breathed deeply. "And it was a terrible time for Aunt Corrie, too. When my mother was so sick, Aunt Corrie got a telegram that her husband had been killed. He was on a navy ship in the Pacific Ocean at the end of the war when it was hit. Aunt Corrie told us not to tell my mother and she stayed with her all day and night until the end."

Will put his hands on his thighs, leaned forward, and looked out over South Loomis.

"The funeral for my mother was in Peoria, at the cemetery. After that, Aunt Corrie and her two children, my cousins, came to the farm, waiting for word that her husband's body had returned. We walked around the farm day after day, Aunt Corrie showing us spots where she and my mother used to play, telling us stories about the farm, and showing us where she fell at the back barn."

Will sat back on the bench. "I'm not surprised. Corrie was a big part of my summer there. She used to twirl when she walked and she even taught me how to wash my clothes. We watched the Fourth of July fireworks together. And her ankle. And Roy. When I left, I told her I'd miss her, and I have." Will paused and shook his head. "My daughter even twirls like she did. I loved it there." He looked down. "Since my wife died, I often think about."

Inga sat straight. "You should go to the farm. They'd all be so happy to see you. Aunt Corrie is there."

"Corrie's at the farm?" said Will.

"Oh, yes," said Inga. "After her husband died, she moved back there. Her children are grown now, married. She said how much she loves being back home, working again at the farm."

But with Vlinder gone, should he go to the farm? Go to see Corrie? It was too much to consider. "What about you, Inga?" Will asked. "You live here in Chicago?"

"Yes," said Inga. "I live and work here in Chicago and I'm engaged to be married this summer. In fact, we're getting married at the farm. I still go down there whenever I can."

"You work here in the city?" asked Will.

"Yes, I opened a shop just down the street," Inga said. "It sells women's clothing."

"You're definitely your mother's daughter," Will said. "She always wanted her own store. Did she ever open one?"

"No, life didn't go like that for her. But before she was sick, she talked to me about my own business. We walked around Chicago and looked at different stores." They were silent on the bench, and then Inga looked at Will and said again, "You should go to the farm. I know Aunt Corrie would love to see you."

"Oh, I don't know," said Will. "So much has happened. She has her own life now. I doubt she remembers much about me."

Inga laughed. "Oh, no. She remembers you alright. In fact, she talked about you just this summer. At the cemetery. We were planting forget-me-nots on the family graves when she picked up a stem. She twirled it and wondered if you ever got the one that she put in your shirt pocket the day you left the farm."

Will spun and stared at Inga. "That was Corrie?! She put the flower in my pocket?!"

"Yes," Inga said. "Did you think it was my mother?"

"Well, I assumed," Will said sitting straight, his eyes darting. "I didn't know."

"No, it was Aunt Corrie," said Inga, smiling.

Will looked forward and rocked slightly on the bench. "I kept it. Kept it in the family Bible. I'd take it out and hold it sometimes.

Important times. It's still there." Will breathed deep and looked out across South Loomis again, the evening traffic beginning to slow.

But he turned quickly toward Inga, surprised. "Wait! Corrie was on the front porch the day I left. She was still using crutches. How could she have put the flower in my pocket?"

Inga shrugged her shoulders and smiled at Will. "I don't know. You'd have to ask her."

CHAPTER 39

Will stopped by the feed and supply store in the morning and told his cousin, Joe, that he'd been called away and couldn't come for lunch today. "I'll stop by when I come back through town," Will told him. He cancelled his ticket to Pittsburgh and settled into his 9:45 a.m. train seat from Chicago to Peoria. Will bought two newspapers for the trip, but they remained folded and shoved between his seat and the next one. He stared across the open land, little changed from thirty-two years ago. He'd get to Peoria at 3:20 p.m., take a taxi to the farm, ask it to wait, say hello and return to Peoria, Chicago, then home. It was a safe story and he hid within it.

At 3:30 p.m., outside the train station in Peoria, Will looked up to buildings that remodeled the skyline. Paved streets. No wagons. Yes, things always change on the outside. He stared at a row of taxis waiting for passengers from the Chicago train. Up to now, Will knew he could turn around, go back to Chicago, back to Pittsburgh. But if he stepped into a taxi, he'd be going to the farm.

"I'm going to Helgeveld Farm," Will said to the taxi at the front of the line. "Do you know where that is?"

"Sure. Hop in," the taxi driver said. "I know the farm."

The taxi sped through the outskirts of Peoria onto a hardened road and past several new buildings and homes. Will knew the fields, the harvest almost complete. The seventeen-year-old boy who'd made the trip to Peoria so many years ago wasn't as nervous as Will was now. The ride was too quick. Up ahead was the Van der Beek farm. Next, would be Helgeveld.

Will sat forward from his back seat and he peered through the windshield. The farmhouse appeared and stood unchanged, just two new silos to the side. Is that someone on the front porch?

Two cars sat out front as the taxi pulled up. "Can you wait?" Will asked the taxi driver. "I might be just a few minutes."

"Sure, no problem," the driver said.

Will got out of the taxi and waved to Corrie who was standing on the porch. He walked toward her, stopping at the bottom of the steps. "I told you I'd wave when I saw you again," Will said. "I hope you haven't been waiting on the porch all this time."

Corrie smiled. "No. Inga called last night and said she saw you in Chicago. I thought maybe you'd take the train from there today. Then, maybe you'd take a taxi from Peoria. And then I thought maybe you'd be getting here just about now. It seemed worthwhile to walk out on the porch to see for myself." She held out her hands. "It's good to see you, Will."

Will walked up the front steps and took her hands in his. "It's good to be here, Corrie. It's good to see you."

"Come on inside," Corrie said. "I know there are some people who'd like to see you." She took his hand and brought him through the front door, through the big room, and into the kitchen. Anika looked up from a mound of bread dough she was kneading. She stared and stood straight. "Will! Is that you, Will?" She rushed around the table and hugged him. "What a wonderful surprise! Corrie, did you know he was coming?"

"Just a guess," said Corrie. "Not enough to tell anyone."

"Did you drive your car here?" asked Anika.

"No, I took a taxi from Peoria. It's waiting outside," said Will.

"Waiting? You tell him he can go back to town," Anika said. "You've got to stay for dinner and a night or two if you can. We'll get you back to Peoria later."

Will paid the fare and sent the taxi on its way. When he got back, Alwin and Gerwin were in the kitchen, as excited as Anika to see Will again.

They shared stories and histories. Alwin and Gerwin still lived at the farm, their families living in two homes built out back. Corrie's twin, Hans, and her brother Bram, had families and both lived in Bloomington. Lotta and her family had moved to Chicago. Will's mouth opened when Betty Granger came into the kitchen. She had married Gerwin and they had four children and two grandchildren.

"Betty!" said Will. "You're still here! Last time I saw you, you were coming back the next summer since you and Gerwin had been talking."

"Guess we just kept on talking," smiled Betty moving over next to Gerwin.

"It's still a little while until dinner," Corrie said to Will. "Let's walk around out back and I can show you what's changed."

They walked out the kitchen door and past the only remaining bunkhouse, Bunkhouse 1. Even that was only half full during the harvests, she told Will. "Machines are taking over everything," continued Corrie. "Summers are so different now. It's noisier," she paused, "and quieter. I miss all the people."

Corrie pointed to Bunkhouse 2 which had been converted into a hen house. Bunkhouse 3 had been torn down. They walked on and Corrie shared stories of events that shook the farm: the droughts, the dust, the heat of the mid-1930s, and an unexpected fire in 1937 that took Aunt Olivia's daughter and much of the main farmhouse. But the years since then had been strong.

They each shared their stories, the losses that shook them, and the joys. Corrie had a married daughter in Indianapolis and a son with a family up in Rockford. Will told Corrie about Hillary, Tom, and Julia.

"I guess I was surprised when Inga said that you hadn't forgotten me," Will said.

Corrie laughed. "Well, it was tough to forget you. You probably crossed my mind every time I put on my socks or pajamas." Corrie reached down, pulling up her pantleg and lowering her sock.

Will stared at a faded tangle of purple scars that still surrounded Corrie's ankle. He looked up at her. "Can I ask you something?" he said. "How did you put that forget-me-not in my pocket the day I left Helgeveld? You were still on crutches."

Corrie smiled. "I remembered that you told me that forget-me-nots were your favorite flower. So, the day you left, I came downstairs on my crutches and picked one from the pot next to the piano. I gave it to Lotta and told her to go to the bunkhouse and sneak it into your shirt. But when she got there, she said there were four bags and she didn't know which one was yours. So she brought them to the house first. I knew yours, so that's when I put the stem into your shirt pocket. Then, Lotta brought the bags down to the wagon."

The two continued past the bunkhouses back up to the path behind the farmhouse. Will watched her, wondering what he was looking for. "Do you know whatever happened to Moses and Isaiah?" he asked.

Corrie laughed. "Well, Isaiah lives down in Springfield, married to a lady he met. He's got five kids. He opened his own repair shop there. But Moses, Moses still lives right here, in Granddaddy's House."

"Right here!? Is he here now??" Will asked.

"Probably, or at the back barn. I was going up there next to surprise you." Corrie paused at the door to the kitchen. "Moses was so helpful when I lost my husband, and then lost Vlinder. He always thinks things will turn out for the best. In fact…wait here." Corrie left Will and went inside the house. She returned a few minutes later. "Moses told me everything would turn out alright and he gave me this." Corrie held something in her palm, wrapped in tissue paper. She unwrapped it and there was the 1909 Lincoln Cent. "Moses said Granddaddy gave it to him and Isaiah, but he said they'd had all the good luck they needed. He told me that you never know when the luck will show up, so he told me to keep it close. And I have."

Will looked at the penny and looked at Corrie. He reached into his pants pocket and pulled out the other two Lincoln pennies, worn almost smooth, and showed them to Corrie. "There were three pennies that summer," Will said. "These are the other two. Isaiah and

Moses mailed them to me after my father and brother died. I always carry them."

Corrie and Will stared at each other, not quite knowing what to make of this.

Will took his two pennies and put them in Corrie's palm next to the 1909 penny. "Moses always said they work best when they're together," he said. "Why don't you hold them for now?"

Corrie looked at Will and closed her hand over them.

"Will!? Is that you, Will?" Up the path hustled Moses, grinning and shaking his head. "I declare. It can't be!"

Will took the hand of his friend in both of his. "Moses! I just found out you never left. You're still here, still living in Granddaddy's House."

Moses gave a quick turn and pointed at his house behind the stables. "Yes, indeed. Me and the Missis. We made a few additions to it over the years, but we're still there. Granddaddy, he died, oh, near onto twenty years ago. Died workin' down in the barn, just like he hoped."

"Missis? Not Celia by any chance?" said Will.

"Sure is," Moses laughed. "I remember meetin' her that summer. I kept going to Peoria to see her and after a time, she said it made more sense marryin' her and savin' the trip. Celia, she's a good woman, even got me sleepin' in a bed again. Got four kids, all moved away now." He paused and recollected. "Bought a building in Peoria a while back and got my own business, *Moses Repair Shop*. Two o' my sons run it and they can fix most anything, even all this modern stuff."

Will nodded at Moses. "Heard Isaiah lives down in Springfield."

"Sure does. He fixes most anything down there, too." Moses laughed. "Got five kids and a wife who's too good for him. I see him at least once a year."

Anika came out the kitchen door. "Dinner's ready, you two." She looked over at Moses. "Moses, can you and Celia join us for dinner?"

"I believe I can speak for Celia," said Moses. "I'll go up to the house and we'll be back shortly."

As Corrie, Will, and Anika walked through the kitchen into the big room, Anika said, "Will, we made up a room for you at the end of the hall upstairs. We'd love to take you around the farm tomorrow, catch up on all the years. Maybe you could stay until Sunday? If you need to, make a phone call to let anybody know."

"Thank you, Miss Anika. I have no firm plans, so staying a little longer isn't a problem."

"Miss Anika!?" Anika laughed, putting a hand across her chest. "Hardly anyone calls me that these days."

The dinner talk covered thirty-two years. Joys and pains. Children, family. Joren Helgeveld. The 1918 flu. Will's father and brother, Emma, Vlinder, Jakob, Corrie's husband Paul, Granddaddy, Will's splint on Corrie's leg, Moses fixing the Dodge, Anika keeping Alwin at the farm during the Great War.

Owen? Nobody knew. Elmer? Moses said he married that lady from the Van der Beek farm and they moved up near her family in Madison, Wisconsin. He went into law enforcement, Moses heard. And Roy? Some years later, Alwin learned that after Roy turned 21, he transferred from St. Charles Reformatory School to prison for five years. In the 1930s, the Peoria police chief told Alwin he had seen a wanted poster for Roy, describing him as an enforcer for Chicago's Touhy gang and responsible for two murders. Lotta added that she was sure she saw him once on a street in Chicago.

But it was a happy night. Stories of sour pickles, Moses' magic tricks, the Fodgabaker, even cow painting.

Will was sitting next to Corrie and watched the laughter and closeness of everyone around the table. He leaned over to Corrie. "I see why you love living back at home. I'm sure you'll live here forever."

"You're right. I love it here so much," Corrie replied. "I'll stay. Probably."

"Probably?" said Will. "What do you mean? Where else would you want to go?"

Corrie thought for a moment. "It's funny. I never think too much about those things. As long as I'm around people I care for, it's never made much of a difference where I was or what I was doing."

It was late. Anika said she was tired and everyone else agreed. When they all got up from the table and headed to the stairs, Will turned and said, "It's good to be here, seeing all of you again." He gave a quick smile to everyone, adding a nod to Corrie's.

* * *

The next morning, Will rose early, dawn hinting at the eastern horizon. He looked out his window and could make out the sycamore, standing as before, its arms spread over and around the back of the farmhouse. Will pulled on his clothes and headed down the stairs, out the kitchen door, and onto the back path. There had been a frost that night and Will walked through the cold, up behind the farmhouse to the spot he and Vlinder shared so many years before. The Milky Way was fading, giving in to the daylight ahead. The horses were stirring in the stables, crunching their morning hay.

Will looked down at the spot he had once lain next to Vlinder in 1917, holding her and kissing her under the ceiling of stars. He looked up and across the fields, dimly lit, bare, silent, unchanged. He closed his eyes. He took a deep breath, and her vision appeared before him. He reached out and took her hand in his. He smiled and put his other hand alongside her cheek. And then Will leaned in and kissed Vlinder goodbye.

* * *

After breakfast, Alwin took Will around and showed him what was new at the farm: two new self-propelled combines, two new silos filled with hay and soybean silage for winter feeding, and the dairy barn completely rebuilt with concrete floors and automatic milking machines. At the back barn, Moses was out front, rebuilding a tractor engine. "After lunch," Alwin said, "we can take the wagon into the fields. I want to show you what's new and show you the beef cattle. I'm heading up to the house. Why don't you stay here with Moses for now."

Moses took Will around the back barn. "I swear, Will, everything's changin'," Moses said. "Hardly use horses anymore. All tractors." The two stood in front of a disassembled tractor body. "Lot easier givin' the horses some hay than fixin' these." They walked behind the barn and there sat the Fodgabaker. "Haven't driven it for a while, but she still runs. Kids like it when I take it out for a drive and we go backwards."

Will looked over and pointed at Moses left arm, shiny, scarred skin stretching from his elbow to the back of his hand. "What happened there? Looks like a burn or something?"

Moses held up his arm, turned it, and chuckled. "Yeah, got that back when the farmhouse nearly burned. Almost lost the whole place. Aunt Olivia, she was living with the family at the time. Her daughter, Anna, had come up for a visit with her two grandkids. She couldn't make it out. She died in the fire." The two sat silent.

"I remember Olivia," said Will. "She came out a few times that summer. To Joren's funeral. I didn't talk to her, but she looked like part of the family."

Moses stood and Will followed. "Yeah, nice lady. Losin' her daughter was tough for her," said Moses. "Fire started on the side of the house. Middle of the night. Never made sense." Moses nodded toward the farmhouse. "After the fire, Isaiah came up, and between him, me, Alwin, Gerwin, and a couple of the Van der Beek's, we got it rebuilt pretty good." They walked toward the tractor. "When you leavin', Will?" asked Moses.

"Looks like tomorrow," Will said. "I'll go to church with all of you and take the noon train to Chicago."

"Gotta tell ya," said Moses. "Your name still comes up from time to time. Corrie, she mentions you a coupla times each year."

Will nodded.

* * *

In the afternoon, Will and Corrie walked to the dairy barn, around the two new silos and ended back at the stables. A horse came over to Will and he rubbed her snout. "She's as friendly as Lily was."

"I'm not surprised," said Corrie. "This is Whisper, Lily's daughter. She had one other mare and two stallions. They're all around here somewhere."

Alwin rode alongside them in a buckboard and Will hopped up next to him, Corrie and Anika on the seat behind. They took the road toward Peoria, turning right and stopping by the beef cattle. All four got off the buckboard and hung over the fence watching the cattle feed.

"Still a few posts left from the 1917 fence," said Alwin. "And that cattle contract we started with the government? Can't imagine the farm without them now."

They stood together, watching the cattle. A calf came over to Corrie and she rubbed its head.

"What brought you down here, Will?" asked Alwin. "Corrie said you were up in Chicago?"

"Yes," Will said. "We had a store in Chicago that my uncle opened many years ago. He died, so we gave it to his family. I came out to sign the papers."

"That was a feed and supply store?" asked Alwin. "Like the ones you have back in Pittsburgh?"

"Yes, pretty successful, too," said Will. "Supplied farms around northern Illinois, I understand."

Alwin turned toward Will. "Your uncle wasn't Clive was he?"

Will looked at Alwin, surprised. "Yes, Clive. It was Clive, my father's brother. I'm going to stop and see the family when I get back to Chicago."

"Well," said Alwin. "That was some real bad news for us, too. He was a great guy and we got all of our seed and a lot of equipment from him, clear up in Chicago. Not sure what we're going to do now. No place in Chicago can handle everything we need. Might have to go down to Springfield to find somebody."

Will hesitated and then looked over at Alwin. "No place in Peoria?"

"Not that can handle what we need. All the big farms around here, we don't know what we're going to do. We all worked with Clive."

"Wouldn't be that hard, really," said Will. "Just need to know the farms and the distributors."

"Well," said Alwin. "Nobody's done it."

They stood silent and then Will stepped away and walked along the fence, stopping and putting his hands on his hips. He breathed deeply and looked past the cattle to the horizon. Corrie walked just behind him.

"Pasture looks a little bigger," Will said, looking down, then up again. "Still got a 100 head here?"

"Almost 200 now," said Corrie.

*　*　*

Pastor Jannsen embraced Will at the Dutch Reformed Church in Peoria and told him how good he still looked. "We steel talk aboot you Will. Dat was a summer wee weell never forget."

Moses was now part of the Sunday service, giving a weekly reading from the Bible in front of the congregation.

"Today's readin' is from Ecclesiastes in the Old Testament," said Moses, smiling at Will and looking out across the parishioners. "It's a book about findin' purpose in life. And havin' someone to do it with. This here section is from Chapter 4, verses 9 and 10." Moses cleared his throat. *Two are better than one, because they have a good return for their labor. If either of them falls down, one can help the other up. But pity anyone who falls and has no one to help them up.*

Moses closed the Bible and smiled at the assembled worshippers.

After the service, everyone gathered out front. Will looked at his watch. "Well, I've got to head to the train station. This was a wonderful visit. It answered so many things I'd wondered about."

Anika stepped up and took Will's hand. "I hope to see you again, Will."

Will nodded. "I hope so, too." He waved at his gathered friends.

"I'll walk with you," said Corrie. Will nodded and smiled.

The train station was some distance, but it was a chance to walk along the streets of Peoria again. Everything different, but still the same.

They walked and talked, Corrie pointing into stores that brought Will back to paydays in Peoria. They found themselves in front of L. E. McKown jeweler, which had changed little inside. "Look, Corrie," Will said. "This is where I bought your silver necklace."

Corrie pointed to her neck. "This one?"

Will stared at it. "It couldn't have lasted all these years?" he said.

"No," Corrie said. "It wore out a few times, but I kept buying the same design. Herringbone." She pulled the necklace out and there hanging from the bottom was the gold charm of the man and woman dancing. Will looked at the charm and up at Corrie and she continued. "Vlinder gave it to me just before she died. It wasn't sad at all. She laughed and said she never got a chance to dance with you again." Corrie paused. "Then she said maybe I would."

Will looked at the charm in Corrie's hand. He looked up at Corrie and asked, "Why did you put that forget-me-not in my pocket when I left."

Corrie shrugged her shoulders. "So you wouldn't forget me."

"All those years," said Will, "it was you in the flower. I think it saved me."

Corrie smiled sadly, nodded, and looked at Will. "Yes, that was me. But I'm not Vlinder, Will. I loved her so much. I miss her so much. But we're different people. If you came to the farm to find her, she's gone."

Will put his hands on Corrie's shoulders and looked straight into her. "I knew Vlinder wasn't here when I came." He paused. "It's strange. It was talking to Vlinder's daughter that got me to come here to see you." Will took Corrie's hands. "One time you told Vlinder that you liked the stars because they're perfect the way they are. You can't compare them to anything. All you can do is be grateful. That's why I came to the farm, came to see you, perfect just as it is, just like the stars."

Corrie moved in and Will held her. He kept his chin on top of her head, then he pulled back and lifted her head towards his and kissed her. He held her face and kissed her again.

"All aboard!" the conductor yelled.

Corrie looked up at Will. "I'll see you again?"

"Yes," Will nodded.

Corrie smiled back. "Last time you said that, it took thirty-two years. I'm not sure I can wait that long."

"I have to come back soon," Will smiled and shrugged his shoulders. "You've got all three pennies."

*   *   *

Will called Corrie each Sunday and on the Sunday after Thanksgiving, Corrie said, "Why don't you and your family come down here for Christmas? There's always so much going on and everyone would love to see you."

CHAPTER 40

At the front door of the farmhouse on Christmas Eve 1949, Will introduced his mother to Corrie. "It's so good to meet you," his mother said, "and Will was right. You're very pretty." Corrie smiled back, offered her hand, and Will's mother took it in both of hers. "It's wonderful to be here," she said.

"And this is Anika," Will continued the introductions. "And Anika, this is my mother, Sarah." There was a smile and a handshake between the two of them, more like old friends than a first meeting.

Will stepped to the side. "And this is my daughter, Julia."

Corrie moved toward her and took her hand. "I'm so glad you were able to come, Julia."

"Me, too," said Julia looking around. "It so Christmassy in here. It's beautiful."

"Please, come in," said Anika. "I hope the drive from Peoria was alright for the taxi. We all try to keep as much snow off the road as we can."

Inside, they took off their coats and put down their travel bags. Will saw that there was nothing in the big room without a decoration. The Christmas tree sat between the two front windows, pine cones, homemade ornaments, and strings of electric Christmas lights filling its branches. Garlands of red and green surrounded the room and cutouts of Santa Claus, reindeer, and elves filled empty spaces. A clear glass vase with Christmas ornaments sat on the piano, the forget-me-not plant next to it, holding a green garland.

"My other children, Hillary and Tom, had to stay in Pittsburgh to keep the stores open," said Will. "I'm always surprised at how much summer merchandise sells around Christmas time."

Travel bags and coats put in their place, Anika took Will's mother and Julia for a tour of the house. Corrie and Will walked behind them, Corrie giving Will stories of the house beyond a first time visit. She took him into the room that she, Vlinder, and Lotta had shared, over the kitchen, with the stubborn door that Moses and Isaiah had fixed.

"This is my room again," said Corrie. She pointed to the other side of the room. "Vlinder was in that bed for her last few days. Lotta and I propped her up so she could look out the window. Inga was in here too. She slept on the floor."

Will looked at Corrie, went to her and held her. "It's so good to see you," he said.

Corrie held Will. "And I'm so glad you're here, Will. It makes Christmas special."

Lives were set, established. Corrie had her life at the farm. And Will and his family had two feed and supply stores in Pittsburgh. Would he continue to call her on Sundays for another year and come back next Christmas? And the next? Share stories about their children, grandchildren, how the store is doing, how the farm is doing, talk about Moses and Alwin? No. This was their future. He had to say something.

But it was Corrie who spoke first.

∗   ∗   ∗

Christmas morning saw the children and grandchildren opening so many presents.

At Christmas dinner, Corrie and Will sat next to each other, different stories weaving around the table. Will looked down to see Gramma Luna's white dinner Christmas plates, circled in lavender. The purpose he felt with Vlinder, then Emma, had moved on. But now, at the Christmas table, it stirred in him again.

Dinner, dessert, and coffee went into the evening. Groups left or moved to other rooms. Julia ended up talking with Betty and

Gerwin's children. Moses' sons talked to Alwin about the newest farm equipment, and Corrie and Will shared missing pieces from thirty-two years.

Anika and Will's mother shared tea at a side table until Will's mother excused herself and said how tired she was after the long day. Will got up from the table and walked his mother to the bottom of the stairs. She turned and stood in front of her son and smiled. "Now you know," she said.

"Yes," Will nodded. "Now I know."

She put a hand on the side of her son's face. "Good night." She turned and headed up the stairs.

The crowd in the big room thinned. The table had been cleared, and soon, only Corrie, Will, Anika, Alwin, and his wife Laura, sat around the table in the big room.

Finally, Alwin said, "I've got to get to bed, Will. I'll say my goodbyes now. I'm heading to Springfield early tomorrow. Maybe even St. Louis if I can't find a feed and supply wholesaler in Springfield. All the farms around here are having trouble getting what we need. We really need someplace closer."

Will sat silent, looked straight ahead, and then turned toward Corrie. She looked back at Will, took his hand, and smiled. "If you ever need help opening another store, let me know."

* * *

In July, Inga stood in Corrie's bedroom, adjusting her bridal gown in front of the mirror. "It looked better in the store," Inga said. "It doesn't hang right."

"No. It's beautiful," said Corrie. "Here, stand sideways." Inga twisted right and looked in the mirror. "Look," said Corrie. "The front and the back are balanced. And your grandmother's pearls as a head wrap? They'll look perfect through the veil." Corrie stood in front of Inga, pulling, fluffing, and straightening. "There, what do you think?"

Inga turned from one side to the other, making a final examination. "Yes, okay, that looks good. How much time do we have?"

Corrie looked at the clock on her night table. "Fifteen minutes. We should probably leave in ten."

"Your turn," Inga said and smiled. She stepped back and looked at Corrie's lavender dress. She pulled at the sleeves, evening them out and straightening Corrie's collar. "I love your shoes."

"They were your mother's. But I don't think she ever wore them," said Corrie. "She said they were a little too dressy for her, but I love them." Corrie twisted her right foot to look at all sides.

Inga went over and took two bouquets of white daisies surrounding lavender forget-me-nots. She handed one of the bouquets to Corrie and smiled at her. "What a beautiful bride you make, Aunt Corrie."

*   *   *

To the side of the farmhouse, Pastor Jannsen stood in front of a field of chairs, full of family, friends, and well-wishers. Along with Will's children, Hillary, Tom, and Julia, many other family members were there. Across the aisle were Corrie's children, Hans and his family along with Gerwin and Betty. Aunt Olivia sat in the next row, her two granddaughters seated on one side, and Aunt Elisabeth and Aunt Mina on the other. In the next row sat Moses, Celia, their two sons from Peoria, along with their three grandchildren. Next to Moses sat Isaiah.

The piano had been brought outside. Anika sat at it and began the processional. Down the center aisle came Inga, arm in arm with her brother Jensen, followed by Corrie, holding the arm of her brother Alwin.

Up front, Inga took the arm of her future husband, Allen, and Corrie took Will's arm.

Pastor Jannsen stepped in front of the gathering. On a small stand sat the family Bible that Will's mother had given them, the pressed forget-me-not still sitting between two pages. Pastor Jannsen opened the Bible and looked out over the two couples and the assembly of wedding guests. He raised both arms and smiled. "Welkom! Welkom! To dis special day," the pastor started. "We are gathered here to join dis man and dis woman, and dis man and dis woman in holy matrimony…."

At the end of the ceremony, Will took no time in lifting Corrie's veil to kiss the bride. He stood back and looked at her. "So beautiful. And your dress. It's perfect." Corrie smiled and twirled, spinning her dress out and drawing cheers from nearby well-wishers. Will eased toward her and held both of her hands, closing a thirty-two-year-old past and starting fresh. "I never could have imagined this, Corrie," Will said.

"Me neither," smiled Corrie.

Will leaned in and kissed her again. Then they turned and waved at the crowd in front of them.

Inga looked over at Will who stood next to her. She took Will's hand in both of hers. "I'm so happy you're here. I'm so happy you're part of the family," she told him.

Will and Corrie then went to their mothers, Sarah and Anika, who stood arm in arm. Anika reached out and took Will's hand. "I'm not sure who's happier, you two, or your mother and I."

Will's mother stepped forward and took Corrie's hands in hers. "You were with my son in the forget-me-not for the last thirty-two years. I hope you're in each other's hearts for the next thirty-two."

Handshakes, kisses, and good wishes followed them through the crowd. Then Will saw Moses coming toward them. At his side walked Isaiah, their smiles reaching back more than three decades. Will went to Isaiah and hugged him. "Moses told me you might come. I'm so glad you made it."

"Had to come," Isaiah nodded and smiled. "Some things just too important." Isaiah stepped back and looked at Corrie and Will. "And Moses tells me you openin' a feed and supply store right here in Peoria." Isaiah shook his head. "This endin' just too good to imagine."

"What do you mean?" Will asked. "Didn't it have to happen just like this?" He looked over at Corrie and smiled. She reached into her dress pocket, pulling out the three Lincoln pennies and holding them in her palm for all four to see.

Moses looked at the pennies and put his arm around his brother's shoulder. He smiled, shook his head and said, "I gotta say. Corrie, Will, you two here. Married. Livin' close by. And them three pennies. Don't know if it's all luck, but sure is serendipitous."

If you enjoyed *One Summer at Helgeveld Farm*, please consider leaving a review on Amazon, Goodreads, or wherever you purchased your copy. Your words really do help others find the story.

And if you noticed a few storylines left hanging, those will be addressed in an upcoming book. story.

www.ingramcontent.com/pod-product-compliance
Lightning Source LLC
Chambersburg PA
CBHW050023120726
47903CB00006B/1883